1989

TIANANMEN SQUARE
TO
EAST BERLIN

First in the Code Name: Jaqui Walnuts series

JACK GODWIN

AUGUST WORDS PUBLISHING
augustwords.org
WRITE WELL DO GOOD

Published by **August Words Publishing**

AUGUST WORDS PUBLISHING
augustwords.org
WRITE WELL. DO GOOD.

www.augustwords.org

Copyright © 2015 by Jack Godwin, PhD

Thank you for buying an authorized edition of this book and for complying with copyright laws by not reproducing, scanning, or distributing any part of it in any form without express permission, except for short passages for educational purposes. In complying you actively sustain the copyrights of writers, which fuels creativity, encourages diverse voices, promotes free speech, and creates a vibrant culture. Your support of working writers allows August Words Publishing to continue to publish books for readers just like you, but also allows support of literary and literacy charities which is the heart of augustwords.org.

ISBN: 978-1-942018-04-9

Publisher's Note: This is a work of fiction and entirely an intentional product of the author's imagination in the pursuit of telling an original tale to reach a higher truth. As such, any names, characters, places, and incidents are fabricated or are used fictitiously, and any resemblance to actual persons (living or dead), businesses, companies, events, or locales is entirely coincidental and surely unintentional.

DEDICATION

For Daniel, my brother

From Stettin in the Baltic to Trieste in the Adriatic an iron curtain has descended across the Continent. Behind that line lie all the capitals of the ancient states of Central and Eastern Europe. Warsaw, Berlin, Prague, Vienna, Budapest, Belgrade, Bucharest and Sofia, all these famous cities and the populations around them lie in what I must call the Soviet sphere, and all are subject in one form or another, not only to Soviet influence but to a very high and, in some cases, increasing measure of control from Moscow.

~ Winston Churchill, 1946

It was the first female-style revolution: no violence and we all went shopping.

~ Gloria Steinem, 1989

1989
TIANANMEN SQUARE TO EAST BERLIN
JACK GODWIN

PART ONE

1989
TIANANMEN SQUARE TO EAST BERLIN
JACK GODWIN

1.

THURSDAY, NOVEMBER 9

What're you doing? Oh, nothing, this batch of stamps came in the mail today. I'm just sorting through them. Can I watch? Sure. C-C-C-P. What's that mean? That's the Cyrillic alphabet. It means U-S-S-R, the Union of Soviet Socialist Republics. Who's that man with the beard? That's Karl Marx. Was he one of the Marx brothers? No. He was a writer. Deutsche Democratische Republik. What's that mean? Let me see. That's East Germany. What's that with the chariot on top? That's the Brandenburg Gate in Berlin. Here it is again on this one. Deutsche Bundespost. That's West Germany. Wow. Magyar Posta. What's that mean? It's Hungarian. It means Hungarian Post or something. There's the bearded man again. Who's that bald man next to him? That's Vladimir Lenin. Who's he? He was a writer too and a politician. Is he dead? Yes. He died a long time ago. They both died a long time ago.

I didn't know where I was at first. Then I remembered. The physical effects of sleep deprivation were bad but the emotional effects were even worse. I wondered how much longer I could last. I mean, I knew how it was going to end, with an execution, a Stasi-style execution. I just didn't know if I could take much more.

1989
TIANANMEN SQUARE TO EAST BERLIN
JACK GODWIN

Would I get a last meal or was that only on death row? Pepperoni pizza, cherry coke and cheese cake, please. That's what I wanted. I wasn't even hungry, disoriented mostly, cold, tired and furious with myself for getting caught. I wasn't afraid to die. Everybody dies. That wasn't the problem. The problem was the idea of summary execution, which felt like losing and I hated losing. I really wanted to take one more with me, help one more die for his country before I died for mine. And when the game was over, and I was dead, at least I'd still have a country. That was something.

My left eye was swollen shut, my mouth was bleeding and my heart was pounding. Sweat was rolling down my back into my butt crack, even though the November air was cool. I knew I was in East Berlin, pretty close to the border crossing because I could hear the cars lined up honking their horns. And I could hear West Berliners pounding on the other side and celebrating, or getting ready to celebrate. They were chanting something, which I couldn't quite make out, but it sounded like the song they sing at soccer games. *Olay-OLAY-Olay*. The guard heard it, too because he kept glancing up at the high window without moving his head. Just his eyes moved but not his head or the barrel of the pistol.

"It does not matter," he said. "It is too late for you."

"Maybe," I said. "Maybe you'll retire on a pension and get to spend your days playing with your children and grandchildren. You got children, Sgt. Schultz?"

"Shut up."

"I don't think so."

The chanting got louder through the window. Then the door opened and in came a Stasi colonel named Gazecki, Konrad Gazecki.

"Jaqueline Olvera Nogales," he said, "You've been busy."

"Colonel Gazecki, how's the shoulder? Sorry about that. I'm not as good with a borrowed weapon. That was a Makarov nine millimeter wasn't it. I'll get you one for Christmas if we both live through this. I was just telling Sgt. Schultz here, maybe he'll get to retire on a pension and spend his summers on the Black Sea coast. What do you think?"

"Stand her up," said Gazecki. The guard holstered his pistol, grabbed my collar and hoisted me to my feet.

"Remove the handcuffs," he said. Gazecki and the guard exchanged a glance, but Gazecki reassured him with a nod. The guard unlocked the cuffs. I rubbed my wrists and Gazecki took a step forward to scrutinize me. The chanting outside was very loud now and the cell vibrated every time the West Berliners pounded on the wall. There was a crumbling, crashing noise followed instantly by bright light pouring in through the high window. The crowd roared in triumph and I held my breath.

1989
TIANANMEN SQUARE TO EAST BERLIN
JACK GODWIN

2.

SUNDAY, MAY 28

I was in Los Angeles for my father's funeral. It was a heart attack the doctors said. Before we went to the cemetery I noticed his belongings at the house, the little things he wore or kept in his pockets. It was strange, especially seeing his wedding ring. He never left the house without his wedding ring. He was funny the way he always turned it into a ritual. Standing in front of the entry table, he would announce everything he was putting on or putting into his pocket—like he was suiting up for something. But all his stuff was right there on the shelf, his watch, his wallet, car keys, wedding ring. He was funny that way.

I only cried once. It was at Kramer's on Dupont Circle and I saw a stack of Robert Ludlum's new book. I wondered if Dad read that one yet. Oh, that's right. He's dead. He's in heaven, so of course he's read it. That's the only time I cried, standing in the aisle at the bookstore. I couldn't believe he was gone. I couldn't believe it would ever stop hurting.

The casket was on a table surrounded by burning candles and herbs. My father didn't have many close friends, but all our neighbors were there to say goodbye. The priest introduced a man I remember being at the house occasionally, one of Dad's business associates I think. He was wearing a black suit and limped up the aisle toward the podium. He looked at my mother, at me and my brother Billy, his wife and their kids sitting in the row behind us. Hector Nogales was a great business partner he said. Death is part of life, and Hector's death is a great loss to the community. He was also a great friend and I'll miss him very much.

Everyone took turns throwing a handful of dirt on the coffin before the grave was filled and then left for the wake. I waited until everyone was gone and stood staring at the grave.

A voice behind me—a man's voice—said "Jaqui Walnuts?"

"Don't tell me," I said turning around.

His right hand was inside his jacket. Could be a weapon, I thought.

"Jaqui Walnuts," he said again, but it wasn't a question the second time.

"Omega three," I responded. "Who the hell are you?"

"Basil Warburton," he said, but didn't draw a weapon. Instead, he handed me an envelope. "I've been seconded from Her Majesty's Government."

"You've been *seconded?* Who talks like that anymore? How'd you know where to find me?"

He laughed through his nose, not quite snorting, not quite smirking.

"Can't this wait?" I gestured to the fresh pile of earth.

"No. I'm sorry about your loss, but this can't wait. There's a situation in Beijing. Tanks are being deployed all around Tiananmen Square. They're blocking all the main roads and all the major arteries in or out. Infantry are right behind. The Chinese government has had enough. We have to get there before too late."

1989
TIANANMEN SQUARE TO EAST BERLIN
JACK GODWIN

"You're talking about the protests? I guess you better brief me, but not here."

We took separate cars to the Federal Building on Wilshire. I called home and my brother answered. He asked where I was. At work I said, something came up and I'd be home in a few hours. He started lecturing me about showing respect for the dead so I said goodbye and hung up.

"Okay, Mr. Basil Warburton from Her Majesty's Government, what's so important to make me late for my father's wake? I've been following the Tiananmen Square story on CNN, but that's all. You better start from the beginning."

"The protests started when Communist Party General Secretary An Song died in April.

"Who?"

"An Song. More than a hundred thousand people gathered at Tiananmen Square for the funeral, and there were demonstrations in several other large cities. Some students and a few intellectuals began advocating for political and economic reform. The movement has been non-violent so far, but the government is losing patience. Premier Jian Cheung has declared martial law."

"Wasn't Milton Friedman there giving a speech about the virtues of the free market? I read that somewhere."

"That's right. General Secretary Gun Zeng invited Friedman. Zeng is now under house arrest or dead. We don't know. Anyway, the reforms took too long. There was corruption, nepotism and influence peddling. This led to chronic shortages and higher prices for everything. The Party put the brakes on economic reform and went back to central planning, which made matters worse and irritated everyone."

"Now what?"

1989
TIANANMEN SQUARE TO EAST BERLIN
JACK GODWIN

"The students started gathering around a monument in the middle of Tiananmen Square. They built little shrines, even a miniature Statue of Liberty. They call it the Goddess of Freedom. It's all over television."

"That much I know."

"A few thousand students from Peking University and Tsinghua University joined the protesters. People gave speeches, sang Bob Dylan songs and issued a list of demands. *Here.*" Warburton handed me the Station Chief's report.

"They expect the government to publish the salaries of party leaders and their family members?" I scoffed.

"They want freedom of speech, freedom of assembly, democratic elections, and the whole shebang."

"Are they suicidal?"

"Not until now. A small group of protesters tried to occupy the Zhongnanhai Building adjacent to the square. Police kept them out but then the students staged a sit-in. There were no arrests and the government promised all would be forgiven if the students went back to class. With Zeng under arrest or dead—like I said we don't know—Jian Cheung became *Acting* General Secretary. Cheung took a hard line and accused the students and protesters of conspiracy to overthrow the government. Of course, Cheung was acting under orders from the party."

"And then what?" I asked.

"Mikhail Gorbachev made an official state visit. The point, at first, was to normalize relations between the world's two largest communist countries. First time a Soviet chief visited China since Khrushchev in fifty-nine. Because of the protest, the Chinese were forced to relocate the welcoming ceremony away from Tiananmen Square. Some students from

1989
TIANANMEN SQUARE TO EAST BERLIN
JACK GODWIN

Beijing University, and I mean thousands of students, invited Gorbachev to speak but he refused. The Chinese were so worried they cancelled any and all official business. Gorbachev's visit became purely ceremonial. The Chinese government was humiliated. As a rule of thumb, communists don't like to lose face, especially in front of another communist."

"Isn't Gorbachev worried about a coup back home?"

"Well, that's the ticking time-bomb, metaphorically speaking. After Gorbachev returned to Moscow, the students in Beijing went on a hunger strike. Jian Cheung went to Tiananmen Square himself and tried to give a speech but the students frightened him off. So Cheung declared martial law and the People's Liberation Army started mobilizing. They intend to clear the square one way or another, without force if possible, with force if necessary. For the moment, there's a stalemate because some of the protesters surrounded the tanks and armored cars and blocked their way. Some of the students even lectured the troops and asked them to join the protest."

"Were there any takers?"

"No, but with all the media and all the cameras around, it put the government in a difficult situation. The students looked peaceful and reasonable, hardly terrorists, counter-revolutionaries or conspirators plotting to overthrow the government. Most important, there's a stalemate now which can't go on forever. The students intend to sit, starve themselves, protest or whatever until the government meets their demands. They don't have an exit strategy."

"So it appears," I said.

"President Bush held a press conference in Washington and said he supports freedom of speech, freedom of assembly, freedom of the press, and so forth. And clearly, he supports democracy. Bush didn't want to give advice to the Chinese, but suggested they familiarize themselves with Martin Luther King's method of nonviolence. A few days later, Bush made a longer statement with some pretty strong words. He called on the Chinese government publicly and through private channels to refrain from violence. Then he talked about the turmoil in the Chinese leadership, in the party but also in the army. That part made the Chinese very uncomfortable, like they weren't really in control."

As Warburton briefed me, I flipped through the pages of the Station Chief's report.

"Why does the Chinese government think we're there? Do they have proof that we're involved in the student movement? Is that just a guess? Did someone break cover or were they working for the Chinese, too?"

"That I don't know. Everything's so compartmentalized," he said.

"But that's the mission, isn't it? One of our agents *is* involved and now we have to extract him."

"That's it exactly. His name is Spencer Pang. He's one of the hunger strikers."

"Is he strong enough to travel?"

"I don't know. He hasn't had much sleep since it started and not much if anything to eat for several days, but the hunger strike was necessary to maintain his cover."

1989
TIANANMEN SQUARE TO EAST BERLIN
JACK GODWIN

3.

SUNDAY, JUNE 4, a.m.

After a week's worth of mission briefings, I found myself in the rear seat of a modified Schweizer SGS 2-33 glider flying due west from South Korea to Beijing, with Warburton at the controls. The plan was to bail out at low altitude and land at the Peoples' Football Stadium, three kilometers from the square. We would jog in from the stadium while the glider, wired to detonate when the altimeter hit one-hundred meters, crash-landed on the other side of the city. By the time the Chinese authorities sifted through the wreckage, we'd be long gone.

"Where'd you get the glider?" I asked.

"We borrowed it from the Air Force Academy and repainted it with North Korean Army colors and insignia."

"You borrowed it? How'd you manage that?"

"Tactical dislocation, Darling," he said. "May I call you Darling?

I ignored the question.

"By the way," he said. "We have to cover the three kilometers from the stadium to the square as quickly as possible. Should we give ourselves twenty minutes? I would rather detour than fight unless we have to, of course. Think you can cover the distance in twenty minutes?"

"I ran in college. But my last fitness score was in the ninetieth percentile."

"Ninetieth percentile is not bad."

"For men," I said "ninetieth percentile for men." Warburton's eyebrows registered this new information. "Let's see if we can get there in less than fifteen, since they already know we're here."

"They may suspect we infiltrated the student protest, but they don't know who he is, and they don't know we're coming to extract him. Now then, after we get to the square and recover the asset, we'll go on foot back to the stadium or use available transport if necessary." Warburton nodded and winked at me.

"Did you just wink at me?"

He just smiled and tapped his wristwatch with his index finger. "Altimeter" he said, "time to go!" And then he shouted *Semper Occultus* as we jumped. Our glider immediately started losing altitude and disappeared into the night. Floating down through the darkness, I could see fires burning in Tiananmen Square in the distance. The football stadium was straight below.

We made good time covering the ground between the stadium and the square. The streets were quiet. I hoped it was because the state-owned radio and television stations told people to stay inside. That would make everyone's job easier, theirs and ours. When we got to within a block of the square, I could see the army had not closed every entrance, just the ones wide enough for the tanks.

We ducked into an alley to avoid a column of tanks rumbling toward the square. Troops set up checkpoints at

1989
TIANANMEN SQUARE TO EAST BERLIN
JACK GODWIN

every major outlet, where they detained any suspected protester or sympathizer. That's when residents living nearby panicked and started flooding every street leading away from the area. Not all the protesters were in the square though. Some were hiding in apartment buildings and threw Molotov cocktails or dropped them from the upper floors. We ran to the other end of the alley, to the edge of the square just in time. The local PLA commander gave the order to open fire on the upper floors of the buildings adjacent to the square. There'd be fewer witnesses that way. I couldn't see everything, but was sure anybody watching from their balcony or any open window would've gotten hit if they didn't take cover.

The PLA commander ordered teargas to drive the protesters out, but they were ready. Many of the protesters wore wet towels and handkerchiefs over their mouths and noses. A few others even had gas masks. Fires were burning and the smoke mixed with the teargas. Rickshaws carried wounded protesters to an improvised triage station near the Goddess of Liberty. I was impressed by how organized they were.

During a lull in the fighting, the PLA commander ordered people out of the square but gave them until dawn to comply, but he also gave them an additional incentive. Anybody who came out now would get amnesty. No questions asked. A few foolish ones took his offer and died at point blank range. An hour later, he gave the protesters one more chance, but no one took his offer this time.

The protesters fell back behind rows of makeshift barriers and waited for the inevitable attack. They took cover the best they could behind whatever they could, but the square was mostly wide open. There was no protection. There were too rather detour than fight unless we have to, of course. Think you can cover the distance in twenty minutes?"

"I ran in college. But my last fitness score was in the ninetieth percentile."

"Ninetieth percentile is not bad."

"For men," I said "ninetieth percentile for men." Warburton's eyebrows registered this new information. "Let's see if we can get there in less than fifteen, since they already know we're here."

"They may suspect we infiltrated the student protest, but they don't know who he is, and they don't know we're coming to extract him. Now then, after we get to the square and recover the asset, we'll go on foot back to the stadium or use available transport if necessary." Warburton nodded and winked at me.

"Did you just wink at me?"

He just smiled and tapped his wristwatch with his index finger. "Altimeter" he said, "time to go!" And then he shouted *Semper Occultus* as we jumped. Our glider immediately started losing altitude and disappeared into the night. Floating down through the darkness, I could see fires burning in Tiananmen Square in the distance. The football stadium was straight below.

We made good time covering the ground between the stadium and the square. The streets were quiet. I hoped it was because the state-owned radio and television stations told people to stay inside. That would make everyone's job easier, theirs and ours. When we got to within a block of the square, I could see the army had not closed every entrance, just the ones wide enough for the tanks.

We ducked into an alley to avoid a column of tanks rumbling toward the square. Troops set up checkpoints at

1989
TIANANMEN SQUARE TO EAST BERLIN
JACK GODWIN

every major outlet, where they detained any suspected protester or sympathizer. That's when residents living nearby panicked and started flooding every street leading away from the area. Not all the protesters were in the square though. Some were hiding in apartment buildings and threw Molotov cocktails or dropped them from the upper floors. We ran to the other end of the alley, to the edge of the square just in time. The local PLA commander gave the order to open fire on the upper floors of the buildings adjacent to the square. There'd be fewer witnesses that way. I couldn't see everything, but was sure anybody watching from their balcony or any open window would've gotten hit if they didn't take cover.

The PLA commander ordered teargas to drive the protesters out, but they were ready. Many of the protesters wore wet towels and handkerchiefs over their mouths and noses. A few others even had gas masks. Fires were burning and the smoke mixed with the teargas. Rickshaws carried wounded protesters to an improvised triage station near the Goddess of Liberty. I was impressed by how organized they were.

During a lull in the fighting, the PLA commander ordered people out of the square but gave them until dawn to comply, but he also gave them an additional incentive. Anybody who came out now would get amnesty. No questions asked. A few foolish ones took his offer and died at point blank range. An hour later, he gave the protesters one more chance, but no one took his offer this time.

The protesters fell back behind rows of makeshift barriers and waited for the inevitable attack. They took cover the best they could behind whatever they could, but the square was mostly wide open. There was no protection. There were too few barriers and no more Molotov cocktails. The PLA opened fire with assault rifles and grenades and came into the square from almost every direction. Then the tanks rolled in, flattening everything and everyone. There was panic now and people ran in every direction. Some were shot in the front, some in the back.

There were a few more shots fired. Then it got quiet, except for the cries of the wounded. Bodies were everywhere. I couldn't make an accurate count, but my best guess was five thousand dead and another five thousand wounded in and around the square. Did the army let the protesters leave the square and then open fire in the streets and alleyways? I couldn't see anything, no paramedics, no ambulances, no rickshaws, nothing.

"You stay here," said Warburton. "I'll find Spencer Pang."

"No way," I said. "You're too English. With your complexion, they'd see you're not Chinese from a mile away. *You stay here.* Anyway, I need you to watch my back."

Warburton looked dejected. "We can still talk." I tapped my earpiece. "You can tell me all about your wife and kids."

"Very funny, charming, but if you want to know if I'm married, then you can just ask me."

"Tell me about all your girlfriends then. Good-looking guy like you, steady job, I'll bet you've got lots of girlfriends." This made him laugh.

"There's the pickup point," he said. "Can you see it?"

"I see it," I said as I charged into the square armed with my handgun plus a backup (not on my ankle because I can't run that way) plus spare ammo, knife, knuckles, smoke, silencer and a grenade.

I always carry a grenade when I'm on the job. I got that from Matthew Ridgeway. I heard him talk once at school. He

1989
TIANANMEN SQUARE TO EAST BERLIN
JACK GODWIN

must have been in his eighties by then. He always wore a grenade on his chest. It wasn't for show, he said. A grenade could get you out of a tight spot. *Old Iron Tits* they called him, but probably not to his face.

I went straight for the rendezvous point, jogging not running because I didn't want to attract attention. Spencer was there. I gave him the code and he responded.

"Are you okay?" Spencer nodded yes. "Well enough to travel?" Again he nodded yes.

"Warburton, I've got him," I said into the two-way. "We're making our way toward you now."

I couldn't see Warburton anymore, but I could see the alley where I left him. Spencer and I started running, which I realized was a mistake almost immediately when a PLA soldier approached us. Spencer and I slowed to a walk and I put my head on his shoulder, kept my eyes down and smiled. Meanwhile, I put one hand inside my vest and felt around for my pistol, thumb on the hammer, index finger on the trigger.

We tried to slip past the soldier, but he barked at us and shoved Spencer with his rifle butt. I gave the soldier a double tap to the head. He went down and we covered the body with a discarded sleeping bag. I looked around to see if anyone was watching but couldn't see any immediate threat. But I still felt exposed, way too exposed and decided we needed a diversion. I rolled my smoke grenade on the ground toward where the crowd was thickest, hoping to add chaos to the chaos.

When the grenade popped, everyone turned toward the red smoke. That is, everyone except for an officer standing on a tank looking through binoculars. He saw us.

"Let's go Spencer. Go now. There's Warburton."

1989
TIANANMEN SQUARE TO EAST BERLIN
JACK GODWIN

I could no longer see the officer with the binoculars because we were running hard. I could feel him watching us, though. He was looking for movement and we were moving fast. I was thinking what I would do in his shoes, and I knew what was coming. I saw Warburton now in the shadows right where I left him, a hundred yards away.

I felt Spencer squeeze my hand and then I heard the report. Spencer went down and pulled me down with him.

"I'm hit," he said and let out a growl to suppress the pain. Then I heard shouting and more shooting, and the bullets really started whizzing overhead. I ripped open Spencer's pant leg to expose the wound.

"What happened? Are you hit?" I heard Warburton in my earpiece.

"Not me. It's Spencer. Looks through and through," I said. "Nothing broken but there's plenty of blood." I felt around for the exit wound. "Spencer," I was shouting now as I took off my belt and wrapped it around his thigh, "Let's put a tourniquet on it. We need to get under cover, and then we'll fix you up. We've got to get to Warburton now."

"Not too tight or I can't run," said Spencer.

I hoisted Spencer to his feet and he let out another growl.

"Where's Warburton?" That way, I pointed and Spencer started galloping, careful not to put too much weight on the bad leg. I kept my pistol out, but pointed down. All I wanted was to get everyone back to the stadium and back to the base in South Korea.

"Warburton, I need you to secure transport, anything with wheels," I shouted into the two-way. "Spencer won't make it to the stadium on foot." By then, Spencer wasn't galloping because he had his arm around my shoulder. That PLA officer with the binoculars was running toward us, shouting and waiving and pointing. There was a squad of tough looking infantry wearing riot gear in hot pursuit. We made it to the edge of the square. *Where is Warburton?* We had nowhere to go and the squad was closing in. When they got within twenty yards, my hand went up to the grenade on my vest. I was ready to pull the pin if it came to that. Spencer and I were about to get shot when an armored vehicle—with Warburton behind the wheel—came flying by us and slammed sideways into the squad.

"It's time to go, kids," Warburton said.

Spencer perked right up now that he didn't have to walk any farther. He climbed in and quickly surveyed the compartment.

"Toyota *Land Cruiser* 70 Series," he said, "multi-layered glass, reinforced roof, floor, fuel tank and door hinges, and high-grade run-flat tires." He heaved himself over the back seat and tore the canvas cover off the gun mounted in the rear compartment. "This is what I'm looking for: Type 67 General Purpose machine gun," turning to me, "big improvement over the 57, which was a pain to reload."

Warburton stepped on the gas.

"Let's give'em a burst." Spencer sighted his target and pulled the trigger, which dropped the rest of the squad.

"That officer's still standing," I said.

"Slow down so I can get a shot," said Spencer as he switched to semi-automatic. Then he sighted his target, exhaled and pulled the trigger once more.

"Nice shot," I said. "Okay, now sit back. We'll be at the stadium in a couple of minutes. I'm sure there's a medic on the chopper."

Warburton took it slow driving through Beijing to the stadium. I caught my breath and signaled that we were on our way. Within a minute, the chopper appeared out of nowhere. Warburton and I delivered Spencer into the good hands of the medic, and then we both jumped in. The chopper climbed so fast I thought my stomach was going to fall through the floor.

"Initial heading, 102 degrees east-southeast, cruising at 173 knots," said the pilot.

"What's your name?" said the medic.

"Spencer Pang, Lieutenant Pang."

"Lieutenant Pang, I'm going to give you something to relieve the pain, okay?"

"Okay. Hey, is this the Sikorsky UH-60L? I read about it in *Jane's Defense Weekly*."

Warburton and I turned toward each other and mouthed the words *janes-defense-weekly*.

"Yeah, I read about it," Spencer said. "This thing's great for cruising at high altitude. It's got plenty of power and lift, yeah? And automatic flight control and carries a crew of four and up to eleven troops. You see those two? They're FBI, at least she is. She saved my ass. The other one's English, or he sounds English. Saved my ass! Okay, I'm going to sleep now."

The medic looked at us. "We'll take good care of him," he said over the din of the engines and the rotor.

As Warburton and I settled back for the ride to the base in Korea, we both put on headsets so we could talk without having to yell. You could feel the cabin vibrating and everything running at top speed.

"Congratulations on a job well done," he said after a while.

"Thanks to you, good job with the vehicle procurement, and the driving."

"So, you never answered my question."

1989
TIANANMEN SQUARE TO EAST BERLIN
JACK GODWIN

"What question?"

"May I call you Darling?"

"That depends. Can I call you *English muffin*?"

Just then, I heard a voice in my headset.

"Folks, sorry to jump in, but ah, you're on the crew channel. We can hear everything, just so you know."

I laughed but I could see Warburton was annoyed.

"Listen, Lieutenant, Sergeant?

"Sergeant Davis, sir."

"Then please listen, Sergeant Davis," said Warburton. "Feel free to eavesdrop, feel free to take notes but please do not interrupt."

"Yessir. Maintain heading 109 degrees east-southeast. We'll clear PRC airspace in ten minutes, and arrive at the 121st Combat Support Hospital, Seoul in approximately one hour."

I buckled in and sat back for the rest of the ride. When we got to Seoul, Warburton and I accompanied Spencer as the crew checked him into the hospital. Handshakes all around and then an officer came out of nowhere with two signed-over-the-seal manila envelopes.

"My orders are to take two weeks of family leave and then report to Wiesbaden." I said, "How about you?"

"Budapest," said Warburton, "On the next available transport. Did you say Wiesbaden? He looked preoccupied and I could see he wanted to change the subject.

"That's what I said, yeah. Have you ever been?"

"No. Never," he said, "Well, I hope we meet again Darling, someday when we're not on duty."

There was nothing to do but say our goodbyes, thanks and congratulations without the banter. Then he was gone.

PART TWO

1989
TIANANMEN SQUARE TO EAST BERLIN
JACK GODWIN

4.

FRIDAY, JUNE 16

I didn't need two weeks of family leave. With my family, one week was more than enough. One day, I was watching television with my mother. There was an interview on CNN with the Chinese ambassador, his first one since Tiananmen Square. He claimed the protesters were trying to undermine the Communist Party, overthrow the government and discredit the socialist system, and he called the dead PLA soldiers martyrs.

"Yeah, that's right," I shouted at the television, "Spencer Pang martyred about twenty of your comrades." My mother looked at me like I was insane. Of course, I couldn't explain myself because it was all classified top secret. I thought about Warburton too much for my own good. *Budapest, on the next available transport*, he said. I didn't even know him, and might never see him again. I was lonely and bored and very impatient to find out what my next assignment would be.

I found out soon enough. I flew from Norton Air Force Base to Wiesbaden, Germany and reported for a briefing with Dr. Bernice Benson from the FBI's Counterintelligence Unit, who happened to be my former instructor at the FBI Academy.

1989
TIANANMEN SQUARE TO EAST BERLIN
JACK GODWIN

"Special Agent Nogales," Benson said inviting me into her office. "Please come in."

"Thank you." I surveyed the room. "Nice fish tank."

"They're Siamese fighting fish," she said "Ernst Blofeld, *From Russia with Love*."

"Good one," I laughed. "I always enjoyed seeing you at office hours."

"It's good to see you again. I read your report on Tiananmen Square. Congratulations on that." She paused. "How was home leave?"

My throat hurt too much to say anything.

She walked with a cane behind her desk and signaled with her authoritative chin for me to take a seat.

"Jaqui, I want to introduce you to Major George Tanner from Defense Intelligence. He'll be joining us and you'll be working together on your next assignment. George, you want to take it from here?"

"Things are moving in Central Europe. In April, the Polish government recognized the Solidarity Party," he said. "Last month the Hungarian government dismantled about two hundred kilometers of the barbed wire fence along the Austrian border. Two weeks ago, the Solidarity Party won the election in Poland. That was the first non-communist electoral victory in a long time. And yesterday, a quarter of a million Hungarians gathered at Heroes' Square in Budapest. They were there to show their support for Imre Nagy. Do you know that name?"

"No," I replied.

"Nagy was prime minister in Hungary back in fifty-six, during the revolution. I should say attempted revolution. Nagy tried to withdraw Hungary from the Warsaw Pact. The

Soviets arrested him, charged him and executed him for treason."

"That's it?" I said, "There must be something else. A quarter of a million people don't just get together without a reason."

"There is," said Benson. She nodded for Tanner to continue.

"The Soviets buried Nagy face-down with his hands tied behind his back. Khrushchev wanted to make an example of him, teach a lesson. Now the Hungarians want to rebury him, give him a decent burial and a proper ceremony. Heroes' Square is sacred ground, full of statues of Hungarian leaders going back hundreds of years."

"Got it," I said.

"Agent Nogales, you'll be part of a squad I'm leading into Hungary, where you will make contact with members of the Hungarian opposition parties, the Hungarian Democratic Forum and the Alliance of Free Democrats. We have an agent on the ground, more like a friend really, and he's well connected to Gyorgy Simon, the Hungarian prime minister."

"We're poking a hole in the Iron Curtain," I said.

"Yes and we smell an opportunity," Benson said. "Simon doesn't work for us, but he's taking a big risk. East Germans are allowed to travel on vacation in Hungary, but they're not permitted to cross into Austria, or West Germany or anywhere else for that matter. There's a treaty between Hungary and East Germany, which is still in effect and it forces Hungary to make sure no East Germans escape to the West. As I say, Simon isn't on the payroll, but he is taking a very big risk."

"Okay, first we make contact with the Hungarian opposition, then what?"

1989
TIANANMEN SQUARE TO EAST BERLIN
JACK GODWIN

"You'll receive further instructions," said Benson. "Since last year, Hungarians have been allowed to travel to the west—through Austria—pretty freely. The fence along that border used to be electrified, but Simon ordered the electricity turned off earlier this year. He brought in television cameras and reporters from the west to show the world pictures that the electrified fence is gone but most Hungarians and East Germans seem to think it's some kind of trick. Either the news hasn't spread to East Germany yet, or if it has, most people just refuse to believe it."

"We'll fly into Paris," said Tanner. Then we'll travel by train from Paris to Vienna."

"On the Orient Express, I hope."

"Sorry, no," Benson said as I tried to hide my disappointment, not very successfully.

Tanner stood up and pulled down a map of the region. "From Vienna, it's about seventy-five clicks to the Hungarian border and from there to Sopron, which is a small town inside Hungary, the terrain is mostly farmland. That won't present much of a challenge."

"What's the challenge?"

Benson exhaled. "We have reason to believe the Stasi—East German secret service—is operating in Hungary all along the Austrian border, but headquartered in Sopron. In addition to doing intelligence work all over the world, they do reconnaissance and surveillance through a network of informers all throughout that area."

"So, our job is to neutralize the Stasi agents working the border."

"Exactly," said Tanner, "as long as the Stasi's network is viable, any East German who crosses that border is ... well, let's say we have a duty to protect them."

5.

SUNDAY, JUNE 18

We flew from Wiesbaden to Paris, and took the train to Vienna. We added three more members to the team, who were based at the embassy in Vienna. The new members of the crew were tough-looking and none too talkative. All I knew were their first names: Tom, Jeff and Paul. Then the five of us went by car from Vienna to Neusidler-by-the-Sea, a small resort town on the north shore of Lake Neusidler near the border with Hungary, not far from Czechoslovakia. That time of year there were plenty of tourists, sailors and windsurfers.

We sailed south in a rented commercial fishing boat. Tanner decided that posing as fishermen was better cover than posing as tourists. After the equipment check, it was three in the morning by the time we pulled away from the dock. It was a beautiful night. The moon was almost full and there was no wind. And at that hour, the lake was all ours. The lights in Neusidler (what few there were) receded into the darkness.

The lake was very marshy, so we took it nice and slow, running south by southwest, straight down the middle of the lake. Our ultimate destination inside Hungary was Sopron, population fifty thousand, not too big, not too small and very

1989
TIANANMEN SQUARE TO EAST BERLIN
JACK GODWIN

close to the border with Austria. There was a sizable minority of German-speaking people, which gave good cover for the Stasi and their informants. This, along with its geographic location, put Sopron on the front line for the Cold War.

I went below and dozed off.

Watch how I tie the lure on. Are you watching? First you thread the line through the eye and double it back a few inches. Then twist the end around the line five or six times. Then thread the end through the loop, like that and then pull. It's easier if you use the pliers. The more you pull, the tighter it gets. Then trim the extra line. Now keep your rod up and keep your line clear but let him run. If he's running out, give him slack. If he's running in, take up the slack. If he stops running, that means he's tired but don't try to reel him in too soon. Pump your rod now, that's it. Now lift the tip and lower the tip and crank the reel. Just keep doing that. That's right. Just keep bringing him closer to the bank, just a little closer. Okay, okay, now land him, land him! I got the net. A little closer, that's it. That's it! You did it! Way to go Jaqui!

"Wake up," said Tanner. "It's show time."

I awoke with a start. Everything was quiet. The pilot must have cut the engines. I couldn't hear anything except the prow cutting through the water.

"We're getting close to the drop point," said Tanner, "We'll launch the punt from here. This place is as good as any."

After we anchored the boat, Jeff and Paul lowered a punt into the water. Tanner climbed down into the punt, while Tom handed him all the gear. Then Jeff and Paul and I all took our seats quietly. Tanner sat up front and Tom took the rudder. Tom pushed away from the fishing boat and switched on the trolling motor. There was no hurry. Silence was more important than speed. It was very dark, very cold and very quiet. We passed through a narrow channel. To the north, there was an uninhabited island—and Austria. To the south, there was an uninhabited peninsula—and Hungary. Straight ahead there was the border, just a rusty sign stuck in the lakebed with a stain indicating the high water mark.

"Welcome to Hungary, passports please."

"Shut up."

As we got close to shore, you could see reeds poking up through the surface, short at first then taller. The trolling motor was straining in the swampy mud and Tom switched it off. Without a word, Jeff and Paul stood up and put the wooden punting poles in the water. They worked in tandem on the same side of the boat, planting their poles, pushing and recovering, plant, push, recover. Finally, we ran aground and the punt stuck in the muddy water.

Everybody got out of the boat and into the mud. Jeff and Paul hauled it a few yards out of the water.

Tanner gathered us together. "See there? That's the drainage canal we saw in the satellite image," he pointed "and there's the dirt road."

I could see the silhouette of a small bridge over the canal. On the other side, there was a dirt and gravel road running parallel to the canal and elevated like a levy, which was bad luck. If there was anyone out there—I mean anyone unfriendly—our silhouettes would be easy to spot.

"We've got a choice," said Tanner. "Sopron is eight clicks away. You know what it means if we stay on the road. If we climb down and try to walk through the swamp, we'll get bogged down and be lucky to get there by noon. We're exposed either way but we have to cover the distance somehow."

"I say take the road," said Tom.

1989
TIANANMEN SQUARE TO EAST BERLIN
JACK GODWIN

"What if it's mined or booby trapped?" I asked.

"I don't think so. We're east of town and the Austrian border is west, all the way on the other side of town. If they're trying to prevent mass defections, that's the soft spot, and that's where they'd concentrate, not here. Tom, you take the point," said Tanner, "single file, safeties off."

Tom took the point, then Tanner, then me, Paul and Jeff. From there, we moved south by southwest toward Sopron. It was four thirty and there was still a little moonlight, a slight breeze and nobody else in sight. Blood was pounding in my ears. We spread farther apart the longer we walked. In fifteen minutes, I couldn't see anybody and barely heard boots crunching on the gravel.

I liked how these guys worked, though, very professional. No locker room antics, no horsing around, just business. Everyone knew who was in charge, but Tanner asked their opinions anyway. And when he gave an order, the guys didn't question it because they knew what to do without waiting for orders. That was my idea of teamwork. I was feeling confident and starting to like our chances against the Stasi, even though they had home court advantage.

Up ahead there was a flash of light followed by a short blast. I could hear Tom screaming. He must have tripped a wire or stepped on a landmine. I hit the deck but I could hear Tanner or somebody running forward toward the screams. Within a few seconds there was a second explosion. Now Tom was dead and Tanner was screaming. I rolled off the road halfway down the south side of the embankment. Paul and Jeff went running past me, ignoring my warning.

"Get down goddammit! It's a trap!" Now I was running too, at the bottom of the embankment where the ground was uneven and muddy. I was running and crouching to keep my head below the top of the embankment. Jeff, Paul and I reached Tanner. He stopped screaming but he was badly wounded, both legs mangled below the knee. While Jeff went to work on him, I heard a low plunk and Jeff went down making a gurgling noise. Then another plunk and Paul went down.

"Shit." There was at least one sniper, maybe two. What do I do? *What do I do?* Now I had three dead and one wounded. It wouldn't take long for Tanner to bleed out. I held my breath to try and hear something, but no. Nothing, not even Tanner made a sound. I couldn't just sit there. I checked the time. It was four forty-five. It would be dawn soon and I'd have no cover at all. Where the fuck was the sniper? He must be on the opposite side, I figured, north of the canal or else I'd have heard the bullets whizzing overhead.

I wondered if the sniper was alone. Even if he was, he might have a radio and not be alone for long. In either case, I had to get away from there, stay low behind the embankment, but my life depended on getting away. I wasn't going to get to Sopron like this. Maybe I could get to that village to the north. What was it called? Fertorakos, maybe I could get to Fertorakos, but then what?

I belly crawled away from the bodies back toward the lake. I thought maybe I could get to the boat. I hated leaving Tanner and the others but they wouldn't want me to get myself killed on their account. I just wanted to get away. If there was another tripwire at the bottom of the embankment, I'd find out soon enough. I crawled not too far, not even fifty yards before I came to a culvert. *Ha! Thank you, Lord.* In the rainy season, the overflow from the lake must come through this channel. This is why the road was elevated, to keep it dry

1989
TIANANMEN SQUARE TO EAST BERLIN
JACK GODWIN

during the spring runoff. And this was how I could get to the other side without getting shot.

Ugh, it was slimy in there, but slimy and smelly was better than bloody. Once I got through to the other side of the culvert, I took a peek left and right but couldn't see much. I sure couldn't see the sniper, but I could feel him scanning the area. I could feel him looking for me, looking and wondering if he counted right. Did he see five or only four?

On the north side of the culvert there was a concrete canal running parallel to the embankment. The water lapped against the bottom of the culvert, but there was no telling how deep it was. I took off my boots, vest and shirt, tied the boots onto my pack and stuffed the clothes inside. I slipped into the water as quietly as I could and half-waded, half-dog paddled across the canal. It was so cold I had to clench my jaw to keep my teeth from chattering. I thanked God it wasn't January and I thanked God again when I reached the other side, barely fifteen feet across.

Once I climbed out on the other side, I put my boots and vest back on. I decided to come back for the rest of my stuff later. There're only two kinds of people in this swamp, I said to myself, the dead kind and that other kind. I got back into my belly crawl and went hunting for the sniper, making no sound and making as little movement as possible. My best guess was that he was lying low at least a hundred yards north of the canal. I figured he might even have a regular duty station, which he would have outfitted for himself to keep warm and dry. Those anti-personnel mines along that embankment could only mean one thing. The Stasi knew someone was coming, but I'll bet that sniper was wondering right now if he counted right—and that was why he hadn't moved yet. Did he know he was being hunted?

1989
TIANANMEN SQUARE TO EAST BERLIN
JACK GODWIN

Twenty minutes later, I covered a hundred yards and it was still dark as night. I just hoped he hadn't called it in and didn't have any friends in the vicinity. I had to find a way to get him to show himself. Twenty minutes later and another few yards, my arms started to ache. I was covered in mud that smelled like rotten egg salad. That sniper was really starting to annoy me. This couldn't go on forever. It was going to be light soon and they'd find the bodies, then they'd find my pack and that would lead them straight to me.

I rolled onto my back and unclipped my grenade. I wasn't frightened but my adrenaline was really pumping. I stayed still for a moment to catch my breath and slow down my heart rate. I pulled the pin, got up quickly onto one knee and threw the grenade as far as I could toward where I thought he was. Then I hit the deck.

There was no cover out there and I didn't want to get hit with my own shrapnel, so I counted to five after the explosion before I raised my head. I couldn't see him but I could hear him and ran toward the distinctive plinking sound. I drew my pistol and ran as hard as I could toward him. The shooting stopped because his clip was empty. He was closer than I thought because I was on top of him in seconds. I almost ran past him and tried to stop but the ground was slick and I lost my balance. My feet came out from under me and I broke my fall with my empty hand just as he popped in a new clip and aimed at me. He was up off the ground now and facing me. Bang, bang, I gave him one to the chest and one to the forehead. Without getting off a round, he fell backward holding his rifle while I kept my weapon trained on him.

I checked left: nothing, right nothing, and then behind me still nothing. It was quiet now, but I could see a sliver of light on the horizon. I could barely stand but I had to keep

1989
TIANANMEN SQUARE TO EAST BERLIN
JACK GODWIN

moving. I checked the body for anything useful. He was wearing civilian clothes with the tags cut out, nothing to link him to Stasi, but that was a given. It was Cold War and counterintelligence and everyone wore civilian clothes, including me. I went back to pick up my backpack and check on the other bodies. I didn't cross the canal again, but I could see from this side that Tom was in pieces. Tanner bled out from his legs. Jeff and Paul one shot each to the head, very efficient.

I had to keep moving. I had to get indoors before dawn. I turned north toward Fertorakos hoping maybe there was a farm, a barn, anyplace warm where I could think for a minute. The farther away I went from the canal, the less swampy it got. It was already after six when I came to the eastern outskirts of town. A rooster crowed, the first one of the day. Very faintly I could smell someone baking bread, which made my stomach growl. In the distance there was a man driving a donkey cart with his collar up and his hat pulled low. All the buildings were made of rough bricks with clay tiled roofs. Some of the houses looked many decades old but still unfinished. The roads were unpaved, but smooth like they had been bulldozed. It was probably a nice place I thought, old country charm if not for the trigger happy East German secret police.

There was movement in an upstairs window. Did I see it or just imagine it? If that was another sniper, I was already dead. My hair was tucked under my cap, so from a distance I could have been anybody, just another villager getting an early start—as long as I kept my head down. Just in case, I moved my hand to my pistol. I kept traveling and breathing to calm myself and tried to look as inconspicuous as possible. I was almost to the town square, a big parade ground with the party headquarters situated at one end, decorated with the red, white and green flag. The sight provoked a moment of weakness. *I'd really rather not cross that parade ground right now. I've got four dead, can't even bury them, completely cut off, and I smell like a pile of manure.*

"In here," said a quiet voice in German.

What? A familiar voice, it's not possible. Over my left shoulder I turned and saw Basil Warburton standing inside the doorway of what looked like an abandoned general store.

6.

MONDAY, JUNE 19

"In here before anyone sees you," he said again. This time I did as I was told and staggered over the threshold into his arms.

"You've been busy, Darling," he said. "I've been watching you from the second floor window."

"That was you I saw, or at least I saw the curtain move."

"I was tempted to run out there and greet you with a tea and toast. You look like you could use a bath. Tell me what happened."

"Wait. First, what are you doing here?"

"I told you I've been seconded from Her Majesty's Government. For the time being, let's just say we're both fighting on the same side. What happened?"

"We took off in a fishing boat from the north shore of Lake Neusidler at three in the morning."

"I mean after that."

"We left the boat anchored on the Austrian side and took a punt across the border, me and four others."

"I know, after that."

"I can't think of anything we did that would have tipped them off. Everything was according to plan, at first. We landed a few yards from the mouth of the drainage canal. We took the road that runs parallel to the canal. It was easy, exactly like the satellite image except the road was elevated a few feet. Tom—one of the squad—took the point. He must have tripped a wire or stepped right on a mine. Then Tanner—the squad leader—ran to help. That's when I hit the dirt and rolled off the road, and the other two members went running past me. The sniper was waiting for them. They're all dead, and I would be too but I took him out. I crawled a couple hundred yards and tossed my grenade hoping I'd get lucky."

"I'd say you got lucky," he said.

"What is this place?"

"This is my safe house," he said. The location is very convenient. The upstairs is perfect for observation. That sniper was not out there—no one was out there—at sundown yesterday, I can assure you."

"Do you think they knew we were coming? Or do they post a sniper out there every night? Anyway, the levy was mined and booby trapped. There must have been a second bomb timed to wound anybody who came to help just like Tanner did. Jesus, I'm hungry. Is there some place I can wash?"

Warburton led me downstairs into the basement. "Here we are. Living quarters, well-stocked kitchen, bath or shower, take your pick. What do you think?"

I nodded my approval.

"Excellent. I'll make tea."

"This safe house is yours?"

"It belongs to the British Army actually."

I collapsed into an overstuffed chair and closed my eyes, which made me realize how exhausted I was.

1989
TIANANMEN SQUARE TO EAST BERLIN
JACK GODWIN

"Here you are, Earl Gray. That's the stuff Jean-Luc Picard drinks."

"Huh? You're not a Trekkie. No way," I said.

"Not a Trekkie, but I know who Patrick Stewart is. He used to do Shakespeare in London. Besides, knowing a thing or two about American television goes with the job."

"You say this is what Captain Picard drinks? Thanks. Go on."

"All of Hungary, including right where you're seated now, as well as the eastern part of Austria was in the Soviet occupation zone. The Soviets withdrew from Austria in 1955. We'd been supplying the Austrian resistance for the better part of ten years before that just to irritate the Russians. Some members of the resistance were former Nazis, but they were all good anti-communists, which is all anyone cared about at the time. However, Her Majesty's Government has maintained this little stronghold and operated undetected for the last fifty years or so."

"I really need to shower now because these clothes reek. But thanks for the tea."

"I'd be happy to scrub your back."

"What?"

"I'll scrub your back," he said. "I wouldn't mind."

"I think you wouldn't mind seeing me naked."

"I'll admit. I wouldn't mind seeing you *undressed*."

"Oh, thank you. No."

"Don't be so American."

"What are you talking about? I thought the Germans were the nudists, not the English."

"What?"

"Hey, I'm not the one pitching a tent."

"Can I say something?"

1989
TIANANMEN SQUARE TO EAST BERLIN
JACK GODWIN

"All I'm saying is you can't exactly hide it. That's all I'm saying." I took a sip of tea and let the silence fill the room. "Listen," I said. "I wouldn't call you cocky. You're confident and charming and intelligent obviously, and you know how to make tea. I'm not sure how unusual that is because you're English, a nudist Englishman."

"Can I say something?"

"Sure."

"I was going to tell you where to find the towels."

"Oh, thank you." I handed him the cup and saucer. "That hit the spot."

I turned the faucet on as hot as I could stand, scrubbed everything twice and let my mind wander. What a luxury it was to have a hot shower after crawling through that muck. I was going to have to write a report for Benson and she was not going to like reading *four dead*. At least I got the sniper. Were they expecting us? Better not to speculate. Let Benson handle that. Why did they send Warburton? And why didn't they tell us? Maybe they told Tanner but not the rest of the squad. Yeah, that made sense.

I toweled off and came out wearing a government-issue bathrobe. There was music playing, Madonna's *Like a Prayer*.

"What this?"

"British Forces Radio, live via satellite. How was your shower? I poured you a glass of wine."

"Great, maybe the best shower I ever had, scrubbed off all that crusty, dried Central European swamp mud."

"Oh, now this is a great song," he said.

"Oh, I know this one. Wait, who's that singing? It sounds like the Beatles."

"Yeah, that's Paul McCartney. This is the benefit song. You're thinking of the old version by Gerry and the

1989
TIANANMEN SQUARE TO EAST BERLIN
JACK GODWIN

Pacemakers, nineteen sixty something. This is the new version, re-recorded to raise money for the Hillsborough disaster."

"What disaster?"

"It was for the Hillsborough disaster in April. There was a crush at a football game—sorry, soccer game—near Sheffield. It was bad. Eighty people died, women, children, it was awful. One of the teams was from Liverpool and most of the victims, too."

"It sounds awful."

"It was. The Mersey is a river, just a river, but it empties into Liverpool Bay. But it's a lovely song."

"Dance with me," I said.

"Dance with you?"

"Yes, dance with me, please."

"Jaqui?"

"Yes?"

"We received a fax while you were in the shower, from Bernice Benson's office."

"Do you know her?"

"We've got new orders. Actually, your orders are the same. Neutralize the Stasi network along the border. But mine are now the same as yours. I've arranged a meeting later with some people from the Hungarian opposition."

"Okay."

Then the song ended.

"Why don't you get some rest? You look done in."

I fell onto the bed still wearing the bathrobe and fell asleep instantly.

Daddy, I'm joining the FBI. What do they want with a business major and a lawyer? There's a lot of work internationally, banking, drugs, terrorism. First, I've got to get through law school, then take the bar exam. After that I would go to the FBI Academy. Then I'll swear an oath and carry a badge, a gun and everything. The pay's not great but the work's really interesting. I could always practice law or maybe teach after I serve twenty years. You and your brother could not be more different. Don't you want a family? Don't you want kids? Still, special agent sounds pretty good. This is Special Agent Nogales. Hands up! I liked that movie with what's-his-name. That was Eliot Ness and he was a Treasury Agent. Not him. Never bring a knife to a gunfight! That was Sean Connery, the beat cop. Oh yeah, that's right. I thought he was better in Highlander. There can be only one! Anyway, I'm proud of you. No father was ever prouder, Jaqui ... Jaqui ... Jaqui.

"Jaqui, it's time to wake up."

"Oh, I was dreaming about my father. Oh my God. It was so real. What time is it?"

"It's four in the afternoon. You've been asleep for eight hours. I guess you needed it. Here are some clothes for you. They'll fit close enough and make you look like one of the locals. I pulled out several pairs of shoes for you to try. You can't wear those boots—they look too American. And don't wear any makeup. You're already too good-looking as it is."

I tried not to laugh.

"Are you telling me Hungarian women don't wear makeup? No lipstick? No eye-liner? How's a girl supposed to survive? Can I at least wear some sunscreen? Ouch, this bra is uncomfortable. I mean, it fits okay but it's hideous. See for yourself."

"Clothes make the woman."

"Ha! Everything fits okay, if a little baggy. Can I wear my vest underneath? I have a little routine. I like to know where

1989
TIANANMEN SQUARE TO EAST BERLIN
JACK GODWIN

my weapons are, my hand gun, my spare ammo, my knife, my knuckles, smoke, silencer and a grenade. That way I don't have to think about it. Check, check, check."

"Can't you do something with your hair, tie it back or something?"

"Sure. How's this?"

"Not bad," he said with his hands behind his back imitating Rex Harrison, "not bad at all."

"You watch too many movies."

"You talk in your sleep."

"Do I?"

"No. Not really."

"Did I say anything? Tell me."

"You didn't say anything." I studied his face to see if he was lying.

"Did I mumble or make any funny noises—anything at all?"

"You didn't say anything. You barely moved. Your face looked extraordinarily peaceful, angelic even."

"So you watched me while I was sleeping?"

"I read mostly, read the files and studied the maps. I have a routine when I'm on the job, just like somebody I know."

"For eight hours?"

"Yes."

"Thank you. Thanks for looking out for me." The silence was awkward and I changed the subject. "So, when are we going into Sopron? How far is it?"

"Just about ten kilometers, and we're going by car—less conspicuous that way. We need to reconnoiter. I procured a vehicle, a modified Trabant 601S Universal, what you would call a station wagon. Someone from the Hungarian opposition will join us and then we'll go to Sopron together."

7.

TUESDAY, JUNE 20

"This is Special Agent Jaqueline Nogales," said Warburton. "And this is Josef Tibor, the concierge at the Napsugar campground at Lake Balaton."

"You're Gypsy?" said Tibor. I shook my head.

"Born and raised in California," I said. "How about if I hop in back and you can tell us all about Sopron?"

"Oh, I would not know where to begin."

"The beginning is a very good place to start."

"Very well," said Tibor. "Sopron is an ancient city. The town's history goes back to the Roman Empire. It was just a settlement back then, called Scarbantia. Legend has it that the Scarbantians deserted the city in the eighth or ninth century. Maybe there was a famine, nobody knows for sure. However, the Scarbantia forum was located where the main square is today. Maybe we will visit there if we have time. When the ethnic Hungarians arrived, all the inhabitants were gone and the town was in ruins."

"The Hungarians rebuilt the old Roman walls and built the castle, where King Otakar of Bohemia lived in the thirteenth century. Then there was King Ladislaus of Hungary. Then the Turks invaded in the fifteen hundreds and most of the area fell under the Ottoman Empire. The

Habsburg Empire defeated the Ottoman Empire in seventeen hundred and took over most of the territory north of the Danube River. By the mid-nineteenth century, the Habsburg family was growing weaker and was forced to share power with the Hungarians. The Austro-Hungarian Empire lasted fifty years until World War I."

Tibor continued, "After World War I, the Austro-Hungarian Empire broke up. Sopron was part of Austria briefly, but in 1921 people voted to be part of Hungary. Every year on the anniversary of the vote, there is a city holiday to celebrate Hungary's *most loyal town*. But there is still a large German speaking population, a lot of Catholics, not too many Jews any more. There is a synagogue in the old town and a Jewish cemetery, but both are in bad condition. There were a few Jewish families, old families who lived in the area for hundreds of years—the 'tolerated' Jews they called them—but most died in the concentration camps. The German and Austrian culture has been suppressed since 1945, but that is beginning to change. That is good and bad for us. Good because we work with the Austrians, bad because it allows the Stasi to operate undetected."

"Tibor," said Warburton, "Tell Jaqui who we're going to meet."

"We are going to meet Otto Von Habsburg."

"You must be joking."

"No joke. Otto Von Habsburg is a devoted anti-communist. He is in Sopron right now, waiting for us at Saint Michael's."

Saint Michael's Church sat at the top of a hill on the east side of town. The spire came into view as we wound our way up the steep drive. It was a beautiful old building, a mixture of Romanesque and Gothic architecture.

1989
TIANANMEN SQUARE TO EAST BERLIN
JACK GODWIN

"Tibor, wait. Are you sure this is secure?" asked Warburton.

"Not a hundred percent, but it is worth the risk. Herr Habsburg has many friends and probably some very useful information."

Tibor, Warburton and I stepped out of the Trabant into the afternoon sun. Everything was quiet except for the gravel crunching as we walked past the headstones scattered around the churchyard to the front porch. We passed underneath the spire dominating the west façade and into the darkness of the arcade. You could feel the temperature drop and smell the medieval stones. The walls were decorated with paintings and a large wooden carving of Madonna. Two men wearing dark suits nodded at us. One gestured with his hand toward a small chapel. Inside there was an imposing old man standing and waiting for us, hands clasped behind his back.

"Permit me to introduce the Archduke of Austria, Otto Von Habsburg," said Tibor.

We exchanged greetings and introductions all around.

"Please do sit down. We haven't much time, but we might as well be comfortable since we're all in the country illegally, except for you Tibor of course." Tibor smiled and they both chuckled at this. Then Habsburg looked directly at me.

"I lived in Washington during the war. Did you know that?"

"I didn't know that."

"I lived there almost five years. When I opposed the Anschluss with Nazi Germany, Rudolf Hess issued a death warrant on me. I consider it a badge of honor and perhaps my greatest achievement. You can tell a lot about a man by the enemies he makes. So many friends died." He paused to take a breath. "I've been involved in politics since the thirties, all of my adult life. In the old days, I worked to restore my family to the throne, but I gave that up in the sixties. I lived all over Europe, in Belgium, France, Switzerland, many years in Spain. Francisco Franco asked if I would serve as king, but turned him down. I just wanted to come home. I renounced all my hereditary titles and declared my loyalty, so eventually the Austrian government let me come back. After almost fifty years in exile, I became a private citizen. The first thing I did was visit the family cemetery. I've used my family name to speak out against communism. I never gave up on European integration, on the idea of a unified Europe. I never gave up hope of liberating our friends behind the Iron Curtain, especially our friends here in Hungary."

"How can we help?" asked Warburton.

"Do you know Gyorgy Simon?"

"The prime minister?" said Warburton, "of course."

"How about Laszlo Nagy? He works in the Ministry of the Interior?" I shook my head no. "We've been working together—just talking really—about bringing down the Iron Curtain once and for all. We have a plan but it's still too dangerous with so many Stasi agents in Hungary." He paused and looked at Warburton and then at me. "Are you aware the Hungarian government began dismantling the barbed wire fence along the Austrian border in May? That border is almost two hundred fifty kilometers long."

"We were briefed on it," I said.

"What would you say if we completely eliminated the border restrictions between Austria and Hungary?"

"It could be the fifty-six uprising all over again. It would almost certainly topple the government. The Red Army would probably intervene," said Warburton. "On the other hand, Gorbachev is no Khrushchev."

"I believe you're right," said Habsburg. "It's not the Red Army we need to worry about. It's the Stasi. They're the watchdog of the party, and widely respected within the intelligence community both for their German efficiency and their Bolshevik brutality. The Stasi is perhaps the only thing in East Germany that really works. They conduct all forms of espionage, including surveillance of foreigners, Jews, Gypsies, capitalists and suspicious persons. They do surveillance of mail and telephone, and analysis of garbage, blackmail, and of course executions, usually with a pistol, one shot to the neck. That's their signature. In this part of Hungary, the Stasi employs a total of ten full-time officers, as far as we know."

"Nine," I said, "I nailed one yesterday." Habsburg nodded his appreciation and continued, "That's not counting paid informants and unofficial collaborators. It's getting more and more difficult to recruit informants, especially here. However, those who remain on the payroll are fanatics. I should tell you, there are some Stasi collaborators working in the Hungarian Ministry of the Interior as well as the National Police."

"Let's assume the local detachment is a death squad and treat it accordingly," said Warburton.

"The Stasi are concentrating their attention in two areas. One is Lake Balaton, also known as the Hungarian Sea. It's a popular tourist destination. Josef here knows as much about that subject as any man alive. The other is right here in Sopron. We know this because we've intercepted several reports. The Stasi have developed an elaborate network of informers in the most popular campsites and resorts for East

German tourists. But the Hungarian authorities don't have the resources—or the political will—to support the Stasi anymore. The government is more concerned with homegrown political opposition."

"So, our ultimate objective isn't Budapest, but East Berlin," I said.

"Yes," said Habsburg. "However, at this point most East German tourists have no intention of going back, but they're scared to death and don't know who to trust. Some of the Stasi agents are equally confused. I'll bet Berlin thinks every East German in Hungary is a potential defector—not just the tourists but the spies, too. And there are so many tourists now, hundreds of thousands this time of year. The people most at risk, at least as far as the Stasi is concerned, are those with families in the West. Remember, the Stasi keeps a file on everybody. From experience, they know who is most likely to defect. The Stasi don't have the authority to arrest anyone in Hungary—they're not even here officially. As I said, the Hungarian authorities no longer have the resources or the will to cooperate with the Stasi anymore. This presents us with an opportunity."

"Let's hear your idea," said Warburton.

"We want to organize a picnic," said Tibor, which surprised all of us because Tibor was so quiet. Warburton smirked and didn't say anything, but Habsburg could read his skepticism.

Then Habsburg said, "It's more than two years since President Reagan went to Berlin and gave that marvelous speech at the Brandenburg Gate. Do you remember that? *Tear down this wall!* Two years I've been waiting. They built the damn thing in 1961. That was twenty-eight years ago! I want to live long enough to see it fall."

1989
TIANANMEN SQUARE TO EAST BERLIN
JACK GODWIN

"Hold on," I said, "What did Tibor say about a picnic?

Habsburg responded. "We're thinking about calling it the Pan-European Picnic. We want to hold it on both sides of the border. We intend to invite a few thousand of our East German friends and encourage them to wander across the border into Austria. We'll eat some sausage, and drink some beer, and a little schnapps. The idea is to give people a taste of freedom."

"But we want to announce it and publicize it," said Tibor. "We want a big crowd, but we do not want any trouble. We want no violence."

"You're asking for trouble," said Warburton.

"That's where you come in, and you Ms. Nogales," said Habsburg. This is the first time he spoke my name. "We need you to neutralize the local Stasi detachment, and we think we can help you do it."

"*How?*" said Warburton.

Warburton's tone was impatient and accusatory, but Habsburg ignored this. "We plan to stage a tear-down event in advance of the picnic. The plan under discussion is to have the Austrian foreign minister—that is Johann Bauer—and the Hungarian foreign minister—that's Tamas Lakatos cut a hole in the border fence. We want it to look like a staged event. We'll invite reporters and photographers, of course. Naturally, this will attract the Stasi's attention, and this is the real purpose. If I know them, and I do, they will find it irresistible. I believe we can use this staged event—you Americans would call it a photo opportunity—to induce the Stasi to tip their hand. Every member of the local detachment will be in attendance."

At this, Warburton stood up and began pacing. Tibor, Habsburg and I followed him with our eyes. "We'll need some time to prepare," he said, "When were you planning this photo opportunity to puncture the Iron Curtain?"

"June twenty-seventh," said Habsburg, "which leaves us nine days."

"So at this point, we don't want to kill or capture anyone or even expose their network," I said. "Later, we'll need to neutralize the muscle-end of their operation. For now, we just want to catalog and diagram their organization. We can be sure all Stasi intelligence officers were trained in the USSR. They probably rely on the same structure as the KGB. When the diagram is complete—and accurate—we'll have a hierarchy of collaborators and informants, all of whom report to sub-agents who report to a few resident officers, who report to one special agent—or spymaster. We need names, locations, pictures if you can, plus any other helpful information."

"We need to know who the spymaster is," Warburton said.

"We know who he is," said Tibor. "Konrad Gazecki, *Colonel* Gazecki. We have a dossier on him. The Stasi sent him to the KGB school in Leningrad. We know he worked in Dresden for a while. We know his first overseas assignment was in Britain, where he demonstrated a special talent as a spy-catcher, killed an agent working in the Soviet embassy in London. And we know he's in Hungary now. The only problem is we do not have a photograph of him. Nobody knows what Gazecki looks like. But, we know that he is here now. We are certain. Our source is reliable even though Gazecki has been very elusive so far."

"What's he doing here?" I asked.

"That's for you to find out," said Habsburg, "And you have nine days, plenty of time to leak the information before

1989
TIANANMEN SQUARE TO EAST BERLIN
JACK GODWIN

the event is publicly announced to set up an operation." At this, he stood up and straightened his vest. "I must go. I don't want people to think I've left Vienna. It's no longer an occupied city, but you still have to be careful." He turned to Warburton and shook hands. He shook my hand and held it and smiled at me. "We're counting on you. Good luck and Godspeed."

Habsburg signaled to his bodyguards, who led him out. We heard footsteps on the gravel in the courtyard. The car doors slammed, engine started and the car rumbled down the drive.

"If Gazecki trained with the KGB at Leningrad," I said. "That's where he learned the tradecraft, guerilla warfare, assassination, sabotage, kidnapping, weapons, unarmed combat and explosives."

Half a second later, an explosion rocked the church. A bomb went off outside, which collapsed the chapel wall behind where Tibor was standing. The blast knocked the three of us, Tibor, Warburton and me to the floor. Lying face down, I was choking on the dust, deafened and dazed. I looked up to see light pouring into the chapel through a huge hole in the wall. Outside, men were shouting in German. I could distinguish three or maybe four different voices but couldn't tell for sure because everything was muffled. Someone grabbed my arm. I turned and saw it was Warburton, but he wasn't looking at me. He lifted me up and pulled me out the chapel door and toward the back of the church, opposite of the way we came in.

We were running now. My head was beginning to clear but I had a fantastic headache. My ears were ringing and I could hear men shouting. But they weren't outside anymore.

They were inside the church, and probably came in through the hole they blasted in the chapel wall.

"Wait," I said to Warburton. I couldn't tell if he heard me so I jerked free. I reached for the grenade on my vest and our eyes met. He smiled to show his comprehension. I glanced at Tibor and showed him the grenade. He smiled, too. With the grenade in one hand, I crawled behind the pews back toward the chapel. I pulled the pin and counted to four. "*Say hello to Old Iron Tits*," I swore and rolled the grenade into the chapel. Then I sprinted toward the back of the church as the grenade detonated.

"That evens the odds," said Warburton.

"Maybe, but don't open that door. Let's climb the tower and see how many we're up against."

"Right," he said, "brilliant. Let's go."

There were two stone staircases on either side of the portico. One went down into the basement. The other went up toward the spire. The stairwell wasn't lit, and the higher we climbed the darker it got. It was completely dark by the time we got to the first landing. Then we heard a voice—again in German—shouting orders.

"Wait," I said, "That wasn't a bomb in the chapel. It was a rocket. Down! Get down!"

Half a second later, another explosion rocked the church, raining blocks, debris and dust down on us. We scrambled back down to the portico. Tibor headed straight for the staircase on the other side that led to the basement with Warburton and me right behind him. Down in the basement, it was cooler and dark again and quiet. Twenty-five feet on the left, there was a sliver of light coming through the cellar door. There was a short flight of steps leading up to a pair of rotting wooden doors held in place by a set of rusty hinges.

1989
TIANANMEN SQUARE TO EAST BERLIN
JACK GODWIN

"Here is the way out" said Tibor. "Mind your head."

Warburton turned to me and said, "I'd like to show you around London someday."

"What?"

"London," he said. "I'd like to show it to you someday."

"Sure. Can we talk about it later?"

"Well, that's precisely the point, isn't it, Darling. We may be dead in a few minutes. If we can just make it to the Trabant, I believe our life expectancy will improve immensely. Meanwhile, we shouldn't stop planning for the future. We may as well surrender."

"Let's plan on London," I said as I reloaded.

We drew our weapons and pushed the doors open. Sunlight flooded the basement.

"There they are, and there's the car," I said. "I'll cover you." I climbed the first two steps so I was still behind the stone wall and opened fire. There were four of them on the far end of the parking lot in front of a cluster of trees, just barely within range if I took careful aim. I squeezed the trigger and put one down on the first shot. The other three were startled, but well-trained and hit the deck instantly. They couldn't see where the shots were coming from.

"*Now*," I said.

Warburton and Tibor bolted for the car while I kept the bad guys in my sights. Now that nobody was shooting at them, they all lifted their heads to see what was happening. I put one shot into the dirt to keep them pinned. Tibor started the engine and Warburton flipped open the passenger side door.

"It's time to go, Darling."

I put one more shot into the dirt before I made my break. All my attention now was on the space between the cellar door and the car. But it was like a dream, like wading waist deep through water. Tibor gunned the engine, which sent gravel flying under the spinning wheels. Warburton reached his hand toward me. Time stood still. I couldn't hear anything and then pop-pop and my left leg wouldn't work. I was hit, *God dam rookie mistake what're you saving your ammo for?* Warburton took my hand and pulled me on top of him into the car. The door closed by force of the acceleration, and we were off.

"Fuck! Shit! *Fuckshit*," I roared. Then I saw how much I was bleeding and forgot about being angry. Tibor was flying the Trabant down the hill and I was bleeding all over Warburton. I couldn't see where I was hit and was starting to feel light-headed. I was bleeding so much. Fight back, *now* I told myself. I drew my weapon, plus my backup. Warburton was covered in blood and I was covered in blood and Tibor was flying down the hill. Warburton had his arms around me and I turned backward and started shooting over his shoulders.

There was one aiming a grenade launcher and two firing Kalashnikovs. Those two were foolish to be standing so close together, so I aimed for them first. I emptied my revolver and my automatic, tossed the revolver on the back seat and put in a new clip into the automatic and then emptied everything I had into the one with the grenade launcher. He fell backward but pulled the trigger before he hit the ground sending the grenade high over the Trabant. There was a huge explosion, which sent more blocks, debris and dust raining down on us.

"Warburton, I'm sorry, I can't, *can't*." And that was it.

I don't want people to think I've left. Vienna is no longer an occupied city, but you still have to be careful. Where have I

1989
TIANANMEN SQUARE TO EAST BERLIN
JACK GODWIN

heard that before? It's from the Third Man. It takes place in Vienna after the war. It's with Joseph Cotton and Orson Welles. Don't you remember? We rented it from the video store and watched it together. Is that you, Daddy? What're you doing here? I'm here. What did he mean Vienna's no longer an occupied city? The allies didn't cut Austria in two like Germany, but divided the whole country into occupation zones, including Vienna. The Allies hit Vienna pretty hard and left a lot of the city in ruins, buildings, people, the economy, everything. There was a black market for everything, food, fuel, liquor, cigarettes, even medicine. That's what it's about, the black market. There's a black market for everything. Remember the chase scene in the sewer, splashing through the sweet water that flows into the Blue Danube? Smells like a doctor's office.

8.

WEDNESDAY, JUNE 21

"Why does it smell like a doctor's office?" I felt something cold and then a stab on my arm.

"That's for tetanus. I'm going to give you one more for the infection," said a voice.

"Who're you? Where am I?"

"I am a doctor, friend of a friend you might say. This is my clinic." I looked down and saw my left leg wrapped in gauze. There was Warburton sitting at the foot of the bed, and Tibor leaning against the door smoking. The doctor swabbed my arm with that quick back-and-forth motion the way they always do. "You are fortunate someone remembered to keep pressure on the wound," he said. "You are also fortunate the bullet missed the femoral artery. You lost some blood, but it was not as bad as it looked. You also have a mild concussion. Keep an icepack on it. You may have a headache for a while. If you feel dizzy or start vomiting, then you should come back." He looked at his watch and then turned to Tibor. "I will return in a while. I am sure you have things to discuss." Tibor and Warburton waited for the door to close.

"What's the last thing you remember?"

1989
TIANANMEN SQUARE TO EAST BERLIN
JACK GODWIN

"I got hit. You pulled me into the car and then I started shooting. How'd we get out? How'd we get here? What time is it?"

"It's just after midnight."

"How did the Stasi know we were at St. Michaels? I mean they obviously know we're in-country. How did they know we were at St. Michael's? How long were they waiting? Did they let Habsburg go or did they get there after he left? How do you know we weren't followed? How do you know they aren't waiting for us outside right now?"

"They are not outside," said Tibor.

"How do you know?"

"You killed them all."

"What?"

"You killed them all," said Tibor. "I do not know how you did it, but you did. I saw them go down, one at a time in the mirror. The last one launched a rocket before he died. He missed but that is how you got the concussion. We were not followed. At least we were not followed here. We will be okay for a while, but we should get both of you back to Fertorakos while it is still dark."

"Habsburg gave me an idea when he said we have plenty of time to leak the information about the tear-down event on the twenty-seventh," I said. "We should set up a sting operation."

"I'd love to hear it Darling, but not here. Besides, we had better check in first, see if there's any new information—or new orders—but not now, not here. I trust the doctor's medical skills but I don't want to remain here any longer than you do. Get some rest and we'll get going in a few hours."

At five o'clock that morning the doctor changed the dressing, gave me some pills for the pain and some more in case of infection.

"Try not to put any weight on your leg for a few days. I can lend you a cane or a pair of crutches, your choice."

"I'll take the cane, thanks Doc."

I followed Warburton and Tibor out to the Trabant, limping and pretending the pain wasn't too bad. Warburton opened the passenger side door and helped me in.

"I don't need help," I barked at him and apologized in the same breath. He looked hurt but laughed anyway. He climbed in the back seat and Tibor took the wheel. We made our way through Sopron and back to Fertorakos without disobeying any traffic laws. Tibor parked in a garage around the corner from the safe house.

"Could you help me out of the car, please? Getting out is harder than getting in." I might as well have been getting out of a limousine the way Warburton stood and offered his hand.

"Wait here a moment while I have a look around," he said. It was still dark in the early morning and very quiet. I checked up and down the street, but there was no sound, no movement, nothing. Warburton was gone for not more than a minute.

"All clear," he said. With no doctor watching me this time, I didn't bother pretending I wasn't in pain. Tibor wished me luck and said goodbye, and we went in through the doorway that looked like an abandoned general store. Warburton secured the door and we descended the staircase into the armored vault. Finally I could relax, a little.

"Cuppa tea?" Warburton asked and I nodded affirmative. "I'll get the water going but I want you to watch me carefully and remember it. The water must be boiling when it hits the teabag, right? Water temperature is critical because it brings out the flavor, which means you don't have to let it steep as long. Watch and remember because I'm depending on you to teach other Americans the proper way. And when you've completed this assignment, I will teach you the rules of cricket."

"I don't need you to entertain me."

"I wasn't trying to entertain you. I just want to avoid offending you. Where'd you learn to shoot like that?"

"FBI academy, everyone has to qualify, just like everyone has to master academics, forensics and investigative techniques." I sighed. "It's a law enforcement agency. Counterintelligence and counterterrorism are secondary. Anyway, we also studied *white collar* crime. Do you use that expression? Anyway, a lot of the FBI's work involves fraud offenses, banking fraud, credit card fraud, confidence games. Sometimes it's covered by the RICO Act—racketeering— sometimes not. We call it white collar crime. Like I said, Habsburg gave me an idea about the tear-down event on the twenty-seventh. We should set up a sting operation using a reverse scam. It got me thinking about the hit-man scam. First, a con artist tells a mark he's a hit man whose been hired to kill him. Then, the con-artist-hit-man promises to save the mark's life if he pays him. Usually, it's the same amount as the supposed contract or maybe even more. You'd be surprised how often it works and how much money a good con artist can make."

"But we're not in it for the money," said Warburton.

"That's true, but there's something else I like about the reverse scam operation."

"What's that?"

"We'll also expose Konrad Gazecki."

"Maybe, maybe not," he said.

"How smart can he be?"

"Pretty smart from what I hear. After he attended the KGB school in Leningrad, they sent him to Gaczyna. It's located in Tatarstan, at the eastern edge of the steppes near the Volga River. He speaks English fluently as well as German, Polish, Russian and Hungarian. At Gaczyna, Gazecki received extensive schooling in English history, politics, literature, popular music, films and television. He's English, or at least would appear to be English, in every way."

Gaczyna," I said, "That's *the* spy school especially for agents chosen to work in English-speaking countries."

"I doubt you'll catch him, unless he stops you in the street and tells you his name is Konrad Gazecki, officer in the *Ministerium für Staatssicherheit*."

"Thank you for the vote of confidence. At the meeting with Habsburg, you said we should assume the local Stasi detachment is a death squad."

"Take it easy, take it easy. *After* the meeting with Habsburg, who do you think carried you into the clinic? Do you think you walked in? Never mind. The point is, if we're going to run this sting operation, we need to plan carefully."

"That begins with picking the right mark," I said. "That's the easy part, in a way. The scam works best when the mark is already susceptible, when he believes that someone would actually put out a contract on him."

"Right, so we need to get the names of the other Stasi officers. There's something else. We can't demand money like a con artist would," he said. "They would see right through it.

We have to find a different incentive, something that won't offend their beliefs."

"Let's offer asylum—asylum and immunity from prosecution. I'd have to get clearance for that, of course."

"Of course" he said, "but first things first. The Stasi officers are die-hard ideologues. The money has to be secondary or tertiary. We would need to convince them they're victims, certainly potential victims if they don't cooperate."

"The Stasi are worse than the Gestapo," I said.

"Yes, but that's not how they see themselves. They see themselves patriots, as the sword and shield of the party. That's why money won't work. We would need to offer them protection, shelter from the wrath that's about to rain down on them."

"They're worse than the Gestapo," I said again, "but I'll call it in. Let's see what Dr. Benson thinks."

9.

FRIDAY, JUNE 23

Benson's response came back, but not from Washington or Wiesbaden. She sent it from the American government's auxiliary embassy in Budapest, the massive compound on Tancsics Street. That was interesting.

According to Benson's message, it was okay to offer asylum, immunity, money, and anything else I wanted to promise in order to expose the Stasi detachment. If anybody refused this generous offer, my orders were to terminate them according to the method of my own choosing. I stared at the message for a moment and reread it: terminate them. There was no explanation, no reason given, just orders. The message gave me permission to share it with my "counterpart," which I did.

"You may bag a few Stasi officers, but you won't catch Gazecki. He's an expert in counterintelligence. His job is to spy on the spies. He won't be easily fooled by a planted message," said Warburton.

"My orders are to kill him—and his friends."

"If he refuses, yes" said Warburton, "but maybe he's having second thoughts about abolishing private property. Maybe he'll cooperate."

1989
TIANANMEN SQUARE TO EAST BERLIN
JACK GODWIN

We sent a message to Josef Tibor, who leaked the offer of asylum, immunity and money to associates at the Hungarian Ministry of the Interior. This worked perfectly, which was good and bad. Good because we got word the offer had been received. Bad because it meant the ministry was thoroughly infiltrated.

The tear-down event was set for June twenty-seventh. The location was a short stretch along the Austro-Hungarian border outside Sopron. There was a hedgerow that ran parallel to the fence, but there was a break in the hedgerow accessible by road from both sides, which was important because—we hoped—there would be a lot of reporters and photographers. Warburton and I scouted the location and reckoned it was a good spot for a photo opportunity and a picnic and an ambush. Tibor arranged for the meeting with the Stasi officers to take place in a field a hundred yards from where the ceremony would take place.

There was another hedgerow that ran perpendicular, which would serve as a screen. According to the plan, Warburton would personally escort the Stasi officers across the border, where they would be met by American embassy officials. Of course, there would be no American embassy officials because I'd be in position behind a small berm covered by a thick hedgerow with a sniper rifle. I kept telling myself they're worse than the Gestapo, they know no limits; they feel no shame, no remorse, no compassion.

After Warburton and I scouted the location, we drove back into Sopron.

"Let's stop in town before we go back to Fertorakos," he said. "It's a lovely day and I feel like staying out a little longer. I know a small café near the old Firewatch Tower where we can get coffee and some delicious Hungarian pastries. It's in the main square, very picturesque, very romantic and hopefully deserted at this hour."

"Do you think this is going to work?" I asked.

"I don't know. Even if it does, after the tear-down event Berlin might send in a new detachment. There's that possibility plus the Stasi is very friendly with the KGB. They're in constant communication, which means the Kremlin will eventually hear about it."

"They'll hear about it alright. That's the whole point. It'll be interesting to see who takes the bait. We only need a few, but they have to convince themselves they have nothing to fear—or at least more to fear by not defecting. They must know what's happening around Lake Balaton. Everyone's under surveillance. They must also know the Interior Ministry isn't as eager to help them as they used to be, no matter what the KGB thinks," I said.

"The numbers work to our advantage. There are hundreds of thousands of East German tourists in Hungary this summer. And we have other assets. I told you Josef Tibor is the concierge at the Napsugar campground. It's in Fonyod on the south shore of Lake Balaton. Think about it. It's perfect cover. He sees everyone who goes in or out. The Stasi thinks he works for them. It's not easy being a double agent. He has to give them some information—a lot of information, actually. As far as the Stasi are concerned, every East German that Tibor sees is a potential defector. Any East German tourist with any family members or friends in the West is under suspicion. Anybody—anybody, even a high-ranking state official—who has a beer with a Westerner but fails to report it is considered a potential defector or a collaborator. The Stasi can and will use the tiniest piece of information to blackmail someone even if that person is completely innocent."

"That's going to change," I said.

"Yes, but let's not underestimate them. The Stasi and KGB really are *that good*. Some are brilliant." We finished the last of the coffee and breakfast. Warburton paid the waiter, said thank you and goodbye in Hungarian.

"You speak Hungarian?" I asked.

"Yes, I can say hello and goodbye and thank you and pardon my flatulence in six languages. I can order beer and coffee, brandy and cigars in *any* language, including Klingon." He smiled. "It's a gift."

It was a clear sunny day so we wandered through old town, past the old synagogue and the ancient Roman walls losing ourselves in the winding cobblestone streets and charming alleyways. We didn't talk much because we didn't want to talk about work, which was fine with me. We stepped inside a medieval church where Ferdinand III, Emperor of Austria and King of Hungary was crowned. I lit a candle and said a prayer for my father. We walked outside again and circled around back where there was a sprawling convent. My leg was getting sore and I wanted to sit down. Somehow, Warburton read my mind and suggested we go back to the safe house. There was a tenderness about him that was very charming, but I suspected he was hiding something, probably married, girlfriend or something. Then I remembered what he did for a living.

10.

SATURDAY, JUNE 24

At breakfast that morning, Warburton suggested we pay a surprise visit to Josef Tibor. The Napsugar campsite where Tibor worked was three hours south of Fertorakos. Wobbly fences and utility poles lined the country roads and way up high there were huge nests—storks Warburton explained—but already empty that time of year. We've got herons and egrets in California, but storks? I never saw such big nests and never saw so many. There was nothing but farmland and everything was green that time of year, except for the sun flowers. We stopped at a monastery and the caretaker invited us down into the cellar, where we tasted a spicy red wine. *Kekfrankos* the man called it (which Warburton translated as *Blue Frankish*) and we bought two bottles. It was a perfect day, or at least it would have been if I didn't know what was coming.

Fonyod was more of a village than a town, but full of transients that time of year. There was a marina and a long pier where people stood shoulder-to-shoulder fishing. In the main square vendors were selling local arts and crafts, second-hands goods, flowers and vegetables while a brass band played on the bandstand. Most of the buildings were bleak, except for a few villas in the hills above the lakefront.

1989
TIANANMEN SQUARE TO EAST BERLIN
JACK GODWIN

One was called the Crypt-Villa, made of faded pink marble and perched on a hilltop with a beautiful view of the water.

"Shall we go inside?" asked Warburton.

"Sure, why not?"

There was old lady selling tickets and brochures inside the door. The Crypt-Villa was built by a grieving widower as a memorial to his wife who died very young. Inside there was a bed carved in white marble with likenesses of the man and his young bride sleeping side by side.

I leaned in close and whispered "Did you ever love anybody that much?"

"The way they're laying reminds me of the tomb in Père Lachaise of Abelard and Heloise except their hands are together like this, like they're praying. Abelard was a scholar—a theologian—and Heloise was his student. They had an affair, she got pregnant, her uncle had him castrated, she became a nun and he became a monk. After that, they wrote love letters to each other, very passionate, romantic love letters."

"How do you know this?" I asked, "Did you study in school?"

"I read it in a *Lonely Planet* guide book actually. It was a long time ago. I was traveling in Paris and I met a good looking American girl named Rebecca. She was from Kenosha or Racine, I can't recall. Anyway, she gave me the guide book. I didn't have any money so I offered to sleep with her. She declined. Can you believe it?"

"Poor thing," I said, "I wonder if she ever got over it."

"I wanted to see where Jim Morrison was buried. You know, the Doors? He's buried in Père Lachaise, the same cemetery as Abelard and Heloise."

"Of course I know the Doors. They were an L.A. band. I love *L.A. Woman*, driving on the freeway listening to that song. I forgot he died in Paris."

"Let's get out of here."

"Yeah, let's go see Josef Tibor."

We drove down the hill to the Napsugar campground, which didn't take more than a few minutes. With our East European clothes and dust-covered Trabant, we looked like the thousands of other tourists vacationing at Lake Balaton. Warburton parked in front of a small gray building—more like a kiosk—with a hand-painted sign that said "Registration" in Hungarian and German. The hinges squeaked when we opened the door. There was a strip of flypaper so full I wondered if there were any flies left in Hungary and it twisted slightly every time the fan oscillated in that direction.

There was Tibor, elbows on the counter reading a newspaper. He looked up obviously expecting another couple of East German tourists. It took Tibor a second to recognize me and Warburton, but the expression on his face—for one second—conveyed utter contempt.

Once Tibor recognized us, his face turned from genuine contempt to fake contempt and boredom. You would never have known it unless you were looking for it and only then if you were standing close enough to touch him. He folded the newspaper, positively annoyed by the interruption. He placed both hands on the counter but didn't say anything, not *can I help you* or *welcome to Napsugar* the way an American would. Smiling was out of the question. Clearly the culture of customer service hadn't penetrated the Iron Curtain.

Warburton broke the ice. "We do not have a reservation," he said in German.

1989
TIANANMEN SQUARE TO EAST BERLIN
JACK GODWIN

"We have no vacancies," Tibor replied. Warburton turned to me and discretely pulled out a wad of cash. "I guess we will have to go back into town and look for a hotel."

Tibor scoffed. "There is nothing in town, not this time of year."

"Are you sure there is nothing available here? Can you check?" Tibor scoffed again and put on a show of flipping through the pages of the register. Then Warburton slid the wad of bills across the counter toward Tibor.

"You goddamn Germans," shouted Tibor. "You goddamn Germans think you can buy anything. Get out, now." Tibor picked up the wad of bills and threw it at Warburton's feet. As Warburton bent to pick up the money, Tibor reached under the counter and pulled out a club, which looked like a miniature baseball bat with a leather lanyard. Tibor shouted again—something in Hungarian—and came out from behind the counter. We bolted for the door and Tibor took a swing at Warburton, who ducked. We stumbled outside and Tibor chased us, not shouting anymore but growling like a bear. Now there was a crowd gathering and he chased us around the Trabant. Tibor threw the club at Warburton and hit him in the chest. Warburton was furious now, picked up the club and charged at Tibor, who took off running in the opposite direction with surprising athleticism for a man his size.

"Let's get out of here," said Warburton. He climbed in and started the engine. Then I climbed in and he tossed the miniature baseball bat onto the back seat. Five minutes later, we were back on the road north to Fertorakos. Warburton glanced in the rearview mirror. Satisfied we weren't being followed, he told me to open the knob.

"What?"

"Unscrew the knob," he said. "And let's see how thoroughly the Hungarian Ministry of the Interior is infiltrated."

I twisted the knob counterclockwise and saw it was threaded just like a wooden nut and bolt. The inside of the club was hollowed out, but the walls were still thick enough to do some damage. Inside the club, there were some rolled up photographs, each with biographical data of the subjects.

"Tibor came through for us, everything we need. Wait, I spoke too soon. One, two, three—there should be four at least, shouldn't there? Yeah, Gazecki isn't here."

"Let me see," said Warburton. He pulled the Trabant to the side of the road. I handed him the photos. "Are you sure? There's nothing else?"

"See for yourself."

"I knew it. I knew Gazecki wouldn't take the bait. Maybe after the tear-down ceremony we'll get another opportunity."

"I doubt it," I said.

"I doubt it, too. Gazecki is too smart."

"You said that before. How smart can he be?"

"Let's get back to the safe house and work on the plan. Three out of four ain't bad but only if we eliminate *all* three. Otherwise, it would compromise the mission."

1989
TIANANMEN SQUARE TO EAST BERLIN
JACK GODWIN

11.

TUESDAY, JUNE 27

The event was scheduled for today at twelve noon. We started out before dawn so I could get into position. Warburton dropped me off near his meeting point and drove back to the safe house in Fertorakos. There was no point in both of us being cold. When the tail lights disappeared, I trotted over to my position behind the hedgerow. I found the berm and the break and got into position with my sniper rifle well before dawn. That's the life of a sniper—long hours of monotony. I checked my equipment and checked it again. I set the alarm on my watch for one hour and dozed off.

I'm taking Billy to Francisquito Canyon on Saturday for some target practice. You're going hunting? Not hunting, just target practice. I don't like hunting anymore. We shoot bottles and cans. I want to go. No, you'll get bored. I won't get bored. Can I go? You'll get bored. Please can I go? I guess so. You're too young to handle the Enfield, but maybe you can try the .22. What's that? It's a .22 caliber rifle, doesn't have much of a kick. What's a kick? That's when you fire it and it kicks backward. What's that little one? That's a Smith and Wesson model 63. They call it a kit gun because you keep it with your camping kit. Why is it so shiny? It's stainless steel. Got a nice heft to it, see? Always assume it's loaded. Don't hold it so

1989
TIANANMEN SQUARE TO EAST BERLIN
JACK GODWIN

tightly. Relax your grip, line up the front and rear sights, and exhale. Now squeeze the trigger, just squeeze the trigger. Beep!

It was still dark when my alarm went off. I was lying on my back, one hand on my rifle, one hand on my grenade looking up through the trees and the tall hedgerow. Dreaming again, I must have been nine or ten the first time my Dad took me to Francisquito Canyon. I was never bored, not for a minute, not for a second. I loved going because we'd always stop at Winchell's Donut House on the way home. What was I going to do without him? He always told me how proud of me he was. I thought all fathers said that, all fathers were good. What was I going to do?

Dawn broke red, yellow and orange, the usual ground fog but good visibility. Biscuits and jerky for breakfast, washed down with water. At nine and again at eleven, I saw a pair of uniformed police officers walking along the perimeter enclosed by the hedgerow. Both times, they walked within a few feet of me. They didn't look twice and I never saw them again after their second round. At eleven thirty, I started moving slowly up the berm. I wanted a clear line of fire to the rendezvous point where Warburton was going to meet the four Stasi agents. Maybe we'll get lucky, I thought, and Gazecki would make a surprise appearance. Meanwhile, I heard carloads of dignitaries and busloads of journalists arriving at the border, mostly from the Austrian side.

Shortly before noon, I saw the turbo-charged Trabant arrive at the meeting point. Through the scope, I could see Warburton behind the wheel. He turned the car around so it faced the way he came in, the only way out. He sat for a moment with the motor idling then got out of the car and stood behind the opened driver's side door. Any minute now, any minute now and here they came, driving a green four-

1989
TIANANMEN SQUARE TO EAST BERLIN
JACK GODWIN

door Skoda. The windows were tinted, which made it impossible to count how many, but the Stasi detachment in this part of Hungary was about to lose some of their assets. They stopped fifty feet short, but then rolled slowly forward to Warburton, who was still standing behind the driver's side door. He looked impatient.

One got out of the front passenger side of the Skoda and crossed toward Warburton too quickly for me to take a shot. He was big and he was smiling and he hugged Warburton like he knew him. The Stasi agent didn't let go but pressed his head up against Warburton like he was whispering something. Did they know each other? I didn't have audio and I couldn't read lips in German or Hungarian or whatever language they were speaking. The agent wasn't letting him go and I still didn't have a shot. Now they moved toward the Skoda. Through the scope, I saw Warburton turn his head toward me and mouth the words *shoot him*. I didn't have a clear shot. I couldn't do it. I couldn't see if there was a gun pointed at Warburton's gut.

I could hear the speeches and occasional applause on the other side of the hedgerow. The Austrian and Hungarian foreign ministers must have been getting ready to take out their bolt cutters and start cutting holes in the fence. The crowd clapped and cheered. The big Stasi agent lifted Warburton off the ground and tried to force him into the Skoda. Warburton resisted and shoved the big agent backward and someone from inside the car grabbed Warburton's coat. That's when the big agent went for his gun, but he wasn't quick enough. I squeezed the trigger and pink vapor sprayed from the back of the big agent's head.

Warburton struggled to get free but many hands pulled him into the car. The driver gunned the engine in reverse, which kicked up a huge cloud of dust and drove straight into the dust cloud. I could have tried taking a shot at the driver's side window or the front tire, but decided it was too risky. As the Skoda sped away I ran toward the Trabant, which was a hundred yards away. It took me twenty seconds to get there, but by then the Skoda was nowhere in sight. The big Stasi agent was lying on his back, eyes wide open. I hated having to waste him, but I had my orders. I reminded myself they're worse than the Gestapo. And anyway, I didn't like the way he was handling Warburton.

There was something else, something bugging me. Their comrade was lying dead in the field back there, so they knew Warburton had backup. Did they know each other or was that friendly show just part of the trap? The modified Trabant was fast and I caught up in no time. There was the green Skoda up ahead, black smoke blowing from the exhaust. I had to keep the pressure on, not get too close, and not injure any civilians. We were approaching Sopron from the west. Where were they taking Warburton? Did they even have a plan?

The best intelligence officers are inconspicuous, except when they're threatened because then their survival instincts take over. The Stasi officers were probably feeling an adrenaline rush right now, constricting their blood vessels, increasing their heart rate, their sense of sight and hearing, and even their physical strength. Unfortunately, adrenaline also impaired your judgment, caused you to overreact. That's what I was counting on. Most good intelligence officers are geeks, not adrenaline junkies. It didn't matter now. I had to catch the Skoda first, and then maybe I could get some answers.

1989
TIANANMEN SQUARE TO EAST BERLIN
JACK GODWIN

They were on Somfalvi Way heading for town, with me in hot pursuit. They turned right, then a quick left onto Baross Way right into the rail yard—such a cliché—and stopped at the end of a long street near a deserted and dilapidated loading dock. The Skoda's motor was still running because I could see smoke coming from the exhaust pipe. I stopped at the other end of the long street and turned off the engine. I got out with the sniper rifle and set up on the roof of the Trabant and peered through the scope.

The first one who got out of that car was going to get a .300 caliber Winchester Magnum gunshot wound unless it was Warburton, of course. The back passenger side door opened and out came an expensive looking black wingtip shoe followed by an expensive looking blue suit. It was Warburton and he was wearing handcuffs, but wearing them in front rather than behind his back. That was a rookie mistake. Maybe the Stasi weren't that good, I thought or maybe these guys weren't Stasi. Maybe they weren't fooled by Tibor's offer of asylum and immunity. Maybe Gazecki knew better than to send his varsity team into an ambush. I was looking through my scope and had no idea what I was seeing.

Warburton wasn't moving, just standing there. He didn't look down the street toward me, so I couldn't tell if he knew I was here. Then the driver got out but he was behind Warburton and the car door was between them. No shot unless Warburton hit the dirt. And that's exactly what Warburton did. This caught the Stasi agent by surprise and he was left standing there momentarily dumfounded holding a pistol, gaping at Warburton down on the ground. He moved his gun hand slightly, which was all the reason I needed. I squeezed the trigger. The Stasi agent went cross-eyed and dropped like a marionette whose strings had been cut. Now they knew I was here. Warburton seemed to recognize he had the advantage. He rolled under the passenger door, popped up and reached into the car with his handcuffed hands. There was still one more agent in the Skoda and no way now he would expose himself of his own accord.

Warburton fell backward pulling the Stasi agent out of the car with him. The Stasi's right hand broke free from the steering wheel. Warburton had him by the collar, flipped him and then planted him into the ground. Warburton didn't wait for the Stasi to recover and attacked again smashing the handcuffs into the Stasi's face. The Stasi's nose and mouth were bleeding but he counter-attacked while he was still on the ground, kicking with one foot then the other before they both got back to their feet.

With Warburton in handcuffs, the Stasi had the advantage and started punching with his right, then another right, then his left. Warburton blocked the punches with both hands and backed away, but then stomped on the Stasi's foot and kneed him in the groin. Now they were grappling and the Stasi grabbed Warburton's hair. But Warburton grabbed the Stasi's wrist and rotated it unnaturally. Something popped and the Stasi fell to the ground face first. Warburton had the Stasi on the ground, and had ahold of his wrist with both hands. Now Warburton finished the fight with one quick, efficient strike. It was not very sporting, but very effective.

I looked up from the scope. Warburton let go of the Stasi's wrist and bent over to catch his breath. When I honked the horn on the Trabant, Warburton looked up and waved to me. I hopped in and drove over to the scene. He was rummaging through the Stasi's pockets, looking for keys no doubt. Finding nothing, he checked the other body—the driver lying next to the Skoda.

1989
TIANANMEN SQUARE TO EAST BERLIN
JACK GODWIN

"Bingo," he mumbled.

"Are you okay? Are you wounded?"

"Fit as a fiddle and ready for love." He smiled. "Well then, mission accomplished. Nice shooting back there and here. You're a crack shot. Thank you."

"Thank the FBI academy. I held my fire on this one, but I had you covered all the way. Was that *Krav Maga*? I thought that was Israeli. Where'd you learn that?"

"In London, I used to spar with a Mossad friend, Hungarian Jew he was. *Always use the nearest tool on the weakest point.* He must have told me that a hundred times. Can you help me with these?" He held his hands out to me. I unlocked the cuffs and he rubbed his wrists.

"What do we do with the bodies? Should we give them a decent burial?"

"Let's stuff these two in the Skoda. The big one back in the field is going to have to rest where he fell."

"Don't you want to check their faces against the photos?" I asked.

"What? Oh sure, sure," he said.

"Are you okay? You're not wounded?" I handed him the photos.

"This one matches, yes, and so does this one. How about the big fellow back in the field? Is that him? You must have gotten a good look at his face before you went to work on him?"

"Yeah, that's him," I said.

"And the elusive spy *meister* Herr Gazecki is nowhere to be found." Warburton inhaled and exhaled loudly. "Whew. I'm thirsty. How about you?" he gestured for me to get in the driver's side. "How did the tear-down ceremony go? Could you hear anything? I got distracted when that big one hugged me. He had a pistol stuck in the small of my back, right there."

"Everything went fine as far as I could tell. I got distracted, too."

"Right, well I'm sure we'll read all about it in the morning papers."

1989
TIANANMEN SQUARE TO EAST BERLIN
JACK GODWIN

12.

WEDNESDAY, JUNE 28

Sure enough, in the newspaper that morning there was a big picture of Johann Bauer and Tamas Lakatos cutting the barbed wire fence between Austria and Hungary. The photographer shot the picture through the fence with Bauer and Lakatos standing on the other side both holding bolt cutters and smiling. There was a delegation behind them, officials, more reporters and everyone looking pleased. Phase one was complete. The next big milestone would be the Pan European Picnic.

That afternoon, we went back to the Napsugar campground at Lake Balaton to meet Tibor. Warburton parked the Trabant outside the same small gray building with the hand-painted sign that said "Registration." Tibor was there and this time he was expecting us.

"Let's find a quiet corner and open a bottle of Slivovitz," he said.

"What's Slivovitz?"

"Oh, it's a Hungarian delicacy—plum brandy blessed by the Rabbi no less." Tibor handed me three small stemmed glasses and pulled a green bottle off the shelf. "You are in for a treat," he said. He led us to glade of trees behind the registration building a few yards away where there was an empty picnic table. Tibor filled the glasses as we took our seats.

"First, let us toast your success. To your health," he said. "No, do not sip it. You must empty your glass or risk insulting your host." It burned going down.

"I have a message for you," said Tibor, and he was looking at Warburton.

"You have a message for me?"

"Yes. The business with the Stasi agents at St. Michael's—and yesterday—attracted some attention."

"Go on," said Warburton.

"The KGB has requested a meeting with you. The agent's name is Vladimir Ivanov. He is based in Dresden, at the KGB outpost on the Angelikastrasse. The local Stasi control center is right across the street. Mostly, Ivanov works as a recruiter, but he also receives raw intelligence and sends it to Moscow. It is all very official but very friendly. You do not have to go all the way to Dresden, of course. He wants to meet in Budapest." Tibor poured another round.

"And of course he didn't tell you why," Warburton asked.

"No, he did not."

Warburton inhaled and exhaled loudly, and then turned to me. "What do you think?"

"Tibor, do you know anything about Vladimir Ivanov?" I asked.

"He has been in Dresden four years. He is in his mid-thirties. He recruits agents to spy on the west. He is very friendly with the Stasi, very supportive but this is not unusual. The Stasi gave him a medal a couple of years ago, which is *very unusual*. He speaks English, so you will not require a translator."

As Tibor spoke, Warburton kept shaking his head slightly. It was hardly noticeable, almost like a negating tremor.

"Take the meeting," I said. "I'll cover you." I put my hand on his, which surprised him. Warburton was usually Joe Cool, but not today for some reason.

"Okay," he said. "I'll take the meeting."

"Tibor, tell Vladimir Ivanov that Warburton has agreed to meet, but tell him we'll choose the time and place. Tell him it's non-negotiable." I turned to Warburton. "We need to go to Budapest and scout a location. I want the meeting to be in a public place so I can be armed and ready. But don't look so worried. I won't pull the trigger without a good reason."

Tibor filled our glasses again. "Then I propose a toast. Let's drink to Vladimir Ivanov's good health and to yours."

13.

FRIDAY, JUNE 30

We started out after breakfast for the three hour drive from Fertorakos to Budapest.

"We need to find a good place to meet. It needs to be public, but not necessarily out in the open," said Warburton. "Then I want to walk with Ivanov someplace where you'll be able to see me and you'll have a clear field of fire. My guess is someplace on the river."

We drove into Budapest and stopped for coffee at the Danube Hotel, on the "Buda" or western side of Budapest. It was afternoon by the time we arrived. We took a table at a café in front of the hotel where we could see the Danube flowing through the middle of town. I couldn't help but notice it wasn't blue like the waltz but sort of a greasy gray. The hotel and café must have catered to westerners because I didn't see any way locals could afford it, but there were plenty of people walking along the embankment.

"If you could install yourself on the roof of the hotel, you'd have a clear line of fire to the bridge there," Warburton said. He was pointing to the Freedom Bridge, a big chain bridge decorated with four menacing-looking falcons, which crossed the Danube and connected "Buda" with "Pest" on the eastern side of the river.

1989
TIANANMEN SQUARE TO EAST BERLIN
JACK GODWIN

"Let's finish our coffee and walk across and find a good place to set up the initial meeting. Warburton finished his double espresso and I my cappuccino and we made our way across the bridge which seemed full of pedestrians, especially college students.

"Did you hear that?"

"Did I hear what?"

"Oh, I forgot you don't speak Hungarian. One of the students said *Let's meet at Karl*. Then I heard it again just now. *Let's meet at Karl*. You see that building there, across the river? That's the Karl Marx University," said Warburton pointing. "That's what they must mean."

We walked to the end of the bridge, to the Karl Marx University on the Pest side, slightly off to the right. The place was bustling, students and professors hurrying this way and that but we couldn't see any meeting place.

"Let's go inside," I said. Warburton shrugged and followed. Inside the main building there was a grand foyer and a bronze statue of Karl Marx seated on a marble pedestal. In his left hand, Karl was holding a book, probably his *Manifesto* because *Capital* is three volumes thick. Warburton and I turned to each other. We both said *let's meet at Karl* and together started laughing.

"Okay," said Warburton as we went back outside, "We'll meet at Karl and walk back toward the bridge. I'll stop in the middle and listen to whatever Ivanov has to say. Where do you want to position yourself?"

"This side is too flat. It'll have to be on the Buda side. The roof of the hotel is the best option." We walked back the way we came, stopping in the middle of the bridge.

1989
TIANANMEN SQUARE TO EAST BERLIN
JACK GODWIN

"How far would you say that is, from the roof to where we're standing?" I scanned the scan the area and estimated the height of the hotel.

"Three hundred yards," I said. "The cone-shaped towers make it look taller, but the hotel only has four floors. If we could book that corner room on the fourth floor facing the bridge, yeah, I'd say three hundred yards. You'll be perfectly safe unless he throws you into the river."

"You're charming. What if things go wrong? Where's my escape route?"

"You can't go toward the university. I couldn't cover you, at least not for very long. You'd have to come back toward me, toward the hotel I mean."

"We should also scout for a meeting place for us if the meeting with Ivanov gets ugly. Let's not improvise."

"Okay, but let's first check the dates when that corner room is available."

The desk clerk at the Danube Hotel said the room we wanted was available. We booked the room for the thirteenth and fourteenth, and paid in advance. Then we set out again, along the river toward a hilly wooded residential neighborhood with views of the river. Foot paths crisscrossed in every direction, all leading uphill toward the Buda Castle, which sat on a plateau overlooking the Danube. The castle walls ran parallel to the river along the steep hillside. There were stairways and ramps, an arcade with pavilions, and a courtyard decorated with a spectacular fountain. This side of the castle complex faced away from the river and opened at ground level. There was a carriageway and chunks were missing in the portico walls where the gates used to be. Everything was in such disrepair it made me wonder how it must have looked before the communists gutted it.

1989
TIANANMEN SQUARE TO EAST BERLIN
JACK GODWIN

"We'll park the Trabant here on the fourteenth. If things get ugly or if we get separated, we'll reconvene right here," said Warburton. "That's the plan anyway." Our eyes met and neither of us looked away and he smiled like he wanted to say something.

"Why would we get separated? I told you. You'll be perfectly safe unless Ivanov throws you into the river."

Then we turned back toward the hotel and walked in silence. I took his arm and he pulled me closer and clutched my hand. I couldn't tell if this was still part of our cover or if he felt what I felt. Let's just say I didn't work regular hours and the only men I met were through work. Most were married or already involved, not interested or not *interesting*. I told myself I shouldn't get too attached. But Basil Warburton was funny and charming when he loosened up. If he was interested—seriously interested, not flirting—he could tell me when he was ready. I wasn't going to ask.

On our way back to the safe house in Fertorakos, we stopped at Lake Balaton to inform Tibor about the date, time and location of the meeting. He laughed when we told him about the Karl Marx statue.

"Vladimir Ivanov will find that most amusing," he said.

"I'll send Dr. Benson a coded message to explain the plan," I said.

14.

MONDAY, JULY 10

Benson responded and gave her okay for the meeting with Ivanov. Other than that, there wasn't much action in Fertorakos. My leg wound continued to heal. There was no sign of infection and I started exercising as much as I could within the confines of the safe house, climbing up and down the stairs occasionally. The headaches weren't too bad, which allowed me to catch up on sleep.

The safe house was completely self-contained. Whoever built it knew there would be long stretches of down time. It was just like a stake-out except without the boredom. Warburton was an amiable companion, as though he'd done this before. That was one of the less glamorous aspects of the intelligence business. We spent the weekend reading, cooking, listening to British Forces Radio and watching every movie in the safe house's meager video library. We couldn't go out very often because it would have been too conspicuous, and anyway I couldn't walk far without pain.

Yesterday afternoon we went into Sopron and played tourist. We went back to the café we especially enjoyed, the one in the shade of the Firewatch Tower near the Gate of Faith. After coffee, we climbed to the top of the tower. The weather was perfect, not a cloud in the sky and you could see

1989
TIANANMEN SQUARE TO EAST BERLIN
JACK GODWIN

the Alps. We walked the streets, past City Hall, the Storno House and the Goat Church, and strolled along the old moat that followed the castle wall. Everyone was so friendly I was sure the town would be swarming with American tourists as soon as the Cold War ended.

15.

THURSDAY, JULY 13

It was the day before we were due to meet Ivanov. Warburton and I drove to Budapest and arrived at the hotel late that afternoon. There was a message waiting for us when we checked in, which Warburton pocketed and did not open until we got up to the room.

"Change of plans," he said. "Ivanov wants to see both of us. He insists." He handed me the note.

The note was in German and I translated as I read aloud. "*Dear Herr Warburton, Let's meet at Karl, tomorrow morning at nine o'clock. I would like Fräulein Nogales to join us. Her reputation as a ~~marksman~~ markswoman precedes her. No reply is necessary.*"

"What do you think? Is it a setup?"

"No," I said. "He asked for the meeting. He wants to talk. Now he wants to talk to both of us. But if Ivanov thinks I'm less lethal from three feet than three hundred yards, he's a fool."

"I don't think he's a fool," he said. "Ivanov is the opposite of a fool. But things could get ugly, which means we should not plan on coming back here. Let's leave the Trabant outside the castle, right where we agreed. The keys will be on top of the rear passenger side tire."

1989
TIANANMEN SQUARE TO EAST BERLIN
JACK GODWIN

16.

FRIDAY, JULY 14, a.m.

That morning we took a taxi across the river. Warburton asked the driver to take a different bridge, the Elizabeth Bridge to the other side and then drop us off at the Great Market Hall behind the university. At nine o'clock, the university was full of students and we walked up to the Karl Marx statue, where Vladimir Ivanov was waiting for us. Blond hair, athletic, five foot eight, I guessed. His expression didn't change, but you could tell he recognized us. After we exchanged greetings, Warburton said *follow me* and disappeared through the double doors while Ivanov and I hurried to keep up.

We got to the middle of Freedom Bridge. Warburton stopped and turned to face Ivanov. Cars and buses rumbled past, causing the bridge to bounce and sway.

"You asked to meet," Warburton said in German, "What do you want?" Ivanov looked slightly offended, but mostly irritated.

"We can speak English, if you prefer." Ivanov then turned to me. "Introductions first," he said, "My name is Vladimir Ivanov. I am a colonel in the KGB, posted in Dresden." He paused a moment. "I wanted to congratulate you for your work in Sopron, and you especially Ms. Nogales for your work in Fertorakos. I am sorry about your colleagues."

"Thanks," I said, "anything else?"

"I have been monitoring the situation in Hungary very closely, and in East Germany of course. Most high-ranking party members are oblivious, unable or unwilling to see the signs. However, there are some who are, shall we say, more realistic about the future. I am deeply committed to my country, to the best interests of my country. I am not trying to deceive you. And I will not waste your time with diplomatic small talk. If we are to have a constructive relationship, let us speak frankly."

"Let's get to the point," said Warburton.

"Did you know the Communist Party lost seats in the last election? Did you know that? In March, for the first time since 1917, there was a real election in the Soviet Union and the communists lost seats. That has never happened before. That was the end of the party's monopoly on power. Elected officials have begun questioning Gorbachev in public, openly criticizing him on television. Do you not see what this means?"

"What? You want to defect or something?" said Warburton.

"Thank you, no." said Ivanov. "What did Prime Minister Thatcher say about Mr. Gorbachev? *We can do business together.* He is not the only one you can do business with."

"That was a long time ago," I said. "Why should we trust you?"

"Perhaps I am wasting my time. Gorbachev's situation is precarious. That is putting it mildly. The hardliners—on the Politburo and in the KGB—consider him a traitor. They want him out."

1989
TIANANMEN SQUARE TO EAST BERLIN
JACK GODWIN

"Do you think there will be a coup?"

"Eventually yes," said Ivanov, "and it may or may not be successful. But something much bigger will happen sooner or later. The Soviet Union is going to collapse."

The Soviet Union is going to collapse. Warburton's expression, his posture, his whole body was now a mix of annoyance and skepticism. Ivanov paused while we absorbed this revelation. He looked at Warburton and then me with his head slightly cocked. I noticed his mouth was higher on one side of his face, which made him look like he was smiling even when he wasn't. Better not underestimate this guy I thought, he could be useful.

"We would like to encourage this picnic you are planning near the Austrian border," he said. "Quietly of course, nothing too obvious, but we can provide intelligence and logistical support."

"What picnic?" said Warburton, "What're you talking about?"

"Mr. Warburton, you said get to the point. That is the point. Is it not? Three intelligence officers, one—*shall we say*—British, one American and a Russian, are standing on a bridge over the Danube. One is offering assistance."

"And the other two want to know why they should trust the no good communist son of a bitch." I was thinking *Oh shit here we go* but Ivanov just smiled.

"Please keep my mother out of this. And who told you I was a communist?"

"It's those cheap shoes you're wearing. You can always tell by the shoes."

"Why do you insult me? You do not trust me I understand, but why insult me?" Ivanov looked down at his shoes and then at Warburton's. "Yours are made by

1989
TIANANMEN SQUARE TO EAST BERLIN
JACK GODWIN

Church's. *Munich wingtips*, it says in your dossier. Unfortunately, I cannot afford them on a colonel's salary. I bought these in Thuringia." Ivanov shrugged. "My shoes should tell you something else about me. I do not accept bribes. Most of my colleagues do and maybe I should, too but I do not. Maybe I am a fool."

"I don't think you're a fool," I said, "or a communist."

"Ms. Nogales, you are as intelligent as you are elegant."

"Thank you," I said, "Look, it's not exactly a state secret that Gorbachev was in Beijing back in May. His official state visit to normalize relations turned into a completely ceremonial and totally humiliating fiasco. He must have seen what happened in Tiananmen Square. My guess is Gorbachev doesn't want to go down in history as a mass murderer. Does he? No? That's what I thought. At least we're finally getting to the point." Warburton looked like someone just flipped a switch inside his head.

"Well?"

"As I said, Mr. Gorbachev's situation is precarious. But the real problem is not Moscow but in East Berlin. The problem is Joachim Schmidt, who has never hesitated to use force, not since he became president and party secretary. Did you know Schmidt is planning a huge parade in October to celebrate East Germany's fortieth anniversary? His country is falling apart and he is organizing the world's largest military parade. Moscow is embarrassed frankly, but also worried how East Berlin will respond to events in Sopron."

"How will Moscow respond?" said Warburton.

"I believe Ms. Nogales articulated Moscow's position quite well. Mr. Gorbachev does not want another Tiananmen Square. He wants a peaceful transition."

"Transition to what?" I asked.

1989
TIANANMEN SQUARE TO EAST BERLIN
JACK GODWIN

"That is a question for the people to decide, Ms. Nogales. Your focus should be on the task at hand, which is to neutralize the Stasi network in Hungary. If Hungary and Austria can open their border, it will isolate East Germany. As a show of good faith, let me help you."

Ivanov reached inside his jacket and removed a small handset. "Do you see the two Skodas parked on the street in front of the university?" He pointed with his chin to the Pest side of the river.

"What about them?" said Warburton as he and I turned that direction.

"Watch the one in front."

Ivanov pressed a button on the handset and the car in front exploded into a ball of flames. All heads turned toward the noise. After the initial blast, everyone and everything was quiet. Then, people started running and shouting and then came the familiar claxon of European police sirens. Then four men in suits jumped out of the other Skoda, the one in back and Ivanov betrayed no emotion as he watched the fallout. Warburton and I watched the scene unfold until Ivanov spoke.

"Two carloads of Stasi agents arrived in country yesterday."

"I wonder what they wanted."

"Berlin sent them to kill you" said Ivanov turning to me, "in retaliation for your excellent work in Sopron and Fertorakos. I would not worry too much. There are many more where those came from." He smiled. "However, you must proceed with your plans for the nineteenth of August. The picnic is a prerequisite for the real work, which must take place in East Germany. I can help you there as well, through the KGB liaison office. Good luck. Oh, there is one more thing." He turned to me. "Konrad Gazecki was not in that car. Goodbye."

A car pulled up to the curb, a big black Mercedes. Ivanov got in back and just like that he was gone. The explosion must have been the signal.

"These people are a little too organized," I said.

"*As a show of good faith, let me help you,*" said Warburton imitating Ivanov's Russian accent.

"I don't like this," I said. "Look at the second Skoda. The guys in the front seat look pretty bad, but the two in back are headed this way. They don't look too happy. Oh, shit. Now they're really coming. Somehow, I doubt they'd believe us if we told them the KGB planted that car bomb."

"Yeah, let's get out of here."

We walked away from the explosion toward the Buda side, as fast as we could without running. The two Stasi agents didn't seem to care how much attention they attracted because they were running flat out over the bridge toward us. There were a couple of uniformed police officers close behind, who probably just wanted to question them because two guys in gray suits running away from an explosion never looks good. We decided to pick up the pace and started running, too.

The two Stasi and the two uniformed Hungarian police were halfway across the bridge by the time we got back to the Buda side. We turned right, away from the hotel, ran across the street dodging cars going this way and that. There was an eight foot high brick retaining wall all along the other side of the street. Adjacent to a niche with a bench and a grungy bust of someone, there was a brick staircase leading up through the park, which we hoped would eventually lead to

1989
TIANANMEN SQUARE TO EAST BERLIN
JACK GODWIN

the Buda Castle. Just as I turned around, a bullet ricocheted off the brick wall near my head.

"By God, that does it," I said. Warburton took my hand but I shook him off. "*No!* One of them took a shot at me and now I'm going to nail his ass."

I took cover on the staircase behind the wall and drew my weapon. The two Stasi and the two officers were right across the street. The two Stasi both looked the same, same suit, same shirt, same commie haircut. I couldn't tell who took the shot, so I took aim at the one in the lead and squeezed off one round and down he went. We didn't wait to see if his comrade came to his aid or if he got up again. Warburton took my hand again and up we went.

It was a steep hill. There was a landing every twenty steps or so, each with a wooden bench and an unobstructed view across the river but no view back down the way we came, so we didn't stop to rest, just kept climbing. My heart was pounding even though I was in the best shape of my life. I wanted to rest but there wasn't any safe place to stop.

"We've got to get inside the castle, then we'll take a breather, then we'll lose them. Keep moving."

There was a passage with three square columns and row of windows on either side. At the end of the passage were three large wooden doors, one of which was unlocked. This brought us into an inner courtyard on the eastern side of the castle.

"Wait a minute," I said. "This is a perfect spot for an ambush."

"No, let's keep moving."

"Then at least let me rig up a booby trap," I said. Warburton gestured surrender with his hands. I unclipped my grenade from my vest and strung it low across the passage inside the doorway. "The wooden doors will absorb some of the blast, but maybe we'll get lucky."

Warburton and I ran to the other end of the courtyard.

"Do you have any idea where we are?"

"This must be the lower court," he said. "Let's go through here." We passed through a wrought iron gate into a small, rectangular private garden. Everything was overgrown, the walls were stained black and everything covered in dust. There was a cistern in one corner.

"Oh, somebody's secret garden," I said. Just then, there was an explosion behind us. The grenade detonated, which I hoped would buy us more time to make it to the car. Our situation did not look good. It looked like the only way out was the same way we came in. We went through an arched doorway and into what looked like a subterranean vault. The curved ceiling was supported by massive pillars the length of the room. The ceiling near us was partially collapsed and the ground covered with dirt and rubble. As we moved forward, more of the ceiling was intact and you could see gigantic barrels lining either side of the long room. It smelled moldy and seemed to slope downward. There was a gutter running the length of the room and the water flowed slowly downhill. The walls were dark and wet and stained. We were slipping and stumbling, trying to keep our feet and Warburton took my hand to keep us both from falling.

"Where are we?" I asked.

"We're beneath the castle, of course. This must be some sort of drainage conduit, probably runs into the river, not too sweet. We've got to keep moving."

"How do we get out?" Behind us we heard someone crunching and sloshing, making their way along the wet pavement. There was a gunshot and a muzzle flash and an

1989
TIANANMEN SQUARE TO EAST BERLIN
JACK GODWIN

echo. The deeper went into the cellar, the narrower and the darker it got.

"Stay close to the wall," Warburton whispered.

"Halt!" shouted a voice from behind. The beam of a flashlight fell on us.

"Get back!" said Warburton as he shoved me behind a column. I drew my weapon and got off two rounds. I shot out the flashlight but missed whoever was holding it. As if to prove the point, he raked the entire cellar with a machine gun. The sound was deafening. The echo traveled from one of end of the cellar to the other and back again, and then you could hear wine spilling and splashing on the ground.

"Halt!"

"Run!" said Warburton, "Run! We'll meet afterward."

"Are you sure?"

"Yes, now run!"

Now there was more shouting and echoing, and more gunshots. Now I could hear people running toward me, away from me, I couldn't tell. There was a small passageway branching off to the right. *Where's Warburton?*

"Basil," I whispered, "you there?" *Are you there?*

The passageway got smaller and soon I was walking in a crouch through the muck, but now it seemed to be moving uphill. The sound of distorted echoing voices got more distant. I couldn't see anything, so I turned back and tried to retrace my steps. It was like being lost in a maze. I called out Basil's name and waited, straining my ears to hear his voice. Then everyone started shooting, everyone, all the bullets, all the magazines emptied. I listened until it stopped.

I didn't know which way to turn, so I turned toward the only light I could see which led me to a cast iron spiral staircase. Before I climbed, I turned back one more time to

1989
TIANANMEN SQUARE TO EAST BERLIN
JACK GODWIN

look down the passageway, but there was nothing, no sound, no movement, no nothing. Above me there was a metal grill, which I pushed open. I hoisted myself up inside a walled enclosure with window niches open to the Danube.

Which way to the Trabant? I ran through a rectangular court covered with a glass roof, climbed a staircase and ran through another passageway which led into another courtyard decorated with big stone lions. I wondered how I was ever going to find the car. I ran past a chapel, past a tomb, past a long hall with alternating columns, square, then round, square, round and tall arched windows lining the sidewall—must be the ballroom, I thought, maybe the banquet hall. No time to admire the crystal chandeliers. *I bet old Otto could explain what it all meant.* I climbed more stairs, came around the corner and to my right saw three arcaded doorways and the stately complex came to an end just like that. There was the car!

I felt for the keys and found them on the rear passenger side tire. I unlocked the doors and started the engine, expecting Warburton to appear any second. I waited and waited but he never came. I decided I had to go find him. I fished a flashlight out of the glove compartment and retraced my steps back along the arcade, past the long ballroom/banquet hall, the tomb and the chapel, through one courtyard then another courtyard and down the wrought iron spiral staircase again. There was the walled enclosure and there was the metal grill. I descended the spiral staircase into the darkness. I paused at the bottom to catch my breath, let my eyes adjust and listen. There was nothing, nothing. I made my way through the passageway back to the subterranean vault, which was easier now that I had a flashlight.

1989
TIANANMEN SQUARE TO EAST BERLIN
JACK GODWIN

I took a knee behind a column and tried to control my heartbeat. I shined flashlight on the floor where I last saw Basil standing, but there was still nothing. Everywhere I shined the light there was water mixed with red wine splashed on the floor, on the walls and everywhere else. There was blood there and there. I tried to follow my forensics training from the academy, except I didn't have gloves, forceps or canisters. On the plus side, I didn't have any of those annoying chain-of-custody legalities I could never remember during my exams. It was a crime scene, in a way, but I would just have to do my own analysis because there was no way to submit a request to the lab in Quantico. I had no camera, no pencil or paper, so tried estimating the dimensions of the cellar visually, the placement of the columns, entrance, and the two exits, at least the only two I was aware of, the way we came in and the way I went out.

Okay, I said to myself, *what are the facts?* There were multiple shooters confirmed by the shell casings here and here. So, there were at least two shooters and two guns from different manufacturers. Did Basil fire back? I didn't see any shell casings that would have belonged to him. Did he have a revolver or did he not fire at all? There was blood where the guy with the automatic was standing, and there was blood on the surface of the water. And there was a shoe print. What did Ivanov say about Basil's shoes? Some English brand or other, I couldn't remember. I wished I had a camera. Any personal effects, any bone fragments, any tissue? No sign.

"What's that?" I said aloud. I shined the flashlight on a small piece of something on the floor. It looked like part of a tooth, a chipped tooth. No telling whose it was, maybe it broke off when Basil fell somehow or other. So, Basil might have a gunshot wound and a chipped tooth. And then the

1989
TIANANMEN SQUARE TO EAST BERLIN
JACK GODWIN

Stasi took him away—for medical attention and then interrogation? What did Habsburg say? The Stasi didn't have the authority to arrest anyone in Hungary—they weren't even here officially. Were those two uniformed police officers in on it? I did not like this at all.

I pocketed the chipped tooth and took one last look around. Then I climbed out of the cellar for the second time today. As I climbed out and walked through the castle grounds, I turned things over and over in my mind. I made my way back to the Trabant and climbed in. He said *if things get ugly I'll meet you right here*. Things got ugly. I rolled the chipped tooth back and forth in the fabric of my pocket and felt sick. What if Warburton was dead? I considered my options and decided my only choice was to pay an unscheduled visit to Dr. Benson at the compound on Tancsics Street. She hated unscheduled visits. I would have to make my apologies.

1989
TIANANMEN SQUARE TO EAST BERLIN
JACK GODWIN

17.

FRIDAY, JULY 14, p.m.

I dug through the glove compartment for a map of Budapest. I'd never been to the compound before, never had any reason. There it was, fifteen kilometers north of here near the Matthias Church at the other end of the castle district. I drove along the west bank of the river, parked the Trabant down the street from the church and walked the short distance to the compound. There was a knocker on the arched double doors. I looked around first, up the street and down then knocked three times. A small door opened at eye level, revealing two suspicious eyebrows.

"Yes?"

"Jaqui Walnuts," I said.

"Wait."

The small door closed again. I heard footsteps on gravel walking away. And I waited. Then I heard footsteps again, two pairs this time, walking back toward the arched double doors. The small door opened again, this time revealing a pair of reading glasses perched on a brown nose, and two dark eyes which quickly changed from suspicion to recognition. The small door slammed shut and the one of the big doors swung inward to reveal a long courtyard with two rows of arches along each side. Dr. Bernice Benson was standing on the other side.

"Jaqui Walnuts," she said.

"Omega three," I replied.

"Special Agent Nogales, she said. "My goodness, we weren't exactly expecting you. Are you wounded?"

"No Ma'am, I'm okay."

"That's good. Do come in," she said holding her cane in one hand and one finger to her lips. "How did you come, by car?"

"Yes," I said.

"Where is it?"

"It's around the corner near the Matthias Church."

"Give me the key." I handed it to her. "Zoltan, bring the car into the compound. Please make sure it gets repainted and the license plates replaced. Get another one from the car pool and get it ready by tomorrow morning." She gestured to follow. I stepped over the old-style threshold into the compound. We crossed the courtyard and entered a three-story building in the middle of the compound. Thick walls and grilled windows told me maybe that's where they stored the gunpowder in the good old days. Now it served as secure communications facility for the United States government. Inside, the three-story building consisted of one great room with a vaulted ceiling, partitioned into cubicle-style work stations except for one that was raised off the floor a few feet and completely enclosed top and bottom and all four sides. In we went, while a man in a dark suit closed and sealed the door with three cranks of a big handle from the outside. On the inside, it looked like any old conference room with a polished wooden table and at least a dozen leather chairs, except you could feel the whole room vibrating slightly.

1989
TIANANMEN SQUARE TO EAST BERLIN
JACK GODWIN

"Please sit down," Benson said, "Would you like some water, anything?"

"Water, please," I said. Benson withdrew a bottle from a low cupboard at one end.

"Were you involved with that car bomb in front of Karl Marx University?" she asked.

"Indirectly, yes but it wasn't our operation. Vladimir Ivanov's people must have planted it. He's the KGB colonel we were meeting today. We didn't know anything about it until it detonated."

"Where is Mr. Warburton?"

"I don't know."

"Tell me what happened," she said.

"A couple of days after the tear-down ceremony, I mean after we eliminated the three Stasi agents, Warburton and I went to Lake Balaton to see Josef Tibor. You know him?" Benson shook her head. "Tibor is the concierge at the Napsugar campground at Lake Balaton—and a key member of the opposition. Tibor's the one who told us that someone from the KGB wanted to meet Warburton."

Benson nodded to continue.

"The day before the meeting, Ivanov sent Warburton a note saying he wanted to meet both of us—Warburton and me—together. Anyway, Ivanov said the Soviet Union was going to collapse and he wanted to do business together. He seemed to know all about the picnic. Then he pulled out a detonator and killed a carload of Stasi agents. The blast wounded a couple of others. We got into a shootout with a couple of their comrades. We weren't looking for a fight. They came after us, chased us up onto the plateau and into the castle grounds. I killed one, I think, but that's where they got Warburton. I don't know if he's dead or alive. I got out but had a bad feeling so went back, found a lot of blood and this."

I reached into my shirt pocket and dropped the chipped tooth on the conference table. Benson stared down at it for a moment then pinched the bridge of her nose with her thumb and forefinger.

"What is it?" I asked. "Is it something about Warburton?"

"Basil Warburton is a double agent."

"What?"

Benson held up her hand as if to say stop.

"Basil Warburton is a double agent," she repeated.

"Who's he working for?"

Benson held up her hand again. "Would you please let me finish? Mr. Warburton is a double agent who has passed *every* loyalty test we've given him, but this ... I should never have approved this."

"You think Warburton is working for the Russians?"

"No," said Benson.

"Do you think he's a rogue agent?"

"I don't know, nor do I know why you were ambushed on a deserted levy outside of Fertorakos last month. Tanner and your teammates should still be alive. I don't think the Stasi just happened to be there. Someone is feeding them information."

"I'm sure you're right," I said. "There's a leak somewhere but it's not Warburton or Ivanov. I was on the bridge when Ivanov detonated that bomb. Before that, I noticed something."

"What was that?"

"For one, they can't stand each other. I don't know why. Warburton insulted him and Ivanov just took it in stride like it wasn't the first time. Also, Ivanov seemed pretty well informed. He knew about the picnic. Warburton played dumb when Ivanov mentioned it, which told me Ivanov could not have gotten that information from Warburton."

"Just because they don't like each other doesn't mean they aren't working together."

"That's the thing," I said. "Ivanov offered to help. I think he wants to work together, sincerely. He's an opportunist. There's no doubt about that. But he thought he was doing us a favor by taking out those Stasi agents. So what if he wanted to show off?"

"I dislike that kind of high-profile tradecraft," she said. "We're supposed to be in the clandestine service. I wonder what Ivanov wants."

"I don't know. But it's safe to say Ivanov hates the KGB as much as Warburton hates the Stasi."

"That's ironic."

"What do you mean?"

"Never mind," she said. "I forgot to tell you. Spencer Pang is here."

There was a buzzer and a red light on the door. Benson pushed a button on the intercom. It was Spencer. The crank to unseal the door spun three times and there was Spencer Pang waiting outside.

"Why Spencer Pang, last time I saw you, you were flat on your back on a south bound Sikorsky. Let me look at you. My goodness that is the ugliest Aloha shirt I've ever seen." Spencer laughed and he ran over to hug me.

"How's the leg?"

"Good as new," he said, "Where's your boyfriend?" Dr. Benson raised her eyebrows.

"He's *not* my boyfriend. And he's been kidnapped or killed."

"Let's go get him."

"Not so fast," said Benson, "You've got orders. In any case, Mr. Warburton's loyalties are divided and his priorities are in question."

"He's a British serving officer," said Spencer, "We've got to go after him Chief, even if it's just to put him on trial."

"Your enthusiasm does you credit, but no. I'm sending you to Sopron with Agent Nogales. Opening the border with Austria is still top priority. Besides, if the East Germans suspect even half of what we can confirm, then Mr. Warburton is probably dead, or worse." Hearing this, I must have given something away because Dr. Benson gave me a look of sympathy mixed with suspicion. "Agent Nogales, is there something you want to tell me?"

"No, Ma'am." She leveled her gaze on me but this time I was more careful.

"You'll spend the night in the compound" Benson said, "First thing tomorrow I want you and Mr. Pang to drive back to Fertorakos and Sopron. There's plenty of work for you there before the big event." She stood up, which signaled the end of the meeting. Spencer and I exited the secure conference room and stepped out into the courtyard.

1989
TIANANMEN SQUARE TO EAST BERLIN
JACK GODWIN

18.

SATURDAY, JULY 15, a.m.

I saw you last night. What? I saw you taking my tooth away and then you put money under my pillow. Maybe you were dreaming. Was that you? Yes. I thought it was the Tooth Fairy. Well, I am the Tooth Fairy—me and Mommy. I guess that's okay. What about the Easter Bunny? We're the Easter Bunny, too. What about Santa Claus? We're Santa, too. Then, who ate the cookies? I did. You mean there's no Santa? That's not what I said. I said me and Mommy are Santa, the Easter Bunny and the Tooth Fairy. Oh. That's what my friend at school said. Your friend told you there's no Tooth Fairy? No, she said it's your parents. Do you believe that? I don't know. What happens next time I lose a tooth? You put it under your pillow same as always. Can I? Of course you can. Nothing's changed. Nothing's changed.

This morning I awoke to the church bell clang, showered, dressed, and met Spencer for breakfast in the canteen in the basement of the compound. Over coffee, hard boiled eggs, cheese, and fresh bread that never smelled so good, we planned our day.

"If we drive due west through Gyor, we'll get to Sopron in about four hours."

"I don't like that idea very much," said Spencer not looking up. "There's plenty of time to get out to the border. We should look into Warburton's disappearance. I'm not sure where to start. I'm not the investigator—that's your gig. Anyway, I'm not sure there's much we could accomplish in Budapest without giving ourselves away."

"Well, we could take a detour, do a little sightseeing."

"Oh, yeah?" asked Spencer.

"I already went back down into the cellar where I last saw Basil. I don't think going again will offer any clues. There are two people I want to talk to. First is Vladimir Ivanov."

"He's the KGB officer you met at the bridge and who detonated the car bomb?"

"Right, but he's probably out of the country already and back in Dresden. Second is Josef Tibor. He's with—or somehow connected with—the Hungarian Ministry of the Interior. He took us to meet Otto von Habsburg. He got us some good intelligence about the Stasi network operating in Sopron. But he also received the request from Ivanov to meet and facilitated the communication. He's been very helpful. I'm not saying he's compromised. I just want to talk to him."

"I'm ready when you are," said Spencer. "Let's go to the motor pool and get some wheels."

The guy at the motor pool gave us another Trabant, this one a very rusty looking two-door. Spencer walked around it, nodding his head in approval.

"Model P601 deluxe limousine," Spencer giggled. "The body is stock, but the engine, transmission, drive train, suspension, and even the tires have been upgraded. It's sort of a turbo-charged sleeper that still looks and sounds like any old Trabant. God, I'd love to bring one of these back to Honolulu. It would be perfect for cruising Kalakaua Avenue

1989
TIANANMEN SQUARE TO EAST BERLIN
JACK GODWIN

on a Saturday night. I wonder if I could just ship it back to Fort Shafter."

"Spencer," I put my hand on his shoulder, "*Earth to Spencer.*"

"Can I drive?" he said.

With Spencer behind the wheel, we left the massive compound on Tancsics Street, crossed the river and drove southwest out of the city toward Lake Balaton, the Napsugar camp site in Fonyod—and Tibor. It was Saturday, so the traffic wasn't too bad. Young couples strolled along the river bank and young mothers pushed strollers. The chairs and tables outside every café were full as though everyone had plenty of time and money. City buses spewed out the blackest exhaust I've ever seen, which didn't just float in the air but clung to the walls of every building, especially the older, stylish ones.

"On a day like this, Budapest really is a beautiful city," I said, "except for the buses. The smog here is worse than the worst day I ever saw in Los Angeles. If the Sierra Club saw what's coming out of these exhaust pipes, they'd never say another unkind word about capitalism. Anybody who thinks socialism is environmentally friendly is a fool."

"You should come to Hawaii," said Spencer.

"It's on my list."

"Did you know the air in Hawaii gets entirely replaced every seven minutes?"

"What're you talking about?"

"Yeah, because of the trade winds the islands have a natural ventilation system. The trade winds brought the first immigrants, explorers, traders, whalers, the missionaries and the tourists. And the trade winds wash and rinse the air in Hawaii every seven minutes."

"You were born in Hawaii?"

"Yes I was."

"Is Pang a Hawaiian name?"

"No, my family is Chinese but I have Hawaiian ancestors, not many but enough to qualify for the Kamehameha school, where I went until the University of Hawaii. I was in the ROTC and then I joined the army when I graduated."

"How did you get to Tiananmen Square?"

"Well, I grew up speaking Chinese at home, so I'm fully bilingual. Defense Intelligence came looking for me, said they had a job for me, quick promotion and all that."

"I hope they gave you a purple heart."

"They did! They gave me a purple heart and made me captain at the hospital in Seoul while I was recuperating."

"And you subscribe to *Jane's Defense Weekly* and you read every issue cover to cover."

"How do you know that?"

"You talked a little after the medic gave you the pain reliever, nothing embarrassing."

"I don't remember that. I don't even remember getting shot. It's been more than two months."

"You don't remember getting shot?"

"No."

"You don't remember running out of the square and getting into the *Land Cruiser*?" Spencer shook his head. "I guess you never read my report. You jumped over the back seat and got behind the mounted machine gun and wiped out a whole squad. Warburton drove us to the stadium in Beijing and we took a chopper to the base on South Korea. We checked you into the 121st Combat Support Hospital in Seoul."

"I remember the hospital."

1989
TIANANMEN SQUARE TO EAST BERLIN
JACK GODWIN

"You talked about *Jane's Defense Weekly* when we were in the chopper. You were very talkative. I think the medic gave you something and you told him that Warburton saved your ass, well, me and Warburton."

"I did?"

"Yeah, you did. And you're right. He did save your ass."

19.

SATURDAY, JULY 15, p.m.

We arrived at the Napsugar camp site in Fonyod shortly after noon. Spencer parked in front of the same small gray building with the hand-painted sign. There was Tibor again with his elbows on the counter reading a newspaper. He never got around to oiling the squeaky hinge. He didn't even bother to look up.

"Hello, Tibor," I said barely above a whisper. He looked up at me, and then his eyes darted to Spencer, to me, and then back to Spencer head to toe as if to assess the threat. Only then did he fold his newspaper and stand up.

"What happened?" he asked, "Where is Basil? No—he is not, not Basil Warburton. I refuse to believe it." He wasn't sure he could convince himself.

"Introductions first," I said. "This is Spencer Pang. He's with us."

"You're Chinese?" Tibor eyeballed Spencer.

"Chinese-American, yes, Hawaii born," Spencer said. After we all shook hands, I took a deep breath and told the tale.

"The meeting with Ivanov went according to plan, except for the grand finale. He detonated a car bomb—a car full of Stasi agents. No problem—they're worse than the Gestapo—

except their friends took off after Basil and me. Ivanov had a car waiting and got away immediately."

A couple came into the little kiosk just then. Tibor stood up and greeted them. They exchanged a few words, Tibor handed them a key and they were gone. Tibor stood on his tip toes, looking over Spencer's shoulder until they were out of earshot. He nodded for me to continue.

"They chased us on foot into the Castle District and into the castle. I shot one and got another with a grenade I think, but there was a gun battle. We got separated. We were supposed to meet at the car but Warburton never showed up. I went back to the scene, found a lot of blood and a part of a tooth. The scene was pretty contaminated. There's no way of knowing whose blood it was, but there was a puddle right where I left him."

"If they killed him, why take the body?" Tibor shrugged and held both hands palms up. "This makes no sense."

"And if they didn't kill him," Spencer said, "there are only two scenarios, two possibilities. One is they took him and the other is he got away. In either case, he may be seriously wounded and needing medical help or maybe dead already."

"I don't know. There was a lot of blood. If he was wounded, he can't have traveled very far." The little kiosk fell silent except for the oscillating fan. Tibor folded his arms, frowned and stared at me. I could hear children playing outside and splashing in the lake.

"I have many friends at the Ministry of the Interior. I will make inquiries. Come back in two days. Now, please excuse me." Tibor rushed us out of the little kiosk and padlocked the door. "Come back in two days. I may have something for you. You cannot stay here." He turned away from us and followed a foot path into the trees.

"Now what," Spencer said.

"Now we wait. But we can't stay here, obviously, too many tourists. Let's go to the safe house in Fertorakos. That's where Benson expects us to be. You drive. I'll show you the way."

"Speaking of Benson," said Spencer as we climbed into the Trabant, "What did she mean *Mr. Warburton's loyalties are divided?*"

"I don't know exactly. Before you came into the conference room, she told me he's a double agent. You know, I love everything about espionage, except that."

"What's that?"

"Everybody is lying, maneuvering and scheming. You never, ever know who to trust."

"It's the *Great Game*," he said.

"What great game? Is that the one where every fucking player is self fucking employed?"

"What did you study in college?" Spencer asked.

"Business school and law school, followed by the FBI Academy," I said.

"That explains that. The *Great Game* was the rivalry in Central Asia between Russia and the British Empire in the nineteenth century. Back then India was the jewel in the British Empire. India became independent in 1947, but long before that, Pakistan was part of India and shared a border with Afghanistan. The competition in that region, especially west of the Himalayas, was nonstop for a hundred years. World War I and the Bolshevik revolution changed all that, but the *Great Game* never really ended."

"There's no checkmate."

"That's right. Just think about the last ten years. In May 1979, Iran became an Islamic Republic. In December the

1989
TIANANMEN SQUARE TO EAST BERLIN
JACK GODWIN

same year, the Soviets invaded Afghanistan. If you think Washington was worried about Iran, then you could double that for Moscow. Seventy-nine was when the Kremlin started getting seriously worried about losing the southern republics. Turkmenistan, Uzbekistan, Tajikistan, Kirghizstan. What am I forgetting? At this Spencer raised his right hand and pointed at the windshield like he was reading a map, "Oh yeah, the big one, Kazakhstan."

"All the Stans," I said.

"All the Stans," he repeated. "You know, Harry Truman predicted this back in 1953." Spencer turned his head toward me nodding. "Yeah, nineteen fifty three, Truman's last week in office he gave his farewell address. He said the Soviet Union is going to lose the Cold War because it's fatally flawed. There's going to be a coup someday, he said, maybe a revolution, maybe the republics will all go AWOL, or maybe the Kremlin will just give up."

"Truman said that?"

"Yeah, you know what Rudyard Kipling said?"

"What?"

"When everyone is dead the *Great Game* is finished. Not before."

"Everyone except Basil Warburton you mean."

"I hope you're right," said Spencer. "I feel like I owe him for getting me out of Tiananmen Square."

"Warburton saved your ass," I said.

When we arrived at the safe house in Fertorakos, I showed Spencer where to stash the car. We went in through the doorway of the abandoned grocery store and descended the staircase.

"I read about this in the *British Army Journal*," said Spencer. "The Royal Engineers built this in 1939. In 1940,

Nazi Germany forced Hungary to declare war on Britain and America, all the while secretly negotiating with Britain *and* America. But in 1944, Hitler discovered Hungary was double dealing, and the Wehrmacht occupied Fertorakos until the Soviet Red Army invaded in 1945."

"You are such a geek," I said.

"This is no ordinary safe house," he said. It's a citadel with a high-tech armored vault, command and control center, weapons facility, storage facility, and living quarters all rolled into one. It's outfitted with secure communications equipment to monitor activity outside of the building. It's got blast protection, tough enough for almost anything but a direct hit from a nuclear attack. The walls are reinforced concrete, access points are reinforced with bullet-resistant fiberglass. The buried pipes guarantee ventilation, potable water, waste removal and an escape shaft."

"It's even got a fax machine," I said. "Maybe we should check in with Benson so she knows we arrived."

20.

SUNDAY, JULY 16

Spencer and I made a site visit to the field where the Pan-European picnic was scheduled to take place. It was a perfect venue because the field straddled the border, with a fence running through the middle where there was a big gate which would be thrown open on the day of the picnic. There was plenty of open space on both sides for people, tents, musicians, vendors, portable toilets and everything. It all seemed like a waste of time with Warburton missing and maybe dead. Back at the safe house, I spent the rest of the day checking the gear, cleaning weapons, checking the gear again, and killing time.

21.

MONDAY, JULY 17

Spencer and I piled into the car and drove to Lake Balaton to find out if Tibor learned anything from his friends at the ministry. It rained most the way from Fertorakos but it let up eventually and the sun broke through. We passed through the rolling countryside, past beech, birch and oak trees. By the time we arrived, tourists were lining up at the food stalls and jamming the small sandy beaches, while kids splashed in the shallow water.

"Not exactly Waikiki Beach, is it?"

"Huh?"

"Waikiki Beach," Spencer said, "Honolulu."

"I'm sorry. What?"

"We're here, Jaqui. You can breathe now." Spencer cut the engine but kept the key in the ignition for a moment before removing it. "Maybe Tibor will have information, maybe he won't. Maybe Basil is alive, maybe not. Be ready for anything, okay?"

"Okay, yeah thanks."

My stomach was in my throat as I opened the door to the little gray kiosk, ready to receive whatever news Tibor would deliver, but he wasn't there. There was a newspaper folded on the counter, but Tibor wasn't there.

1989
TIANANMEN SQUARE TO EAST BERLIN
JACK GODWIN

"Son of a bitch," I said. "That's great, just great. What do we do now?"

"Now we wait," said Spencer.

"I don't feel like waiting. The Stasi probably has—or had—Tibor under surveillance, monitoring his movements. Let's look around."

"I'm sure they would consider us undesirable," Spencer shrugged. "Maybe he's somewhere in the campground."

"Okay," I said, "Let's take the foot path Tibor took the last time we were here. It was that way. Remember?"

"Lead the way," said Spencer.

There were still plenty of children playing and splashing in the lake. If anything, the campground felt more crowded than ever. We followed the path through the trees, which led to a large car camp, a tent city with picnic tables, makeshift canopies, clothes lines, and hundreds of people on holiday. The car camp was bare dirt except for the weeds clumped around the rusty fence posts. People were eating, drinking, cooking, smoking, talking and laughing. Nobody paid us any attention as we walked.

"Do you see all these families? How many of these people do you think are potential defectors?"

"Good question," said Spencer. "Wait. Do you hear that?"

"What?"

"German," he said, "They're all speaking German. And check out the license plates."

"What about them?"

"The first letter tells you where the car is registered. S is for Leipzig, I for East Berlin, R for Dresden. There are fifteen districts and these are all East German. There is *no way* the local Stasi detachment is going to stop these people without help from the Hungarian government. Even the Stasi wouldn't gun down entire families, would they?"

"I don't know. They might," I replied.

At the other end of the car camp there was a gray kiosk identical to the one Tibor usually occupied. There was a picnic table under a shade tree next to the kiosk, and there was Tibor, thank God, sitting at the table. There was someone else sitting across from him with his back to us. They were both smoking, chain-smoking judging by the pile of cigarette butts in the ashtray. I was hoping Tibor would smile when he saw us but he didn't smile or speak, just invited us to sit down with his hand.

"I have news," he said, "But introductions first. Jaqueline Nogales, Spencer Pang, this is Laszlo Nagy, with the Ministry of the Interior. These are the Americans I have told you about."

"Ms. Nogales, Mr. Pang, pleased to meet you," said Nagy as he presented his calling card. "Forgive my attire. Officially, I am not even here."

"Forgive me for saying so," I said, "but we're a little exposed here. Is this secure? We're surrounded by Germans."

"My security detail is here, undercover," said Nagy. Spencer and I looked at each other and shrugged. "Thank you for asking. Tibor tells me you are good friends to know, especially you Ms. Nogales."

"Tibor talks too much," I said. Tibor guffawed.

"I understand Tibor introduced you to Otto von Habsburg, you and Basil Warburton."

"Yes," I said. "That was in June. That's when we first heard about your plans to eliminate the border restrictions with Austria. Congratulations on that. Basil Warburton and I were working behind the scenes at the tear-down ceremony.

Before that, when we met with Habsburg, we also heard about your plans for the Pan-European picnic."

"So far so good, as you say."

"So far so good, except that Warburton has gone missing," said Spencer. Nagy looked at Spencer and tapped his cigarette.

"We should talk about that," said Nagy. The location where the car bomb went off is not far from the parliament building. The police informed the ministry that the occupants of both cars were Stasi agents. That is all we knew until Tibor contacted us and informed us of Vladimir Ivanov's involvement. Let me assure you that the Stasi has very limited authority in Hungary, limited and decreasing on a daily basis. The Stasi continue to have a presence, they maintain a network of informants, but they have no authority to arrest anyone, and certainly not to kill or kidnap anyone."

"Maybe they were acting without authority," said Spencer.

"This is possible of course but highly unlikely. Stasi agents are German, and Germans follow orders. This is one of their greatest strengths, from an operational point of view, but also their greatest failing. Stasi executions have a signature, a single pistol shot to the neck, very methodical, very economical. In any case, they did not kill or capture Basil Warburton."

"How do you know?"

"I cannot tell you how I know. However, it appears that Mr. Warburton deliberately faked his own death and it appears he did so with Ivanov's cooperation."

"Why?" asked Spencer.

"We do not know," said Tibor. My mind was reeling and Nagy was staring at me while I was trying to compose myself.

"Ms. Nogales," he said, "You seem troubled to be hearing this. I appreciate your concern, but we are receiving conflicting reports. We assume such reports are part of a disinformation strategy. My office has resources of its own, Ms. Nogales, friends in the intelligence community. Vladimir Ivanov is a friend."

"And a colonel in the KGB," I said. "I met your friend. I was standing this close to him when he detonated the car bomb."

"Yes, we know," said Nagy. "Ms. Nogales, we appreciate your efforts, the work you have done, and the work you *will do* on behalf of our cause. Thank you, and thank you Mr. Pang. The American government has been very supportive."

"But?" said Spencer.

"But things are perhaps more complex than your political leaders suggest. Calling the Soviet Union an *evil empire* may be very pleasing to Christian evangelicals in the American south, but perhaps the threat of Soviet expansion has come and gone. Perhaps there is a new threat, not expansion but disintegration. If that is the threat—disintegration and perhaps revolution—then we need friends inside the KGB, friends inside Stasi, all kinds of friends including Vladimir Ivanov, whose anti-communist credentials may not be apparent to you."

"Ivanov is working to bring down his own government?"

"Yes," said Nagy, "and he is not working alone. Everyone can see the corruption, the internal decay—everyone except the most conservative party members. If you can see it, you cannot help but have contempt for it. I would say Ivanov has more faith in opportunism than communism. By hastening the end of a brutal regime, he is furthering his political ambitions and positioning himself for the future."

1989
TIANANMEN SQUARE TO EAST BERLIN
JACK GODWIN

"He's an employee of the brutal regime," said Spencer.

"Yes, from the American point of view, Ivanov's conduct is hypocritical. But from the European perspective, it is merely ironic. You can judge for yourself which perspective makes more sense." Nagy looked at his watch and rose from the table. "Ah, it is getting late and I have to get back to Budapest. I have enjoyed meeting you and you Ms. Nogales. Please do not get up. There is something else Tibor would like to share with you." Nagy signaled with his hand and a black Mercedes appeared out of nowhere. Before he got in, he turned and flashed a politician's smile. Then the Mercedes disappeared in a cloud of dust.

"Tibor, what the hell is going on?" I said.

"We do not know for certain, but our sources tell us Basil is in Dresden, East Germany."

"Dresden," I said, "That's where Ivanov is based."

"Yes," said Tibor, "He is stationed in the KGB office across the street from the local Stasi office."

"What are you saying?" asked Spencer. "Basil is working for the Stasi?"

"I do not know," said Tibor. Tell me, when you met Ivanov, did you notice anything unusual?"

"Like what?"

"Anything unusual means *anything unusual*," said Tibor. "Think."

"Ivanov sent Basil a note asking me to attend the meeting. That was a surprise. We met at Karl—at the Karl Marx statue—no surprise there. We walked to the middle of the bridge. Basil kind of barked at Ivanov and asked him what he wanted. Ivanov switched from German to English, and introduced himself to me. Wait, that's it. He introduced himself to me but not to Basil. *That's it*," I said. "Ivanov and Basil knew each other. They've met before."

"You're speculating," said Spencer.

"Tibor, I need to get to Dresden."

"No way, no how," said Spencer. "What am I supposed to tell Benson?"

"Tell her I'm in the field. Tell her I'm reconnoitering. Tell her I'm following up on a lead. The picnic isn't for another month. Dresden is what, seven hundred kilometers from here? Tibor and I could get there and back in a few days. Right, Tibor?" Tibor sat up straight and pointed at himself.

"You mean to drive, through Czechoslovakia?"

"Yes. Exactly, we'll just fall in with the crowd driving home to East Germany after their vacation. It'll be easy."

"Easy you say."

"Not easy but doable," I said.

"And then what?" said Spencer. "When you get to Dresden, what are you going to do? Are you going to stake out the KGB station? I won't stop you. I'll even try to cover for you the best I can, but let's think this through."

"Spencer is right," said Tibor. "Getting in—this is doable as you say. But getting out, and this means getting out with Basil Warburton, this will not be so easy."

"And what if he doesn't want to go? What if he resists? What if Benson is wrong and Basil's loyalties *aren't* divided? What if he's been working for them all along?"

"Are you saying Basil Warburton is a collaborator? Who do you think he is? Do you think he's been playing us? You do remember waking up in the army hospital in Korea, don't you? Listen to yourself."

"Yeah, sorry about that," said Spencer.

"Tibor, are you in or out?"

1989
TIANANMEN SQUARE TO EAST BERLIN
JACK GODWIN

"I will drive you, but we cannot leave now. I do not want to get detained at the border. We need documents and pictures for you and me and for Basil, too if possible. Are there any photographs of Basil that we can use at the safe house?"

"I don't know but I can check," I said.

"Plus, we will need something to trade, American cigarettes and Scotch whiskey. Blue jeans if you can find them, it does not matter if they are new or used. Come back with whatever you find first thing tomorrow," said Tibor, "and meet me at the kiosk. Is that where you left your car? Come now and I will walk with you. Walking helps me think."

Tibor, Spencer and I walked back along the path through the trees. My mind was still reeling. When Spencer and I told Tibor about Basil's disappearance two days ago, it never occurred to me it would lead to this, to driving halfway across Europe to rescue a colleague who may not really be a colleague and who may not even want to be rescued.

22.

TUESDAY, JULY 18

At the safe house, Spencer and I rummaged through Basil's belongings and found a British passport with Warburton's photo using the alias Gerald Roberts. Tibor would have to destroy it to use the picture but there was no other way. In the stockroom we found five cartons of Marlboros, a case of Johnnie Walker and a pile of Levis jeans in various sizes. After that, I filled a small duffel bag with enough guns, ammo and hardware to respond to most contingencies.

"You have to inventory all this stuff," Spencer said, "government property you know."

"Do I have to keep track of every bullet I use? I'm not going into East Germany unarmed."

"Not the bullets," said Spencer, "just the cigarettes and the liquor. Are you going to bring the sniper rifle?"

"Not for this job," I said. "A shotgun is better for close combat."

"It might come in handy," said Spencer.

1989
TIANANMEN SQUARE TO EAST BERLIN
JACK GODWIN

23.

WEDNESDAY, JULY 19, a.m.

We woke up and loaded the car and got on the road before dawn. By the time we pulled up to the kiosk, it was mid-morning and Tibor was sitting on a rickety wooden stool holding a cup. He stood up and came to the driver's side window.

"Good morning," he said.

"Sorry to interrupt your coffee break," said Spencer.

"What?"

"Coffee," said Spencer, pointing at the cup and mimicking.

"Oh this," he said grinning, "This is not coffee." Tibor drained the cup and set it on the stool. "Do you have pictures? Good, I will show you where to go. We can walk from here."

We headed uphill away from the lake and campground. Tibor guided us through town left, right, left until we came to a small shop. The sign in the window told me it was a locksmith.

"Here," he said. The place was empty when we filed in except for a middle aged man wearing an oil stained apron. He peered over his half-rim glasses, and without acknowledging Tibor or us, walked around us and locked the front door. He flipped a sign in the window and signaled with his head for us to follow. We went behind the counter to the back of the shop and descended a staircase into the basement. The locksmith pulled a cord, which illuminated a very large room, part photographer's studio, part workshop. I noticed all the machines were German or Japanese and all state-of-the-art. I handed Warburton's passport to the locksmith. He nodded in approval. Tibor said something in Hungarian, a few sentences then he turned to Spencer and me.

"I explained we need a new passport for Basil and one for you. Do you have a photograph of yourself?"

"No," I shook my head. Tibor spoke to the locksmith again. He nodded again.

"Sit on the stool over there in front of the screen and he will take your picture." The locksmith set up the lights then came over to me. With one hand on my shoulder and the other at the small of my back, he straightened my posture and then tilted my head down. He said something in Hungarian.

"Do not smile," said Tibor.

"I never smile." I said. He took five or six shots of me all the while speaking to Tibor.

"The locksmith thinks the best cover is to make us a married couple. He will make an East German passport for me and a Bulgarian passport for you. If anybody asks, we were here on holiday visiting your family."

"Tibor, do you speak German well enough to pass as a German?"

"As a matter of fact, yes I do."

"Too bad you don't speak Bulgarian," said Spencer.

"I speak Bulgarian," I said.

"What do you mean?" said Spencer.

"*What do you mean* what do you mean? The FBI sent me to language school. Study Bulgarian they said, so that's what I studied." Spencer looked impressed.

"The locksmith says to come back in three hours and he will have new passports and identity papers ready."

Tibor, Spencer and I passed the time having a long lunch at a café on the lake. The food was good and the beer was cold and Tibor regaled us with stories about his life, Hungarian history and scandalous stories about the Hungarian royal family.

"They were not all gentlemen like Otto von Habsburg," Tibor said. "In the late nineteenth century, years before the British had to deal with King Edward and Wallis Simpson there was Crown Prince Rudolf, Franz Joseph's son and heir to the throne. Rudolph was married but he was unhappy and drank too much. He had an affair with a beautiful young baroness. She was only seventeen years old. Of course the emperor ordered Rudolph to get rid of her but Rudolph refused. Nobody knows for sure, but they say Rudolph and the girl had a suicide pact and both took poison at Rudolph's hunting lodge in Mayerling, near Vienna. Franz Joseph was so distraught he converted Mayerling into a convent. The nuns still say prayers every day for Rudolph's soul."

"How is Otto related to Franz Joseph?"

"Franz Joseph was Herr Habsburg's uncle. Rudolph was Franz Joseph's only son, so when Franz Joseph died, his brother Charles became emperor. That was 1916, during the war. His reign ended in 1918 when the war ended. Charles was Herr Habsburg's father."

"That's fascinating."

"Oh, what a tangled mess," said Tibor, laughing and slapping the table with both hands. He checked his wristwatch. "I think the locksmith should be ready by now. He usually works very fast."

We walked back to the small locksmith shop, where the "closed" sign was still hanging in the window. Tibor knocked and we waited for the locksmith to appear. He let us in and we descended the stairs into the well-equipped studio/workshop. He showed us over to a project table with three piles, one for Basil, one for Tibor, he said, and one *for the lady.*

"National identity card, driver's license and passport," said Tibor, "with entry and exit visas, excellent."

"Floriana Varga," I said inspecting my documents while Tibor looked over my shoulder.

"That is a Gypsy name. I think he likes you." The locksmith said something in Hungarian to Tibor, and Tibor nodded. "You were "born April 10, 1962 in Sopron. Your father was Gypsy and your mother Bulgarian. The locksmith said he wanted to call you *Gypsy Angel Rose* but it did not translate into Hungarian so he called you Floriana. Some American singer he heard on the radio, spring time, spring roll or somebody. He talks crazy."

"Springsteen," said Spencer.

"Springsteen," said the locksmith nodding vigorously, "Bruce Springsteen." He tapped Tibor on the arm with the back of his hand and spoke in Hungarian again.

"He says this singer was here last summer traveling all over Europe. He even played in East Berlin," Tibor translated.

"Now I know we'll win," I said.

"Yes," said Tibor.

"No, translate for me. Tell him *now I know we'll win.*"

1989
TIANANMEN SQUARE TO EAST BERLIN
JACK GODWIN

Tibor translated and the locksmith laughed, played air guitar and raised both fists over his head in a triumphant rock 'n' roll pose. Thank you he said in English, thank you, patting us all on the back as he ushered us upstairs and out the door.

"That was interesting," said Spencer glancing at me discretely.

"Okay," I said, "Tibor, what's next?"

"We could leave tonight if you want, but I think we should get an early start tomorrow.

"Tonight," I said, "right now, as soon as possible. Let's get loaded and get going. We can sleep on the road if we have to."

Spencer and I walked back down the hill to where we left our car at the kiosk, while Tibor veered off in the other direction. A few minutes later, Tibor pulled up in a Trabant with East German plates.

"Maybe we should switch cars," I said.

"No, it is better to have German license plates," said Tibor.

"Then let's change the plates," said Spencer. "You've got a thousand kilometers or more there and back. Besides, this one's got smuggler's compartments. See?" Spencer lifted the fabric on the floor in front of the passenger seat.

"Ah, very good, but we should leave a few packs of cigarettes and one or two bottles of whiskey where the border guards can find them. Even if they do not find them, we can offer them as gratuities. And you," Tibor said to Spencer, "Take care of my car please, no joyriding."

"Don't worry Tibor. I'll take good care of it."

24.

WEDNESDAY, JULY 19, p.m.

We finished loading and said our goodbyes. I got behind the wheel and Spencer wished us good luck and good hunting. We headed east toward Budapest then northwest toward the Czechoslovakian border crossing near Bratislava. We had the windows open, which helped a little. Air conditioning in a Trabant would be suspicious even if the innards weren't supercharged. Tibor tuned the radio to the state run station, which played folk music and whatever else I couldn't understand. Once we got on the main road out of Budapest—I wouldn't call it a freeway—Tibor dozed off. Two hours later, I woke him up.

"Tibor, Tibor, wake up. We're about thirty minutes from the border. We should switch places and anyway, I have to pee."

We stopped briefly at a roadside stand where we ordered coffee and rolls. Unfortunately, there were no restrooms, so I scrambled through the weeds out back and squatted. It wasn't the first time. The coffee came in little plastic cups with half an inch of sediment at the bottom. The rolls, which they called *rollicki,* came with a slice of salty cheese. There weren't any chairs, so we stood at the waist-high tables and ate in silence.

1989
TIANANMEN SQUARE TO EAST BERLIN
JACK GODWIN

Tibor got in behind the wheel pulled onto the road. It was getting dark and there wasn't much to see at this hour, just a few lights behind us and a few more going the opposite way. It was thirty minutes to the Czech border, where we would certainly find out whether the blacksmith's forgeries were any good. Did I say blacksmith? I meant locksmith. Blacksmith uses a forge. Locksmith makes forgeries. The folk music wafting from the radio made me drowsy—even with the coffee. I thought maybe I would pretend to be asleep when we got to the border. That way I wouldn't have to answer questions. What if there was trouble? No, I better stay awake I told myself, I better stay awake.

Daddy, wake up. What? What time is it? There's somebody outside the tent, somebody in the camp. Shush. It's a bear. He's sniffing around. Listen. He found the canister. Daddy, I'm scared. Come here. Where's the flashlight? Shine it over here. Okay, I've got the pistol. Turn that off and be quiet. Listen. He's playing with the canister. Uh oh, is he coming over here? Quiet now, be still. Okay, he's gone now, everything's okay. That was close. Did you hear him snuffle the tent? That was close. I'm glad I didn't have to shoot. Jesus, that was close. I'm glad we're going back down tomorrow. Yeah, tomorrow, now get some sleep. He won't be back. It's a short hike to the car tomorrow. We'll be at the trailhead before noon. We'll have pepperoni pizza and cheesecake for lunch. Okay? Okay. Can I have a cherry coke? Anything you want. Hold my hand until you fall asleep.

We started slowing down. Were we slowing down? Yes, I had to shield my eyes from the lights. And there was the border crossing.

"Passports, something, something," I heard.

"Something, something, Sopron," Tibor said, "something, something, Dresden."

While the border guard inspected our passports, Tibor opened a pack of Marlboros, tapped it against the steering wheel, pulled out a cigarette and lit it. The guard noticed the American brand and Tibor pretended not to notice that the guard had lost interest in our passports. Tibor offered a cigarette to the guard and then casually offered the whole pack. The guard pocketed the cigarettes, said thanks and Tibor said something I couldn't follow but I'm sure it was more than *you're welcome*. The unsmiling guard pounded both passports with a rubber stamp, and with a wave, signaled us to go.

"What did you say to him?"

"I told him we might be traveling back this way in a week or so, and that I hoped to see him again."

"That's it? C'mon."

"No. He is almost at the end of his shift. We will drive a few kilometers and pull off to the side of the road. I will give him a carton of Marlboros and a bottle of Johnnie Walker, and maybe one more of each if he brings a trustworthy colleague. This way, when we come back next week with Basil, we will have no problems, I hope."

"You're taking an awfully big risk."

"Maybe but I do not think so," said Tibor, "The real risk is getting through the Czech-German border and into East Germany. I do not think one or two Czech border guards is much of a problem. In any case, it is good to have friends. Look there, there is a good place to pull off the road and wait."

I didn't like it. We were sitting and waiting on the side of the road and I just didn't like it. Cars and trucks were rolling

1989
TIANANMEN SQUARE TO EAST BERLIN
JACK GODWIN

past us and the western sky was turning yellow orange to black. I told Tibor I wasn't waiting in the car.

"You get the cigarettes and whiskey out where you can reach them," I said. "I'll get the shotgun in case there are any misunderstandings."

Tibor looked horrified, as though I was challenging his tactical know-how.

"Haven't you read *The Art of War*? "I asked. "A Chinese general named Sun Tzu wrote it a while back. You've got to know when to fight and when not to fight. You have to consider the context, the timing and all the resources at your disposal." In that context, at that time, I wanted a shotgun at my disposal, just in case those border guards hadn't read Sun Tzu either.

I took a knee a few yards into the bushes where you'd never notice me unless you knew exactly where to look. A few minutes later, two men in a car pulled off the road right behind ours. They left the engine running for a minute, then turned it off but left the headlights on. I could see there were two of them. They were just sitting there talking, probably wondering if the East German tourist traveling with his Gypsy wife would be an easy mark. The doors opened simultaneously. The border guards got out on either side and slowly walked toward Tibor, who was leaning against the trunk smoking.

I recognized the one who greeted Tibor. The other walked past them and peered into the passenger side. He said something to his partner, probably in Czech, which I didn't understand. My guess was "the woman is gone" or words to that effect. Then his partner, the one I recognized, spoke Tibor in German.

"Where is the woman?"

At that moment, I stood up, pumped one shell into the chamber and pressed the butt of the shotgun against my shoulder. The double action pump made that distinctive click-clack sound, mechanical and oily, somewhere in the range between tenor and bass. Everybody turned my way and I walked toward them, angling to my left to stay out of the beam of the headlights.

What do you say at a moment like this? I really wished I had something prepared because all I could think about were lines from Brian De Palma movies. *Say hello to my little friend.* I couldn't say that, but I had to say something that inspired the same shit-in-your-pants fear as the click clack of a pump shotgun. I couldn't just stand there, could I? Then occurred to me it didn't matter what I said if they didn't speak English.

"*Nobody brings their girlfriend to a gunfight!*" I snarled. Even Tibor looked terrified. "Tibor, translate word for word, you hear me, word for word. And put your hands down, God damn it. Okay, you and you get one bottle of whiskey and one carton of cigarettes, American cigarettes—each. Translate that. We'll be coming back this way in a week and you're helping us get through customs. Translate! We'll give you more whiskey and cigarettes and American dollars if you help us. Do we have a deal? Okay, good, Tibor, hand over the merchandise. Now get in your car and go."

I waved my hand as the border guards pulled way. Tibor frowned at me but then laughed and shook his head.

"What're you laughing at?"

"You made exactly the right impression. I am sure they will remember you at least until next week when we come back through. I am sure they will never forget you. I am certain they are talking about you right now."

1989
TIANANMEN SQUARE TO EAST BERLIN
JACK GODWIN

"It ain't a popularity contest. As long as we get Warburton out of East Germany, back where he belongs, those guys can tell the Surgeon General to go spoon a goose."

"Sometimes I do not understand. I mean, I understand your words but not your meaning."

"The Surgeon General, you know, smoking is hazardous to your health. Read the label."

"Oh, I see. And what was that you said about the goose?"

"Spoon a goose. That's a polite way to say *fuck a duck*."

"You Americans, you have the most wonderful obscenities."

"I don't know about that. The British can be very colorful. I think it's the cold weather."

Tibor looked puzzled but opted not to ask. He got behind the wheel. I stashed the shotgun out of sight and got in the passenger seat.

"I will drive for a while," said Tibor. "From here to Prague it is five hours, and then from Prague to the East German border, it is maybe ninety minutes."

25.

THURSDAY, JULY 20, a.m.

North of Bratislava, we crossed over the western tip of the Carpathian mountain range, what they call the "Little Carpathians." I'm sure the scenery was beautiful, charming vineyards and alpine lakes, but these mountains were more like foothills, and anyway it was pitch black outside and I couldn't see a thing. Besides, the roads in Czechoslovakia weren't as well maintained as Hungary and my spine was taking a pounding with every pothole. We passed by or through many towns and villages, Malacky, Zavod, Podivin, Rackice on our way through the woods and down to the meadows and farmlands. In ninety minutes we reached the outskirts of Brno, a much bigger town than Bratislava.

"See that sign?" said Tibor. I was so lost in my thoughts I forgot he was there. "That is the way to the Spilberk Castle. It was built about seven hundred years ago. During the Austro-Hungarian Empire, it was used as a prison. It was impossible to escape. Nobody escaped."

"Like Alcatraz Island."

"Worse than Alcatraz because it was a prison inside a castle, but then in eighteen fifty something, Franz Joseph dismantled the prison and converted it into a military barracks."

1989
TIANANMEN SQUARE TO EAST BERLIN
JACK GODWIN

"Otto's uncle," I said, "The same Franz Joseph with the crazy romantic suicidal son?"

"The same one," he said.

"I'd definitely like to stop there on the way back. We don't have any castles in California, not real ones anyway. We have plenty of prisons. And shopping malls, we've got a lot of shopping malls. Nice beaches in the south, Sierra mountains up north. Have you heard of Yosemite?"

"I want to visit San Francisco someday."

"That's where I went to law school, right there in the civic center. It's a pretty tough part of town these days. I lived in North Beach, in the Italian section with three roommates in a one-bedroom apartment. In my second year, my mother and father came up from Los Angeles to visit me. We were walking to my favorite restaurant, called Tommaso's. They have the best calzone. Anyway, the three of us, my mom and dad and me were walking from my apartment to the restaurant. There's a famous strip club on the corner, the Condor Club and there was a barker outside. Do know that expression?"

"No," said Tibor.

"Sometimes they're called carnival barkers and they stand outside a circus tent or a theater and call out to people and try to get them to come inside to see the show. So, my mother and father and I were walking past the Condor Club and the barker saw us and called out to my dad, *Come on in, bring both your lovers!*"

"No!" said Tibor.

"Yes! My mother was horrified of course. My father thought it was hilarious, of course."

"Bring both your lovers!"

"What about you, Tibor? Do you have a family, wife and kids?"

1989
TIANANMEN SQUARE TO EAST BERLIN
JACK GODWIN

"No. I am what the English call a confirmed old bachelor. I would be a world traveler if I could. But in San Francisco, the weather gets very cold in the summer, does it not?"

"It does. It gets foggy in the summer. I remember the first time we visited. My parents took us there on vacation. I must have been twelve or thirteen. We went to a baseball game. The Dodgers were in town against the Giants and we made the mistake of rooting for the Dodgers."

"I do not understand this game."

"Yeah, the rules are complicated, too complicated to explain. One thing you need to know is that Dodger fans and Giant fans hate each other. Another thing is that summers in San Francisco are cold. The fans, at least some of the fans, drink to stay warm. But I didn't know that at the time. We were just kids and we were on vacation and we were just rooting for our team. Well, a few of the locals got offended. They started by insulting the Dodgers. And when we didn't react, they insulted Dodger fans. And when we still didn't react, they insulted *the mothers* of Dodger fans."

"They sound like English football fans, hooligans."

"Yeah, my father had enough. He chewed them out."

"He chewed them out?"

"He scolded them. My father was a big guy. He got up, walked over to the hooligans and chewed them out in two languages, Spanish first, then English and then in Spanish again. Family is important in my culture and mothers are off limits. I've never seen him so angry. His face was purple. God, I haven't thought about that forever. It's baseball season now. I wonder how the Dodgers are doing."

"See there, we are coming up to Prague," said Tibor. "What time is it?"

"It's early still."

141

1989
TIANANMEN SQUARE TO EAST BERLIN
JACK GODWIN

"Good. We should keep driving until we get through town. Then we should get some rest, and give the car some rest, maybe two hours. And we should find something to eat. I want to get to the East German border early."

"How far did you say it is from here to the border?"

"One hour thirty minutes," said Tibor.

"When we stop, let's find a place off the road so we can put the shotgun away and repack everything. I'll put the cigarettes and whiskey where the guards can find them. We may not get searched, but we should make them work a little. I'll keep my pistol handy in case I'm not satisfied with the customer service."

"Service with a smile and socialism with a human face," said Tibor.

"I'm sorry. What?"

"I was making a joke."

"I still don't get it. What's socialism with a human face?"

"That was the Czechoslovakian Communist Party's slogan in 1968. It lasted a few weeks before the Soviets declared martial law. There was a new party secretary. I cannot remember his name, but some writers and intellectuals got him thinking about political reform and democracy. You have never heard of the Prague Spring? It was like 1956 all over again."

"What happened in fifty-six?"

"That was the first time people fantasized about democracy."

"Not the first time," I said.

"No. Not the first time, just the first time in Hungary. In 1956, the Soviets responded exactly the way the Chinese did in Tiananmen Square. They were ruthless. They killed thousands of people, imprisoned thousands and sent hundreds of thousands into exile. You see? First Hungary in the fifties, then Czechoslovakia in the sixties, and then it was Poland in the seventies and eighties. The communists outlawed Solidarity and declared martial law, all because some shipyard workers wanted to unionize."

"Maybe it will be different this time."

"Do you think so?" he said, "first Hungary, then Czechoslovakia and then Poland. What is missing from this list?"

"I give up. What's missing?"

"East Germany—straight ahead," he said, "Socialism with a human face. I must be a fool."

"Let's give them a bloody nose," I said, "Face first into a meat grinder. Then it'll be socialism with hamburger face. Better still, socialism with a cheeseburger face, secret sauce and a sesame seed bun."

"You are angry."

"You're God damn right I am. You want some fries with that? The bastards are holding our friend Basil Warburton."

It was still dark as we passed through Prague, which looked like another beautiful city I hoped to visit, maybe someday. We passed a wooded area on the edge of town and Tibor found a secluded place to park, where we rested and repacked. I set the timer on my wristwatch for two hours but I was too wired to sleep and couldn't stop thinking about Warburton. Niggling doubts grew into major reservations until the beeper woke me with a jolt. As usual, I didn't know where I was at first. Instinctively I reached for my weapon. The sun wasn't up yet, but I could see light in the eastern sky. I nudged Tibor with my elbow.

1989
TIANANMEN SQUARE TO EAST BERLIN
JACK GODWIN

"Wake up," I said opening the car door on my side. I stepped out of the car to stretch and forced myself awake. "Tibor, wake up."

We took our time methodically checking and rechecking the gear. Moving around helped loosen my stiff joints from the long drive. We worked in silence until—with a loud exhale—Tibor said *that should do it*. We climbed back in with Tibor behind the wheel and found our way back to the main road. The sun was up now but hiding behind a layer of clouds. Not yet seven o'clock and it already felt hot, humid and unstable, perfect conditions for a thunderstorm. All we needed was something to trigger it.

There was a sign in three languages that said the German border was five kilometers. The traffic slowed to a crawl and a line began to form at the border crossing.

"You've got the passports handy?" I asked.

"Yes," said Tibor. "Remember to keep your cover. Your name is Floriana. You are half Gypsy, half Bulgarian. You were born April 10, 1962 in Sopron. Do not speak to the agents. Do not even look at them. If one of them asks you a question, use simple words and keep your voice down. Do you understand?"

"Roger that."

Up ahead, I could see the checkpoint. There was one guard stopping every vehicle, cars and trucks. I saw the pattern. First, he checked the passports. After that, he gave the passports back and waved the drivers forward. Or he kept the passports and sent drivers off to the right for a closer inspection. Off to the right there was a lane with concrete barriers on both sides, but it looked like almost every car was getting waived forward. We inched our way up to the border, fifth in line, then fourth, third, second.

We got to the head of the line. The guard said *passports* and Tibor complied. He flipped the one open and glanced at Tibor. Then he flipped the other open and glanced at me. I watched the guard's eyes move over the page. Keep breathing, act casual, just play the part I told myself. Everything was cool. Everybody was cool. Then he lifted one page by the corner and slowly rubbed his thumb back and forth. Tibor was resting his arm on the door and staring straight ahead, not even paying attention. It was hardly noticeable, but I could tell the guard wasn't reading anymore. He was feeling the paper and thinking.

My face felt hot. *He knows. He's not going to give the passports back. He's going to keep the passports and send us off to the right and his buddies are going to rummage through the car.*

And that's what happened. The guard kept the passports and directed us toward the lane with the concrete barriers.

"Do not worry," said Tibor out of the guard's earshot. "We planned for this contingency. Do not worry."

There was one car ahead of us. One guard carrying a Kalashnikov watched while two others searched the car. The one with the Kalashnikov looked bored until the guard holding our passports walked over and placed them on what looked like a concierge desk. They exchanged a glance and the one carrying the Kalashnikov moved his index finger inside the trigger guard. The other two guards finished with the car in front of us and we pulled forward until one of the guards signaled to stop and told us to step out. He started asking Tibor questions while the other poked around, first opening the glove compartment, checking under the front seats, and rummaging through the back seats. He opened the

1989
TIANANMEN SQUARE TO EAST BERLIN
JACK GODWIN

hatch, lifted the tarp and that's when he found the Johnnie Walker and Marlboros we planted.

The guard scolded Tibor and accused him of buying goods on the black market. Tibor offered to pay duties to import the cigarettes and whiskey but the guard just confiscated everything. Fortunately, they hadn't discovered the hidden compartment and the weapons, at least not yet. Meanwhile, the other agent—the one from the checkpoint who took our passports—walked over. There were a few cars behind us in line, but he must have waived them on because we were the only ones left. The morning rush was over, I guessed. It was awfully quiet. Something was wrong. The one with the Kalashnikov pulled the butt close to his shoulder. I looked away casually and yawned, and put one hand in my pocket, feeling for the pistol grip.

The one who found the whiskey and cigarettes started shouting and waiving at Tibor. When Tibor didn't respond, the guard slapped him hard in the face with a carton of cigarettes. I kept my eyes on the guy with the Kalashnikov, who still had his index finger inside the trigger guard. The other guard was shouting and Tibor just kept his cool until the guard pointed at me and said something I didn't understand, *zig-oy-ner-rin* something. I couldn't understand. Then Tibor completely lost it. He grabbed the guard by the collar and hit him in the face. One deafening shot from the Kalashnikov dropped Tibor.

I drew my weapon and put two rounds into the shooter's chest. I trained my weapon on the other three still standing. They were all armed, but their pistols were holstered. The one who shouted at Tibor went for his gun and I put two rounds into his face. That was two down, two still standing. I couldn't take my eyes off them—not for a second—and couldn't even look at Tibor to see if he was alive or dead. The two left were standing close, the one who thumbed the passports and the one who first questioned Tibor. I shifted my aim from one to the other and back again. Who was it going to be? Both of them, as if on cue, reached for their side arms. I already had one of them in my sights. I didn't know how much time I had and couldn't take the risk, so I put two into his chest. That meant I had two cartridges left. An eight round magazine calls for economy, so I put one into the last guard's forehead and saved the eighth round just in case.

No need, everything was calm. The gunshots were echoing in my head even though everything was quiet now. Five bodies on the ground, not one of them moved. Nobody moved, nobody breathed, and nobody made a noise.

"Jaqui."

I looked down and saw Tibor on his back, one hand outstretched, the other holding the side of his head. I knelt down and tried to move his hand away to inspect the wound. I couldn't tell but head wounds sometimes look worse than they really are. He was covered with blood and so was the pavement beneath him.

"Jaqui, we must go. We must get back to Czechoslovakia. Help me to the car."

"Okay, keep your hand on the wound. Let's sit up nice and easy. Put your arm around my neck just like that. That's it, nice and slow." I eased him into the passenger seat and unbuttoned my top to dress the wound. "Hold this against your head Tibor. I'm sorry it doesn't smell very good." One of the guards was blocking the car so I pulled his body out of the way by the ankles.

I spun the car around and passed through the checkpoint back into Czechoslovakia. Still not a soul in sight,

1989
TIANANMEN SQUARE TO EAST BERLIN
JACK GODWIN

we got lucky in that department. The shock was wearing off, for me and Tibor. He was in pain but at least he was conscious. We were racing down the road away from the scene. Jesus, he looked pale. We had to find a doctor.

"When you get to the crossroad, turn left toward Tisá. It is only a few kilometers," said Tibor, "I know a clinic there." The clinic was just opening for the day when we arrived. I left Tibor in the car, ran inside and explained the best I could. The doctor or whoever understood some English but not much. Or maybe I was talking too fast. I said Tibor's name—Josef Tibor. *Outside*, I gestured and pointed and mimicked with my hand pointing at my temple. The doctor got it and ran outside with me. Tibor was right where I left him, semi-conscious and moaning.

Examining the wound, the doctor spoke softly to Tibor barely above a whisper and Tibor seemed to recognize him and understand. *Help me inside* said the doctor and signaled for me to help him carry Tibor into the clinic. We laid him on a bed in a dingy examination room and the doctor went to work. I got up to leave but Tibor held out his hand and waved for me to come back.

"Jaqui," he said.

"I'm here Tibor. The doctor's here."

"I lost my temper. It is my fault."

"That doesn't matter now. The doctor's going to fix you up."

"The border guard made me angry."

"Hush now Tibor." The doctor was working on Tibor's right eye. The shooter's aim was off otherwise Tibor would be dead, but there was a long gash on the side of his face. His right eye looked bad. It was hanging out like there was no bone, no eye socket left.

"The border guard insulted you. He called you a Gypsy and then called you the most vulgar thing you can call a woman." Tibor let out a loud grunt and squeezed my hand so hard it hurt. The doctor was working, mumbling something and shaking his head. There was a lot of blood.

"Thank you Josef Tibor. That was heroic. Be still now and let the doctor work." It went on like this for awhile, a few minutes or longer, I don't know. There was that familiar hospital smell. I blinked from the alcohol fumes burning my eyes and looked around the room at the peeling paint and the wall clock ticking away. Everything was quiet now except for the surgical instruments clinking and the birds warbling and chirping in the distance. Tibor loosened his grip on my hand. He took a shallow breath and exhaled and died. I was still holding his hand and it was still warm but there was no life in it.

"I am sorry," said the doctor. "I am sorry." Carefully the doctor placed his instruments on the surgical tray and wiped his forehead with his sleeve. He staggered toward the sink to wash his hands and face. He pulled a fresh towel from a pile in the corner, turned to me and said "Who are you?"

"Floriana Varga," I said, "from Sopron, Hungary. My father was Gypsy and my mother was Bulgarian."

1989
TIANANMEN SQUARE TO EAST BERLIN
JACK GODWIN

26.

THURSDAY, JULY 20, p.m.

I explained to the doctor the best I could what happened at the border checkpoint, omitting all the important details, of course. Well, Miss Varga, he said, I will have to sign the death certificate and prepare the body for burial. In the space for *Cause of Death*, I will write gunshot wound. This will initiate an investigation, which will mean many questions—questions for which there are no good answers.

"Sorry but I can't help you there. I don't know anything about Tibor's family. I know he wasn't married, that's all. Why can't you just notify the Hungarian authorities? I can't be transporting a dead body halfway across the continent."

"You are going back to Hungary then?" I nodded yes. "I know a little about Tibor's work, a little but not much," said the doctor, "The least you could do is reassure me he died in a good cause."

"No. I mean yes. We were on a mission, if that's what you mean. But we never got there. We had some trouble at the border."

"Then, Miss Varga, at least you can reassure me whoever did this to Tibor is dead."

"Yes," I said, "him and a few of his friends."

"Good," he nodded. "You should go. Do you have a change of clothes? You can wash up in here if you want. While you are doing that, I will find a bucket and something to clean the bloodstains in the car in case you get stopped."

I did not get stopped. At least I don't think I did but I don't remember much from the long drive back. I just followed the signs to Prague, Brno, Bratislava, then to Budapest. Crossing the border into Hungary was easy this time. I fell into the long line of travelers headed south on vacation. It was like crossing from Nevada into California. Just don't try to sneak any fruit or vegetables past the agricultural inspectors. *Exotic invasive species may be hitchhiking!* Everyone slowed down as they passed through the checkpoint into Hungary but nobody got stopped. If there was a border guard, I didn't see one.

Was Tibor dead because of me? *He called you a Gypsy and then called you the most vulgar thing you can call a woman.* What did I care? We were on a mission! He could have called me whatever he wanted! What was it with men? Half of them wanted to insult you. The other half wanted to defend you. I didn't need defending. We were on a mission! And now Tibor was dead, Warburton was still missing and I was coming back empty handed. How was I going to explain this to Spencer? *He called me the most vulgar thing.* But that's not why I shot him. I shot him because he shot Tibor. I shot the other three in self-defense. I didn't need defending. What was it with men?

Besides, it's never a good idea to get into a Mexican standoff with an actual Mexican. Isn't that one of those unwritten rules like never going against a Sicilian with death on the line? Of course, those border guards didn't know who they were up against. Not that it mattered. They were bench

1989
TIANANMEN SQUARE TO EAST BERLIN
JACK GODWIN

warmers compared to the Stasi. What did Habsburg say? The Stasi is the watchdog of the party. The Stasi is the only thing in East Germany that works. It does surveillance against all foreign enemies, including Jews, foreigners, capitalists ... and Gypsies. That's their mission. That meant fighting them was my mission. Suddenly, I was inspired.

It was dark by the time I got to Budapest. I pulled into the Grand Hotel to use the telephone and call Spencer.

"Hello?"

"Spencer, it's me Jaqui."

"Where are you?"

"I'm at the Grand Hotel in Budapest."

"Are you wounded?"

"No, I'm fine but Tibor's dead. We had trouble at the German border. That's as far as we got. I'll tell you the whole story when I see you. I'm not sure when that'll be. I'll spend the night here and maybe drive over to Fertorakos tomorrow. There's something we have to discuss but this line's not secure. It'll have to wait. See you soon."

I checked into the hotel and headed straight for the bar—foreigners only, hard currency only. I was on my second shot of tequila when a man wearing a dark suit appeared in the doorway. I avoided eye contact and used my peripheral vision to study him. I noticed the earpiece and the sexy bulge under his left armpit, which meant he was carrying. I thought I recognized him from the compound, but wasn't sure. The shoes were definitely American. I emptied the shot glass and turned it upside down on the bar to distract his attention away from my other hand, which was handling my pistol. Even if he was American, he might not be friendly and I wanted to get the drop on him.

He looked around the bar, but instead of coming in he stood aside with his back to the wall. In came Dr. Benson leaning on her cane but still larger than life. She looked right at me showing no emotion at all, just hobbled toward me with that authoritative chin of hers.

"Keep your weapon holstered," she whispered. "Bartender, two more please, at that booth over there." She motioned with her head to follow. I slid into the booth and she sat down with some effort. She leveled her gaze on me the way she always does while we waited for the drinks. When the bartender withdrew, she lifted her glass, put a twenty dollar bill on the table and carefully set the glass on Andrew Jackson's face. She took a deep breath after a moment and spoke.

"To your health," she said.

"Uh, toast," I coughed.

"What are we drinking anyway?"

"Tequila," I said.

"Have you eaten anything?"

"I was going to order room service."

"Good. You're staying here tonight?"

"Yes."

"Good. Keep your receipts so you can get reimbursed. Since you're not going anywhere and since my body guard over there is also my driver, let's have one more. I already know what happened to Tibor, or most of what happened, but I still need you to come in tomorrow morning, not too early and submit a report about your unsuccessful *and unauthorized* mission."

"Yes ma'am."

"Jaqui."

"Yes ma'am."

"If you ever pull another stunt like that, you will be arrested and prosecuted, and you will go to jail. You won't just lose your job. You will lose everything."

"Yes ma'am."

"You have an assignment. That Pan European Picnic we're planning may seem trivial to you, silly even. But people are risking their lives to make it happen. We're fighting a war. We call it cold because it's unconventional and ideological and tactical and mostly symbolic. Lots of threats and nonstop propaganda, the arms race, those are the parts we broadcast. It's Cold War on television, but not for us and not for poor Tibor." She raised her glass then drained it and tried not to wince. *Doggy* she said shivering like one after a bath. "For us, Cold War means espionage. Sometimes it turns into a shooting war but we try to avoid that because, because … it's sloppy tradecraft for one thing. We can't broadcast it."

Benson paused then continued. "Cold War is very peculiar in that way. There's *The* Cold War, which I believe we're very close to winning. After the big celebration things will settle down again but we'll have to deal with the new normal. First we've got to win this one. And that means you've got to do your job, you and Mr. Pang. And that is to neutralize the local Stasi detachment before the picnic so the Austrians and the Hungarians can open the border for a few hours. Clear?"

"Yes ma'am."

"Alright then, drinks are on me." As Dr. Benson slid out of the booth, she stood up with the aid of her cane. The bodyguard said something inaudible into his wrist, then turned and led her out of the bar. Through the window I watched them leave the hotel and step out onto the cobblestone drive. The bodyguard held the door and Dr.

1989
TIANANMEN SQUARE TO EAST BERLIN
JACK GODWIN

Benson climbed into the back seat. He scanned the area one last time then climbed behind the wheel and I watched the red tail lights disappear around a corner.

Arrested and prosecuted she said, arrested and prosecuted. What did I care? Where'd I put my room key? Which room was I in? Ugh, that was nasty stuff. What did I care? I'd sleep it off and give Benson my resignation tomorrow. What did I care? Warburton: Missing, Tibor: Dead, Jaqui: Busted. Where the fuck was that elevator? There. I just wanted to get up to the room and lock the door and go to bed. I was exhausted, depressed and lonely, so lonely. I hated myself. What did I care? Okay, sixth floor, now all I had to do was find room 621, which was that-a-way. I didn't want to puke even though I always felt better afterwards. I tried to get to my room so I wouldn't puke in the hallway. I skipped brushing teeth and just fell into bed.

Did I ever tell you about the time I got fired? I was a forklift driver in Santa Maria. It was my job to unload the pallets from the trailers and drive them into the reefer. We called it the reefer. It was a big refrigerated warehouse. Did you ever dump a load? Yeah, that's how I got fired but it wasn't my fault. There was a pallet full of strawberries and the pallet was broken. I lifted it off the trailer, and I was turning the forklift toward the reefer when I heard the pallet crack. And then the whole load—this tower of strawberry boxes—started leaning. I tried to turn the forklift and save it, but no way. The tower just kept leaning and leaning until it fell to the pavement. The foreman came running over shouting and swearing at me. I tried to tell him the pallet was broken, but every time I tried to talk, he shouted strawberry jam, strawberry jam! And that's when you got fired? Yeah, plus I had to clean up the mess.

1989
TIANANMEN SQUARE TO EAST BERLIN
JACK GODWIN

27.

FRIDAY, JULY 21, a.m.

A sliver of light coming through the drapes stabbed me in the eye. What time was it? No time for breakfast, just coffee before I had to report to the compound on Tancsics Street. I sat up slowly because my head was pounding and that's when I noticed the red light on the telephone was flashing. Was it flashing before I went to bed? I called the front desk and the operator said there was a message for me. I figured it was from Benson reminding me to submit the report.

When I went to check out, the clerk handed me an envelope with my name and room number hand written. It was hotel stationery.

"When did this arrive?"

"I do not know. My shift started at seven o'clock this morning."

"Thank you," I said as I tore open the envelope.

Jaqui Darling,

I'm writing to tell you I'm alive and well. Sorry to disappear like that. I'll explain when I see you. I hope the boss didn't come down on you too hard. Sorry about our Hungarian driver. Remember what our majestic friend said. Never give up hope of liberating our friends behind the Iron Curtain. See you soon, love, B.

P.S. I cherish the memory of splashing through the sweet water with you.

He's alive, I told myself. I found an empty chair and read it again. I turned the page over to see if there was anything on back and peered inside the envelope. I glanced around the lobby half expecting to see him, knowing it was impossible. He cherished the memory of splashing through the sweet water with me? *What the hell?* It was written on hotel stationery, which meant Warburton was here. He was alive and he knew about Tibor and he knew—or at least suspected—Benson would reprimand me. Was he in the bar last night? No way! What was with the cloak and dagger? I stuffed the letter in my pocket and drove to the compound on Tancsics Street.

Everything seemed familiar except the last time I was there, all I had was Basil's chipped tooth in my pocket. Now I had proof of life. After the guard let me in, I trudged across the long courtyard trying not to make eye contact with anyone. Writing my report was going to be hard enough even without Warburton's little surprise. It took me four hours and several drafts to tell the story, the locksmith, the road trip, the shootout, all ending with Tibor's death at the clinic. I proofread it, signed it and slid it into one of those button-and-string "buckshot" envelopes every federal agency uses.

I tried to deliver it to Benson personally but when I reached her office, the door was closed and the guard stopped me in my tracks—the same guy from the bar last night wearing the same dark suit. Dr. Benson is not available he said, and held out his hand palm up. The finality of his tone and nonverbal communication told me my towering screw-up was famous, at least within the walls of the Tancsics Street compound. In agency parlance it was called

1989
TIANANMEN SQUARE TO EAST BERLIN
JACK GODWIN

having a high profile. And in the clandestine service, a high profile is sloppy tradecraft. What did Benson say? We can't broadcast it. For a moment, I stood there feeling humiliated and irrelevant, wondering if my career was finished. I handed the envelope to the guard and turned back the way I came in.

I might have protested. I might have mentioned the letter in my pocket, but no. That's not something I wanted to share at that moment. I needed to think. Who was Basil working for? *Mr. Warburton is a double agent, she said.* There was no way Basil Warburton was working for the Russians. No way. Was Basil self-employed? I couldn't see any profit in it. How about a third party? If so, it might explain what happened the day of the tear-down event. It might explain why the Stasi agents wanted to kidnap him and maybe kill him. When that big Stasi agent first got out of the Skoda, he smiled at Basil like he knew him.

Plus Ivanov knew him. It couldn't be a coincidence that Warburton disappeared so soon after the meeting with Vladimir Ivanov. I wanted to talk to Ivanov, but how? Tibor was the go-between, and now Tibor was dead. If Warburton was working for a third party, then what was his relationship with Ivanov? Who the hell knew? That wasn't a rhetorical question. Who knew? I could talk to Spencer but he wouldn't know any more than me. I could talk to Habsburg, if I had any idea where he was. I could talk to Warburton, if I had any idea where *he* was. Then I remembered that guy at Lake Balaton, the one Tibor introduced us to. What was his name?

This is Laszlo Nagy with the Ministry of the Interior. He seemed to know Tibor pretty well, and knew about our meeting with Habsburg. He knew the guys who died in the car bomb were Stasi agents. He knew Ivanov was involved, but he wasn't surprised or even a little bit concerned. He knew for certain the Stasi didn't kill Warburton. Spencer asked why he was so sure, but Nagy wouldn't say, just that Warburton faked his own death and did it with Ivanov's cooperation. He was very confident and a little condescending. *My office has resources of its own, and friends in the Stasi and the KGB.* He called Ivanov "a friend" and seemed pretty sure Ivanov was working against his own government. What the hell was going on?

Well, at least I knew my next move. I had to talk to Laszlo Nagy. Didn't he give me a business card? Bingo. His title was Special Assistant. That could have meant anything. The ministry was on Josef Attila Street, on the Pest side of the river, walking distance from Karl Marx University where the car bomb went off. I decided to pay him a call. I left the Trabant at the compound on Tancsics Street, walked downhill for a few minutes and took a taxi across the river to the Pest side.

Fifteen minutes later, I passed through the giant carved double doors of the Ministry of the Interior. Everything looked very grand: wood paneling, high ceiling, parquet floor. But it didn't look like there was anything in the budget for maintenance. Grand but deteriorated, the windows were filthy, the brass on the staircase was tarnished, and there wasn't anyone to empty the lovely art deco ashtrays. Behind a big desk a security guard was eyeballing me. When I scowled at him he shifted in his seat and looked away.

"I'm here to see Laszlo Nagy."

"What is your name, please?"

"Jaqueline Nogales."

"Wait." He picked up the telephone, dialed three numbers and said something I couldn't understand. He put the handset back in the cradle.

1989
TIANANMEN SQUARE TO EAST BERLIN
JACK GODWIN

"Wait," he said again. I looked around at the grand room and noticed a plaque hanging next to the double doors. I must have walked right past it without noticing. It said Imre Nagy with the dates 1896-1958. Imre Nagy, Imre Nagy. Where did I know that name? The briefing I got from Benson and Tanner! Quarter of a million Hungarians gathered at Heroes' Square to show their support for him. He was prime minister back in the day. The Russians murdered him, tied his hands behind his back and buried him face-down, the bastards. *We're sending you to Hungary said Benson, to make contact with members of the Hungarian opposition.*

Just then, I heard heels clicking toward me on the parquet floor.

"Hello Miss Nogales. If you follow me, I will take you to Mr. Nagy." As we ascended the staircase, I took one last look at the plaque and put two and two together. What was the relationship? Could be his father, but I guessed grandfather probably. Either way, it explained a lot. The opposition party would never want to be too high profile. But it made perfect sense to be as well placed as Laszlo Nagy was. No wonder Tibor knew him.

"Ah, Miss Nogales, I have been expecting you."

"Mr. Nagy, it is kind of you to see me without an appointment." *He's been expecting me?*

"Please sit down. Make yourself comfortable. Would you like a cup of tea?"

"Yes I would, thanks."

Nagy nodded to the secretary.

"So, what's your relationship with Imre Nagy, the former prime minister?"

"Prime Minister Nagy was my grandfather."

"So *that's* why you went into the family business," I said. Nagy nodded. Maybe I should've kept my mouth shut but it was too late now. Benson said to make contact with the opposition, and I was making contact. "I've got family, in California." I continued, "My mother and my brother live there."

"California," he said.

"Yes."

"Is it beautiful?"

"Very. On my mother's side, my family goes back all the way to the early settlers and the missionaries. They built the missions. My father's side came later. My great grandfather, Emiliano Nogales rode with Pancho Villa."

"Revolution is in your blood then," said Nagy. "You are perfect for this assignment even if you do not know it."

"I don't know, maybe." Suddenly, I was feeling less sure of myself. "Listen," I said. "You heard about Josef Tibor by now."

"Yes," he said. "I was sorry to hear it, terribly sorry. I was the one who introduced Tibor to Basil Warburton."

"It was all so unnecessary. Tibor had a bad gunshot wound to the head. It was bad. I got him to a doctor quick as I could. The doctor was treating him and Tibor said one of the border guards said something about me, something offensive. Tibor lost his temper. It was brave, but totally unnecessary."

"More unnecessary than you know," Nagy said.

"What are you saying? And what do you mean you've been *expecting* me?"

I was expecting the secretary to return with the tea. Instead of clicking heels, I heard heavy footsteps belonging to a man. Something tickled my antennae when the door creaked. I leapt out of my chair and drew my weapon. The guy in the doorway—holding a big silver tray—stopped in his tracks.

"Drop it!" I said before I realized who it was. Then I recognized the face, the eyes. It was Basil and he smiled and guffawed so it echoed up and down the ornate hallway.

"I'm unarmed. Lower your weapon, please." He continued into the room, put the tray on the conference table and raised his hands in surrender.

I crossed the room and fell into his arms.

After a time, Nagy cleared his throat.

"Oh, Laszlo old friend, I forgot you were there," said Basil.

"I apologize for intruding, but the tea is getting cold."

We all took our seats around Nagy's conference table. Basil poured the tea and I couldn't take my eyes off him. My heart was pounding.

"Where have you been?" I asked.

"I'll explain later," Basil said. "Let's just say Tibor wasn't in possession of all the facts. The picnic's the thing wherein we'll catch the conscience of the king." Basil turned toward Nagy. "Is it still on for August nineteenth? That's less than a month away. We'd better get busy publicizing it. I don't think we need to worry about the Stasi anymore, at least not in Sopron."

"Habsburg plans to distribute pamphlets publicizing the picnic. Soon he travels to northern Czechoslovakia, not as far north as East Germany, but all along this side of the Czech and Polish border," said Laszlo.

"That's where Tibor and I were," I interrupted.

"Yes," Nagy continued. "Herr Habsburg leaves tomorrow. He intends to come back on the Friday before the picnic with as many busloads of people as he can. He is going to distribute presents, food and money to everyone on the buses. And every shilling is coming out of his own pocket. I agree we no longer need to worry about the Stasi. I think our biggest problem may be our own border guards. Officially, they still have orders to shoot-to-kill anyone who tries to cross. The border guards are not under the Ministry of the Interior. They are under the authority of the National Police. It is possible they might intervene."

"Well then, let's start there," said Basil. "I'll square it with Dr. Benson."

"Does Benson know you're back?" I asked.

"No, but I'm sure she'll see me."

Of course, I remembered what Benson said about Basil being a double agent. I was tempted to say something, but not in front of Nagy.

"What?" Basil said looking at me.

"Nothing," I said. I must have been staring without realizing it.

"We'll talk on the way to Tancsics Street."

"You mean go now?"

"Yes. We'll talk on the way."

1989
TIANANMEN SQUARE TO EAST BERLIN
JACK GODWIN

28.

FRIDAY, JULY 21, p.m.

We left Nagy's office, walked along the paneled hallway and descended the ornate staircase. I could feel where soles of thousands of shoes had worn away the marble. The staircase spilled out into the grand room and we crossed the parquet floor. I took one last glance at the plaque to honor Imre Nagy as we passed through the double doors.

"Where's the car?" asked Basil.

"I took a taxi, but never mind that," I said. "Let's find someplace to talk. We need to talk before we go see Benson."

"Let's go that way," said Basil pointing south. "We can walk along the river. Nobody will hear us."

As we walked along the east bank, I told Basil everything that happened after we got separated in the cellar beneath the castle. I just kept moving toward the light, I said, even after all hell broke loose below me. I told him how I kept climbing and came out somewhere inside the castle walls, and went to the car to find a flashlight, and retraced my steps back down into the cellar. By then you were gone, I said, and everyone was gone. I figured you'd been killed or captured because there was blood on the floor and nothing but a chipped tooth.

Basil was walking with his head down, hands in his pockets. When I paused, our eyes met and he smiled and poked his tongue through the gap left by the broken tooth. He chuckled and nodded for me to keep talking. I told him how I inspected the scene the best I could and decided to go back to the car in case you were there. When I didn't know what else to do, I went to the compound and reported it to Benson. She already knew about the car bomb, but not about Ivanov. Anyway, that's when I told Benson you were missing. And that's when Benson told me you were a double agent. (I omitted the part about her suspecting Basil might be the source of the leak.) Then Spencer Pang came in! We went to see Tibor together at the lake. That's where we met Laszlo Nagy. That's how we cooked up the plan to go to Dresden. And that's how Tibor got killed.

"Okay, now there's something I need to tell you. My name isn't Basil Warburton. I'm not even English. My name is Konrad Gazecki and I'm an officer in the Stasi, the East German Ministry of State Security. My specialty is counterintelligence. I'm mole-hunter and a damn good one, if I may say." He paused here to observe the effect on me. During this pause I studied his face to determine if he was teasing me or telling the truth. He wasn't.

"Uh-huh," I grunted and shifted my weight from one foot to the other. "Does Benson know? I mean, does she know you're Gazecki?"

"Of course she knows. She's been my handler since I was assigned to the Soviet embassy in London. I feed her all kinds of information, lists of Stasi and KGB intelligence agents, intelligence reports, signal intercepts, that sort of thing. Do you know what Bernice Benson, Ph.D. does exactly? She chairs the Counterintelligence Analysis Group/Europe or

1989
TIANANMEN SQUARE TO EAST BERLIN
JACK GODWIN

CAGE. It was created in eighty-two after Brezhnev died. At first, the primary purpose of CAGE was analysis, you know, producing special reports and that sort of thing. Now, the goal is to finish the Cold War. Hardliners on both sides want it to go on forever. Benson wants to finish it."

"Does Laszlo Nagy know?"

"No."

"Does Vladimir Ivanov know?"

"Yes."

"Did Tibor know?"

"No."

"He wasn't in possession of all the facts he says with his phony fucking accent."

"My accent's not phony. I went to school Gaczyna. Don't you remember? We talked about it with Habsburg and Tibor at Saint Michael's in Sopron. Remember the explosion?"

"Yes, I remember the fucking explosion! How do you know Ivanov?"

"My family is Polish and German, originally from Gdansk. My family fled to Dresden, where I was born. When the Stasi recruited me, they sent me to the KGB school in Leningrad. That's where I met Ivanov."

"Did Tibor know?"

"I said no. If you and Tibor made it all the way to Dresden, it is likely you would have both been killed. Tibor generally knew I was cooperating with the Stasi and the KGB, but he didn't know all of it. He didn't know my true identity because if he did, he would've done things differently. Wouldn't he?"

"Okay. Okay. Then where have you been all this time?"

"First I had to eliminate those Stasi agents who chased us as well as the two survivors of the car bomb. I couldn't risk leaving them alive whether or not they saw my face. Then I went to the KGB outpost in Dresden to see Ivanov, and then to the Stasi headquarters in East Berlin."

"Doing what?"

"Checking in with my superiors at the counterintelligence directorate," he said. "But let's go see Benson. That way I don't have to tell the story twice. And maybe I can rebuild a few bridges. My life rather depends on it."

Basil and I crossed over the river again to the Pest side, and within forty minutes we were in the compound, sitting inside the sound-proof, vibrating conference room waiting for Benson. She came in accompanied by her security detail. Benson hooked her cane onto her forearm and the guard helped her climb the short wooden staircase into the conference room. She sat at the head of the table while the guard sealed the door from the outside with three cranks of the big handle. She set an expensive looking pen on top of her yellow legal pad, clasped her fingers and leaned forward.

"Good afternoon Mr. Warburton. I'm pleased to see you among the living."

"Anyone among the living has hope, even a dog."

"Ecclesiastes," said Benson. "*Hope is the thing with feathers that perches in the soul.*"

"Ah, those were the days," said Basil, "studying nothing but English all day every day for three years—literature, history, politics, music—I never wanted to leave."

"That's not how it works though, is it?"

"No unfortunately, no" he said.

"Your employer has certain expectations," said Benson. Warburton interrupted her.

1989
TIANANMEN SQUARE TO EAST BERLIN
JACK GODWIN

"I'm an independent contractor, not an employee, not *your* employee. And anyway, I'm no good to you dead," he said.

"I agree," she said, "You're no good to us dead." Benson levelled her gaze at Basil and continued speaking. "As I was saying to Ms. Nogales yesterday evening, you have an assignment. And that is to neutralize the local Stasi in and around Sopron in advance of August nineteenth so the Pan European Picnic may take place, as planned without incident. A corollary to this assignment, unwritten if not unspoken, is to perform your duties according to the highest standards of tradecraft. Do you understand your assignment?" Benson turned to me, to Basil and back again. "Do you?"

"Yes. No," I said. "The thing is we've just been to see Laszlo Nagy at the Ministry of the Interior."

"Oh? What information do you have?"

"Nagy told us Otto Von Habsburg leaves tomorrow for Czechoslovakia," I said. "He plans to distribute pamphlets about the picnic all along the border. Habsburg plans to show up in Sopron the day before the picnic with as many busloads of East Germans as he can persuade. He's giving away food and money, begging and bribing as many people as he can."

I paused long enough to catch my breath but not long enough to let either Basil or Benson speak. "Nagy also thinks we don't need to worry about the Stasi in Sopron anymore. He's more worried about the border guards, who aren't under the Ministry of the Interior. They're under the National Police and they'll shoot anyone who tries to cross into Austria."

Benson unclasped her fingers and sat back in her chair. She didn't interrupt, so I kept going.

"I think Basil and I should stay in Budapest. I think the work is here. I think we need to help Laszlo Nagy put pressure on the National Police. I think we better get busy."

Benson looked exasperated but I didn't get why. This was solid.

"Mr. Warburton, do you agree? Is it your wish to stay in Budapest and work with Laszlo Nagy?"

"It is," he said. "I agree with Jaqui."

"Why," she demanded.

"Since my disappearance, I've been to Dresden and to Stasi headquarters in Berlin. My comrades are well aware of what's going on at Lake Balaton and they're extremely anxious. They would like to prevent East Germans from traveling to the West through Hungary, but they're paralyzed for some reason. I've never seen anything quite like it. The Stasi's network of informers in Hungary is extensive. Berlin has been receiving regular reports from Budapest and elsewhere. They're watching Napsugar and Fonyod, so they suspect something's going to happen but they're worried about their Hungarian counterparts faltering. They're also worried about the KGB."

"What do you mean?" I asked.

"There is a lot of unrest in East Berlin, which is extremely unusual. That's one. The other is even more unusual. And now I'm speaking as a Stasi officer. Normally, we'd never worry about the KGB backing us. We'd never give it a second thought. But things have changed in Moscow, which means things have changed in East Berlin."

"The Stasi have ninety thousand people on the payroll, plus another two hundred thousand paid informants," said Benson. "Are they planning for the worst case scenario?"

"That depends on who you ask. The Stasi's culture of impunity is legendary, so there's always a lot of cheeky talk. But Jaqui's right. We should stay in Budapest and work with Laszlo. For now, that is. After the picnic, I'll go back to Berlin. But for now, our top priority must be preventing the border guards from shooting at their own people. That would be catastrophic."

"Yes, we agree on that," said Benson. The room was silent for a moment and now you could really hear the low hum and feel the vibration. "You can't stay here though. I want regular reports but I can't have you two coming in and out of the compound every day. We've got an apartment, a safe house on the Buda side. You can get the keys from the GSO. I want a detailed plan of the operation on my desk on Monday. Take the weekend. You have your instructions."

Benson lifted herself out of her chair and tapped her cane on the door. The handle cranked counter-clockwise three times from the outside and the guard swung the door wide. Basil and I sat there while Benson cleared out.

"That went well," he said looking relieved.

"A plan of operation within forty-eight hours," I said. "You got anything in mind?"

"Yes. Let's kidnap Mihaly Csikany."

"Who's he?"

"The National Chief of Police," he said.

"And then what?"

"And then we use our powers of communication and persuasion to convince him it's in his best interest to cooperate with us."

"Right, we'll convince him to join the fight for free markets and multi-party democracy."

"Okay."

"Okay." We both laughed and got up to leave.

29.

FRIDAY, JULY 21, late

The safe house apartment was on the fourth floor of one of those monolithic Eastern Bloc buildings. Ours was one of four facing a large leafy courtyard overgrown with weeds where all the neighbors spent the warm evenings socializing and smoking, and letting their dogs run and their children play. The apartment was small but well-equipped. The bedrooms were tiny and we had to share the bathroom, but it was luxury living compared to the safe house in Fertorakos. All in all, I'd say it was a perfect base of operations for two weeks.

"Let's go shopping," said Basil. "There's a small store on the ground floor of Building No. 3. We'll get something for breakfast, tea, coffee, that sort of thing."

"Okay."

Once we made it to the small store, I took a look around. "Hey, this place isn't bad," I said. "They've got everything I need."

"Everything you need for what?"

"I'll cook dinner. Let's see. Tell her I need flour, salt and oil. Never mind. I'll just point. They've got dried beans. These are like pinto beans. Good. I need garlic and onions and chili powder. Ask her if she has chili powder. No? Okay. What's that? Ask her what that is."

"Smoked paprika, she says."

"Can I smell it? Ask her. Mm, that'll do. We'll take it. How about tomatoes, canned tomatoes? Okay. Finally, we need cheese. Something like cheddar but it doesn't have to be cheddar. Yes? We'll take it. Okay, finished."

"What are we having?"

"We're having burritos. When we get home, I'll start the beans boiling. Those'll take three or four hours. Meantime I'll roll the tortillas. When the beans are soft, I'll mash them and then refry them and then sauté the onions, garlic, tomatoes and paprika. We should get some beer or something. Ask the lady."

"Not here, she says. Beer and wine are sold in the shop on the ground floor of Building No. 2." Basil carried a plastic bag in each hand and we walked around the courtyard to the next building. The layout of this store was exactly the same except plastic cases filled with beer and water and soft drinks were stacked along the walls and everywhere else you looked. The selection was not great. Basil saw a brand he recognized with a lion on the label, looked at me and shrugged.

"Let's get a case." He handed me the shopping bags, paid the unsmiling shopkeeper and lifted a case from the top of a stack.

"Isn't that heavy?"

"It is a little, but we haven't got far. Let's hope the elevator works."

Back in the apartment, we unloaded the bags and put the beer into the fridge. The kitchen was tiny compared to the average American kitchen, not even big enough for two people but I had everything I needed. I disliked cooking in an unfamiliar kitchen. I've always disliked it. Soon enough though, the water was boiling and the beans were cooking. I glanced around to make sure I remembered all the ingredients. I wished I had some green chiles or jalapenos but that would have been asking too much. Besides, I didn't know Basil's tolerance for spicy food. He was German-Polish, not English but maybe he acquired a taste for English cooking at Gaczyna.

I found him sprawled on the couch in the front room with his shoes off, stocking feet hanging over the armrest.

"Are you asleep?" I whispered.

"Yes."

"No you're not. Move over."

"There isn't enough room."

"C'mon, move over Konrad."

"Ouch."

"Ugh."

"Is that okay?"

"Okay, but don't touch me."

"Don't touch you?"

"Do I have to explain?"

"No."

"I'm mad at you," I said.

"No you're not. You're mad at Benson for keeping you out of the loop."

"You mean the counterintelligence group? Oh, please. Benson was my instructor at the academy. Compartmentalization is standard operating procedure. Oh shit, the beans, I've got to check the beans."

Basil followed me into the kitchen and stood there looking like he needed something to do, so I told him to rinse a couple of beer glasses and find me a rolling pin. The beans wouldn't be ready for a while, so I started on the tortilla mix. It was a messy chore so I excused myself and went to the bedroom to change into a t-shirt. Plus, my bra was bugging me. I reminded myself to go to the mall next time I took home leave. I thought maybe I'd write to Mom and ask her to mail them. She knew what size I wore. I needed to write to her anyway. It was three months since Dad's funeral, but seemed longer.

Back in the kitchen, Basil watched while I added flour, salt water and oil into the mixing bowl. My mother used lard but not me because the whole idea made me sick. I sprinkled flour on the counter-top, rolled out the dough, kneaded it and punched it. Basil looked amused and fascinated.

"What? You never watched your mother make tortillas? Where's that rolling pin?"

"I can't seem to find one," he said.

"The dough can sit for a few minutes. Open a beer and we'll use the bottle as a rolling pin."

"Cheers," he said.

"Prost. Here, give me the empty. I'll soak the label off and then we can use it to roll out the tortillas."

"What can I do?"

"Well, if you want to, you can pinch off a piece of dough like that. Then roll it into a ball. We need about eight tortillas, so try and make eight balls about the same size. They don't have to be perfect. Wash your hands first."

After I peeled off the label, the empty bottle worked perfectly as a makeshift rolling pin. I would have liked a real one, but I wouldn't have wanted to be anywhere else in the world right then. It felt natural. When I told Dad I was joining the bureau he was so proud of me. I hope he was proud. *Don't you want a family? Don't you want kids? If you met the right guy, would you give it all up?* Why did I have to give it up? Why? I'll tell you why. I wasn't sure I was even going to be alive a month from now. Basil might not either. Or he *still* might not be who he says he is. No. Benson would have said something. It looked like she approved. Of course she approved. Did she? I didn't know.

"Basil?"

"Yes Darling."

"Open another beer."

"Yes Darling."

"The tortillas are almost ready. They don't take very long, not even a minute on each side, just long enough to blacken the dough in a few spots. See?"

"They smell good."

"The beans are done. Let's heat the oil so we can sauté the onions and garlic. Is there a potato masher? I need something to puree the beans. While I'm doing that, open the can of tomatoes and stir them in. I wish we had some chili powder. I don't know about this smoked paprika. Where's the cheese grater? Did you see a cheese grater? This isn't going to be authentic, but it'll taste okay."

"Prost," he said.

"Cheers," I said. "Grab a couple of plates for us. I'll bring the tortillas and the beans. We can sit on the floor and eat at the coffee table. Let's talk while we eat. I'm too tired to think but Benson gave us only forty-eight hours to come up with a plan."

"Okay, right. What do I do now?"

"First, we have to flip the whole pile of tortillas upside down so the first one we cooked is on top. Okay, now watch me. Take a swig of beer. C'mon, take a swig. Are you watching? Put a tortilla on your plate. Add a spoonful of beans, not too much otherwise you'll tear the tortilla when you pick it up. Then sprinkle some cheese. Then fold the tortilla and roll it like that. Then take another swig, say grace, and chow down."

He exaggerated each step.

"And the verdict is."

"A triumph," he said, *"truly scrumptious."*

"I used to live on this stuff in college. It's healthy, except for the salt. Too bad we don't have any Tabasco. What're you smiling at?"

"I was just thinking how nice it is shopping together, cooking together and drinking beer together."

"I cooked. That means you wash dishes. Togetherness has nothing to do with it."

"Why are you always joking?"

"I'm not always joking. I'm still mad at you, furious in fact. But I am joking right now because I recognize that look on your face."

"What look?"

"It's the same look you had in Fertorakos when I came out of the shower wearing that ugly bathrobe."

"I don't know what you're talking about."

"Ha! Yes you do."

"I'm a model of old Prussian virtue."

"No, but I will say this. I like it that I can take you anywhere, tuxedo to blue jeans."

"Thank you."

"And here we are sitting on the floor."

"It's not just any floor," he said. "It's a US Government safe house in the middle of Budapest."

"I went back to look for you," I said. "I thought you were dead."

"If you thought I was dead, then why did you come looking for me?"

"I didn't want to believe it. And I didn't want to wait around for the stupid picnic. Besides, Spencer thought going to Dresden was a good idea. So did Tibor."

"But you didn't tell Benson you were going."

"No. But the mission was good and the plan was good. The execution was a total fuck up. We even had documents made."

"Did you really?"

"Yeah, Tibor had a contact in Fonyod. He was a locksmith. He made new passports and documents for me and Tibor and even one for you in case we needed to smuggle you out of East Germany."

"Did the locksmith know about the plan?"

"I don't know. No. Why?"

"You said he made a fake passport for me. Did you give him a picture of me?"

"Yes, of course."

"Where did you get it?"

"We found your British passport at the safe house. We gave it to the locksmith. Why do you ask?"

"He's seen my picture. It doesn't matter. The damage is done."

"C'mon. He's a counterfeiter, a forger. He's nothing but a doc jock. Are you saying he tipped off the East German border guards? What's the difference? Floriana Varga was on the jay-oh-bee."

"Who's Floriana Varga?"

"Hello. My name is Floriana Varga. *Prepare to die.*"

"Who's Floriana Varga?"

1989
TIANANMEN SQUARE TO EAST BERLIN
JACK GODWIN

"That's the alias the locksmith gave me. He's a Springsteen fan. Heard him on the radio last year and wanted to call me *Gypsy Angel Rose* but it didn't translate. Basil, relax. We'll go to Fonyod and visit the locksmith if you want. Take it easy. This beer is good."

"It is good, but this meal really calls for a sweet German wine, like a Riesling."

"Mexican food and German wine," I said. "What a great idea! All we need now is some hot Polish sausage. *Whoa Nelly*, this beer is pretty strong. I better go to bed."

"I think you'd better," he said. "I'll clean up. Give me your plate."

"Yeah, we'll decide what to do about Mihaly Csikany tomorrow. Kidnapping him seems like a lot of trouble. Let's waste him. Be done with it. Okay bed now, night, night."

Daddy, you're staring at me. I'm not staring, I'm watching you. And watching you devour a chocolate doughnut is one of my favorite things. I never knew a girl who liked doughnuts as much as you. Just don't tell Mommy. If she asks, don't lie but don't bring it up if she doesn't ask. Okay? Okay. Do you know what you said to me the first time you tasted a doughnut? You said doughnuts are made out of bread ... and sprinkles. Yes, you did. You just don't remember. What should we do next? I don't know. How about a movie? Sure. Let me see. Oh, here's one, Three Days of the Condor. It's playing at the Chinese Theater in Hollywood. We should go. Okay. Finish your doughnut. We'll get tickets and check out the footprints before the show. What footprints? In front of the theater, movie stars put their footprints in the concrete. Is that for real? Yeah. Finish your doughnut so we won't be late.

1989
TIANANMEN SQUARE TO EAST BERLIN
JACK GODWIN

30.

SATURDAY, JULY 22

I awoke to find Basil in the kitchen making coffee with one of those Italian stovetop espresso makers. The coffee smelled good. My stomach was a little queasy but otherwise I was okay, just a little embarrassed to show my face. He said good morning *Darling* and kissed me on the cheek. Sleep well? He went out for breakfast rolls while I was still asleep. The whole neighborhood was still asleep, he said except for him and the bakers. Have you ever had these? Hungarians call them *rollicki*. Here, have some coffee.

"I found the *International Herald Tribune* and the *Financial Times*," he said, "It was easier said than done."

"You read the *Financial Times*?"

"Of course" he said, "I used to read it every morning in Gaczyna."

"You told Benson you never wanted to leave."

"I did and it's true. Now I read it to keep track of the stock market."

"You own stocks?"

"I'm no billionaire, just a small investor. I live on my Stasi salary, which isn't much. But I invest every penny the British and American governments pay me. Lately I've been buying up shares in a software company in Redmond. It's in Washington State."

"You're a capitalist?"

"Why's that surprising?"

"It's not surprising, just interesting," I said. "That's all."

"Having a horse in the race makes it interesting."

"We should talk about Mihaly Csikany, I guess. Upon sober reflection, I don't think we should waste him."

"Who said anything about wasting him?"

"I did, last night. Don't you remember? Oh, never mind."

"I knew that was the beer talking. It doesn't matter. When I was in Berlin, I learned a few things."

Next, Basil informed me he belonged to the foreign intelligence section, known as the General Reconnaissance Administration, or GRA, which operated a network of informants in all the Warsaw Pact countries, including Hungary. He was privy to a lot of political and business-related information about West Germany and all the NATO countries. The GRA had informants in almost every major factory, university, hospital—even large apartment buildings—in the region. Most informants didn't do it for money or because they were being blackmailed or coerced in any way. They were eager to perform the service because it made them feel important.

"That's the key with Csikany," Basil said. "We need to come up with a scheme that makes Csikany feel important or that makes him feel as though he's on the right side. If he feels like a conspirator, we'll never co-opt him."

The Stasi were having serious trouble maintaining their intelligence network. There was always a high turnover of informants, in any situation. But lately, there was so much unrest that the Stasi's methods were becoming well known beyond their network of informants. The Stasi's methods were becoming public. And this created a political problem. People just weren't as afraid of them anymore.

The Stasi's reputation had gone from ruthless to parody, he said. Some Stasi officers were trying to *rebrand* East Germany as a politically stable, investor-friendly country. They were panicking. The Stasi officers who had devoted their lives to serving as the sword and shield of the Communist Party thought they could attract foreign investors and sell consumer goods to the West. This was pretty hard to believe and made me wonder whether it was just cover for high-ranking officers trying to secure their financial future, for themselves and their friends.

The main thing for us, said Basil, was the Stasi couldn't rely on informants at the Hungarian Ministry of the Interior any longer. Keeping East Berlin happy used to be a major policy issue for the Hungarian government, but not anymore. The Hungarian opposition parties were pressing for change and they weren't intimated anymore. Laszlo Nagy deserved some credit for that, he said. The Hungarians simply stopped caring about preventing East German tourists from leaving. The defectors were better organized now and the problem of *illegal* border crossings was building like a wave. Everyone had friends who watched the border in Hungary and in Austria. They knew the weak points because they had the guards' timetables and routines memorized.

Not only that, Basil said. Potential defectors communicated with their relatives living in the west. They planned holidays together. They arranged to go on vacation at the same time and place—and Lake Balaton was one of their favorite places. Family members living in the west hauled their relatives' luggage and belongings back to Austria or West Germany in preparation for a defection at a later date. Why can't family members hide defectors in their cars? I asked. They can and they do, he said but the risk of getting caught is very high. Not too many are audacious enough to attempt it. If the Hungarian border guards caught an East German trying to defect, he said, they would hand you over to the Stasi, who would haul your ass back to East Germany. After that, your life expectancy could be counted in days.

"And you could always rely on American newspapers to report the successful escapes, especially the most sensational ones," I said.

"Yes! And enough of those stories got through East Germany's information blockade, which meant that enough East Germans heard about the stories to maintain the illusion."

"But it works both ways, doesn't it? Most people probably think about defecting, but would never actually try it. It's a very small percentage of those who convince themselves they can make it out. It's the same mentality that makes people buy lottery tickets. The odds are always against you, overwhelmingly against you. It's totally irrational."

"Maybe it's not the lottery mentality," said Basil. "Maybe it's the second marriage mentality, you know, the triumph of hope over experience."

"Who said that?"

"Oscar Wilde maybe, I can't remember. But that's not the point. Everybody's under surveillance. Everybody is watching everybody and nobody trusts anybody. East Germany is falling apart and so is the Stasi."

"Where does that leave us?" I asked. "You said the key is to make Csikany feel important. Make him feel as though he's on the right side. How do we do that?"

"Let's run another con."

"When we ran the hit man con, we had orders to terminate Stasi agents, including Colonel Gazecki, if you recall. Csikany is Hungarian. Our plan can't involve the use of force."

"I thought you studied con games at the FBI Academy? Think of something."

"Well, maybe we could send Csikany on a fool's errand."

"How would that work?"

"Normally, the idea is to send the victim to find something that doesn't exist. It's a wild goose chase. It's more of a practical joke than a con game, but what if we told Csikany there was a leak? What if there was an informant—or better still—a double agent at the National Police leaking information that compromised Csikany?"

"Are you mocking me?"

"*No!* What? He'd be consumed with finding the informant. He'd be so distracted from performing his regular duties that he'd forget all about the illegal border crossings."

"Okay, that's the con," Basil said. "But Csikany is the National Chief of Police. He won't be easily fooled."

"Does he know you?" I asked.

"You mean does he know Gazecki?"

"Yes. Does he know you? Has he ever seen you?"

"Darling, nobody has seen me."

"You're that good, eh? I think you mean nobody except for Ivanov."

"Yes," he said, "Except for him."

"Then Konrad Gazecki needs to pay a friendly call on Mihaly Csikany and inform him that the *F-B-I* has him under surveillance. We should check with Benson to see if the bureau has some actual dirt on this guy. That way you can approach Csikany—as Gazecki—and tell him you intercepted some information about him. If Csikany already knows the information is true, he'll never question your source."

"In a way," said Basil, "It'll be amusing to watch Csikany try to hunt down the phantom informant."

"It'll keep him preoccupied," I said, "but it won't kill him. We need him preoccupied for a couple of weeks. After the picnic we can let him in on it, as far as I'm concerned."

"You'll clear that with Benson first."

"Yeah, let's see how it goes. Csikany may not be so forgiving."

"He will," Basil said, "if we win."

"At least we have something to go on. Let's write it up and present it to Benson."

31.

MONDAY, JULY 24, a.m.

We met Benson in the secure conference room at the compound on Tancsics Street. Basil and I took turns presenting the plan and she listened without interrupting. When we were finished, she nodded her approval and leaned forward.

"I like it," she said, "but there is a downside. I wish I could see a way around it."

"What is it?" I asked.

"Normally, I would expect such a significant flaw to be addressed as part of the plan. However, I'm sure Mr. Warburton has taken it into consideration."

"I think we're on the same page," he said. "This will blow my cover, at least in Hungary. For this to work, I'll have to expose myself. Nobody in Hungary knows what Konrad Gazecki looks like, nobody except Laszlo Nagy and the people in this room. And Ivanov, but he's back in Dresden. And somebody else."

"Who do you mean?" said Benson.

"We talked about this on Friday," I said. "The guy in Fonyod who made the fake documents, he calls himself The Locksmith. He was Tibor's contact. He made new documents for me and Tibor and Basil. We gave him Basil's photo."

Turning back to Basil, I said "We'll go to Fonyod and see him. Or we'll send Spencer if you want. I told you. Take it easy."

"No," said Benson. "Assume your cover is blown. It'll remind you to be careful. This operation is critical. We neutralized the local Stasi detachment before the picnic so now we're going to neutralize the National Police. Let's practice careful tradecraft and mitigate the risk. You will almost certainly be needed elsewhere."

Benson always had an authoritative way of ending a meeting. She stood up and tapped her cane twice on the door. The handle cranked and her guard swung the door open. Once again, Basil and I were left sitting in silence for a minute or so until Basil leapt from his chair and dashed out of the conference room. I ran after Basil, who was running after Dr. Benson. He caught her as she was waiting for the elevator. Benson's body guard was startled. He drew his weapon, took half a step backward and took aim at Basil's chest.

Basil reacted by raising his hands in surrender. Basil had his hands up saying okay, okay, okay, and then pushed the guard's gun hand to one side and wrapped himself around the guard's arm. Now Basil and the guard were facing the same direction and the gun was pointing at the ground. Benson's bodyguard was struggling to pull the gun away and Basil seemed to be playing with him. Basil put his right hand over the gun barrel and his left hand underneath. He rotated the gun and disarmed the guard almost effortlessly. Now Basil had the gun and he was backing away from the guard, laughing and wagging his finger.

"May I have that weapon, please?" Benson held out her hand.

1989

TIANANMEN SQUARE TO EAST BERLIN

JACK GODWIN

Benson's guard was absolutely fuming. I think he wanted to murder Basil and would have tried if he could. The doors to the elevator opened with a ping. Basil checked the chamber, ejected the magazine and handed Benson the gun as the elevator doors closed.

"Thank you," she said pushing the button to call the elevator back. "Now what is it you wanted?"

"There's just one more thing. Can we bring Laszlo Nagy in on this?" Basil was about to explain the reasons why, but Benson cut him off.

"No need to explain," she said. "The answer is yes. Laszlo is friendly, and well placed for the future I might add. By all means take him into your confidence. Explain the plan. Make sure he understands the United States government is taking this action to preclude violence. We may injure Mihaly Csikany's pride, but nothing more. We'll make it up to him. Understood?"

"Yes ma'am" said Basil respectfully, "Thank you ma'am." Then he bowed, which I'd never seen him do. She turned and went in. The bodyguard backed in scowling. *Auf Wiedersehen* said Basil as the doors closed.

"Mr. Frowny Face didn't look too pleased," I said. "Was that more Krav Maga? Your Hungarian Jewish Mossad friend taught you well young grasshopper. *When you can take the gun from my hand, it will be time for you to leave.*"

"What?"

"Master Po," I said, "Never mind. You totally embarrassed him."

"What a ghastly thing to do," Basil said, "challenging me like that in front of Dr. Benson. What was he thinking?"

"He doesn't trust you, for starters."

"Oh, how American you are. And you went to business school? No wonder the Japanese are cleaning your clock. People worthy of your trust—hence trustworthy—are dependable. It's analogous to the word *quality*, which means conformance to a standard. It's got nothing to do with loyalty and everything to do with reliability. If you aim a pistol at my chest, for example, you may rely on me to take action."

"I know. I do," I said. "Let's get out of here. Let's go."

"Not yet," he said. We've got to check Csikany's file, which I've been informed is in the archive. It's not a lending library and they don't deliver, so we'll have to visit the basement."

Basil pressed the down arrow with his index finger.

"Benson was just going on about tradecraft. Wasn't she?" Basil asked. "Why does she keep that gorilla around?"

I figured it was a rhetorical question and ignored it. We got into the elevator and went down two floors into the catacombs below the compound.

1989
TIANANMEN SQUARE TO EAST BERLIN
JACK GODWIN

32.

MONDAY, JULY 24, p.m.

The elevator doors opened to a small foyer where there was a reference clerk seated behind an enclosure. Behind the clerk were rows and rows of sturdy shelves holding hundreds of file boxes full of background information on every high-profile individual in the country, including party members, government functionaries, artists, writers, intellectuals and high ranking law enforcement officials.

We gave the clerk Mihaly Csikany's name. *Spell that,* said the clerk and tapped the name on his keyboard. He squinted at the screen and made a clicking noise with his tongue and disappeared into the rows. Five minutes later, he reappeared carrying a two-inch thick manila folder marked Top Secret. He directed us to a small room off to one side with a small metal conference table and chairs. We were allowed to read but not permitted to make copies or take photographs, he said. Basil and I sat side by side at the table and got to work.

Every agency in the federal government used the same forms for background investigations. Csikany's file started with the basics: name, birthdate and place, schools attended, current address and current occupation. There was an envelope stapled on the left-hand side when you opened the file. Inside there was an unsmiling, official-looking black and white photograph of Csikany in his police uniform. There were sections on marriage, divorce and family history, military history, criminal history, salary and financial history, personal habits (including spending habits, alcohol and drug usage), sexual preferences and proclivities, a skills assessment, medical history and a psychological profile.

We started by building a behavioral profile and went from there. He was a widower. Wife died ten years ago in a car accident, and there was a baby in the car, too. We looked for but couldn't find any evidence of alcohol or drug use. Csikany drank brandy, but not to excess. He drank something called Palinka, a fruit brandy, which was probably the same stuff that Tibor drank. He enjoyed Turkish baths, especially the Gellert Baths located in the basement of the Gellert Hotel. The place had a swimming pool, which he also used. That would be an ideal place to make contact, we agreed. It was public, but not too public. We made a note of that.

We looked at his finances. Basil asked if I ever read the Sherlock Holmes story when Holmes pretended to be an accountant. I didn't know that. Yeah, it was *The Stock Broker's Clerk*, he said. It made perfect sense if you thought about it. Sherlock Holmes would have been a great forensic accountant. It was all about making deductions based on the evidence. But you had to know what you were looking for. We weren't necessarily looking for fraud or money laundering or any kind of criminal activity. We were looking for patterns, earnings, payments, cash flow problems.

I didn't see an opening. Money was usually a reliable motivational tool for spies because so many were already having financial problems. It wasn't as though we were going to blackmail him or ask him to sell state secrets. Unless there

1989

TIANANMEN SQUARE TO EAST BERLIN

JACK GODWIN

was something missing from the file, it looked like Csikany was a good cop, an honest cop. He lived within his means and did his job. That meant we wanted keep him in place and on the job. It worked to our advantage. I would have had no problem compromising Csikany—or anybody else—if we knew he was already dirty. No problem whatsoever. I remembered what Benson said about Laszlo Nagy. He was friendly and well placed for the future. For now, we decided to use the same approach with Mihaly Csikany.

We decided to try and convince Csikany that he needed help from the West. To do this, we would have to manipulate appearances, spread disinformation and mislead him into believing East Berlin—meaning Konrad Gazecki—was out to get him. But Csikany couldn't know, he could never know, he was being manipulated. Whatever the ruse, it must paralyze Csikany into inaction, at least in the short run. That was an absolute necessity. In the long run, we had some latitude but our goal was to drive Csikany into the American camp. Benson said no violence. We could injure Csikany's pride, but that was all.

"Right," said Basil. "Let me think out loud for a minute. For this to work, the best thing would be for you to contact Csikany first."

"Keep going."

"You contact him first and make him an offer, not a generous offer but one that will get him thinking. Then withdraw. Don't give Csikany any way to contact you. If Csikany tries to find you or tries to contact the embassy, they should deny everything. Throw him off balance and keep him off balance."

"He's the National Chief of Police," I responded. "We'll have to give him something."

"True. In that case, the embassy can confirm there is a Special Agent named Jaqueline Nogales if they want. But they should deny everything else and deny that anyone named Jaqueline Nogales is in Hungary."

"Let's make sure Benson is in on this part."

"Of course," he said.

"Okay, then we let him stew for a few days. He'll try to track you down but you'll have disappeared. You'll be impossible to find."

"And then?"

"And then Colonel Gazecki makes a grand entrance."

"And says what exactly?"

"I'm still thinking out loud. Gazecki tells Csikany that he's being watched. Sources have informed Berlin that Mr. Csikany has come into contact with a woman, a beautiful *foreign* woman. But he has not reported this contact. Berlin wonders why. Berlin demands to know why. Is he hiding something? Mr. Csikany knows he must report all contacts with foreigners. Mr. Csikany should know better."

"Oh yes," I said. "The National Chief of Police should definitely know better."

"The woman, she is an American or maybe a Gypsy."

"Okay. That'll do."

"She has long brown hair, almost black, and brown eyes and skin the color of *café au lait*. The surveillance photos show her long legs and muscular athletic buttocks."

"Shush! The clerk, Basil, he can hear you."

"Yes. How to say in English—*spektakulär*—yes this woman she looks spectacular with her muscular athletic buttocks when she wears the blue jean. Yes. I think so."

I was laughing so hard I stopped caring whether the clerk heard or not. Somehow, it was like laughing in church because it was so quiet down there. I closed up the file folder and gathered my things. Basil was looking very pleased with himself. I walked over to the enclosure and slid the file through the opening back to the clerk. He didn't appear to have been listening, which relieved my embarrassment. He barely even looked up. Basil was waiting for me in front of the elevator and pushed the button. He was smiling. At that moment, he was the handsomest man I'd ever seen.

When we got into the elevator I kept my head down and my eyes focused on the floor. *I'll be glad when this mission is over.*

"Will you?" he asked.

"What?"

"Will you be glad when this mission is over?"

"What?"

"You just said you'll be glad when it's over."

"I didn't say that."

"You just did."

The elevator opened with a ping and we stepped out onto the ground floor.

"Do you think there is any need to update Benson on our plans?" he asked.

"I don't think so. She never gets too deeply involved in the details of any operation, except when it goes wrong. So, what's our next step?"

"Next was for Jaqui Walnuts to introduce herself to Mihaly Csikany," he said. "Make sure you do it out in the open."

"How about the front of the National Police building," I suggested.

"No, that would be too public. You aren't trying to humiliate him. You aren't trying to frighten him either. That's

Gazecki's job. You're trying to befriend him. We know he goes to the Gellert Baths. Why don't you approach him there?"

"You want me to go in wearing a towel? I could wear a holster underneath."

"No, they segregate men and women," said Basil. "Maybe you could come out of the women's side at the same time Csikany comes out of the men's. I could signal you. He'd be relaxed after his bath and more approachable. Flash your smile, flash your badge and invite him for a drink. That would get his attention surely. It might startle him, so you better be cool. Charm him but don't flirt. Don't ask him for anything. We know he's a decent chap, at least that's what his file says. Wear a dark suit if you've got one, professional all the way. Approach him like a colleague. Never forget he's law enforcement, which means he started out wearing a uniform just like everybody else."

"Police officers everywhere all have that *us versus them* mentality," I said. "It goes with the job. At this point in his career, he's more of a political animal than a crime fighter. But he'll respect the badge."

"He will. The FBI is well known in law enforcement circles, but not as much in the intelligence community. He'll do a background check, count on it. The most important thing is for the two of you to be seen together in public, not in any compromising position, just *seen in public*. So much the better if you meet more than once. It doesn't have to look suspicious. In fact, it's better if it looks innocent because it will be innocent. That'll work to our advantage. If anything, Csikany will be more worried precisely because he knows he's innocent. Nothing bothers a cop more than a false accusation."

"And Gazecki will see us together," I said.

1989
TIANANMEN SQUARE TO EAST BERLIN
JACK GODWIN

"He'll see you together," Basil said. "Csikany is supposed to report all contacts with foreigners. Are we counting on him not reporting the contact? No. That won't matter to Gazecki. I'll make sure of that. Anyway, I've already laid the groundwork."

"What do you mean?"

"Konrad Gazecki has a nasty reputation. The myth has taken root. The more Csikany protests and proclaims his innocence, the nastier I'll get. I'll threaten him with blackmail, torture, death, whatever it takes. If that doesn't work, I'll improvise. But I'll keep insisting until he tells me everything I want to know about the beautiful foreign woman."

"But he won't know anything."

"That's right but I can convince Csikany that I'm certain he's withholding information."

"Don't you think that's a little dangerous for you? Csikany didn't get where he is by being stupid. Plus, he's got the home court advantage. And he's got resources. If you push him too hard, you could get killed, easily."

"Oh, I don't think so," said Basil. "You think he'd have me killed? Have a Stasi colonel killed? Maybe but I don't think so. He's terrified of the Stasi. Everyone is."

"Except you," I said. "You're not terrified."

"But I am terrified. I know their methods. I went through the training. My security clearance gives me access to a lot of information. Death squads assassinate people or kidnap them. People just disappear and family members never know. People land in prison for no reason, for telling jokes! They get exposed to low doses of radiation in prison and slowly die of cancer. It's horrible when you think about it."

1989
TIANANMEN SQUARE TO EAST BERLIN
JACK GODWIN

"Ivanov thinks the Soviet Union is going to collapse. Even Benson thinks we're close to winning. It'll be over soon. "

"Let slip the dogs of war that this foul deed shall smell above the earth."

"Is that all you did at Gaczyna? Read Shakespeare?"

"I never wanted to leave."

"So you said. Sometimes I think you're not cut out for this business."

"I'm not. I know I'm not," he said. "The job chose me. I didn't submit an application. I got called into the headmaster's office at school one day. There was someone from the Ministry of State Security with a list, and my name was on the list. I showed an aptitude they said. From that day forward, I went to special schools. My parents got an extra stipend, not much but something."

"What did they do to you?"

"Nothing," he said. "It was rigorous of course, but I worked, I studied hard and got rewarded. What do you mean?"

"I mean tens of thousands of people work for the Stasi. But there's only one Basil Warburton."

"I told you I was born in Dresden, but I'm part Polish. My family is from Gdansk. Most of them died in the late thirties when Hitler invaded. A few got out. The allies destroyed the city, then the Soviets liberated it—some say invaded. The allies carved up Poland at the Potsdam Conference. The Russians took a chunk for themselves, and the whole country moved west about four hundred kilometers. My father's family—the Gazecki side—settled in Dresden. That's where he met my mother and that's where I was born."

"Did the Stasi or the KGB know about your family history when they recruited you?"

1989
TIANANMEN SQUARE TO EAST BERLIN
JACK GODWIN

"I don't know," said Basil. "Gazecki is a Polish name."

"Well, then they recruited the wrong man, didn't they?"

"Darling, there's no question they recruited the wrong man but not because of that. Like I said, I'd rather be teaching English literature somewhere, maybe Southern California. Do you remember the day we met? Are there any universities near there?"

"Yes, I remember the day. I remember the exact moment," I said.

"Oh, I'm sorry, of course, I'm sorry."

"It's alright."

"No, it's not alright."

"Basil, really it's alright."

"I'll be glad when it's over."

"That's what I said."

33.

FRIDAY, AUGUST 11

For several days Basil and I shadowed Csikany on foot, focusing on the area between his office and the Gellert Hotel for several days. We never got too close and never worried about losing him because there were only two of us. If we lost him, and we did a few times, we were able to catch up with him again. Early on, we couldn't tell if Csikany knew he was being followed or if he was just well trained and highly disciplined. He never kept a bodyguard with him, but it sure seemed like he knew he had a tail. He stopped and stretched and checked behind him without it looking obvious. Another time, he stopped abruptly in the middle of the sidewalk and pretended to tie his shoe. Yet another time, he dropped his wallet.

One afternoon, we shadowed Csikany all the way to the Gellert Hotel. Basil went up to the café on the mezzanine level and read the *Financial Times*, while I continued to tail Csikany. He headed straight for the entrance to the baths, and fortunately I wasn't following too closely. He stopped abruptly in the doorway, patted his chest pocket on one side, then the other, snapped his fingers and turned right around. If it had been Basil tailing him, he and Csikany would have been standing face to face. Basil would have been burned

1989
TIANANMEN SQUARE TO EAST BERLIN
JACK GODWIN

and the operation ruined then and there. But the café on the mezzanine was a perfect place to watch the main doors of the hotel and the entrance to the baths and Basil saw the whole thing. This convinced us it would be a big mistake to underestimate Csikany. But it also gave us an idea. We could use Csikany's training and self-discipline to our advantage.

It was Friday, and Csikany left the office an hour early to go to the Gellert. Rather than tail Csikany all the way from his office, Basil staked out the café on the mezzanine with his cup of tea and newspaper, while I waited on the corner a block from the hotel. We knew what time to expect Csikany and sure enough, he brushed past me—walking alone—at about four thirty.

I started shadowing him closely with no thought for good surveillance technique. My goal wasn't purposely to get burned, but to get so warm that Csikany would naturally get suspicious. I followed him through the big glass doors into the lobby. He made a beeline for the bank of public telephones in the corner. This was a little unsettling because we had to pass underneath the mezzanine where Basil couldn't see us. Csikany walked up to the phone farthest in the corner, inserted a coin and punched the numbers. I walked up to the pay phone right next to him. Fortunately, we were the only ones there.

Csikany positioned himself with his back to the wall to check if he was being tailed. Our eyes met when he looked up but he broke eye contact immediately. I fished my badge out and waited for the right moment. Csikany continued the charade, but I had enough. I held my badge up where he couldn't miss it. The brass caught the light just right. Csikany's eyes went to my badge, my photo, my face and back again. He was deeply engrossed in his fictitious phone call and I was losing my patience. I cleared my throat and Csikany switched from Hungarian to English.

"Who are you?"

"Special Agent Jaqueline Nogales," I whispered, "F-B-I."

"I can see that. What is it you want?"

"If you were a gentleman, you might offer to buy the lady a drink."

He nodded and put the phone back on the hook.

"You didn't say goodbye to whoever that was."

He scoffed and gestured for me to follow. We took the big staircase up to the mezzanine. Basil didn't bother to look up from his newspaper as we walked past him toward a table in the farthest corner.

"You are American?"

"Yes."

"You do not look American," said Csikany. "You look Gypsy."

"I'm American, born and raised in California."

"Yes. What is it you want?"

"The official policy of the United States government is to establish a multi-party democracy and a free market economy in Hungary."

"Very suddenly this has become very tedious. Tell me what you want."

"Mr. Csikany, we're planning to have a picnic next week. We're calling it the Pan European and we're going to have it in Sopron, not in town but west of town near the Austrian border. You know where Johann Bauer and Tamas Lakatos cut a hole in the border fence a few weeks ago?"

"Yes."

"That's where. We've invited some friends to join us, friends from East Germany because during the picnic we're

1989
TIANANMEN SQUARE TO EAST BERLIN
JACK GODWIN

going to throw the fence wide open and let people wander back and forth, you know, into Austria if they want."

Up to this point, Csikany's facial expression was neutral, very hard to read. The coffee came and I stopped talking. Csikany took his time adding milk and sugar, stirring very slowly focusing all his attention on the spoon, the cup and saucer. Finally, he exhaled and inhaled like he forgot to breathe and looked up at me. I continued.

"The United States government would appreciate it, that is, we would take it as a gesture of goodwill, because you're in charge of the National Police and therefore in charge of the border guards, we'd appreciate it if you would take no action to prevent the picnic from taking place. Furthermore, we'd appreciate it if you would make sure the ban on border crossings is not enforced and make sure the border guards all hold their fire. This is temporary, you know, just during the picnic."

"What you are asking is impossible."

I took a sip of coffee. I pushed my chair back from the table, stood up and said "We thought you might say that." Then I turned and walked away. As I went down the stairs to the lobby, I really wanted to look over my shoulder and see Csikany's face but I knew Basil was keeping an eye on him. And I knew he'd fill me in on Csikany's reaction when we met up later. But I did my job. At least I hope I did. The seed was sown.

On the way back to the apartment, I stopped at the same small store on the ground floor of Building No. 3. Then I spent the next couple of hours reading, listening to music, cooking and waiting. Basil arrived in no time at all. I greeted him at the front door and we kissed and we celebrated, but never mind. After that, I debriefed him.

"I watched you walk down the big grand staircase and out the big glass doors," said Basil. "Csikany stayed there for a few minutes thinking, jiggling one foot. Whatever you said, it worked. You got to him."

"I told him about the picnic and I told him the United States government would appreciate it if he would make sure the border guards held their fire during the picnic."

"What did Csikany say?"

"*What you are asking is impossible*, quote, unquote. What happened after I left?"

"He went downstairs and into the baths and I followed him."

"Did you approach him?"

"No," said Basil. "Now he knows he really is being followed. He knows his instincts were right. But he thinks it's the Americans."

"So you didn't approach him?"

"No. But I followed him into the locker room and into baths. I never made eye contact but made sure he got a good look at me. It's hard to tell someone's nationality when they're naked. As far as he's concerned, I could have been anybody. But I could have been another American. The point is, when I do approach him, I want Csikany to recognize me.

"If you paraded around naked in front of him, I'm sure he'll remember you."

"I wore a towel," he paused "on my head."

"Okay, okay, so now what?"

"Now we've got the weekend to ourselves. What are you cooking? It smells delicious."

"Rellenos, stuffed peppers, I bought veggies on the way home, more onions and some mushrooms and rice. I used up the rest of the cheese."

1989
TIANANMEN SQUARE TO EAST BERLIN
JACK GODWIN

"It smells delicious."

"Mamacita taught me. I wish we had some chili powder. There was an unopened bottle of Tabasco at the safe house in Fertorakos. Remind me next weekend, if we're still alive."

34.

MONDAY, AUGUST 14

I waited for Csikany where he regularly took a shortcut through the park to the Gellert Hotel. He walked with his head down and his hands clasped behind his back. And I startled him when I stood up and called out to him.

"Hello Mr. Csikany."

"Not you again," he said.

"Yes sir."

"You ask the impossible. I said so already."

"I'm asking you not to kill your own people. And you tell me that's impossible?"

"East German defectors are not my people."

"Who said anything about defecting?"

"Would you lower your voice, please?"

"Who said anything about defecting? It's a picnic," I said. "The prime minister—your prime minister—wants to open the fence for a couple of hours. He wants people to come and go across the border. Nobody said anything about defecting. And by the way, they already poked a big hole in the fence outside of Sopron. Maybe you heard about it. It was in all the papers."

1989
TIANANMEN SQUARE TO EAST BERLIN
JACK GODWIN

"You are too young to remember what happened the last time. It was before you were born. Is your government one hundred percent sure it knows how Moscow will respond?"

"No."

"Well then?"

"The border guards can't hold their fire for two fucking hours?"

"It is not so simple."

"You're worried the Russians are coming to get you? Is that it? Let me tell you something," I said poking him in the chest. "If the border guards *don't* hold their fire, I'm coming to get you." Then I turned and walked away. But I was walking with much less bravado than the first time. Maybe I shouldn't have threatened him. That was Basil's job. Mine was to offer a pleasant alternative. I blew it. I hoped not.

Basil and I caught up back at the apartment.

"So, how'd things go with you?" I asked.

"Well as could be expected," said Basil. "I ran into Csikany in the baths, confronted him, told him he was being watched, you know. I made all sorts of threats to ruin him."

"And?"

"And what?"

"And how did he take it?"

"Oh, he didn't take it well. Fortunately, he wasn't armed or he would have killed me I'm sure. We were in the baths you see, no place to conceal a weapon. I suppose he could have snapped his towel at me, but he didn't do that, either."

"What did he say? Did he say anything?"

"Yes, he did. And what he said would make you blush. Well, not you maybe, but what he said would make a sailor blush. And if that's any indication, the Hungarians aren't afraid of the East Germans anymore. He's Chief of the

National Police, so he must have his own intelligence sources."

"Are you sure Csikany believed you?"

"How do you mean?"

"I mean, are you sure Csikany believed you were Konrad Gazecki?"

"Oh yes, quite sure," said Basil. "He remembered me from the other day when I followed him into the locker room and into baths. He wasn't the least bit surprised when I introduced myself. He knew me. I mean he'd heard of Gazecki and wasn't surprised, wasn't intimidated, wasn't worried." I exhaled loudly upon hearing this. "No, no, no Darling. That doesn't mean our plan is kaput. Csikany may still try to contact you. But don't wait because he may not. Wait a day, then approach him again and make your case."

35.

TUESDAY, AUGUST 15, p.m.

I staked out the Gellert Hotel lobby that afternoon.

"Hello Mr. Csikany."

"I was wondering when I would see you again."

"Oh? Why's that?"

"Let us find someplace where we can talk."

"Lead the way."

We climbed the staircase to the mezzanine coffee shop and took our places at a corner table. The waiter took our order and disappeared. Csikany reached into his coat pocket, took out a three-by-five photograph, and handed it to me.

"Do you know this man?"

It was a picture of Basil bare-chested with a towel around his waist, probably taken somewhere inside the baths.

"Yes," I said. "That's Konrad Gazecki. I recognize the face." I placed the picture face down on the table as the waiter arrived. Csikany leaned back to make room. I was sitting up straight with my hand on top of the picture trying to keep my cool. When the waiter left, I leaned forward. "He is a Stasi colonel, a spy-catcher."

"Are you sure?" He said, "Take another look."

"I don't need to. I'm sure."

"That is interesting. We have a dossier on Colonel Gazecki, a very detailed dossier but no picture. Are you sure this man is Konrad Gazecki? If so, this may be the only known photograph of him."

"Where did you get it?"

"It was taken yesterday, in the Gellert Hotel baths."

"The Hungarian National Police put cameras in the baths? I said, "I must make a mental note." My mind was racing. "Why are you doing this? Gazecki's your comrade, isn't he?"

"Gazecki is a comrade with a nice smile and iron teeth." Csikany hesitated for a moment and smiled. "I have another photograph. I was wondering if you would look at it."

"Sure."

Csikany reached into his coat pocket again and took out another three-by-five photograph. This time he didn't hand it to me. He looked at it and smiled and then he placed it on the table between us. It was Basil again, this time with Vladimir Ivanov standing in front the bronze statue of Karl Marx. I breathed in and out as slowly as I could. When I looked up, Csikany pulled another picture out of his coat pocket. He smiled again, a tired smile and placed another photograph on the table. It was Basil and Ivanov again, *and me*, standing next to them on the Freedom Bridge.

"This photograph was taken on July fourteenth, a few moments before a car bomb exploded near Karl Marx University." If Csikany's intention was to shock me and distract me, it wasn't working. As I met his gaze across the table, I sensed something behind me. I reached for my coffee cup with my left hand and threw it directly behind me. I couldn't see behind me, but I could see Csikany reaching inside his coat again, so with both hands, I pushed the table

1989
TIANANMEN SQUARE TO EAST BERLIN
JACK GODWIN

away from me. Csikany fell backward in his chair with the table and everything on top of him.

Then I drew my weapon and spun around to see what was going on at six o'clock. Sure enough, there was a suit—a coffee stained suit—looking mad as hell. He had his gun out but he was too slow. I already had the drop on him and he knew it. If he twitched, I'd have killed him.

"Sit there," I said and motioned for the goon to take my chair. "Drop your gun to the floor, gently." There was a thud on the carpet. I stood behind the goon and kicked his sidearm toward me, but kept an eye on Csikany, who looked very disappointed as he got up from the floor and straightened the table.

"Empty your pockets, please." When the goon didn't respond immediately, I pressed the barrel up against the base of his skull. This time he got the message. All he had was a leather badge wallet, which told me he was with the National Police. I tossed it back on the table. Csikany was watching me the whole time, not moving anything but his eyes. I picked up the goon's weapon with an exasperated sigh and pulled up a chair from another table. I checked the chamber, ejected the magazine and placed the goon's gun on the table.

"You may go," I said. The goon looked at Csikany, who gave him a curt little nod. "You can take that, but I'm keeping the magazine. Mr. Csikany can have it when we're finished." Oh, he scowled at me. Then Csikany and I were alone again.

"Where were we?" I asked. "Mr. Csikany, perhaps you could tell me what *you* think I was doing on the Freedom Bridge when that car bomb went off."

"You Americans ..." he said but couldn't finish his sentence.

"Yeah, and you know what? When you fuck with me, you're fucking with the American government. It's a Cold War and *as somebody said*, Cold War is very peculiar. But we're going to win and we want you on the winning side, our side."

"Tell me what you want."

"I told you." I lowered my voice. "Your government and the Austrian government are having a picnic. We want the border guards to hold their fire. We want you to make sure they hold their fire. *Oh come on*, you must have checked it out. If you've got all these pictures, you must have checked it out already. What's the problem? Tell me what the problem is. Maybe I can help."

"I told you. It is not so simple."

"What's not so simple?"

Csikany looked like he was going to vomit. He reached into his coat pocket and took out another three-by-five photograph.

"A surveillance camera outside my home took this yesterday."

The picture showed a distinguished looking man helping a red headed woman into an armored Lincoln town car.

"This woman is my fiancée," he said. "Do you recognize this man?"

"Yes," I said.

36.

TUESDAY, AUGUST 15, late

I called Basil. I told him to contact Benson and get over to the compound on Tancsics Street on the double. I had something.

I told the story of my encounter with Csikany and laid the pictures on the table.

"Francis Irvine," said Benson, "Orange County real estate developer, attorney-at-law, top political donor, and United States Ambassador to Hungary." Benson picked up the receiver and pushed a button. "Get me Ambassador Irvine on the phone for me, please." She looked at me with a crooked smile while she was on hold. "Yes, this is Dr. Benson calling from the compound. I need to speak with the ambassador. Oh, he's not there. Can you transfer me to the residence? Thank you." I could feel the conference room vibrating under my feet. "Yes, Dr. Benson calling for the ambassador. Yes, I'll hold."

"Francis, this is Bernice. Hello. This is an encrypted line and I'm in the secure conference room at the compound. I've got FBI Special Agent Nogales with me. I'm going to put you on the speaker phone." Benson pushed a button and placed the handset in the cradle. "Are you still there?"

"I'm here," said Irvine. "What do you want?"

"Mr. Ambassador, we've got a little bit of a problem. Agent Nogales just came from a meeting with Mihaly Csikany, the National Chief of Police."

"So?"

"So, I'm holding in my hand a photograph of you and a woman. It appears to have been taken outside…"

There was a click and then a dial tone. Dr. Benson punched the speaker phone button. "Well, I guess that confirms the photo is genuine," she said.

Basil asked to see the photograph.

"What is it?" I asked

"I know this woman. I mean, I recognize her."

"Don't leave us in suspense," said Benson. "Let's hear it."

"Her name is Maria Borodina, but at Gaczyna I knew her as Ginger Bush."

"Wait. What?"

"At Gaczyna, they had a huge English language library, and she loved Ian Fleming. You know how women in the Bond books have silly names? She wanted a name like Honey Ryder or Pussy Galore, so she called herself *Ginger Bush*."

"Will wonders never cease?" said Benson.

"Then after Gaczyna we went to sex school together."

"Wait," I said. "You and this woman were lovers?"

"Let him speak," said Benson.

"Not lovers, no. I said we went to sex school together. In the Soviet Union, everything belongs to the state, including your body. She's a good looking woman. As a girl, she would have been recruited or at least considered for intelligence work. Sex school was part of the training."

"I've heard of this but I never wanted to believe it," said Benson. "The San Fernando Valley and the Evil Empire have something in common."

1989
TIANANMEN SQUARE TO EAST BERLIN
JACK GODWIN

"We never even knew where we were. They loaded us into an armored personnel carrier blindfolded. When we got out, we had no idea where we were. It could have been anywhere. We all lived in a dormitory together, ate together and attended class together."

"And slept together," I said.

"Shush. Let him speak," said Benson.

"We watched live demonstrations and learned different techniques. At night, we were assigned different partners."

"Homework," I said. "Did you have to bone up for final exams?"

"Would you let him speak?"

"We'd have a different partner every night. Sometimes, our encounters were videotaped and they'd show the tape to the rest of the class to, let's say, critique it. Everyone was embarrassed at first, but it didn't take long to lose your inhibitions."

"Or your sensitivity," said Benson.

"Or your sensitivity," said Basil "We were conditioned so we could have sex without hesitation and without feeling any emotional connection whatsoever."

"With no more sympathy than you'd feel killing someone," said Benson, "because your body belongs to the state. Thank you for sharing this information, Mr. Warburton."

Benson picked up the receiver again and pushed a button.

"Get me with the reference desk, please. Thank you." Benson waited to be connected. "Yes, this is Dr. Benson. Do we have a file on Maria Borodina? KGB," she said, "Borodina, yes, could be an alias, yes. Bring it upstairs to the secure conference room."

"What now, call in the Hostage Rescue Unit?" I asked.

"I don't think that's necessary," Benson said. "Besides, the closest HRU is in Wiesbaden. Anyway, I don't believe the ambassador is being held against his will, if you catch my drift. Let me think. Can you contact Mihaly Csikany? We need to keep him calm. Make sure he lets us handle it. Then we need to contact Washington. The White House is not going to like this. What does the old fool think he's doing?"

"An old fool is a complete fool," I said. "What do you want me to do?"

"Meet me at my car in one hour. I have some work to do first. Then we'll go see Ambassador Irvine together. You can ride with me. I'll knock on the front door and you can come in from the back. Mr. Warburton, you'll have to sit this one out."

The Ambassador's residence was located in a leafy neighborhood surrounded by an eight foot high brick wall topped with razor wire. There were surveillance cameras at the main gate and the pedestrian entrance, plus more cameras at the service entrance. There were city streets on three sides of the compound, not too busy but busy enough. One side of the compound abutted a public park and there was one section—maybe fifty feet long—with overgrown trees and dense foliage.

"Let me out here," I said. "This is where I'll go over the wall."

In addition to the razor wire on top of the wall, there was barbed wire not visible from the street. My knee caught on a barb, which sliced right through my pants and opened a bloody gash. I lost my balance going over and landed awkwardly inside the compound. I laid flat on my back and went through my routine in case I lost anything: handgun, spare ammo, knife, knuckles, smoke, silencer, grenade:

1989
TIANANMEN SQUARE TO EAST BERLIN
JACK GODWIN

check, check, check. I felt like puking but took deep breaths until it went away and bandaged myself up. I got up to a crouch, so far so good. It hurt when I put weight on it but I'd be okay if I kept moving. I knew it would hurt tomorrow morning though.

Dusk turned almost dark. All the lights were on and there was music coming from the residence fifty yards away. I looked around and couldn't see any security. Budapest must be a cushy post I thought. If this were anywhere in the Middle East, there would be five or six Marines guarding the place round the clock.

"Dr. Benson, this is Jaqui. Do you read?"

"Go ahead Jaqui."

"I'm inside the perimeter looking at the residence. The lights are on and there's music playing. I don't see any staff or security, no movement at all." I moved slowly around the mansion, which was bow-shaped and three stories high in the center. I could see Benson's car roll up to the front entrance and stop.

"Go around to the garden and find a way inside."

There was a wide terrace overlooking the garden and three glass doors. The first one I tried was locked, but not the second one. I stepped into a huge rotunda that seemed to extend all the way to the front of the house. There was a staircase to the second floor where the guest rooms or bedrooms must be. It looked like the ground floor was for entertaining. Not a soul in sight, but I could smell cigar smoke. Double doors led me into a very cozy library, where I would have lingered, if only I could. At the other end, there was a long corridor, bow-shaped just like the house, and a passage that opened up into a salon with red and gold drapes, oak paneling and built-in bar. Sure enough, there sat

Francis Irvine, United States Ambassador to the People's Republic of Hungary, coolly smoking a cigar. And there was Dr. Benson, leaning on her cane. She had a file folder in her other hand.

"Right behind you, ma'am."

"Thank you," she said.

"I see you travel with your own assassin," said Irvine.

"Mr. Ambassador, this is FBI Special Agent Jaqueline Nogales."

"I know who she is."

"Mr. Ambassador, I have to ask you. Is the woman here?"

"Yes," he said.

"May I? It's been a long day." Irvine gestured for her to sit. Benson placed the file on the coffee table and withdrew the photo Csikany gave me, the one with Maria Borodina climbing into the Ambassador's town car. "Mr. Ambassador, this photo was taken by a surveillance camera outside of Mihaly Csikany's home."

"So?"

"Francis, you're a single man. Under normal circumstances, I would say *make yourself happy*. Unfortunately, circumstances are not normal."

"It doesn't matter," he said. "We're in love."

"As I say, carrying on an affair with a foreign national wouldn't get you recalled, under normal circumstances," said Benson.

"What then? Is it because she was seeing Mihaly Csikany? She broke it off. She told me so."

"Francis, this is very awkward." You could sense Benson's discomfort by the way she adjusted her glasses. She opened the file on the table. Clipped to the inside flap there was a black and white mug shot of a younger Maria

1989
TIANANMEN SQUARE TO EAST BERLIN
JACK GODWIN

Borodina, one front view, one side view. In the front view picture, she was holding a placard with Cyrillic lettering on it. Benson showed this to Irvine."

"So what?" he said, "so what? She's got a past. Who doesn't?"

"Not everyone is KGB for one thing," said Benson.

"What?"

"She's KGB," said Benson. Irvine's face went white as a fish belly. At first, he looked like he wanted to protest but slowly it dawned on him.

"Is that the file on her?" Irvine asked.

Benson nodded.

"I didn't know," said Irvine, "I swear I didn't know."

"How long has this been going on?"

"Since May," said Irvine. "We met on the Grand Boulevard at the May Day celebration."

"I admit it's more creative than we're used to seeing from KGB. She played both of you, Csikany and you."

"I can't believe it," he said.

"You'll be recalled for failing to report an intimate relationship. Washington will want to debrief, of course. They'll be interested to know if you leaked any classified information. But I wonder if you could satisfy a point of curiosity. During your pillow talk, you didn't happen to mention anything about that team we brought in to deal with our Stasi friends operating near the Austrian border?"

"You mean Tanner and his little moonlight incursion? What's that got to do with anything?"

"Oh nothing, just a point of curiosity," said Benson.

"I thought she loved me."

"Oh Francis," she said. "You're not exactly the first government official targeted for sexual entrapment. It happens in books more than real life. I mean, ambassadors don't know enough to do much damage. Frankly, I'm more worried about Borodina's relationship with Mihaly Csikany. He might have leaked information to her incidentally without knowing its value."

Benson turned to me. "I radioed the deputy chief of mission on the way over. He should be waiting outside by now, along with the chief of security and a couple of Marine guards. Could you please tell them to come in?"

"Yes ma'am."

I walked back along the long bow-shaped corridor to the front entrance. There were two black armored Chevy Suburbans idling. The driver's side power window opened when I approached.

"I have a message for the DCM from Dr. Benson. She says to come in and bring the guards. I think you'll be taking the ambassador into custody."

When we all came back to the salon, Benson was standing at the built-in bar pouring something, which looked like scotch.

"Try this," she said. "It's Macallan single malt, eighteen years old. It comes from a village in northern Scotland." She took a swig. "Oh yeah, this is the good stuff." She handed me an expensive-looking glass and offered one to the DCM. "I'd offer one to you gentlemen," she said to the Marines, "but not while you're in uniform. I'll drop by the Marine House on Friday and buy a round. How's that sound?"

The embassy's chief of security hoisted the ambassador to his feet and escorted him out of the room, followed by the two Marine guards. Dr. Benson and the DCM (a thirtyish career Foreign Service Officer named Joe Watkins) sat down around the low table sipping their scotch.

1989
TIANANMEN SQUARE TO EAST BERLIN
JACK GODWIN

"Pretty smooth," said Watkins.

"Good, isn't it? It's well balanced with a smoky flavor," said Benson.

"I'm not talking about the scotch. I'm talking about you: smooth, pretty smooth."

"Oh, I have a little experience in that department. Do you remember Ambassador Janeway in Costa Rica?"

"Of course I remember him."

"Well, back in eighty-five, Janeway decided containment wasn't working anymore, said we should start supplying *material support* to anti-communist movements in Third World countries. He convinced the Costa Rican government to let him build an airbase near the Nicaraguan border. Costa Rica is the Switzerland of Central America. Can you imagine? That's how Iran-Contra got started. That's how the plan to sell arms to Iran and then use the proceeds to fund the Contras in Nicaragua got started. You know what the Contras are? They're terrorists, not freedom fighters. God, what a creep Janeway turned out to be. He reminds me of that guy from *Strangelove*, the guy who took control of the air force base. Who was that?"

"That was Brigadier General Jack D. Ripper," I said.

"That's him. General Ripper, meet Ambassador Janeway. Washington recalled him, too. What is it with these amateurs anyway?"

"Pretty smooth," Watkins said again.

"Well Joe," said Benson." "You're chief of mission now. What do you want to do about Mihaly Csikany?"

"Apologize to him, I guess, unofficially of course."

"Csikany is friendly and so is Laszlo Nagy," said Benson. "We want them to remain friendly when this is all over, right?"

"This is Mihaly Csikany we're talking about," Watkins said.

"I know. I know. Joe, you can handle him. Empathize with him. Tell him we all got played. Remind him she's KGB and that the Russians are the enemy, not us."

"Do you think he'll go for it?" I asked.

"Like I said, we want to be friends when this is all over. Give him an incentive. C'mon Jaqui, I'll give you a ride home."

"Yes Ma'am. What about Maria Borodina? The ambassador said she was here."

"I remember. Let her go. She's an administrative detail. C'mon Agent Nogales, let's go. Joe, show me a draft before you send the report to Washington."

"Sure thing Dr. Benson. I'll need your help filling in a few of the blanks anyway. Good night."

We climbed into the back seat together and Benson's driver peeled away.

"Are you sure it's a good idea to let her go?" I asked.

"What's the alternative?"

"Take her into custody. Interrogate her."

"I told you, we're getting close to wrapping this thing up. Why do you want to interrogate her? Do you think its sloppy tradecraft?"

"Well, yes," I said.

"You're right of course. But politics supersedes tradecraft, and this is a case in point. I don't think she got much out of Irvine. She was investing in the future, really just beginning to cultivate the relationship. He allowed himself to be entrapped, which is scandalous but not exactly criminal. What can we do, really? We can't arrest her for goodness sake. The best we can do is to expose her to

1989
TIANANMEN SQUARE TO EAST BERLIN
JACK GODWIN

Csikany, and we'll do that. Watkins will take care of that tomorrow. For us, Cold War means espionage just like I said. Csikany and Irvine allowed themselves to be used. And in doing so—especially Irvine—they interfered with our plans." Benson paused for a moment and smiled sadly. "Besides, now we know where the leak was. That's the important thing. It removes the cloud hanging over Mr. Warburton."

"Can I see the file?" She handed it to me and asked *what for.* "I just want to study the photograph, that's all."

"Jaqui, we can wrap this thing up in a few months, weeks if we're lucky. Appearances are important. And it must appear as though this movement—this final push—isn't coming from us. The Hungarians must do it themselves, along with the Austrians."

"She's got an intelligent face," I said.

"Let me see. Yeah, look at the eyes. She looks formidable."

I closed the file and laid it on the seat between us. The safe house apartment was still a few blocks away, but Benson told the driver to stop so I could get out without attracting attention. I cut across the leafy courtyard, past the small store on the ground floor, which was closed at this hour, and then up to the fourth floor. I unlocked the door and let myself in, where Basil greeted me.

37.

WEDNESDAY, AUGUST 16

Basil and I made our way over to the compound on Tancsics Street to help Dr. Benson write her report. She's the one who approved the original operation on Csikany, which was successful on paper even though it didn't quite go according to plan. That's how the intelligence business worked. You developed a plan and then you put the plan into the field knowing that reality would always intrude, as it did the moment Csikany showed me that photograph of Maria Borodina—a Russian KGB agent—getting into the American ambassador's car. Sometimes you got lucky, sometimes not. We got lucky on that one.

"It's not the first time the KGB has employed a woman to obtain information," said Benson. "It won't be the last."

"Irvine could have been a gold mine of information in his position, and even more valuable depending on his next assignment. It is also possible Borodina was simply planning to murder Irvine," I said.

"No, I don't think so, not as long as he held an official position in the government. He was a real estate developer and a big donor and a dilettante. His reward was this cushy ambassadorship. Later on when Irvine was a civilian and no longer had access to classified material, Borodina might have killed him just to be done with him."

"If it went public, it would have been one hell of a scandal," I said.

"Yes, if it ever went public," she said. "I don't believe Borodina would ever have let it go that far. When Irvine was no longer useful, he'd be found dead and her gone without a trace. But that's not what bothers me. Clearly, Borodina was still in the process of recruiting and cultivating Irvine. It bothers me that we'll never know what information Csikany shared with her or what, if anything, she shared with Moscow or Berlin."

38.

THURSDAY, AUGUST 17

The State Department issued a press release announcing Francis Irvine's retirement, which proved Washington can move with surprising agility when it wanted to. Former Ambassador Irvine was now out of the country and on his way home. The embassy's General Service Officer, known as the GSO, was supervising the tedious process of packing up Irvine's personal effects for shipment back to his home in California. And Joe Watkins, career Foreign Service Officer, was now serving as acting chief of mission until the president nominated, and the senate confirmed a new ambassador.

Joe Watkins paid a call at the Ministry of Foreign Affairs to present his diplomatic credentials. Presenting one's credentials—and having them formally accepted by the host government—is mostly ceremonial but it was also a legal requirement. It was politically advantageous to be considered the official representative of the American government, and that called for official recognition from the host government. When Joe arrived at the Hungarian Ministry of Foreign Affairs and stepped out of his Lincoln Town Car (yes, the same one) a military band played the *Star Spangled Banner*. The Deputy Minister of Foreign Affairs escorted Joe up the stairs of the Parliament Building and into the Carpathian

1989
TIANANMEN SQUARE TO EAST BERLIN
JACK GODWIN

Heritage Room, where the Minister of Foreign Affairs was waiting. Joe bowed (but not too low because it looked bad back home when Americans bowed) and presented his letter of credentials. They shook hands, posed for a few pictures, and ten minutes later it was all over.

We climbed into the back of Dr. Benson's car and followed the ambassador's official limo back to the embassy. The rain drizzled down the windows as the cityscape whizzed past looking like a smudged painting.

"Good work dealing with the Stasi," she said. "I'm sorry we lost Josef Tibor."

"Yes ma'am."

"You've got the talent. You need more experience. Fortunately, there's a cure for that. We got a telex about your next post. Charlottenburg House in West Berlin," she said. "You and Spencer Pang report August twenty-first."

"August twenty-first," I said. "That's two days after the picnic."

"That's right. Congratulations."

"Thank you."

"Berlin won't be a picnic I can assure you. You better hit the books. Berlin is where it started. And that's where it's got to end."

"Yes ma'am."

"I suggest you begin by familiarizing yourself with the Berlin Wall. In forty-eight, Stalin tried to blockade Berlin and Truman responded with the Berlin airlift. That went on for almost a year until the Russians backed off. By sixty-one, more than two million East Germans had crossed over to the west. There were talks between DC and the Kremlin, but then the Russians shot down our spy plane and captured the pilot. Meanwhile, East Germany was losing ten thousand people a month—ten thousand a month! Of course it wasn't exactly a spontaneous occurrence. We'd been encouraging people to defect for years."

"So they didn't just build it to keep people from leaving. They built it because we were meddling."

"That's not the official version, but yes. That was in sixty-one. It's more than a wall though, which is why I'm telling you to hit the books. The Berlin Wall is a death trap for anyone trying to cross in either direction. And I'm not saying that to be melodramatic. Behind the wall, on the East German side, there's a double row of fences topped with barbed wire all monitored, mined, booby trapped and patrolled by armed guards around the clock. I want you to familiarize yourself with it."

"Yes ma'am."

"See you at Charlottenburg House," she said.

1989
TIANANMEN SQUARE TO EAST BERLIN
JACK GODWIN

39.

SATURDAY, AUGUST 19

The last couple of days before the picnic went by quickly. I spent most of it in the catacombs beneath the compound on Tancsics Street. There was plenty of reading to do before I got to Berlin, and I was eager to learn as much as I could when I found out what my assignment would be. Basil's story about sex school bugged me. I meant to ask him if they had class reunions next time I saw him. I don't know what it was. Something about Maria Borodina still bothered me. Something told me it was a mistake to let her get away.

The picnic went exactly as planned. Basil was there—unrecognizable in disguise—wearing oversize glasses, a black curly wig, prosthetic teeth and nose, and dressed like an East German tourist enjoying his Hungarian vacation. He must have gotten theatrical makeup training on top of everything else. The glasses and wig would have been easy to find, but not the teeth and nose. Those were custom-made. The nose made his voice sound a little nasally, which added to the effect. The more beer he drank the deeper into character and the funnier he got.

Spencer Pang was there and so was Otto Von Habsburg. Boy, it seemed like a long time since that meeting at Saint Michael's Church. Our eyes met and Habsburg walked over to say hello. His eyes were smiling and he was obviously pleased with the turnout. It didn't matter how much it cost, he said, it was worth every *pfennig*. Habsburg spoke to Basil in German and asked Basil where he was from. Basil said his name is Dieter and he was from Leipzig. Habsburg whispered something to Basil I couldn't quite hear. He turned to me and explained he just told my friend there would be a very short ceremony at three o'clock and they would open the border to Austria for a few hours. Habsburg then turned back to "Dieter" and pointed to the fence and whispered into Dieter's ear. Dieter recoiled and shook his head in disbelief. Habsburg patted his forearm and spoke in a gentle, reassuring tone but Dieter still looked doubtful. Finally, Habsburg reached into his pocket and handed Dieter twenty Austrian shillings, patted him on the back and chuckled as he walked away.

At three, people started to congregate around the small platform. There was a sizable crowd on the Austrian side, which you could see through fence. Representatives from the Austrian and Hungarian governments made speeches about friendship, freedom and Glasnost, and then threw open the gates. People began pouring through the opening into Austria. There was an even larger crowd holding back, waiting. But nothing happened, no shouting, no shots fired, just hundreds of people—men, women and children—shuffled toward the border into Austria. The Hungarian border guards were on duty, but stood aside to let people cross. Some people kept walking and never came back. Other people crossed a few feet into Austria, and just sat down in the grass laughing and crying in disbelief. Were we making history? Was this the beginning of the end? Or was this just the best picnic ever?

1989
TIANANMEN SQUARE TO EAST BERLIN
JACK GODWIN

PART THREE

1989
TIANANMEN SQUARE TO EAST BERLIN
JACK GODWIN

1989
TIANANMEN SQUARE TO EAST BERLIN
JACK GODWIN

40.

MONDAY, AUGUST 21

I arrived in West Berlin last night, and reported this morning to Charlottenburg House, the American consulate in West Berlin. But Charlottenburg House was much more than a consular office. By that, I don't mean it was almost an embassy. The real embassy was in Bonn, six hundred kilometers to the west. On the ground floor of Charlottenburg House, the State Department issued visas, replaced passports and provided assistance to American tourists. On the second floor, the Foreign Commercial Service and the American Chamber of Commerce promoted American business interests. But since 1945, the real mission of Charlottenburg House was fighting the Cold War. That happened on the third, fourth and fifth floors.

Charlottenburg House was located walking distance from the train station at the Zoological Garden, what they called "the Zoo Station." This was where West Berlin came together, where all the spokes of public transportation in the city came to a hub, and from where you could catch a streetcar across town, an express train to West Germany, a regional train to Western Europe and even the Trans-Siberian railway to

1989

TIANANMEN SQUARE TO EAST BERLIN

JACK GODWIN

Vladivostok if that was your destination. It was a colorful neighborhood full of bars and cafes, restaurants, nightclubs, strip clubs, pickpockets, prostitutes and junkies.

If you looked down the street right or left you wouldn't find a single empty parking space. American and German cars filled the streets. You'd never know there was a world war forty years ago. You'd never know there was a Cold War now. No bombed out buildings. No military cemeteries. There was a Jewish cemetery, but that was on the other side of the wall in East Berlin. There was one big war memorial on this side, in the Tiergarten, which the Soviets built before the wall went up. It was in the British sector, and British soldiers stood guard to ward off vandals and graffiti artists.

Other than that, all the repairs had long been completed, all signs of war-torn Berlin gone. Not a scaffold in sight, just brightly lit shops selling jewelry, expensive watches and luxury goods, and teenagers smoking Marlboros, wearing Levis and posing like movie stars. It was like Vegas without neon. Defiant was the word. All neat and polished, as though cleaning crews came out at night and scrubbed the cobblestones with tooth brushes. And it all came together at Zoo Station.

Checkpoint Charlie was exactly five kilometers east. The first thing that stood out was the red flag with the yellow hammer and sickle. Sandbags were piled chin high around the little wooden whitewashed guard station. The sign in four languages, English, French, German and Russian told you that you were leaving the American Sector. On the other side of Charlie, the bright lights and fancy retail stores came to a sudden stop. Everything was covered in soot, rust-stained and crumbling. Nothing looked new except the young GDR border guards wearing crisp gray uniforms and shiny black boots. They looked so young. It was easy to scoff at the idea of a worker's paradise. Even if the GDR hired one of those big time advertising agencies, it wouldn't have helped. East Germans were competing with the Marlboro Man and it wasn't a fair fight.

41.

TUESDAY, AUGUST 22

Dr. Benson assigned a thirty-something Foreign Service Officer to brief Spencer and me and to help develop a strategy. This document was in the packet of briefing materials he prepared for us:

BERLIN WALL 1989: FORTIFICATIONS OF THE GERMAN DEMOCRATIC REPUBLIC (GDR) IN AND AROUND EAST BERLIN

Background

In July 1945, Germany was divided into four zones and occupied by Russia, France, Britain, and the US. In May 1949, France, Britain and the US consolidated their occupation zones and created the Federal Republic of Germany (FRG.) The Russian (or Soviet) occupation zone became the German Democratic Republic (GDR.)

Berlin, like Germany was divided into four occupation zones. The French, British and American zones became West Berlin, while the Soviet occupation zone became East Berlin. The Berlin Wall separates East Berlin from West.

The wall is approximately forty (40) kilometers long and runs north-south inside the boundary formally occupied by the Soviet Union.

Fortifications

The Berlin Wall consists of a series of fortifications. First is a twelve foot (12) high concrete wall that sits entirely on the East German side of the border and is visible from the FRG. On the other side, there are two (2) metal barriers running parallel to the wall. The metal barriers are fitted with sensors that do not deliver an electric shock, but send a signal that identifies the exact location upon contact with the barrier. The metal barriers consist of six (6) foot wide panels fitted together with a tongue and groove joint and buried below the surface to prevent tunneling.

There is an anti-vehicle ditch, six (6) feet deep and twenty-five (25) feet wide running between the two rows of metal barriers. All trees and bushes have been cleared from this V-shaped ditch to ensure a clear field of fire. The area between the wall and the outer metal barrier (closest to the wall) is installed with a network of mines and sensors. Different types of mines have been installed over the years, so there is no consistency. However, newer models are directional and target defectors rather than intruders when activated. No accurate count is possible, but the GDR has laid more than a million mines according to best estimates.

1989
TIANANMEN SQUARE TO EAST BERLIN
JACK GODWIN

There are concrete poles with floodlights every twenty (20) yards and concrete watch towers every one hundred (100) yards. The wall is patrolled in all weather, twenty-four hours a day by armed East German border guards. In total, there are four hundred sixty-five (465) watch towers. For every ten (10) watch towers, there is a specially fortified command tower where supervisors monitor the wall and other towers, communicate with guards, and monitor electronic sensors in the metal barriers.

Surveillance

There is a patrol road running parallel to the inner metal barrier. This is where the "Restricted Zone" begins. Civilians are prohibited from entering the Restricted Zone during daylight hours without special permission. At night, during curfew hours civilians are absolutely prohibited from entering the zone.

Between the patrol road and the inner metal barrier, there is a six (6) foot wide strip of bare ground covered with fine silica sand. This sand is raked every day, patrolled by guards with guard-dogs, checked for footprints every morning and raked again before curfew hours. The purpose of this security measure is to discourage GDR border guards from defecting, which occurs with some frequency. [Note: the number of GDR border guards who have successfully defected remains classified.]

There is a special unit within the Stasi that regularly screens border guards, interviews and inspects them. Anyone with family in West Germany, anyone with strong religious beliefs, or anyone considered ideologically "unreliable" is discharged or in some cases imprisoned. Guards always work in teams of three. They have standing orders not to permit each other out of sight. They also have standing orders to shoot anyone, including other border guards, caught attempting to defect.

"Jesus," I said. "They thought of everything, didn't they?"

"No they didn't," said Spencer. "The wall isn't just a symbol. It's a concrete reminder of everything wrong with the system. Forget about the propaganda and ask yourself this. If they built the wall to keep intruders out, then why do the anti-personnel mines face inward? Why are they directional, facing inward?"

"Because the incentive to leave is overwhelming," I said.

"That's right," said the FSO "especially for anyone with skills, anyone who's young or single, or anyone who has relatives living in Western Europe. I mean, the standard of living in East Germany is much higher than in any other Warsaw Pact country. But it's still lower than the even poorest country in Western Europe. The shortages are getting worse and the lines are getting longer."

"Where can we hit them?" I asked.

"Their roads and railways and most buildings are falling apart. There's a chronic housing shortage and long wait times—years—for cars and household appliances.

Occasionally, there are acute shortages of basic consumer goods."

"Where do they get hard currency?"

"The Trabant factory in Saxony," said the FSO. "It's the best-selling car in East Germany and it's exported to other countries, not just the Soviet bloc but to Africa and South America, too. It's the only heavy industry in the GDR and one of its few sources of hard currency."

"What else?"

"The other major source is the monthly payment from West Germany to use the autobahn into Berlin. There is essentially no other foreign investment."

"Can't we ask West Germany to stop the monthly payments?"

"No way," he said. "I mean, we could but they'd just close the autobahn in retaliation. We don't want another airlift."

"No. But we do want to hit them economically and cripple them politically. I want to hear some ideas," said Benson. The table fell silent. The FSO spoke first.

"What about the black market? We don't have precise information, but we estimate that twenty to twenty-five percent of GDR's economy is black market. Everyone's involved—even though there are severe penalties for getting caught."

"That's good but too small scale," said Benson.

"Wait, I have an idea. You said everyone's involved. I assume that means party officials, too."

"That's right," said the FSO.

"Is there any official government involvement in the black market?"

"Yeah actually," said the FSO. "East Germany doesn't have any natural resources except for some minerals, which they export to Russia. But Russia doesn't pay in hard currency. They pay with crude oil, sometimes with natural gas."

"So?"

"So, the last time the GDR received a big shipment of oil from the Soviets, they sold it. The GDR didn't distribute it domestically." The FSO flipped through a file as he spoke. "They sold it on the international commodity exchange. They sold it for hard currency, and sure enough, there was an energy shortage that lasted for more than a month. I never put two and two together."

Dr. Benson leaned forward smiling.

"That's our scam," I said. "When I was stateside, I worked white collar crimes and racketeering. We could pose as buyers, couldn't we? But we wouldn't pay. Not only that, we could blast the whole shipment and the whole oil distribution facility to hell. Is there a refinery or a distribution facility?" Everyone was looking at me.

"What!" I said.

"There is one called Leunawerke, not far from Leipzig," said Benson. "It's the biggest. The oil comes to Leipzig via the Druzhba oil pipeline from the Russian Far East, through Belarus and the Ukraine to East Germany. Druzhba means friendship. It's perfect."

"Great," I said. "Who do we talk to?"

"Bart Lowry," said the FSO. "He's down on the second floor in the Foreign Commercial Service. We can't invite him up. You'll have to meet him in his office."

A few hours later, Spencer and I were sitting across the desk from Bartholomew Lowry of the United States Foreign Commercial Service. Lowry introduced himself.

"How can I help you?"

1989

TIANANMEN SQUARE TO EAST BERLIN
JACK GODWIN

"My name is David Huang. This is my associate Floriana Varga. We represent Mutual Petroleum, which is a subsidiary of Kendall-Brown Petroleum. We're interested in buying Russian crude oil, benchmark grade."

"What quantity?"

"Two million barrels," said Spencer. The little commercial officer with the bulbous nose and purple face was suddenly interested. "We're not shoppers. We want to start the transaction today. But there is a catch. We can't do all the logistics ourselves. We prefer to take delivery at the Leunawerke distribution center near Leipzig."

"I understand completely. The East German government has lately gone into the resale business. I know someone. He's an Assistant Deputy Secretary in the Ministry of Coal and Energy."

"That sounds perfect. Tell him we'll pay a premium if he can load it into rail cars."

"Today's price is twenty dollars a barrel. How much of a premium are you willing to pay?"

"Twenty-one is the highest we'll go."

"Let me do the math. Two million barrels is sixty-three million gallons. At twenty dollars a barrel, that's forty million. If we go as high as twenty-one, that's an extra two million bucks. Now, if we use the seventy-five thousand gallon tankers, you'd need eight hundred forty cars. That's a long train, too long. We can split it up into multiple shipments. Would that okay? It might cost more."

"That sounds good. When can we meet your friend at the ministry?"

"I'll call him today. Where can I reach you?"

"We're staying at the Hyatt," said Spencer. "Give me one of your cards and we'll call you tomorrow."

Back on the third floor of Charlottenburg House, Spencer and I met with Dr. Benson.

"While you were downstairs, I did some checking," she said. "The Druzhba pipeline has a maximum capacity of 1.4 million barrels a day. The southern branch, the one that goes to Leipzig, has a slightly smaller diameter, so the capacity is 1.2 million per day. How much did you ask for?"

"Two million barrels," said Spencer.

"Next I suppose you're going to ask me for money."

"Yes," said Spencer. "If you want to end the Cold War this year, it's going to cost the government a few million bucks. But don't worry. You won't have to pay up. As soon as they load the first shipment, we're going to torch the whole train and the distribution facility. We'll need an advance of ten million. And then, you can stop payment, or at least try even though that's nearly impossible with an irrevocable letter of credit."

"If this doesn't send their economy into a tail spin, then I'm going to start looking for a new line of work," I said.

"Makes you feel sorry for them, does it?" he said.

"Not quite," said Benson.

1989
TIANANMEN SQUARE TO EAST BERLIN
JACK GODWIN

42.

WEDNESDAY, AUGUST 23

Spencer and I contacted Lowry again. Lowry told us the meeting with his contact at the Ministry of Coal and Energy, someone named Markus Schmidt, was set for August thirty-first.

"Did you say Schmidt? Is he any relation to Joachim Schmidt?"

"Yes. President Schmidt is his uncle," said Lowry. "East Germany is like anyplace else. It's all who you know."

"This gets better all the time," said Spencer. And I kicked him under the table.

"It never hurts to have connections," said Lowry. "And Markus Schmidt is certainly well connected."

"The US Foreign Commercial Service arranges a meeting with a top official from the GDR ministry official, just like that?"

"It happens all the time," Lowry said. "He'll do business with the West, but he never crosses into West Berlin. He insists on meeting you. If you want to make the deal, you'll have to meet him in East Berlin."

"It sounds dangerous," I said.

"You'll be perfectly safe," said Lowry. "We do this all the time."

1989
TIANANMEN SQUARE TO EAST BERLIN
JACK GODWIN

The week-long wait gave us plenty of time to arrange all the documentation we needed, fake identification, letters of credit and business cards. We planned to meet at the big fountain in Alexanderplatz in East Berlin's central district. It was a big public square so personal security would be no problem. That was the thing about socialism. There was almost no petty crime.

43.

THURSDAY, AUGUST 31

That morning, Spencer and I met Bart Lowry outside Charlottenburg House and the three of us took a cab as far as Checkpoint Charlie. This was the only place where diplomats, allied forces and foreigners could get into East Berlin legally, and back again. I expected we would all have to be frisked by Schmidt's people, not just for weapons but for wires, too. In general, getting into East Berlin was easier than getting out. But you know what they say: add up the number of times you cross a checkpoint. If it adds up to an even number at the end of the day, be grateful.

On the other side of the checkpoint, the three of us caught another cab to Alexanderplatz. You could see the huge TV tower out the window. It was so tall the top disappeared from view the closer we came. At the edge of the square the driver let us out. We walked fifty yards or so through the crowds to the fountain. At the base, there was a big circular pool with a bench around it where people could sit. In the middle of that, there was another pool, taller but smaller in diameter and covered with brightly colored tiles. Rising out of that were seven or eight metallic shafts that opened at the top like abstract flowers or something. The water cascaded down from the flowers into one pool and then the other.

We were right on schedule according to my watch, but there was nobody waiting for us. Lowry, the fidgety little commercial officer, said that was the problem with socialism. Good old German punctuality wasn't as high a priority on this side of the great divide. What a weasel. Standing with my back to the fountain, I turned and saw someone heading straight toward us and he was walking with a purpose. I figured that must be Schmidt. He had someone with him, maybe an assistant maybe a body guard. Who brings one guy? Nobody brings one guy, especially when you have home court advantage. Always bring superior manpower and superior firepower. That was standard operating procedure.

Then I remembered. Check six. There they were, two more in plain clothes behind the fountain. Without being too conspicuous, I scanned to see if there was a sniper positioned on one of the rooftops. When you did business with a paragon of Cold War corruption, you had to expect that sort of thing. As Schmidt approached, I got a good look at him. He was impossibly handsome, if you go for that blond, blue eyed Aryan type. Schmidt stood back while his assistant frisked Lowry, Spencer, and then me. The goon gestured "hands up" and patted me down starting at my armpits, then down my sides and back. He felt around my belt and squeezed my pockets. Then he ran his hand up the front of my blouse along the row of buttons and then down the lapels of my jacket. I tried not to flinch. He was not just looking for weapons. As I suspected, he was looking for a wire. That told me Schmidt was as worried about secrecy as he was about security.

1989
TIANANMEN SQUARE TO EAST BERLIN
JACK GODWIN

"Mr. Markus Schmidt," said Lowry "This is Mr. David Huang and this is Ms. Floriana Varga of Mutual Petroleum." Spencer and I presented the cards we had made at Charlottenburg House. Schmidt handed them to his goon without a glance. Spencer handed the phony letter of credit from Kreditanstalt Dusseldorf. This Schmidt did not hand to his goon. He read it carefully.

"Why is it I have never heard of Mutual Petroleum?" Schmidt spoke flawless, unaccented English.

"The Mutual Petroleum Corporation is a wholly owned subsidiary of Kendall-Brown Petroleum, the largest gas and oil distributor in California. KBP has thirty thousand employees and operations in North and South America, North Africa and the Mid-East with an income of two point three billion dollars on annual revenues of twelve billion. "That's nineteen percent, Mr. Schmidt. We're pleased with this rate of return, but KBP's growth strategy depends on development of a new supply chain." Spencer paused. "We have been informed that you have a connection in Leipzig to the Druzhba oil pipeline from the Russian Far East. We need a reliable source and a reliable distributor. We contacted Mr. Lowry here in the hope he could make an introduction. We would like to buy two million barrels of benchmark Russian crude, broken into several shipments and loaded on rail cars at the Leunawerke distribution center."

Schmidt examined his cuticles while Spencer spoke. I think he was trying to look nonchalant.

"Thank you, Mr. Huang. I think we can accommodate you. The price is $22 per barrel."

"We hope this would be the first of *several* shipments," said Spencer.

"Twenty-two," said Schmidt.

"Nineteen," said Spencer. "We know how much VUNeft charges you at the Volga-Ural Oil Fields. We've done our homework."

Schmidt held up one hand signaling for Spencer to stop.

"We will not haggle here in such a public place."

"I want to tour the facility," Spencer said.

"You Americans, with you it's always I want this, I want that."

"Our creditors insist on it," I interjected.

"A tour may be arranged," said Schmidt, "after we finalize the terms of sale."

"Twenty dollars per barrel," said Spencer. "At today's exchange rate, that's forty million dollars—seventy million deutschmarks—five percent payable in advance, and the remainder with an irrevocable letter of credit. And we want to tour the Leunawerke facility *tomorrow*."

Spencer extended his right hand for Schmidt to shake but Schmidt did not reciprocate.

"Come back tomorrow," said Schmidt, "same time, same place. I will give you a tour of the Leunawerke facility. Thank you, Mr. Lowry. Your services are no longer required." With that, Schmidt turned and walked back the way he came and disappeared into the crowd.

44.

FRIDAY, SEPTEMBER 1

Spencer and I made our way from Charlottenburg House through Checkpoint Charlie to Alexanderplatz. We were waiting by the fountain no more than five minutes when a big East German Air Force Helicopter came down in the middle of the square. The rotors were still spinning after the helicopter touched down and people scurried out of the way holding on to their hats. A uniformed East German airman came running toward us and invited us aboard. After we buckled in, the airman signaled for us to put on headsets.

"What're we flying in, Mr. Huang?" I asked.

"Oh, this is a turboshaft Mi24, seventeen hundred horse power, maximum airspeed of three hundred kilometers per hour, carries eight passengers. This one's Russian-made. The body is armored and impact resistant. We'll be in Leipzig in less than an hour I guess."

"That's very impressive, Mr. Huang" said a disembodied voice in the headset. It was Schmidt. "How do you know this? Do you subscribe to *Jane's Defense Weekly*?" Spencer (Mr. Huang) glanced at me and suppressed a giggle.

"Yeah, I read it cover to cover every week, even the classifieds." Spencer said, "sort of a hobby of mine. You know in *Rambo III*, that wasn't a real Mi24. That was a French-made 330 Puma with plywood wings and fake rivets.

"You Americans watch too many movies."

"Yeah, that's true. Both the Mi24 and the 330 Puma have four blades, but the Puma has twin engines, which is what gave it away because the Mi24 has a single engine. That's also what makes the Mi24 vulnerable to heat-seeking missiles, you know, because of the exhaust." Spencer discreetly mimicked hoisting a Stinger to his shoulder, clicked his tongue and winked at me.

Less than an hour later, we arrived at Leunawerke. Schmidt pointed out the major landmarks as the pilot circled the giant facility. Everywhere you looked the ground was stained black. There were thousands of pipes running in every direction. And there was one big one on stilts with a wide swath of oily dirt on either side coming out of nowhere on the eastern horizon, rising and falling, up and down again with the terrain. From a distance the pipeline moved with the long, graceful curves of a railroad. Up close you could see how it was made. Thousands of long straight sections of pipe riveted together, leaky at the couplings, patched in places all pouring into a giant manifold with giant valves leading to giant storage tanks painted white and surrounded by earthworks to keep the oil from spreading in case of a spill.

There were two rail lines heading into the facility from the northeast and two heading out again to the southwest. There were dozens of switches which branched into ten or twelve lines for receiving and loading. There were bridges over the tracks, signals, electrical lines and more pipes running in every direction. Hundreds of intermodal and tank cars sat at terminals waiting to be loaded. Junked cars, rusting locomotives, wheels and spare parts were scattered

1989
TIANANMEN SQUARE TO EAST BERLIN
JACK GODWIN

throughout the yard. As we got closer to the ground, you could see the faces of men in greasy coveralls clustered around dilapidated shops, smoking and looking defeated.

There was a helipad inside the fence at the main entrance where we touched down as the pilot cut the engine. Schmidt led us to a long two-story building, made of reinforced concrete on the ground floor. But the top floor looked like an elongated control tower with rows of windows leaning outward at a forty-five degree angle. Schmidt punched a keypad to open a strong metal door and ushered us inside. We climbed the staircase to the second floor into the control room and were greeted with a panoramic view of the entire facility, the pipeline, storage tanks, distribution center and the rail depot. Away from the row of consoles, which lined the windows, there was a round conference table covered with a white table cloth and elaborate place settings.

Schmidt suggested we have lunch before the tour. It was quite a spread, starting with an assortment of cold cuts, salami, liverwurst, tomato, cheese and rolls on the side. The main course was mixed sausages with grilled onions, sauerkraut and potato pancakes all washed down with beer. Every German city has its own local brew, said Schmidt, and in Leipzig the specialty was some cloudy stuff called "Gose," which came from a town called Goslar. It was hard to find these days, he said, because only a few breweries still made it. *Do you like it? Take a bottle with you with my compliments.* After that came dessert, Black Forest chocolate cake with cherries and whipped cream, and coffee. I started feeling so good from the food and drink I almost forgot what we came for.

I wished Spencer and I could talk, but we had to stay in character until we got far away from there and safely back to

1989
TIANANMEN SQUARE TO EAST BERLIN
JACK GODWIN

West Berlin. I really wanted to wreck as much of the pipeline as possible, plus as many storage tanks and tank cars as possible. I wanted to cripple the economy without killing anybody, if possible. Planning was the key. I yearned for architectural drawings of the facility or schematics. I wished I could take photographs but wasn't even going to bother asking. I wished the workers here wouldn't smoke so much, not because of lung cancer but because I didn't want any premature detonation, and I didn't want the blast or the fire to get out of control, if possible. Whenever I worked with explosives, I never wanted anybody near me who even carried cigarettes, matches or a lighter.

After lunch, we got a quick walking tour. One of the senior engineers accompanied us and Spencer peppered him nonstop with technical questions. Frankly, the place looked more impressive from the air. The tour ended where it started, outside the door of the long concrete building. Spencer asked one final question. When could we expect delivery of the goods? Schmidt deferred to the senior engineer. Usually it took two weeks from the date of the order, he said. The oil fields were on Yekaterinburg time, Western Siberia so it was four hours later. Today, they were already closed. If we put the order in on Monday the fourth, we could receive the shipment by the eighteenth. That was an educated guess. As the oil moved through the pipeline, we would receive updates. The closer it got, said the engineer, the more precise he could be.

"We'll let you know on Monday," said Spencer. We shook hands with the engineer and walked with Schmidt toward the helicopter. The ride back to Alexanderplatz seemed shorter. As soon as we touched down, Schmidt disembarked with us and the pilot took off again. Schmidt said he had a busy

1989
TIANANMEN SQUARE TO EAST BERLIN
JACK GODWIN

schedule. Otherwise he would give us a lift to the checkpoint. Thanks anyway, we said and cut across the square heading southwest toward Checkpoint Charlie.

When we got to the edge of the square, a taxi driver approached asking in English if we needed a cab but Spencer waved him off. Spencer coughed and covered his mouth and said we're being watched. It was two and a half kilometers to the checkpoint, he said, *let's walk*. We were under surveillance, visual and audio. Remember, Spencer said, the Stasi is in charge of surveillance of foreigners, and that includes any and all Westerners traveling and doing business in the country.

45.

FRIDAY, SEPTEMBER 1, late

When Spencer and I returned to Charlottenburg House, we briefed Dr. Benson on our day touring the Leunawerke facility with Markus Schmidt. When I lamented the lack of architectural drawings or schematics or photographs, Benson brought in an aerial surveillance technician.

"Unlimited aerial surveillance is still part of the original occupation agreement," the Tech explained.

"Did you take these from a Blackbird?" asked Spencer.

"No. Blackbirds are designed to operate at high speed and high altitude, which means the detail isn't any better than a satellite photo. We fly a converted B-47 bomber with cameras installed in the belly. All the occupying powers have the right to enter all East and West German airspace. So, we can take all the aerial reconnaissance photos we want. These were all shot at low altitude. Take a look at that detail," said the Tech. I could tell Spencer had a new best friend.

"Schmidt says the shipment will be delivered on the eighteenth," I said. "We'll receive updates as the stuff moves through the pipeline, but the eighteenth is a Monday, so the goods will be en route the Sunday before, when the facility will have a skeleton crew. Before they can load the train, they'll have to keep the oil in the storage tanks, at least overnight. Our best bet is to set the charges on Sunday, September seventeen."

"That's very risky. Why don't you just call in an airstrike?" said the Tech. "You'd have zero friendly casualties with the same result."

"Let's operate within the rules of engagement, shall we?" said Benson. "Cold war means espionage, in this case industrial sabotage."

"How about we use a Trojan Horse?" I suggested.

"Go on," said Benson.

"What did Lowry say? We'd need more than a thousand tank cars to hold two million barrels. What if we hid explosives in the tank cars? We could plant the explosives beforehand and detonate remotely, which would eliminate two risk factors. If we worked it right, we could take out the train, most of the rail yard and the storage tanks and maybe part of the pipeline, too."

"You forgot about the oil," said Spencer.

"That's right. And everything in the Leunawerke facility would get a fresh coat of benchmark grade Russian crude oil."

"I'll set up the logistics," said Benson.

"How's that work?"

"I'll call Deutsche Bundesbahn in Frankfurt" she said, "and talk to a shipping advisor about prices. Mutual Petroleum will need to complete a credit application before we can submit a shipping order. We're going to have to provide a lot of details so DB can review designated routes and transit times. On top of that, we'll be leasing their equipment. Even though we're going to blow up a couple hundred of DB's tank cars, everything should be professional in order to be totally convincing."

"Yeah, about that," said Spencer. "They're not going to be too happy about having a couple hundred of their tank cars blown up."

"That's what insurance is for," said Benson. "After it's all over, we can quietly approach DB's top management, tell them as much as they need to know, and compensate them for any losses not covered by insurance. I expect there to be some environmental damage, although I don't know how the GDR would file such a claim. No matter. It's worth whatever it costs."

Everybody nodded in agreement. Dr. Benson stood up with the aid of her cane and disappeared down the hall. I opened a copy of the *International Herald Tribune*.

"Spencer, listen to this."

"What is it?"

"They're demonstrating in Leipzig," I said.

"No kidding?"

"No kidding," I said, "Right in the middle of Karl Marx Square. There was a prayer meeting or something outside of the big Lutheran church. One of the pastors made a speech and called for people to resist the government. A big crowd started gathering and demanded freedom."

"Are there any reports of violence?"

"Not so far," I said, "but ever since Tiananmen Square, every time I read or hear about another protest, I think it's going to be the last straw and the Red Army's going to roll in guns blazing."

"I know the feeling."

1989
TIANANMEN SQUARE TO EAST BERLIN
JACK GODWIN

46.

MONDAY, SEPTEMBER 4

Dr. Benson informed us that everything was in motion. It's a good thing we got started, she said, because it takes two weeks for setup and processing. DB asked a lot of questions, and fortunately we had the right answers about the commodity, number of barrels, origin and destination of the shipment, name of the shipper, name of the receiver, the name of freight payer, and all the credit information.

"As far as Deutsche Bundesbahn is concerned, Mutual Petroleum is shipping two million barrels of Russian crude at the Leunawerke facility for delivery at the Panamax port in Marseille, in the south of France. As part of the order processing, DB will take care of all logistics door-to-door, and even have their own representative at the Grand Port in Marseille to make sure the shipment clears customs. The first shipment will be two hundred ten J-type tank cars, 75,000 gallon capacity. That comes out to fifteen million, seven hundred fifty thousand gallons. If we calculate thirty-two gallons to a barrel, that is exactly half a million barrels, at twenty-one dollars a pop that's ten million five total." She smiled.

"Any have any ideas how, where or when we'll set the charges?" I asked.

"The train with the empty tankers will pass through Vogtland on the way to Leipzig. Here, I'll show you." Dr. Benson pulled down a giant map of Central Europe. "Here's Leipzig, and here's the rail line which crosses through Vogtland and connects the southern part of East Germany, Saxony and Thuringia with Bavaria, Munich and other cities farther west. These are the Bavarian Alpine foothills here. There are several rivers flowing out of the Alps, the Weiss, Zwickauer, Goeltzsch and Saale." She pointed to each one in turn. "And you can see the tracks cross several river valleys, here, here and here. All these rivers mean viaducts and bridges and lots of opportunities."

"All we have to do is pick one."

"I have an idea," said Benson. "See this section here? This is the Erzgebirge Pass. You can't really see it on this map, but the grade on the western approach is quite steep here. Instead of climbing straight up, the tracks circle around and keep gaining elevation until they're high enough to get over the pass. But look right here where the track actually crosses over itself. That's the Erzgebirge Helix. It's a marvelous piece of German engineering. They built it in the late nineteen hundreds and somehow it survived two world wars."

"And the train slows down enough for us to hop on?" I asked.

"That's exactly right. You can wait right there on the bridge. German trains always run on time, so you'll know exactly when it's going to pass." Benson tapped the map with her finger.

"What do we use as an explosive device?" I asked.

"We could use Turtle Mines," said Spencer. "They're magnetic anti-tank grenades. They can penetrate two inches of steel plate, and the hull of a tanker isn't nearly that thick. Normally, they come with a delayed action fuse but that wouldn't work for us. We'd have to modify fifty or so with remote detonators and deploy them to the outside of the tanks cars, one at a time."

"They work like a sticky bomb?" I asked.

"We haven't used sticky bombs since WWII, but yeah."

"That seems labor intensive."

"True," said Spencer. "If all you wanted to do was to blow up the train, an airstrike would be less risky *and* less labor intensive. But we want to blow it while it's in the depot *after it's loaded*. Timing is critical. You have to arm these things before you attach them. Once they're armed, you can detonate all of them simultaneously. The only downside is the detonator has limited range."

"How limited is limited?"

"It depends on how many turtles you're firing at once. With this many, I'd say you'd have to be no more than a hundred yards away from the furthest one."

"That's the tricky part then," I said "because you've got to have cover and be clear of the blast."

"What if we had two detonators? There are two of us. What if we positioned ourselves at opposite ends of the train, or at least opposite ends of the depot where they sort the cars? Wouldn't that work?

"That would work," Spencer nodded.

"Okay," I said. "We've got the how and the where. Now all we need is the when."

"Let's plan on Sunday the seventeenth," said Benson. "Spencer, check with the armory to see how many Turtle Mines we have in inventory. I want you to start modifying the detonators immediately. Jaqui, you can check with the motor pool, something inconspicuous please, and collect whatever gear you'll require." Benson paused. "After you've completed attaching the mines, then what?"

"We'll have to get off the train before it pulls into the depot, preferably while it's still dark," said Spencer. "If the plan is to detonate after dark on Monday, we'll need someplace to hide out during daylight hours while they're loading the oil."

"I have an idea," said Benson. "We have a safe house in the *Tote Taeler*, the Dead Valley Campground, approximately thirty kilometers from the Leunawerke facility. It's just a cabin, but it's a legitimate safe house. If you go north toward Leipzig, eventually, you'll come to the Saale River. The campground is just across the river. You can't miss it. But you'll be on foot and thirty kilometers is a bit of a hike. Are you sure your leg is fully recovered Mr. Pang?"

"Yes ma'am."

"Okay then. The safe house is cabin number ten. The key is lodged under the front window. Just pull the sill toward you and slide it to the left. You've got your assignments. Good hunting."

47.

SUNDAY, SEPTEMBER 17

We departed Berlin early morning with me behind the wheel and Spencer riding shotgun. Berlin was an island inside East Germany. Our first task was to get out of East Germany on the special "foreigners only" autobahn. We headed west to get out as fast as possible before we made a big left turn and started heading south toward the Erzgebirge Pass. The farther south we went, the more spectacular the scenery got, like driving through a fairytale. As we crossed the alpine foothills of southern Bavaria, we drove over dozens of bridges and through dozens of tunnels as the road wound its way past one charming village after another, with lakes, castles and high mountain peaks decorating the landscape.

The sun was setting by the time we reached the pass. There was no paved road at the helix, so I pulled off to the side and far enough into a grove of trees so the car was out of sight.

"Let's leave the gear in the car and hike up to the helix," I said. "But bring the binoculars. I'd like to reconnoiter before dark."

"Lead the way," said Spencer.

We walked back to the road and followed it until we came to a dirt path that looked promising. We started climbing gradually and I could tell we were gaining altitude because my chest was pounding. The terrain was amazing. On one side, there was a steep drop-off thick with fir trees which plunged hundreds of feet down to a river. The maps and satellite photos we studied at Charlottenburg House didn't do this place justice. The air was so clean and clear it made the sun seem brighter even as it was setting. Up ahead, I could see where the trees had been cleared for the roadbed and train tracks. I checked left and right. "I don't see any happy wanderers. Let's follow the tracks and see what we can see."

"No wonder the Germans like beer. This mountain air is making me thirsty."

"The first round is on me," I said, "after we complete the mission."

"Look. There's the bridge."

We walked to the edge and peeked down. Sure enough, there was another set of tracks underneath. If you followed tracks, they circled around in a gigantic loop until they crossed right where we were standing.

"This is where we hop on?

"That's right."

"When's our train expected?" I glanced at my Ironman. "In about an hour," I said. "Let's hustle back to the car and get the gear. I'd like to give ourselves plenty of time to get into position."

Back at the car, I popped the trunk and pulled out two large black backpacks each carrying twenty-five turtles and a detonator. I put mine on and went through my equipment check: hand gun, backup, ammo, knife, knuckles, smoke, silencer and a grenade. I've always stuck to my little routine—because it's gotten me this far. Since this was an overnighter, I also carried water, energy bars and chewable caffeine tablets. We each had handheld radios and set them to the same frequency. I wiped the car clean and left the keys in the ignition.

We walked along the road again until we found the dirt path up to the helix.

"Can you find your way again?"

"No problem," I said.

In a few minutes, we were standing on the Erzgebirge Helix looking down at the track crossing below.

"I know what you're thinking."

"What's that," said Spencer.

"You're wondering if I'm going to put my ear on the rail and listen if the train's coming."

"The idea never occurred to me." Spencer laughed.

"You do it then," I said.

"I was born in Hawaii but I'm Chinese, not Native Hawaiian. We don't do that. They only do that in the movies I think. Maybe Schmidt was right," said Spencer, "too many movies."

"That's exactly what I said to Basil. Did you know the Chinese built the railroads in California?"

"Everybody knows that. Not to change the subject but when the train comes, how about if I go first?"

"I'll go first. I'll let the first locomotive pass—or locomotives depending on how many there are—and the first few cars, and then I'll jump down. Meantime, you let the rest of the train pass and jump onto the third or fourth to the last car. Then we'll plant the turtles on every other car or so, working our way toward each other. We'll meet someplace in the middle. Just make sure nobody in the caboose sees you."

"Nobody will see me. They don't use cabooses anymore."

"Really," I said "Why not?"

"Technology made them obsolete. These days they attach a beacon to the last car to identify the end of the train. The engineers have sensors in the cabin, which sends a signal if any car gets uncoupled or derailed. Besides, cabooses don't generate revenue. They're just dead weight."

The bridge began to vibrate and we heard the big diesel engines rumbling up the steep grade.

"Get down!" We lay flat waiting for the first locomotive to pass under the bridge, then another and then one more. There was the first tanker. Spencer signaled thumbs up and we moved to the other side of the bridge where the train came out. I let one more tanker roll past and jumped down onto the third tanker and took hold of the grab irons. As soon as I was sure of my footing, I turned and saluted Spencer over my shoulder. Two thumbs up.

Might as well get to work I said to myself. The train was barely moving so it would be a while before Spencer got on and a while longer before I met up with him. I flipped the backpack around to my chest, unzipped it and felt around inside. I pulled out a turtle, armed it and attached it to the hull of the tanker. It looked just like another valve. Spencer and I had twenty-five each, plus one handset each. That was one down, twenty-four to go. I closed the backpack and stood up as much as I could without letting go of the grab irons, made my way down the ladder and along the catwalk. My heart was pounding even though the train still was still barely moving. But I wanted to get a few more of these attached before the end of the train made it over the pass and began picking up speed.

I stretched across the couplers but I couldn't reach the grab iron on the next car without letting go. I took a deep breath and leapt to the next car. That's where the training

1989
TIANANMEN SQUARE TO EAST BERLIN
JACK GODWIN

paid off, I told myself. Once more along the catwalk and up the ladder I went. Now I had the routine. That was two down. But I had to remember I only had twenty-three left. Spencer said these were powerful enough to penetrate two inch steel plate. I should make sure to space them out, one every other car. I figured the front of the train must be well beyond the pass by now. We were still barely moving but now it felt like we were losing altitude, gradually descending. I wondered how Spencer was doing.

48.

SUNDAY, SEPTEMBER 17, late

It was too dark to count how many turtles I had left, but as I worked my way toward the middle of the train, I could feel the backpack was almost empty. I'd been at it two sweaty hours and was shivering in the night air even though it wasn't that cold. Just before I jumped to the next car, I glanced to my left, up ahead to the first locomotive. There were lights clustered on both sides of the track. That couldn't be the Leunawerke facility. Could it? I didn't recall seeing a train station on the satellite photo or the map. Besides, Benson said this line was for freight only, and no passenger trains. Where were those lights coming from?

Then there was a jolt and I almost lost my grip on the grab iron. Somebody must have hit the brakes hard because we started slowing down.

"Spencer, come in. *Spencer, come in.*"

"What is it?" said Spencer.

"Where are you?"

"I'm out of turtles and almost to the middle of the train." I looked back, but I couldn't see him.

"Lights up ahead, two maybe three hundred yards. We have to get off, *now*."

"Roger that."

1989
TIANANMEN SQUARE TO EAST BERLIN
JACK GODWIN

I waited a moment longer because now the train was really slowing down. Lying flat on the catwalk, I could see the lights shining on the first locomotive. The train came crawling to a complete stop. The engines were idling and someone was shouting orders up ahead. I slid backward, toward the end of the car and hopped down onto the gravel. It stank of oil and diesel fuel, but at least it was warm. I checked right and left. No sign of anything. I couldn't see much, so I scrambled down the embankment and into the trees. Ten yards in, I took a knee and listened and waited. No movement, no sound except for the engines idling in the distance.

I clicked my handheld once. Spencer clicked twice in response. Okay. Hold position.

"Halt!"

What the hell? That came from Spencer's direction, toward the end of the train. *Don't move. Don't move. Don't move.*

"Halt!" It came from the same direction but this time it was a different voice. Rifle shot, then another and another and then quiet again. I expected a fourth shot and waited for it, but no. Just muffled talk and then boots went jogging past me along the tracks toward the front of the train. Then I smelled cigarette smoke and decided I better go check it out.

Weapon drawn, I belly crawled toward the muffled talk. *Keep talking morons. That's just what I want.* There they were. Two of them, weapons shouldered looking toward the lights at the head of the train, waiting for their comrade to return. At this range, I could give them both a double tap. If they wasted Spencer, it wouldn't be murder. It'd be a righteous kill. It'd be justice. *It's a Cold War, Jaqui. Try to avoid shooting because it's sloppy tradecraft. Cold War means espionage. We can't broadcast it.*

I got up on one knee behind a big tree. And now, when I peered to the side, the rest of scene came into view. Spencer was dead on the ground. That settled it. I fished the silencer out of my vest and screwed it slowly onto the barrel until it was tight. I stepped out from behind the big tree, took aim and squeezed the trigger twice. *Pop. Pop.* He dropped like a rag doll. The other one turned toward me instinctively. He was just a kid and that was just too fucking bad. *Pop. Pop.* Down he went. I bent down to check Spencer's carotid. No pulse. His backpack was underneath him, still slung over his shoulder. I had to lift his arm and shift his body to remove the pack. If they found it and tested it, they'd find traces of explosives for sure. The important thing was he planted his share of the turtles.

I found Spencer's radio, the backup detonator and also found his weapon. Either they didn't have the time to search him or they never bothered. Lucky chance, it was the same make as mine. I holstered his weapon plus the spare ammo and then I put my pistol into his right hand. I fired two shots with his hand so he had powder burns, even though I doubted they'd do any forensics. Hopefully they'd fall for it and not come looking for me. They'd figure he was mortally wounded but still managed to get off a couple of rounds.

I whispered a prayer over Spencer's body and told him I got the guys who killed him and turned into the trees, moving perpendicular to the tracks. It was a moonless night, which had an upside and a downside. The upside was they'd never catch me. The downside was that I was sure to step in a pile of shit before sunup. When I got two hundred yards away from the tracks, I checked my compass and turned right. I

1989
TIANANMEN SQUARE TO EAST BERLIN
JACK GODWIN

didn't know where I was or how far I was from the Leunawerke facility, and I wouldn't know until I saw a landmark. As long as I traveled northeast, eventually I'd get to the Saale River.

Two hours later, I came to a steep riverbank. There was a footbridge crossing to the other side and a cluster of cabins. Before I put one foot on the bridge, I surveyed the area through the binoculars. It looked like a civilian campground, as opposed to an army camp which came as a great relief. At the other end of the footbridge, there was a small hand-painted sign welcoming me to the *Tote Taeler* Campground. I was exhausted and desperately needed sleep, if only for a few hours. Everything was quiet and all the lights were out, but the campground looked full. There was a Trabant parked next to almost every cabin, except one that looked empty. Number ten, that's the one I was looking for. I found the key right where Benson said it would be, slipped inside and closed the door behind me.

It was one room and very rustic with a wood burning stove, table and chairs, double bed stripped to the mattress. There was a lantern on the table and plenty of kerosene, so I lit it and took inventory. There were some canned goods and bottled water in the cupboards, wood stacked by the fireplace and not much else. But it was clean and warm and I could hardly believe my luck. Benson said the safe house was thirty kilometers from the depot. I could get there in six hours without breaking a sweat. The tricky part would be getting there in broad daylight. I wondered if the fishing was any good—probably not because of all the industrial runoff.

I set my alarm and fell into bed.

Daddy, do you want to play chess? Okay, but I'm going to try to beat you. I'm not letting you win. I'm going to beat myself. What do we call that? Self-defeating! That's right. You're a funny girl. What if I sacrifice my Queen? What's that mean? I start the game without my Queen to make it more even. Okay, I'll sacrifice mine, too. No, don't do that. Keep your Queen and I'll sacrifice mine. Otherwise there's no point. No, I don't want you to sacrifice your Queen. It's not fair. Let's just play regular. Can I go first? Okay. Why did you do that? It's called the Sicilian Defense. Never go against a Sicilian! What? Never mind. Before every move, ask yourself what you're planning to do next. Why? Try to see several moves ahead. Is that what you do? Yes. Remember to guard your king. Checkmate ends the game. What if there is no checkmate? What if it never ends? The game ends when everyone's dead.

1989
TIANANMEN SQUARE TO EAST BERLIN
JACK GODWIN

49.

MONDAY, SEPTEMBER 18, a.m.

Three taps on the door. What was that? At first, I couldn't remember where I was. Oh yeah. What time is it? Four forty-five. Three more taps on the door. I held my breath and tried to keep still.

"Open the door."

I swallowed so hard it hurt.

"Who's there?"

"Open the door, please. There is no time."

I knew that voice. Didn't I? That was Vladimir Ivanov. I drew my weapon, jumped off the bed, and crossed the room. I was still half asleep and my head was pounding. I opened the door, and there he was. He pushed into the room and closed the door.

"We must go, now" Ivanov said. Before I could utter one word, he grabbed me around the arm but I shook him off and ran back for the backpack. We rushed outside where there was a KGB staff car idling.

"Get into the back and stay down," he said. "They found your associate's body and the other two bodies. Something must have made them suspicious and they brought dogs to the scene. They do not know about the safe house, but they are tracking you and now they are closing in."

"How do you know about the safe house?"

"Our friend in Charlottenburg House told me."

"Basil," I said.

"No."

"Was it Bart Lowry?"

"No. Mr. Lowry is not very intelligent and he rarely provides information of any value. Please do not waste your time on him. Is this instance, the information came from Dr. Benson."

"What?"

"The information came from Dr. Benson."

"Wait. Wait a minute. What?"

"After the car bomb in Budapest, she invited me to join the counterintelligence group she chairs. I accepted her invitation."

"Does Basil Warburton know?"

"No," he said.

"Okay. What else do you know?"

"Dr. Benson told me nothing about your mission. She told me only about the safe house in the *Tote Taeler* Campground, cabin number ten. Unfortunately, however, the East German authorities now have your associate's body. Be quiet now. We are coming to a roadblock."

I couldn't see a thing but could feel the car slowing down and the cool air rushing in when Ivanov opened the window. I was holding my breath for the second time this morning, but the car never stopped and we just kept rolling, passing under the bright lights. The guards must have seen Ivanov's maroon colored shoulder boards and waived him through.

"You can get up now," he said. "That was a regular roadblock not an emergency roadblock. I think you are safe, for now."

"Okay, what else do you know? What do you know about the mission?"

"I do not have any information about that, as I said. But I might take a guess now that I know you are in this vicinity. Does it have something to do with the protests in Leipzig?"

"No," I said. "I heard about the big prayer meeting in Karl Marx Square. What else?"

"In Leipzig, nothing else," he said. "But people in other countries have heard about Leipzig and are doing the same thing, every Sunday night. There was one in Prague and it was the largest so far, seventy-five thousand people. The West German ambassador gave a speech from the balcony of the embassy. The train station is across the main square from the embassy. People became overly excited from the ambassador's speech. It was bad timing that a train coming from Berlin happened to stop at the station at that moment. What began as a peaceful demonstration almost turned into a riot. And it would have if not for the police."

"And you believe this is further proof that Soviet Union is going to collapse."

"That is what I believe, yes."

"And you want to help it along?"

"Of course," Ivanov said, "But you already know that."

I needed time to think how much I should tell him. Good tradecraft often involved opportunism and improvisation. It also involved dealing with some pretty sleazy people, at least in my experience. But Vladimir Ivanov wasn't sleazy. He was a KGB colonel, a professional. Basil didn't entirely trust Ivanov, for some reason, and he thoroughly disliked him for some *other* reason I'd probably never know. Maybe Basil was indebted to him. That made sense. Basil was the kind of guy who held a grudge when he should have felt gratitude. How much should I tell Ivanov? After calculating the risks, I decided the mission came first.

"We're planning a Trojan Horse scam at the Leunawerke oil depot," I said. "We posed as buyers from Kendall-Brown Petroleum. We bought two million barrels of Russian crude oil. The first shipment is due to be loaded on a tanker train tomorrow—today I mean—today. We planted magnetic mines on the inbound tanker cars. The train will arrive first thing this morning. Shortly after it arrives, they'll start sorting the cars and loading the tankers. I'm going to blow the train before it leaves."

"The blast and the fire will destroy Leunawerke."

"That's not all. We're also going to stop payment on the shipment. Knowing how desperate for hard currency East Germany is, we're hoping to disrupt the economy, create an energy shortage and seriously inconvenience the Schmidt crime family."

"That part I knew," said Ivanov.

"You knew Schmidt's nephew met with us?"

"I knew he met someone. Mr. Lowry informed me. But I did not know anything about the rest of your plan until now." Ivanov turned to me. "How can I help? Be specific. What do you need me to do?"

"I need to get inside the facility. The detonator has a short range."

"How short?" said Ivanov.

"With so many Turtle Mines firing at once, I need to be no more than a hundred meters from the furthest one."

"That will be a challenge," he said. "It would look very suspicious for a KGB colonel to suddenly appear at Leunawerke. I am known among other Stasi officers, but I am Russian. We need Colonel Gazecki. He is in Dresden and I know where to contact him. He could be here in a few hours especially if I told him you are here and need his help."

"That might hurry him up," I said.

We drove to a big hotel near the Leipzig train station, where Ivanov found a telephone and called Basil. They spoke briefly. Then Ivanov looked straight at me, and said yes a couple of times, and I was sure Basil was asking about me. Then he put the phone against his shoulder and checked his wristwatch, said yes again and hung up. Ivanov took a breath and switched back to English.

"Everything is arranged. He was not expecting a call from me so he was surprised. But he will be here this afternoon. He asked about you."

"I thought so. What did he say?"

"He said nothing. The line was not secure, and he knew to say nothing. There was the sound of relief in his voice." He studied me for a moment with sort of a half-smile half-smirk on his face and said, "You look hungry. We should get coffee and something to eat. I know a quiet place."

"I prefer a crowded place," I said "And wipe that fucking smile off your face."

"You mistake my meaning," he said.

"Do I?"

"Do you remember what I said on the bridge in Budapest?"

"No, but I remember I said you weren't a fool—or a communist." Ivanov laughed at this involuntarily.

"I said you were intelligent and elegant."

"Thanks. You can add hungry, thirsty and tired. And I stink. Let's go to the train station, must be some place to eat there."

1989
TIANANMEN SQUARE TO EAST BERLIN
JACK GODWIN

We walked a few steps from the hotel to Leipzig Central Station. We passed through the tall archway into a domed entrance hall. The room was flooded with light from windows lining the street and skylights which ran the length of the huge building. Big as it was, the place was full of travelers, running, walking, standing in line, sitting at the cafes, sleeping on the benches.

"Is this crowded enough? He asked.

"Enough," I said.

"What are your plans after this?"

"No plans," I said. "At least, I don't decide the plans. I execute the plans. My job is operational."

"May I make a suggestion?"

"You have an idea?"

"Yes," He said. "I would not trouble myself if I were speaking to the average American agent."

"What is it?"

"I know a way inside the Palace of the Republic."

"You know a way inside the palace? Yeah. Sure," I said.

"Yes," he said. "There is a tunnel, an escape tunnel for Joachim Schmidt and his family."

"It must be heavily guarded. It would be suicide."

"For anyone but you, it would be suicide. It is not heavily fortified. You see, very few East Germans know about it. I doubt if Colonel Gazecki knows or any other Stasi officer knows of it. It is a closely guarded secret."

"How come you know about it?"

"I know about it because the Russians built it. The palace was built in 1976. But in the late seventies and early eighties the strikes among the dock workers in Gdansk made Joachim Schmidt very uncomfortable."

"Lech Walesa," I said. "That was in Poland."

1989
TIANANMEN SQUARE TO EAST BERLIN
JACK GODWIN

"Yes, but when General Jaruzelski declared martial law in Poland, Schmidt decided to make contingency plans here. He asked the Russians, specifically the Red Army, to build him a secret escape tunnel."

"The Russians built it?"

"Not army regulars," he said "It was a special unit of coal miners conscripted from the Kuznetsk region in southwestern Siberia. They are all dead now, naturally."

"Naturally," I said. "Where is it?"

"The tunnel leads from President Schmidt's office in the palace, approximately one hundred meters west to the bank of the Spree River. There is a passageway inside the horse stables where it opens."

"That's on the east side of the wall."

"That is correct," he said. "The tunnel is part of his escape plan. There is a boat standing by for Mr. Schmidt, his family and perhaps a few members of the Politburo, which they would board and escape on the river."

"And there is a passageway in the stables on the Spree River," I said.

"Yes," he said.

"That's suicide."

"For anyone but you, yes."

"Why are you telling me this?"

"Because I am a patriot," he said "defending my country."

"I don't understand."

"*The powers of darkness shall be crushed by the spirit of light.* Boris Pasternak said that. The Soviet Union is not an evil empire. There is no need to crush it. I think of the Soviet Union as an unsuccessful political science experiment. A little revolution now and then is a good thing, is it not?"

"Now and then," I said.

50.

MONDAY, SEPTEMBER 18, p.m.

After breakfast, we spent the day killing time waiting for Basil to arrive. At four in the afternoon, Ivanov and I went to the rendezvous point, which was the same hotel lobby where Ivanov made the call. A few minutes later, Basil came in wearing his Stasi colonel's uniform, gunmetal gray jacket and pants, shirt and tie, shoulder boards and collar bars. I was pleased to see him, to say the least. I had plenty to tell him, and a million questions, but had to be cool as long as Ivanov was around. Plus, there was that uncomfortable tension between them.

Basil wanted to leave the hotel the moment he arrived. He brought maps of the facility and the surrounding area but wanted to reconnoiter the objective personally. Ivanov said he knew a good place to survey the topography. We took separate cars—I rode with Basil—out of town toward the Leunawerke facility. We followed Ivanov for almost an hour, when we turned north off the main road toward Leunawerke. I noticed how wide and well paved the road was, probably because of the truck traffic in and out of the facility. We passed a sign saying the entrance was two hundred meters on the left. As we followed Ivanov, the road circled to the left out of the flatland and into the trees. We came to a clearing

1989
TIANANMEN SQUARE TO EAST BERLIN
JACK GODWIN

and Ivanov pulled off the road. We came to a stop behind him and waited for the cloud of dust to disperse.

There it was. The helicopter Spencer and I took must have passed directly over this little bluff where we were standing. There was the big pipeline coming in from the east. And there were the two rail lines. There was the helipad and there was the control tower where Spencer and I had lunch. *Don't worry Spencer. I haven't forgotten.*

"Let's finish this, right now, *right fucking now.*"

"Jaqui," said Basil.

"What!"

"Remember your assignment."

"What're you talking about?"

"I'm talking about Tibor."

"What?"

"You have an assignment. Dr. Benson gave you an assignment. That's your job. The mission is your job. Planning is Benson's job, right?"

It made me dizzy. I thought about Spencer galloping one legged out of Tiananmen Square, lying on his back in the chopper, and then lying on his back by the railroad tracks. He was staring at nothing. And Tibor was lying on the table at the clinic moaning something. What did he say? He squeezed my hand so hard it hurt. *What did he say?* The border agent insulted you. But we were on a mission. That's what mattered, the mission. I blinked twice, three times.

"Right," I said. "If you can get me inside that depot, anywhere within a hundred yards of that train, I'll blow it to hell."

Basil opened the map on the hood of the car. He studied the map for a minute, then lifted his head and surveyed the depot. Then he ran his finger along the map where the main line split into multiple tracks running in parallel.

"Do you see these short tracks? This is where they load the cars, he said. After they're loaded, they shunt the cars here and hold them until they're ready to start forming up the train. Now, look down there. Can you see those rows of tank cars?" I could see them alright through the binoculars. There were eighteen or twenty sidings. And each one had fourteen or fifteen tankers just sitting there. "That's your objective," he said.

"Got it," I said. "How am I going to get out? Where's my egress?"

"I'll pick you up," said Basil.

"Are you sure?"

"Of course I'm sure. The blast will be my signal, and a perfect diversion. There'll be total chaos. Who's going to stop a Stasi colonel? I'll come in through the front gate and wait for you by the control tower, here." He pointed to the map again. It's far enough so it ought to be safe. There'll be plenty of light from the fire, even at night."

"Okay," I said. When do I pull the trigger?"

Basil and Ivanov looked at one another and back at me. Ivanov broke the silence.

"As soon after dark as possible would be best," he said. "The workers will have gone home for the day, which will minimize casualties. But you will need the cover of darkness to get into position."

"He's right," said Basil. "Starting from here, you'll have to hike down to the hill just to get to the edge of the depot. But then you'll have to sit tight until after sundown. From there, it might take you two hours to get into position."

"Let's say *balls-oh-five* then," I said. "That'll give me an extra hour, just in case. Are we agreed?" Ivanov looked at Warburton not understanding.

"Five minutes past midnight," said Basil.

"Balls-oh-five," Ivanov nodded and cocked his head slightly.

"Good. I should start making my way down the hill while there's still some light." I looked at Basil, at Ivanov and back again. "Before I go, please tell me you won't kill each other as soon as I'm gone."

"I promise not to kill him," said Basil.

"What is this?" said Ivanov. "I do not understand."

"Jaqui, you'd better go. I promise not to kill him. You have my word as a gentleman."

"Never mind him Colonel," I said to Ivanov. "He's just jealous. I want to thank you for saving my life. Thank you."

51.

MONDAY, SEPTEMBER 18, late

I put on my gear, made sure I had both detonators and said goodbye one more time as I started down the hill. The depot was directly south, perhaps an hour over rough terrain from this point. The sunset was spectacular, flaming orange and yellow. The evening air was dry and cool. There was no trail to follow, which was probably a good thing, because I didn't want any company. There was no sound except for birds, which was also good. An hour later, I came to the bottom of the hill and took a swig from my canteen. From this point forward, stealth took priority. I redistributed my weight, relaxed my muscles and controlled my breathing.

I came to the edge of the depot where the trees thinned out. There was no fence, so I crouched down, scanned the area for cameras or any other security devices and waited to see if there was a regular patrol. Still in stealth mode, I inched out of the trees and into the depot. The stench was overpowering. The place smelled of rotten eggs, ammonia and gasoline, rusting machinery, cleaning solvent, road-kill, burnt rubber and roasted almonds. It hurt to breathe so I tied a bandana over my nose and mouth. I moved slowly, silently down an aisle of massive crude oil tanks and followed a line of pipes that led to a tall tower with a flame that shot

1989
TIANANMEN SQUARE TO EAST BERLIN
JACK GODWIN

straight up. That was the only sound, like a blow torch fire clicking on and off every few seconds.

Looking left, there were more tanks, taller and narrower, not as massive but still huge. Looking right, there was a row of boxy-looking buildings with pipes coming in, going out and running in every direction, each one with twin chimneys. There was the big pipeline on stilts which meandered in from the east, and crossed my path straight ahead. Still no sign of security, no sentries, no patrols, no nothing but I took a couple of steps backward anyway, held my breath and waited. Off to the left, a tiny red light caught my eye. It glowed for a couple of seconds and disappeared. Then it glowed again, but this time it moved exactly the way a cigarette moves when someone drops their hand after they take a puff. That was him—the lone sentry—standing in front of the long concrete building with the control tower. I watched the routine again and wondered if he was having his first cigarette of the night. That's a bad habit but it gave me a slight advantage because it impaired his night vision.

I checked my Ironman: less than two hours to go. I got down onto my belly and crawled out into the open. The stench was even worse this close to the ground and something stung my eyes. I worked my way underneath the big pipeline until I came to the first set of tracks where the tankers were waiting until dawn when they were due to roll out to Marseille in the south of France. I crawled under one tanker, then another, and then another. From that angle, I could see where the turtles were magnetized to the hulls. At the stroke of midnight, every one of these suckers was going to release an enormous amount of energy and produce a detonation wave that would travel very fast and get very, very hot. The clock was ticking and I had to find someplace close enough for the detonators to be in range but far enough away to be clear of flying debris.

It was a quarter 'til twelve when I got beyond the last siding and into position behind a low concrete wall. Fifteen minutes to spare. I took another swig and checked if the cigarette smoking man was still on duty, but couldn't see him from this angle. At five minutes past midnight, I fished the two detonators out of my backpack and began the countdown. I pulled the triggers simultaneously and discharged the Turtle Mines. I was face down behind the wall so I couldn't see the explosion, but I heard it and I felt it. I don't know what happened to the lone security guard. I never saw him again. I walked over to the long building with the control tower, which was intact except for the broken windows. Basil was waiting for me, standing next to the car with the engine idling.

"Nice uniform you're wearing, Konrad," I said.

Basil spun the car around and we took off through the main gate. Outside of Leipzig, we stopped on the Elsterbecken Bridge where I tossed the backpack with the detonators in the river. We went to Basil's room at the hotel near the train station where we slept until mid-morning. The mission was a complete success, I thought, until Basil showed me the newspaper over breakfast. They interviewed the security guard, who knew nothing and saw nothing. He was a little shaken up but otherwise in good health. The blast and ensuing fire destroyed the Leunawerke facility, the depot, rail yard and a large section of the Druzhba pipeline. Like I said, I thought the mission was a complete success until I heard about the casualties. A family of seven, mother, father and five kids killed in the fire. They weren't supposed to be

1989
TIANANMEN SQUARE TO EAST BERLIN
JACK GODWIN

there, obviously. They were scavenging for fuel or something and evidently were in the wrong place at the wrong time.

That's what triggered the biggest demonstration in the history of East Germany that morning. It took place in Leipzig and it wasn't because of the economic damage. It was because of that poor family I killed. It was impossible to tell for sure, but there must have been more than a million people in Karl Marx Square. It was clear the authorities—by that I mean the local party leaders—weren't in charge any more, not really. The speakers, one after another, were all dissidents and opposition leaders and every one of them was fearless. And they were organized. People distributed pamphlets, brought homemade banners and signs. Something changed as though the revolution had started and couldn't be stopped. The local police were there, plus a few others in military uniforms, and all they could do was stand and watch.

52.

TUESDAY, SEPTEMBER 19

"I need to get to West Berlin. I need to talk to Dr. Benson. Can you help me get across the border?"

"You must be joking. For starters, you don't have any papers. You're here illegally. The only way would be south through Czechoslovakia and Hungary, and then across the border into Austria."

"That's not an option. There are four dead border guards at the checkpoint on the road from Czechoslovakia. They may not have a picture of me, but they'll at least have a description. I can't go back there."

"What do you intend to do? You cannot cross into West Germany. It's madness. I'm afraid you're here for the duration."

"I'm here for the duration?" I asked, "For the duration of what? I don't have diplomatic immunity. If I get caught, I'm dead. Understand?" Basil acknowledged this with a curt nod.

"You'll have to go into hiding. I'll bring you to East Berlin, which ironically may be the safest place for you right now."

"I need to talk to Benson."

"What about," he asked.

1989
TIANANMEN SQUARE TO EAST BERLIN
JACK GODWIN

"I can't tell you, but I need to see her face to face. I'm sure she'll bring you in on it. I hope she will, but I can't be the one to tell you."

"It doesn't matter. You can't cross. I don't think Benson should cross either. She's too high profile. She'd be under surveillance from every direction. The easiest way to get to you would be to follow her. Even if you didn't meet, the Stasi would know something was up. If Benson put her big toe into East Berlin, they'd be on alert."

"Just get me to East Berlin and then we'll figure something out," I said.

It was after dark when we arrived. We argued back and forth about getting me over to the west, but it was no good. Basil simply refused to cooperate. It didn't help that I refused to tell him why I needed to see Benson face to face. Finally, we agreed to a compromise, which involved finding a look alike in West Berlin and sending her through Checkpoint Charlie. That way, we could switch clothes and documents, and I could cross back over into West Berlin. It took two weeks to find someone and we were into October by the time I made my way back to West Berlin.

53.

TUESDAY, OCTOBER 3

I was waiting for Dr. Benson on the top floor of Charlottenburg House when she and Basil Warburton—to my complete astonishment—walked into the secure conference room.

"What're you doing here? How'd you get across?" I said.

Benson held up her hand.

"Mr. Warburton is here at my invitation. Now, tell me about the Leunawerke mission."

My briefing took almost an hour. Basil heard most of it already, but not everything. Despite the civilian casualties—perhaps even *because* of the civilian casualties—Benson considered the mission a complete success. Now there were demonstrations every week in every major city in the east. The economic disruption was very real but secondary to the political fallout.

"Congratulations," said Benson. "I'm recommending you for the Medal for Meritorious Achievement in recognition of your extraordinary and exceptional service to national security."

"Thank you," I said. "What about Spencer?"

"Captain Pang will receive the Memorial Star in recognition of his exceptional act of heroism. I will personally guarantee his family in Hawaii receives it," she said.

"There's something else," I said. "After Spencer was killed, I went to the safe house in the Dead Valley Campground, Cabin No. 10, just like you said."

"Yes?" said Benson.

"The East Germans were closing in. They had dogs tracking me. It was a close call."

"Of course," said Benson.

"That's not it," I said. "Vladimir Ivanov came to the rescue. He came out of nowhere. He knew about the safe house but not only that. He knew I'd be there. At least he knew somebody would be there. Why didn't you tell me?"

"Information security," she said. "Compartmentalization and risk management are imperative."

"I don't think you understand. Ivanov didn't know anything about the mission. Do you know what this means?"

"There's a leak," said Basil.

"It's Lowry." I said, "That weasel Lowry."

"I'll take care of it," said Benson.

"That weasel got Spencer killed, I'm sure of it."

"I said I'll take care of it. Was there anything else?"

"Yes," I said. "And it's the most important thing."

"Yes?"

"What I have to say would normally be classified Top Secret NOFORN," I said, as I moved my eyes from Benson to Basil and back again.

"Understood," she said. "Please proceed."

"After the safe house, Ivanov took me to Leipzig and he called Basil. While we were waiting Ivanov told me about a secret passageway in the Palace of the Republic. It's

Schmidt's escape tunnel." Benson and Basil both shifted in their seats. "Not for us, though" I said. "For us, it could be an entry tunnel."

"Do you know anything about this?" Benson turned toward Basil. He shook his head and scoffed.

"If it sounds too good to be true, it probably is," he said. "I'm sorry. This sounds too good."

"I know. But if not for Vladimir Ivanov, I'd be dead and you'd be sending a Memorial Star to my mother."

"Okay, okay" said Benson. "So there's a tunnel, a secret tunnel. What else?"

"Ivanov told me the Russians built it, Siberian coal miners. And they're all dead, and that's why nobody knows, not even the Stasi."

"This tunnel," said Basil, "Do you know where it is?"

"Yes," I said. "It lets out near the Spree River inside the old royal horse stable. That's according to Ivanov. I haven't checked it out yet."

"We'll need to verify that," said Basil.

"Of course," said Benson. "I'd like pictures if we could manage it. Meanwhile, Jaqui, you don't go near the place. If this tunnel is so secret that not even the Stasi knows it exists, we may or may not send you in, but let's not do anything that might limit our options in the future."

54.

SUNDAY, OCTOBER 8

Yesterday was the fortieth anniversary of East Germany's founding. There was a huge celebration, of course, and a military parade along Unter den Linden toward the Palace of the Republic. Mikhail Gorbachev was on the grandstand next to President Joachim Schmidt beneath gigantic red banners. Gorbachev was the guest of honor and gave a pretty standard speech about his two favorite subjects, glasnost and perestroika, transparency and reform. But he also humiliated Joachim Schmidt when he said *life punishes those who arrive too late*. Schmidt was furious, but the crowd loved it and began chanting "Gorbi, Gorbi" and shouting "Gorbi help us!"

The morning newspaper had a picture on the front page. It showed Gorbachev on the grandstand in his topcoat and fedora looking bored and checking his wristwatch. That said it all. The great celebration of the glory of socialism turned into a fiasco. The Leunawerke explosion left the economy in a shambles and the country was falling apart. East Germans were fleeing through Czechoslovakia and Hungary every day by the thousands, but thousands more stayed behind. The ones who chose not to flee were getting more vocal and better organized with each passing day.

55.

MONDAY, OCTOBER 9

Dr. Benson's reconnaissance team confirmed Ivanov's information. The tunnel was inside the stables, just like Ivanov said. Photos showed a small cluster of buildings, including a barn with a wide center aisle, tack room, wash rack and ten stalls, five on each side. The middle stall on the side closest to the river had a hatch in the floor and a low, T-shaped air vent. The stall was covered with hay, but you could see in the photos the floor was concrete. The hatch looked like any storm door, metal painted battleship gray, handle on one side and a row of heavy-duty hinges along the other.

"The good news is that security is very light. There weren't any uniformed guards. The only people our team saw were staff members, stable hands to feed the horses and clean the stalls. Better assume they're armed, just to be safe," said Benson. Then she turned to Basil. "Mr. Warburton, you've been inside the palace. What can you tell us?"

"It's a five story complex, which includes the East German parliamentary chamber, legislative offices, auditorium, cinema, art gallery, post office—there's even a disco," he said.

1989
TIANANMEN SQUARE TO EAST BERLIN
JACK GODWIN

"We obtained some old architectural plans for the building," said Benson. She unrolled the blueprint and pointed while she spoke. "You should study these carefully, but concentrate on this side, where Schmidt's executive offices and his private residence are located. The executive offices are on the fourth floor and the residence is on the top floor. I doubt there's direct access to the tunnel. There may be an elevator, but they would never use it if there was a real emergency. Look for a staircase. These are the original blueprints from seventy-three, so they may not be entirely accurate. However, there are foundation walls everywhere on the ground floor, and they couldn't move those very easily. The tunnel was built seven years later, so anything's possible, I guess."

I nodded. Benson continued.

"This side of the palace is closest to the river, and therefore closest to where the tunnel lets out under the stables. According to the information from Ivanov, the tunnel is a hundred meters long. If we measure that distance from the stables, give or take twenty meters, the other end of the tunnel must be somewhere here." And she made an arc with her finger back and forth on the blueprint of the ground floor. "That's where you'll come out. That's the best I can do for you."

"What's the mission?" I asked.

"The mission is to plant listening devices in the Palace of the Republic," she said. "One should go in Schmidt's executive office. Another should go in his nearest conference room. The third should go on his telephone, if possible. Improvise if necessary but we want to keep the existence of the tunnel secret. They can't know that we know. That means no lethal force is authorized, not even in self-defense. Those are the rules of engagement."

"Got it," I said.

"You'll be coming out the same way you go in, through the tunnel. You'll be armed with whatever you usually carry, but we'll equip you with a tranquillizer gun loaded with a ballistic syringe, which will immobilize your target."

"It is like a sedative?"

"No. Sedatives aren't an option, one because they work too slowly and two because they're unreliable. The syringe in the dart contains a fast-acting paralytic agent. It won't kill anybody, nor will it knock them out. But it will paralyze them instantly and keep them that way for five or six hours depending on body weight." Benson paused. "There's another task for you, one which you might even enjoy." She handed me a manila envelope. "We want you to plant these pictures. Don't hide them. Leave them in plain sight where somebody will find them."

They were pictures of Spencer Pang and Joachim Schmidt's nephew Markus in Alexanderplatz.

"How did you get these?"

"Never mind that," said Benson. "We're hoping to sow a little internal discord. Stasi spies and informants are everywhere. We're hoping whoever finds them will assume the Stasi took the pictures, not us. Whoever finds the pictures won't necessarily start looking for listening devices."

"Ma'am, the tunnel is an escape route *from* the palace *to* the stables. We need someone inside the palace." I looked to Basil for support.

"I'm with Jaqui on this," he said. "We're asking her to take a big risk. You reconnoitered the best you could on the outside. I'd feel more comfortable if I could have a look inside the palace."

"Okay," she said. "I want you to get back to East Berlin as soon as possible, today. You can brief Jaqui when we send her across."

56.

WEDNESDAY, OCTOBER 11, early

I crossed through Checkpoint Charlie back into East Berlin after midnight and made my way to the stables. There was a clump of trees east of the stables along the riverbank where Basil was waiting for me wearing civilian clothes.

"What did you find?" I asked, "Anything?"

"The other side of the tunnel leads into the wine cellar and then the kitchen. I haven't been inside the tunnel, but your way is clear inside the palace. There's one guard on this end. Other than that, the information we got from Benson's reconnaissance team is all we have to go on."

"Thanks." Our eyes met as we stood facing each other. "Let's plan on London," I said.

"Right, here's a torch. Cheers then," he smiled.

I made my way in the darkness toward the stables. The stable hand was snoozing on a wooden stool. I hit him with a dart without waking him. I retrieved the dart and then found his weapon, which meant he was more than a stable hand, but not much more.

I found the hatch in the middle stall, opened it and crept down the staircase. The walls were stained and the air was stale and damp. The flashlight echoed when I clicked it on. At the bottom of the stairs I shined the flashlight forward and

1989
TIANANMEN SQUARE TO EAST BERLIN
JACK GODWIN

the light disappeared into infinity. It got darker and quieter the deeper I went, but eventually I came to another staircase identical to the one beneath the stable.

Up the stairs I went. At the top, there was a small landing where I stopped to catch my breath. There was a metal door, unlocked thanks to Basil. Before I turned the handle, I peeked at the bottom and couldn't see any light. I pushed the heavy door slowly, very slowly, nervous beyond words about squeaky hinges giving me away. When I got the door open about six inches I stopped and listened. Then I pushed it open just wide enough for me to slip inside.

It was the wine cellar. When I closed the heavy door behind me, it disappeared into the wall perfectly camouflaged. Across the cellar I took the other staircase up to the kitchen. I made my way around the stainless steel work tables toward a set of double doors and into a large dining room. I moved quietly across the room, which brought me to the farthest northwest corner of the building where the blueprint showed a staircase. There it was, concealed behind heavy drapes of red, gold and black. I paused for a moment and thought this would be a good place to plant one or two of the devices. A dining room was as good as a conference room, right? That's what I thought, and planted two underneath the table, one at each end.

I passed the second floor landing and noticed there was no door. I passed the third floor and it was the same thing so I just kept climbing. The fourth floor was different. I paused to slow my heartbeat and control my breathing. I still couldn't see any sign of security, said a silent prayer of thanks and drew the dart gun just in case. The same heavy drapes in red, gold and black concealed the staircase and I parted them to peer into the room. There were carved columns in dark brown wood and wallpaper that was yellow and peeling. It was Schmidt's office!

There was a large wooden desk a few feet away and a leather chair. There were two telephones on the desk, so I bugged the one closest if you were sitting at the desk. Then I pulled the top drawer, but it was locked. I tried one after another but none of them opened. There was a low cabinet behind the desk decorated with framed photos of Schmidt, his wife and family and two small bronze busts of Marx and Lenin. I opened one of the cabinet doors and planted a device inside, behind the top hinge. Then I heard something.

"Wer bist du?" said the voice.

I turned and saw a white haired man wearing a bathrobe. I was so startled my reaction was instinctive. I drew my weapon and took aim, but hesitated because he looked so frail. As long as he didn't call for help, I was sure I could defend myself. He fumbled with his glasses as I crossed the room toward him. I recognized who he was, Joachim Schmidt, General Secretary of the Socialist Party and President of the German Democratic Republic, although he looked ten years older than the pictures in the newspaper. He looked broken.

"Wer bist du?" he repeated, and then "Sind Sie Zigeunerin?"

"No."

"Ah, you are American. You do not look American." I noticed he switched to English effortlessly. "Are you here to assassinate me?"

"No."

"What then, to kidnap me?"

"No."

1989
TIANANMEN SQUARE TO EAST BERLIN
JACK GODWIN

He took a few steps toward me, squinted and studied me from head to toe. I took a step backward and held my aim, not sure what to do. He walked around the desk and flopped in the big leather chair.

"Why are you pointing that at me?"

"In case I have to shoot," I said. "If I don't aim carefully, I might kill you instead of wounding you." I guess his eyesight wasn't that good even with glasses because he didn't notice I was pointing a dart gun at him, not a pistol. He looked so frail.

"Shoot me. It does not matter."

"Maybe I will. But first I want you to listen to me. I'm the one who blew up the Leunawerke facility and the pipeline. You know the dead body they found by the train tracks?" He nodded. "He was my friend and his name was Spencer. I'm the one who killed the two soldiers they found on the ground next to him. Spencer and I posed as buyers. Do you know who the seller was? It was your nephew Markus."

"He is my sister's boy."

"Is he? Well, Markus has been feathering his nest, selling oil for hard currency, a lot of hard currency. He's a capitalist, a real risk-taker. He's got that entrepreneurial spirit we admire so much in America. Here are some pictures of him in the Alexanderplatz talking—negotiating—with my friend Spencer. Here's a good one of Markus and Spencer climbing into his helicopter." I put the envelope on the desk and watched the tremor in his hands and the horror on his face.

"You should think about resigning, maybe tomorrow. No wait. It's already after midnight. You should think about resigning today." Then I walked around the desk toward him, took the dart out of the gun and stuck it into his neck. The paralytic agent went to work immediately. Schmidt looked up at me with a fish mouth. His arms went slack and he dropped the envelope on the floor beside him. I took a look around and slipped back behind the curtain, down the stairs and into the kitchen.

I retraced my steps back through the tunnel, carefully closing up behind me. The stable hand was lying right where I left him. I waited a few hours until I was sure Checkpoint Charlie would be busy and crossed back into West Berlin.

1989
TIANANMEN SQUARE TO EAST BERLIN
JACK GODWIN

57.

WEDNESDAY, OCTOBER 11, a.m.

The listening devices were working perfectly. At Charlottenburg House, we listened to Schmidt and Klaus Fischer—the head of Stasi—get into a terrific argument. Schmidt ordered his personal bodyguards to place Fischer under arrest, but Fischer was a step ahead of him.

Of course, we couldn't see anything but we heard shouting and then a brief scuffle. Fischer had his own men—loyal Stasi officers—stationed outside and they overpowered Schmidt's bodyguards. If Schmidt was younger and stronger, I'm sure he would have had Fischer taken out and shot. But he was powerless now, and nothing proved that better than when the head of state security disarmed the president's bodyguards. This was a coup. Schmidt's bodyguards were allowed the dignity of escorting him to his car, which was waiting in the basement garage. Then Fischer dismissed his men and asked for Bernd Becker—Schmidt's deputy and second ranking member of the Politburo—to be brought in.

"You will have to go on television tonight and announce that Schmidt has decided to step down, due to ill health," said Fischer.

"Yes, of course" said Becker.

1989
TIANANMEN SQUARE TO EAST BERLIN
JACK GODWIN

"We must call an emergency meeting of the Politburo, immediately, today. I want to expel Ulrich Wagner and Dieter Hoffmann. Wagner's policies have made our economic situation worse and Hoffmann has been too liberal with the media. There have been too many negative stories—and too many stories altogether about the demonstrations. I want them both out today."

"Are you planning to install yourself as president?"

"You forget yourself, Mr. Becker. Did you know we have a black file on Joachim Schmidt? Would you like to see it? Would you like to see yours?"

"Thousands of our people are fleeing to the West every day. What would you have me do?"

"I have already told you. Call a meeting of the Politburo and get rid of Wagner and Hoffmann. How can I be any clearer?"

We were monitoring East German television that night when they interrupted their regular programming to announce the resignation of Schmidt and the appointment of Bernd Becker as his successor. Schmidt didn't appear but issued a brief statement citing his poor health. I couldn't help but wonder if he told anyone about the pictures of his nephew. And if he did, I wonder if anyone believed him. Becker read a canned statement that could have been written by the pigs on *Animal Farm* urging the East German people to work harder. He was planning to chart a new course, a change of direction he called it, but I doubted anyone believed him. Bernd Becker certainly looked younger than Schmidt, so maybe there was some hope. Maybe Becker would be the Mikhail Gorbachev of East Germany.

58.

THURSDAY, OCTOBER 12

In the morning papers, congratulations came in from everywhere. President Bush was cautious as usual, said it was too soon to tell. From Moscow and Bonn to London and other European capitals, leaders were hopeful the change would bring about national renewal and a better life for East Germans. In East Berlin, political dissidents were the exact opposite of hopeful. One of the leaders said the solution to socialism wasn't more socialism. Another quoted that old song by The Who, and said the new boss was same as the old boss.

59.

FRIDAY, OCTOBER 13

We continued to monitor the listening devices all day and night. Becker and the Stasi head Klaus Fischer were desperate about the protests. They decided to create a special Stasi infiltration unit armed with clubs and cattle prods and with specific orders to pick fights and disrupt peaceful protests.

"Who is this colonel we are meeting?"

"Konrad Gazecki," said Fischer. "He trained at Gaczyna and worked for us in London. He was recently in Hungary."

"You had quite a few of your agents killed in Hungary."

"Yes, I know," said Fischer.

"Do you still trust him?"

"You asked me for my best officer. If I did not trust Colonel Gazecki, do you think I would have sent for him?"

"We must put a stop to these protests with a show of force. We must respond to this crisis the same way the Chinese responded to the demonstrations in Tiananmen Square, with strength."

"I agree," said Fischer. "We must eliminate the leaders before the situation gets out of hand."

"Yes, but we must have a reason. We cannot simply open fire on peaceful protesters. Moscow would abandon us."

1989
TIANANMEN SQUARE TO EAST BERLIN
JACK GODWIN

"Then we will manufacture a reason."

"Very well," said Becker. "Bring in Colonel Gazecki."

There was dead air for an hour, until Bernd Becker and Klaus Fischer returned and welcomed Colonel Konrad Gazecki into the room. Fischer began.

"Colonel Gazecki, come in. This will not take long. You may remain standing," said Becker.

"Colonel, the Ministry of State Security has an assignment for you. That is, to put an end to the anti-revolutionary criminal protests. Here is a written order authorizing you to reassign members of the Felix Dzerzhinsky Regiment. You know what to look for, specialists in anti-protest tactics, that sort of thing," said Fischer.

"Thank you Herr Minister." Basil's voice was easily recognizable.

"Colonel, you are authorized to use whatever force you think is necessary. I encourage you to emulate the Chinese solution," said Becker.

"If you mean the Chinese government's response to Tiananmen Square, sir, I am not sure that would be effective."

"That is exactly what I mean and I do not care what you think. I was in Beijing earlier this month. I can tell you from personal experience, the Chinese solution is the only acceptable solution. Those protesters are animals. They are pigs. And when I say you may use whatever force you think is necessary, it means I want you to club the pigs into submission. Is that clear?"

"Yes, Herr Minister."

"You are dismissed, Colonel." We heard Basil close the door on his way out. Becker spoke first.

"Are you certain he is up to the job?"

"Oh yes," said Fischer. "Colonel Gazecki has a reputation for brutality. In London he assassinated a spy in the Soviet Embassy who was working for British Intelligence. He is up to the job."

"I am sure he has the necessary skills. That is not my meaning. Is Colonel Gazecki committed to the revolution?"

"Of course he is. But I would never rely on one person. The time has come for new tactics." We heard the sound of a buzzer then Becker said, "Send in Maria Borodina."

"Comrade Borodina," said Fischer. "Sit down. The Ministry of State Security appreciates your [garbled transmission] Charlottenburg House despite your [garbled transmission] as KGB liaison officer.

"Yes, Comrade Minister."

"The ministry has an additional assignment for you now. Are you familiar with Colonel Konrad Gazecki?"

"Yes, Comrade Minister. Colonel Gazecki and I went to school together, in Russia."

"Thank you, Comrade. Permit me to compliment your German accent. However, a simple yes or no will suffice." A moment passed.

"Yes, Comrade Minister."

"Colonel Gazecki has been ordered to [garbled transmission] anti-revolutionary criminal protests. We want you to observe the colonel's activities and report back. You are to deliver your reports verbally, nothing in writing."

"Yes, Comrade Minister. I am to observe and report."

"Yes. Forgive the informality, but I love all people and want only to keep things under control. Sadly, the protesters get bolder every time we make an arrest. And Colonel Gazecki is known to be a hothead. If he or any his men commit any acts of aggression, you must [garbled transmission]."

1989
TIANANMEN SQUARE TO EAST BERLIN
JACK GODWIN

"Yes, Comrade Minister."

60.

MONDAY, OCTOBER 16

Dr. Benson and I met at Charlottenburg House and studied the transcript. We shook our heads trying to make sense of it.

"What the hell? Did Klaus Fischer just say *he loves all people*? He's losing it," I said.

"Did you hear what Fischer said about Charlottenburg House? I couldn't follow."

We replayed the recording, then asked the technician to enhance the audio and then replayed it again several times.

"You called Maria Borodina an administrative detail." I said.

"Ouch. I remember."

"I said take her into custody. You said let her go."

"Obviously it was a mistake, my mistake," said Benson.

"We can still take her into custody."

"How?" she asked.

"Let me go back to East Berlin."

"Alright, but what else do we know about her?" she asked. "The dossier we had on her in Budapest was pretty thin. I'll ask if we have a file here that might be more helpful."

"Good," I said. "I want to keep an eye on her while she's keeping an eye on Basil."

61.

TUESDAY, OCTOBER 17

We already knew Maria Borodina was beautiful, intelligent, charming and fluent in several languages. We learned from the Charlottenburg House file on her that she had the rank of major in the KGB, a vacation villa in the Crimea and an apartment in Paris. She is alleged to have worked as an assassin, and preferred administering a drug overdose. Borodina was sexually uninhibited, which we understood from the details Basil provided. However, she was no run of the mill prostitute spy. Maria Borodina was cold and calculating, meticulous and dangerous, and totally unsympathetic toward her victims.

While I waited for Benson to give me the green light to go back into East Berlin, I monitored the listening devices in the Palace. I learned that the Berlin Theater Ensemble submitted an application to hold a rally in front of the theater in Alexanderplatz. These days, there were protests in every big city throughout the Soviet Bloc, but the Alexanderplatz protest would be the first one since Joachim Schmidt resigned and Bernd Becker took over as party leader and president. Becker's response would tell everyone whether he was serious about changing direction, or if he was nothing but a puppet of the communist hardliners.

At first, Becker and Fischer didn't know what to do with the application. Nobody in the history of East Germany ever submitted such an application before, complete with a list of speakers who would talk about "democratization". They were laughing and couldn't decide whether to prohibit the rally or permit it. In the end, Becker and Fischer decided to approve the application but only because they believed Konrad Gazecki and his crew would disrupt it.

62.

WEDNESDAY, OCTOBER 18

That morning, I crossed back into East Berlin and headed straight for Alexanderplatz. I arrived an hour early while the crowd was still relatively sparse. By mid-morning, there were tens of thousands of people milling around. I watched them build an outdoor stage in front of the Berlin Theater and hang a huge yellow banner with the words *No Violence*. Then I spotted Basil and backed out of sight. He was standing with a crowd of tough-looking men who must have been his crew from the Felix Dzerzhinsky Regiment. I knew Maria Borodina couldn't be far away. And I was relieved we never met face-to-face in Budapest. I knew her but she didn't know me.

At half past ten, the first speaker, a locally famous stage actress came onstage. She was followed by other dissidents, all of them actors, writers and artists, leaders of human rights groups and members of the clergy. Some of the speeches were very bold I thought, as though they wanted to provoke a confrontation. As I listened, I watched Warburton and his crew, who didn't even seem to be paying any attention. Considering their reputation as specialists in anti-protest tactics, there was an awful lot of horseplay. I couldn't help but compare the scene to Tiananmen Square, where the atmosphere was so tense.

By now, people were pouring into Alexanderplatz, thousands of them chanting and carrying signs and banners proclaiming democracy and freedom and denouncing the Berlin Wall. One man next to me was shouting so loudly his whole body shook. Then a woman got up to speak, who said she was a lawyer for one of the opposition parties. She said it was time to rewrite the constitution and do away with the paragraph that reserved all the power for the Socialist Party. She wasn't a very good speaker, but she got the crowd to quiet down so she didn't have to shout over them. She spoke like a lawyer, like she was making a case. When she he was done, she just turned and walked away and got the loudest response of anyone so far.

Then the crowd started moving, shuffling out of Alexanderplatz toward the Brandenburg Gate, which was a stone's throw from the Berlin Wall. I was trying to keep one eye on Basil and his gang when there was a loud bang right behind me. The noise startled everyone and we all turned to see what it was. It wasn't a protester. It was a waiter wearing an apron. He bent down and then he stood up holding a wobbly metal sign which someone must have knocked over. When I turned back, Basil was looking right at me. And our eyes locked. And Maria Borodina spotted us. She looked at Basil and then right at me. *Fuck!* I turned away as casually as I could and tried to disappear into the crowd. I pulled a hat out of my pocket and put it on to change my profile.

Oblivious to this little life-or-death drama, the crowd continued to move like a great herd. There was no way for me to stay close to Basil and simultaneously avoid Maria Borodina, so I just kept my head down and let the wave to

1989
TIANANMEN SQUARE TO EAST BERLIN
JACK GODWIN

carry me out of Alexanderplatz and down Friedrich Engels Strasse toward the Brandenburg Gate. I turned down the first side street I could, hustled down the block and then stopped to check my reflection in a store window. I needed to know if I had a tail. I took off my hat and primped and preened to give my tail—if I had one—plenty of time to catch up but didn't see anything suspicious. Meanwhile, my mind was racing. I was trying to think what I would do if I were in Maria Borodina's place. What would I do if I saw what she just saw?

When I rounded the corner back toward Friedrich Engels Strasse, I was shocked to see Basil crossing the street coming right toward me. I cursed under my breath when our eyes met. The street was full of people going about their business and I needed a place to talk. I jerked my head toward the nearest alcove.

"Why did you follow me?"
"What are you doing here?"
"Why the hell did you follow me? You're being watched."
"By who," he asked.
"Our old friend Maria Borodina," I said.
"What? How do you know?"
"For one, I saw her in Alexanderplatz. We got a tip. We know about your orders from Fischer. You didn't seem that enthusiastic about clubbing the pigs into submission back there. Know what I mean?"
"Thanks."
"They brought Borodina in after you left Fischer's office."
"Okay, but why did you disappear back there?"
"I think Borodina saw me. I don't think. I know."
"Not good," he said. "Not good."

1989
TIANANMEN SQUARE TO EAST BERLIN
JACK GODWIN

"Stay the hell away from me," I said. "They suspect you already. You might have bluffed your way out of it but not now, not after Borodina saw you looking at me. If anybody sees us together, you're dead. *Dead!* I might be able to get back to the West, but not you. They'd never let you cross again. You're a Stasi officer. Get it? They'll lock you up and torture you and give you high doses of radiation."

"Alright, alright," he said "Never mind the rest."

What happened next totally surprised me. Basil clasped my face in both hands and kissed me on the lips. I didn't know whether to laugh or cry. I shook his hands off and shoved him backward.

"They're gonna microwave your balls, Basil. Stay away from me."

"Oh Schuster," he said bouncing his chin up and down the way he always did. He looked up and down the street and stepped out of the alcove onto the sidewalk. Then he turned and walked away.

"Hey," I called out. "Be good."

"*Bueno como un ángel, Señorita Nogales*," he replied.

As soon as he was out of sight, I darted out of the alcove in the opposite direction. For the next twenty minutes, I wound my way through the streets, turning left or right at random. Once I circled the block to identify anyone who might have followed. When I was sure I didn't have a tail, I started moving toward Checkpoint Charlie.

There were twenty people lined up for the border guards to check their papers. I was almost to the end of the line, when I saw Bart Lowry coming the other way into East Berlin through the checkpoint. Something tickled my antennae, so I decided to follow him. There must have been some reason that weasel would be in East Berlin. Evidently, Lowry was

1989
TIANANMEN SQUARE TO EAST BERLIN
JACK GODWIN

unhappy with his career in the Foreign Commercial Service. He was a wannabe. I told Benson there was a leak. I told her it was Lowry. She promised to take care of it. That was a month ago.

Lowry turned left heading north for a kilometer, then right toward Mitte-Berlin. Lowry was walking with a purpose. That was obvious. But he wasn't trained and that was obvious, too. But I wasn't sure. Sometimes amateurs got lucky. As I followed him, I remembered what Ivanov said. Lowry isn't very intelligent and doesn't provide information of any value. *Don't waste your time.* Fuck that shit. Lowry got Spencer killed. Just because I nailed the guy who pulled the trigger doesn't mean the case was closed. There were three dead bodies back there beside the tracks. Two were East German. But one was American. I hated the idea of letting Lowry get away with it. I hated the idea of him *thinking* he got away with it.

Lowry stopped on the sidewalk and made a show of checking his watch. It was comical the way he turned around and looked backward, as though he expected to see someone climbing up his ass. Satisfied with himself, he crossed the bridge over the Spree River, and walked to the end of Karl-Liebknecht-Strasse where the street widens into a plaza. I looked up and saw it was the Palasthotel. East Berlin was dingy, but there were a few upscale hotels for westerners who did business with the east. Lowry crossed the plaza and disappeared into a bar. There was no way I was going in after him so I waited down the street to see who Lowry was meeting.

An hour later, Lowry came out—alone—and walked back the way he came. I waited, watching and expecting Vladimir Ivanov to emerge. Ivanov came to my rescue back at the campground, and I owed him one. But if the information Lowry provided was as worthless as Ivanov said, why would Ivanov waste his time? Perhaps I should not have been surprised, but fifteen minutes later Maria Borodina stepped out of the bar. I ducked backward to make sure she couldn't see me. I had to be sure. Yeah, that was her alright.

Lowry was feeding information to Borodina? Maybe he was working for Ivanov, too. And maybe that's why Ivanov wasn't too impressed. It wasn't because Lowry's information wasn't valuable. Maybe it was because Lowry saved the best stuff for Borodina. That made sense. When Borodina was out of sight, I crossed the street and went inside the bar. It smelled like alcohol and aftershave. There was an exit toward the back, which I discovered wasn't really an exit. It was the doorway to the hotel. A few of the pieces began to fall into place, but I needed to let Benson sort them out and I needed to get back to West Berlin.

Unfortunately, Benson was not pleased to see me when I got back to Charlottenburg House.

"Do you know what this means?" she asked.

"I don't think Borodina recognized me. She couldn't have. We never made contact at the ambassador's residence in Budapest. I never saw her until Mihaly Csikany gave me the photo of her and Ambassador Irvine together. And I saw the few photos in the file you showed me. That's it."

"So from Borodina's perspective, she saw Gazecki make definite eye contact with someone—let's say an unidentified female. Immediately afterward, she met with Bart Lowry."

"Maybe it was pre-arranged," I said. "Maybe her meeting Lowry had nothing to do with Konrad Gazecki and the unidentified female in Alexanderplatz. And that's another thing. I thought you were gonna take out Lowry. That's what you said."

"Careful," said Benson.

"Bullshit! Lowry got Spencer killed. And why the fuck didn't you tell me about Warburton? Why'd you leave it for Konrad fucking Gazecki to tell me his real fucking name?"

"We're in the middle of an operation," she shouted. Benson quickly recovered, reached for her cane and stood up and lowered her voice. "We were keeping an eye on Lowry and feeding him disinformation. We thought maybe, *maybe* Ivanov was his handler. I had to be sure. Now I am sure that's not the case. But I don't want you to whack Lowry, not today anyway."

I cleared my throat and nodded. "Yes ma'am."

"Now, please go upstairs. I'd like you to go through the transcripts from the last few days. See if you can find the missing pieces to this puzzle. There may be nothing to find and we'll just have to wait until Borodina goes back to the Palace to report."

"We could interrogate Lowry."

"We could, but not yet. Upstairs now please," she said.

I couldn't put my finger on it but I knew something was wrong. Why was Benson so defensive? Usually she was derisive. Maybe I was missing something. Maybe Lowry wasn't such a weasel after all. Maybe he was smarter than he looked. Maybe he was a brilliant intelligence operative two steps ahead of everyone. If so, he fooled Dr. Benson and Vladimir Ivanov. *We're in the middle of an operation*, said Benson. Jesus, what if Lowry was running his own operation? I really wanted to take a look at Lowry's personnel file but that was out of the question. I decided to follow Benson's orders and go upstairs. If I went back and read through the transcripts from last week, maybe there was a clue. Maybe somebody said something we overlooked because it seemed trivial at the time.

1989
TIANANMEN SQUARE TO EAST BERLIN
JACK GODWIN

63.

THURSDAY, OCTOBER 19, late

The building was almost empty. I just couldn't resist the temptation and decided to go down to the Foreign Commercial Service on the second floor. The lights were out and the door to Lowry's office was locked. I picked the lock and closed the door behind me. I didn't know what I was looking for, and didn't even know where to start. I flipped through some files on his desk, all having to do with promoting American business interests. That was to be expected. Lowry had to maintain his cover—and that often took up as much time, energy and expertise as the intelligence work. In one of the file cabinets I found some of Lowry's employment records, correspondence, performance evaluations. It was the kind of stuff every employee accumulates who works for the federal government.

Lowry's last post was Moscow. That would explain where he met Maria Borodina. She'd gotten out of Budapest a day or two before me, and there was no way she could have recruited Lowry so quickly. I suspected they must have had a previous relationship, and I was right. After Lowry left Moscow, he was recalled to Washington before his assignment to Charlottenburg House. The circumstances were mysterious. I wonder if somebody in Washington or the

1989
TIANANMEN SQUARE TO EAST BERLIN
JACK GODWIN

Moscow embassy suspected him then. I was combing through Lowry's files and totally engrossed, but hadn't found anything incriminating so far. I jumped out of my skin when the phone rang. *Fucking son of a bitch*, I snarled. I picked up the receiver in the middle of the third ring.

"Bart Lowry's office," I said.

"Who is this?" said the voice. *Russian accent, I screamed inside my head!*

"Mr. Lowry's gone for the day. I'm his secretary. Can I ask who's calling please?" There was a click and the line went dead.

"Don't turn around" came a voice from behind me.

"Okay," I said. "Is that you Bart? It sure sounds like you."

"Shut up. Hang up the phone."

"It doesn't matter. She hung up already. She wouldn't tell me her name but she spoke with an accent. She sounded foreign, maybe Russian."

"I said shut up. And don't turn around."

"I think it was Maria Borodina." Then I felt something hard against the back of my head and everything went black.

You asked to see me? Yes, bad news I'm afraid. Is it about my father? Yes. How'd you know? He's dead, isn't he? Yes, your mother telephoned. I'm very sorry. But how'd you know? I had a dream. He was my best friend. I'm sorry. Take some time, go home. When you get back, come see me. I'm putting together a little task force. Interested? Do I have a choice? Not really. You'll never be an investigator, but you've got an aptitude for counterintelligence work. I'll be working for the CIA? Not CIA no, you'd be working for me. Mark my word, twenty or thirty years from now, people will still be wondering how the CIA missed it. Missed what? The end of the Cold War, that's what.

1989
TIANANMEN SQUARE TO EAST BERLIN
JACK GODWIN

Next thing I remember, I was laying on the floor of Bart Lowry's office. The door was closed and the lights were off and Lowry was long gone. It was still dark outside. It made me dizzy just to sit up. I felt a bump on the back of my head but no blood. Lowry really whacked me good. The desk clock said twelve thirty. I got up slowly and switched the light on. The office looked different somehow, cleaner and slightly emptier. *That was it.* Lowry's personal items were gone. The cabinet drawer where I was looking was closed. It was no use now. Lowry took what he wanted and then took off. At least he didn't kill me. I switched the light off and locked the door behind me. Then I went home, took an aspirin and washed it down with a shot of tequila.

64.

FRIDAY, OCTOBER 20, a.m.

Dr. Benson called me into her office when I reported in the morning.

"Bart Lowry has gone missing," she said.

"Oh?"

"He cleaned out his office last night. A surveillance camera caught him leaving after hours. Did you see him?"

"Me? No. I never saw him."

"Are you sure?"

"Yes Ma'am. I'm sure. I haven't seen Lowry since East Berlin."

"Did you make any headway with those transcripts?"

"No. Not yet anyway, I was going to get started first thing this morning. Maybe we should process Lowry's office. It's a crime scene."

"Good idea," said Benson. "It's on the second floor."

"Yes Ma'am. I know where it is." Then she scrutinized me for a few moments.

"You look tired. Are you feeling unwell?"

"Fit as a fiddle, Ma'am."

"Alright then, I'll let you get to it."

Benson signaled the conversation was over with her index finger. My face was burning but I did my best to look

1989
TIANANMEN SQUARE TO EAST BERLIN
JACK GODWIN

nonchalant as I left her office. That was close. With any luck Benson would never find out. She'd just assume Lowry knew he was under suspicion and decided to make a clean break. She was probably not too happy about whatever disinformation operation she had going, but at least I could say I never lied to her. He cold-cocked me from behind but I never saw him. Now he was fair game. One thing was sure. I wasn't going to forgive and forget. That weasel got Spencer killed. With Lowry gone, there wasn't any operation anymore. Benson said not to whack him, *not today anyway*. Okay, not today.

By the book, I told myself. From here on in we were going by the book. Secure the scene, collect the evidence, establish the facts and work the case. I looked through the files on Lowry's computer and found nothing out of the ordinary, just correspondence with clients about business opportunities and such. There was a box for disks, but the box was empty. I searched the drawers and found nothing but pencil shavings and paperclips. I looked under the desk, found nothing. His calendar and phone book were missing, so he must have taken those with him. Lowry knew what he was doing and covered his tracks while I was unconscious.

I was staring into the blank computer screen thinking this was looking worse by the minute. Feeling defeated, I turned off the monitor and saw a typewriter in the reflection—on the table behind me. I spun around and saw it was an IBM Selectric, the fancy kind with a little typing ball that jumped up and struck the paper when you hit a key. I turned it on and hit the J key a couple of times. Then I lifted the lid to get a better look. This one had a cartridge with two spools of carbon film. It had a memory! Everyone was supposed to remove the cartridge and lock it up for the night, but Lowry must have forgotten. That was a security breach, but what the hell. I removed the cartridge, pulled out a short section of the brown film and held it to the light. You could actually read where the typing ball punched the film because the characters were translucent through the dark background.

Straining to remember my training in cryptanalysis and coded documents, I turned the thumb-wheel a couple of times and pulled out more film. I cut an eight inch section and placed it on the photocopier. Then I cut another section and another and placed those on the copier. I gathered up the strips of film, grabbed the photocopy and ran back to Lowry's office. I realized immediately I didn't need cryptanalysis because this was not coded. It was a love letter:

My Darling Maria,

Things cannot go on this way. I don't know whether it is because I have lost faith in my government or because I love you so much. I have decided to defect to the East. I have cleaned out my desk and will cross over to East Berlin immediately. I will meet you at the same place, same time.

Love, Bart.

Same place—that meant the Palasthotel—but what time was it when Lowry showed up at the hotel? What time! It was noon, twelve noon. I thought I would barf but also thought this was something Benson needed to see.

1989
TIANANMEN SQUARE TO EAST BERLIN
JACK GODWIN

65.

FRIDAY, OCTOBER 20, p.m.

I ran upstairs to Benson's office to show her Lowry's reconstructed note.

"I wonder how he sent this message, dead drop probably. Doesn't matter," she said.

"There's still time. Should I go?"

"I don't know. On a hunch, I checked to see if we had anything about the Palasthotel."

"Anything come up?" I asked.

"Yes," she said. The Stasi owns and operates that particular establishment. They call it the Stasi Nest and it's closed to most East Germans. The Stasi keeps everyone in the hotel under surveillance. There are cameras and microphones everywhere, not just in the public areas but inside all the guest rooms, too. There are several suites on the fifth floor especially equipped to record sexual adventures."

"Fifth floor," I said. She nodded.

"That's where I'd start looking," said Benson.

"What am I looking for?"

"First you need to find him. Then see if you can talk him out of defecting. The operation we were running turned up nothing, by the way. Lowry's not a professional. He's got a low level security clearance but no access to anything that would really hurt us. And he hasn't passed any classified information, so far." *Except for Spencer*, I thought. "The worst we could do is charge him with conspiracy. His career is over and he'd probably have to spend a couple of years in minimum security. But if he gets in too deep, he's going to end up dead."

"What do you think Maria Borodina wants with him?"

"She's just doing her job. She hasn't been in country long enough to develop her own network. She probably inherited Lowry along with a few other assets. And I'll wager she already knows his information is worthless."

"That's bad for Lowry," I said. "What do you want me to do?"

"He's an American diplomat serving in the field. He's got immunity."

"Yeah, yeah, yeah, he's got a black passport, and that comes with certain privileges. So fucking what," I said. "He took an oath." Benson touched her fingertips together and stared at me in silence. Then I said, "Ma'am, what do you want me to do?"

"Go get him, I guess, but not now. Go in after dark."

"The longer we wait, the less of a chance we'll have of nabbing Borodina."

"I don't care about Borodina. I mean, she's not the objective. You asked me what to do. Bring Lowry in. Use minimum force. You can return hostile fire in self-defense but you may not fire on unarmed elements. Those are the rules of engagement. Agreed?"

"Yes Ma'am."

1989
TIANANMEN SQUARE TO EAST BERLIN
JACK GODWIN

"I'll make sure to insert a letter in your file. Take him to No. 24 Kirschestrasse, apartment 2A. Ask for Frau Hecken, Angela Hecken. She's one of ours. Here's her picture."

"I know this woman."

"Where from?"

"She was one of the speakers at the demonstration a few days ago. She talked about rewriting the East German constitution so the Socialist Party wouldn't have all the power. Is she another member of your network?"

Benson nodded. "Bring Lowry to her if you can," she said. "If you can't, go see her anyway."

66.

FRIDAY, OCTOBER 20, late

That night, I crossed back into East Berlin. It always made me nervous crossing through the checkpoint so heavily armed, but there was no way I could leave my weapons behind. This too, was part of the original occupation agreement, and there was nothing the young border guards in their crisp gray uniforms and shiny black boots could do about it. I retraced the route Lowry took to the Palasthotel, north then east toward Mitte-Berlin. I stopped on the bridge to catch my breath and look around. The night air was cool and the river smelled like dead fish and diesel fuel. It was coming up on midnight when I arrived at Karl Liebknecht Strasse and the Palasthotel. Three giant arched windows lit up the sidewalk outside. Someone was playing piano, probably in the hotel bar. *It's now or never*, I said to myself. I checked my gear one more time and took a deep breath to calm my nerves, then crossed the street.

Once inside, I vaguely remembered the lobby from the day before. There was green vinyl furniture and threadbare carpet. I walked toward the reception desk under a huge archway decorated with a hammer and compass and a ring of rye, the East German emblem, in gold leaf. Behind the long desk there was a painting of Lenin with some peasants

1989
TIANANMEN SQUARE TO EAST BERLIN
JACK GODWIN

outside a farm house, an old man and woman, a soldier, two children and their dog. Lenin was sitting on a log wearing that distinctive hat and explaining, I guess, that the best way to kill the Bourgeoisie was by taxing them to death. The clerk's back was turned and I cleared my throat.

"Good evening," He said.

"Good evening," I said. "There's an American on the fifth floor. Tell me the room number, please." I never smile except in the line of duty. I didn't want to kill the clerk, but I gave him a smile just in case.

"Excuse me?"

"I said tell me the room number." The desk clerk was cute, twenty something with curly brown hair, blue eyes and thick lips. So far, he was more annoying than threatening and the rules of engagement precluded use of deadly force for annoyance. Maybe it was the late hour, maybe it was the adrenaline, but I had little patience.

"Okay comrade," I said as I placed both hands on the reception desk. "I'll admit I respect your devotion to duty. Grudgingly, I'll even admit I respect some aspects of German efficiency. But socialism has destroyed your culture and turned you all into a bunch of bureaucrats. All that shit about equality really makes me puke."

And just like that, I vaulted over the desk and landed standing face-to-face with the clerk. I drew my weapon, cocked it and pressed the barrel against the soft spot under his chin.

"There's an American on the fifth floor," I whispered. "Tell me the room number, now."

"Room fifty-two," he said. "You can take the elevator around the corner."

1989
TIANANMEN SQUARE TO EAST BERLIN
JACK GODWIN

"Thank you for your cooperation." I knocked him cold, dragged him into the little office behind the desk, hog tied and gagged him. I strolled past the elevator and found the stairs. The Stasi always took the stairs, never took the elevator. There was something intimidating about the sound of heavy boots coming up the stairs. I wasn't trying to make an impression at the moment, but I took the stairs, too. Anyway, the cute desk clerk gave up a little too quickly. I ran up the first four flights and stopped to catch my breath.

At the fifth floor, I opened the fire door and checked the long empty hallway. No surprise, it was empty at this hour. I couldn't read any room numbers because all the doors were recessed several inches from the wall. At least I'd have some cover if anybody took a shot at me. I moved down the hallway sideways with my back to the wall. The first room was fifty-nine. Number fifty-eight was across the hall diagonally. I put my ear to the door but heard nothing. Halfway down the hallway I heard someone moaning—not what you're thinking—he was in pain, broken and babbling in German. I kept moving with my back to the wall until I came to room number fifty-one. I backed into the alcove and studied number fifty-two. There was light coming from under the door. Nobody in the hallway left or right, so I crossed over and pressed my ear to the door.

Hearing nothing, I turned the knob, which was locked, naturally. Down on one knee holding my breath, I picked the lock working as quickly and quietly as possible. I folded my tools and fixed the silencer onto the barrel of my weapon, and still down on one knee, pushed the door open. There was Lowry alone on the bed propped up against the headboard, hands tied to the bed posts. His eyes were open but his head was drooping at a funny angle and his face was ghostly pale.

1989
TIANANMEN SQUARE TO EAST BERLIN
JACK GODWIN

There was a syringe on the nightstand and a vial with no label. Then I heard water running in the bathroom. I trained my weapon on the bathroom door and moved quickly to the bed to check Lowry's pulse. The faucet squeaked and the water stopped and the door opened.

From my angle beside the bed, all I could see was a pair of hands holding a towel. Then Maria Borodina came partially into view but she stopped short. The door to the hallway was ajar, maybe that was it. My silencer chuffed but I didn't have an angle and the bullet went wide. She darted back into the bathroom. With Lowry confirmed dead, the best I could do now was to eliminate Borodina and get myself out. I ducked down behind the bed and tried to make it to the hallway. This was risky because I didn't know if Borodina was armed but I had to find out. I reached out with the tip of my silencer and swung the door open and she emptied a clip over my head and into the hallway. This sent splinters flying in every direction and I wondered whether the Stasi equipped every room in this hotel with an automatic weapon.

Nonetheless, this tactic changed the odds in her favor whether that was her intention or not. It made one hell of a racket and within a few seconds, several pairs of boots came charging toward us down the hallway. Thinking quickly, I holstered my pistol and grabbed my smoke and grenade, one in each hand. I crawled behind the bed far enough to reach the door, pulled the pin with my teeth, counted to three and rolled the grenade toward the boots. As soon as I heard the blast, I pulled the pin on the smoke and rolled it toward the sound of screaming.

As soon as I heard the pop, I bolted through the door and sprinted down the hallway through a metal fire door and into the stairwell. I slammed the door behind me and felt and heard someone—probably Borodina—empty a clip into the thick metal. It was Maria alright. When the shooting stopped I heard her swear. Then I heard her eject the empty clip. Instead of running downstairs, which she surely would expect, I ran upstairs toward the roof and stopped halfway. While I caught my breath, I looked down at the empty stairwell for something, anything, a fire hose to swing down heroically to the street below, or perhaps a fire axe to bar the door. No luck there.

I decided to make a stand in the stairwell. I got into position one flight up from the dimpled metal door and waited. A shadow crossed the light on the other side of the door. Someone was listening. I held my breath and fingered the trigger. The door moved, pushed open ever so cautiously by the barrel of a Kalashnikov. Then a foot, a black high-top too small to belong to a man propped the door open ever so slightly. Then a shoulder draped in black and a few strands of red hair appeared and quickly disappeared. And then a hand with manicured nails opened the door even more. Then Maria Borodina stepped into the field of fire.

It wasn't my intention to shoot unless she raised her weapon, but I took aim and cocked the hammer knowing it would attract her attention. She looked at me and raised the barrel a fraction of an inch and I pulled the trigger. The silencer chuffed once, twice and she fell gently, gracefully to the polished concrete floor.

I allowed myself to exhale and stepped down from my perch. Looking down the long smoky corridor, I assessed the damage. A grenade sure can do a lot of damage in such a small space. I looked down at Borodina's bloody red head wound as though I were investigating a crime scene and made a preliminary determination of self-defense. *That's*

1989
TIANANMEN SQUARE TO EAST BERLIN
JACK GODWIN

minimum use of force. It occurred to me that more of her Stasi friends were probably on their way and would be here soon, so I stepped over Maria's body and hustled down the stairs. *Adios Ginger*, I said to myself.

67.

SATURDAY, OCTOBER 21, a.m.

Outside in the night air, you could hear the police sirens closing in. I buttoned up and turned toward Kirschestrasse to meet Frau Hecken. Her apartment was five blocks away but I didn't take the direct route. I turned left or right at random and circled twice, and so probably covered ten blocks or more by the time I arrived. I let the cold night air fill my lungs and let the solitude clear my mind. Frau Hecken was expecting me because she buzzed me in before I could push the button.

"Come in," she said in English.

"Lowry is dead."

"Yes. I know." She said, "Heroin overdose administered by Maria Borodina."

"How do you know?"

"Because we intercepted a telephone call she made to Klaus Fischer from room fifty-two at the Palasthotel. Borodina called Fischer as soon as she obtained a piece of information from Lowry that she knew Fischer would want. Lowry must have realized he and Maria were not going away together and tried to bargain with her. So he told her the only valuable thing he knew."

"What was that?"

"The name of Bernice Benson's agent in Stasi," she said "Colonel Konrad Gazecki, also known as Basil Warburton." My mind reeled.

"We have to find him," I said. "If they find him before we do, he's dead."

"After the protest," Hecken said.

"What protest?"

"There's a protest planned for today in front of the Palasthotel."

"Wait a fucking minute. There's a protest planned for today?"

"Yes. We started planning it since the first time one of our agents saw Bartholomew Lowry go into the Palasthotel. That was some weeks ago. The place is notorious, you know."

"Yeah, I know. How long have you known about Lowry and Maria Borodina?"

"Not long, a few days," she said. "He met Borodina on several occasions before you first saw him go in."

"Whoa. Let me get this straight. You've been following me?"

"We're not following you, no. We have many eyes on the street. We are well organized, and we have to be because the Stasi is well organized."

"And you've been planning this protest in front of the Palasthotel for how long?"

"What does it matter? It has been in the planning a few days, like I said."

"It matters because we have new information. It matters because Lowry exposed one of our agents."

"Agent Nogales, there are other lives, millions of other lives and historic issues at stake."

"Don't be so condescending," I said.

"Don't be so parochial," she said. "In a few hours, thousands of people will assemble in front of the Palasthotel, a symbol of everything rotten in this country. We are calling for nonviolence, but we expect the Stasi will have undercover agents in the crowd who will try to provoke a fight. We need your help. I can telephone Dr. Benson if you like."

I was furious, but I knew what Benson would say. There was no need to call. I remembered what she told me in the bar in Budapest. You have an assignment. We're fighting a war. Practice careful tradecraft and keep your head down.

1989
TIANANMEN SQUARE TO EAST BERLIN
JACK GODWIN

68.

SATURDAY, OCTOBER 21, noon

The first protesters began to gather. It wasn't long before thousands of people, maybe as many as ten thousand, filled the plaza. People carried signs and banners, shouted and chanted slogans about opening the Berlin Wall and reunifying East and West. You could tell who the organizers were because they all wore a yellow sash over one shoulder with the words *No Violence*. There were half a dozen uniformed police officers forming a line between the hotel and the raucous crowd. The police kept backing up and backing up not because the crowd was pushing them but because the crowd was growing.

Finally, the police gave up and the crowd surged forward into the building. People ransacked the lobby and smashed everything in sight. There wasn't any violence that I could tell, but a lot of property damage. Anything that couldn't be smashed was thrown into the street. You could see the progress as the rioters reached the upper floors. Suddenly glass would shatter and people would look up from the plaza below. A second later, a piece of office furniture—a chair, telephone or typewriter—would come flying out the window. The crowd would push backward and cheer at the thud. This went on for a while until the rioters came to the fifth floor. Something changed and the cheering stopped.

No broken glass this time. A window opened on the fifth floor and a voice shouted for help. They found the victims—a few victims anyway—of the Stasi's systematic abuse. In a way, these were the lucky ones. The unlucky ones got a pistol shot to the neck and their relatives would never know the charge, sentence, date of execution or the location of the grave. But the mob of angry protesters transformed instantly into an army of liberators quietly going about their work. Then everyone turned in the direction of the sirens. People braced themselves as the sirens grew louder but then an ambulance turned the corner into the plaza and the mood returned to normal.

I found Angela Hecken in a back room going through a filing cabinet. The Palasthotel was much more than a symbol of everything rotten in East Germany. Behind the reception desk there was an office with a carefully concealed door at one end, which led to a passageway and in turn to an underground complex of rooms. It was a rabbit warren of offices, one part traffic control one part fallout shelter, and a tribute to German bureaucracy. Thankfully, the rioters lost their enthusiasm before they discovered all this. There was a bank of computer screens, maps on every wall, communications equipment on every desk, paper shredders, but no technical staff. If these people were any good at all, surely they knew about the angry crowd gathering in the plaza outside and got out while they could. Angela Hecken was already in lawyer-mode when I found her.

"These documents must be secured," she said. "I do not know if they should be opened or sealed. That is not my decision to make. But we must secure these documents. We cannot let Stasi officers get away with their crimes. Read this. Look at these photographs. If this happened to my family, my God I would want revenge."

I flipped through the file she gave me.

"This is evidence," I said. "It could be used to prosecute Stasi members. But there must be millions of files down here, tens of millions of pages."

"It does not matter. At least, people have the right to read their own file. And survivors have rights, too. Maybe they can finally know what happened to the ones who disappeared. You must help me."

"I can't. I have to find Gazecki—I mean Warburton."

"We need your help. We need to safeguard these files before we move them to a central location. It will take years to catalog everything. Every one of these dossiers is evidence of a crime. Klaus Fischer has been head of Stasi for two decades. There may be a way for him to avoid prison, but there can be no way for him to avoid responsibility. And there is no way Fischer can keep his job after Becker promised reforms. I doubt Becker can last much longer."

Hecken was right, of course.

"Oh no," she said. "I found something." In the back of a file cabinet was a red leather portfolio. And inside was Klaus Fischer's own dossier. It was said that Fischer kept a dossier on everyone, political opponents and people he disliked, and even members of the Politburo. That's how he stayed in power so long. It probably never occurred to Fischer—the Original Master of Fear—that he had enemies in Stasi and they would keep a dossier on him.

According to the dossier, the Gestapo arrested Fischer in 1943 and kept him in prison for almost a year. Fischer tried to convince the Gestapo that he renounced communism and was a loyal Nazi. He volunteered to enlist, to go to the front and fight for Hitler. Under the terms of his release, he agreed to become an informer and named dozens of Communist Party members. Fischer must have been very convincing because there was a copy of his release papers signed by the warden of Brandenburg prison. Throughout Fischer's career as Minister of State Security, he was considered a hero and a patriot, received countless medals, but the man was just a Nazi collaborator who enjoyed West German beer a little too much.

"This ought to be enough to sink him. Murdering thousands of your compatriots is one thing, but collaborating with the Nazis is quite another. Can I take this with me?" I asked. "Dr. Benson will want to see this. And I'll make sure the press in West Berlin gets it, too. Anyway, this isn't something you would want to have in your possession."

Hecken nodded and choked out a *good luck* to me. I tucked the red portfolio inside my jacket and left the Palasthotel. There was still a large crowd outside standing around with nothing to do. I made my way back to Checkpoint Charlie and Charlottenburg House. Benson agreed to meet me immediately. When I showed Benson the dossier, it was the first time I ever saw her really and truly impressed.

69.

SUNDAY, OCTOBER 22

That night, we listened to an emergency meeting in the conference room at the Palace of the Republic. Meetings of the Politburo were normally well scripted and absolutely secret, but not this time. It was explosive. Bernd Becker demanded everyone's resignation, including Klaus Fischer. Fischer tried to defend himself. When he got up to speak, he began by addressing everyone as "comrades" but everyone in the room shouted him down. Fischer was finished. Becker ordered him taken into custody. There was a scuffle, more shouting and then it was quiet again. Becker withdrew his demand for mass resignations and finally brought the meeting back to order. Bernd appointed Hans Schlaff as the new head of Stasi, but denied him the title of Minister of State Security.

70.

MONDAY, OCTOBER 23

All the newspapers and television stations in West Germany and elsewhere pounced on the story. Somehow, Fischer escaped custody and slipped out of the country. Rumors were he was on his way to Argentina, where he was given asylum. I think the East German government was glad to be rid of him. What choice did they have? Put him on trial? He knew too much. And there were plenty of people within the Stasi who were still loyal to him. It was ironic if you thought about it. Argentina always had a liberal immigration policy. After WWII, the Perón government admitted hundreds of former high ranking Nazis without asking too many questions. And now there was a new addition to the German-Argentine community.

"Okay," Benson said. "What's next?"

"I don't know. Angela Hecken told me that her people intercepted a call Maria Borodina made to Klaus Fischer. According to Hecken, Borodina told Fischer that Konrad Gazecki is a double agent."

"But Fischer is out and Borodina is dead. I call that a good day's work Agent Nogales."

1989
TIANANMEN SQUARE TO EAST BERLIN
JACK GODWIN

Benson's phone rang before I could respond. I watched her expression change. I motioned with my thumb whether I should leave and she gestured for me to stay.

"Yes, I'll hold for the Prime Minister." She pointed to the other telephone extension and indicated that she wanted me to listen in. She took several deep breaths while we waited.

"Dr. Benson?"

"Yes, Prime Minister."

"Please hold for Prime Minister Thatcher." Benson's eyebrows twitched and she cleared her throat.

"Good morning Dr. Benson."

"Good morning Prime Minister."

"I've recently spoken to President Gorbachev. We had a frank discussion on a range of topics, Namibia and South Africa, and of course the fighting in Afghanistan. He told me he was very disappointed in the American response, thinks Mr. Bush has gone back on his word. What do you make of that?"

"I'm not surprised Prime Minister."

"We talked about Cuba. I asked him why Castro wasn't more supportive of perestroika. He thinks Castro knows what he's doing, when it comes to domestic politics, at least, but it would weaken Cuba's influence in Africa if Castro accepted perestroika. And do you know what Gorbachev said?"

"No, Ma'am."

"He said Britain has a stronger presence in Africa than Cuba does. Well of course, I said! I told him about my trip to southeast Africa last spring. I visited a refugee camp in Malawi filled with thousands of Mozambique nationals. There was a unit of British troops training Mozambique solders in anti-terrorism tactics, training Mozambique solders how to use a Kalashnikov. What do you think of that?"

"That's what I call ironic, Prime Minister."

"There's something else. President Gorbachev is convinced the Americans are afraid of perestroika. He thinks the president's people are panicking, not because perestroika is working but because they fear it's nothing more than a public relations scheme. And he thinks the West Germans have simply lost their minds."

"Do you think we're losing public opinion?"

"I think Mr. Kissinger talks too much," said Thatcher. "I can't imagine why the chat shows keep inviting him. He undermines the president every time his opens his mouth. I know George Bush and James Baker very well. Of course, Mr. Bush is a very different person from Reagan. Bush gives more attention to detail than Reagan did. On the whole, I think Bush will continue the Reagan line."

"What if Kissinger is right?"

"He's wrong of course. And Gorbachev told me so. It all comes down to whether perestroika is Gorbachev's *personal* policy. That's something the West can't depend on, not yet anyway. He even accused me of having reservations."

"How did you respond?"

"I told him his success is in our interest. It's in our interest for the Soviet Union to become more peaceful, more affluent and more open to change. He's got an immense task, hasn't he? The old order is being broken and people don't know what will replace it. Naturally, it makes people feel less confident in themselves and their future."

"He's a man we can do business with," said Benson.

"Now you're quoting me. Congratulations on your success in Hungary. What happened with your ambassador? I can't remember his name."

"His name was Francis Irvine. But I can't talk about it."

"No harm in my asking," said Thatcher. "It's just that Hungary is already three steps ahead of the Soviet Union. All in all, there are positive signs throughout the region but I'm strongly opposed to reunification of the two Germanys. We shouldn't do anything to destabilize the Warsaw Pact. Mr. Gorbachev agrees with me on this. Oh, one more thing. MI6 tells me Basil Warburton missed his last check-in, which should have been two days ago. Do you have any information on his whereabouts?"

"No, Ma'am I don't. It is possible his cover is blown. We believe a Russian agent passed information on Warburton to Klaus Fischer."

"Is that confirmed?"

"Yes. But Fischer is out and the Russian agent is dead, so we may have caught a break."

"Does this have something to do with the demonstration in front of the Palasthotel?"

"Yes," said Benson.

"Please do keep me informed, Dr. Benson if you learn anything."

"Yes Ma'am."

"Right then, goodbye." The line clicked.

"That was shrewd not to mention anything about Bart Lowry," I said.

"You know, I might have said something if she hadn't brought up Ambassador Irvine. But trying to explain to the British prime minister how Irvine *and* Lowry fell for the same woman is just too much, even for me. Don't get me wrong. Margaret Thatcher is one of the good ones, but the job is hard enough already."

"Don't forget Mihaly Csikany."

"Oh yes, first it was the police chief, then the ambassador and then the commercial officer. How did she do it?"

"Maybe she was a great lover."

"It was a rhetorical question, Agent Nogales."

"Yes Ma'am."

"Where were we?"

"You were asking *what's next*."

"Ah, yes. That call was informative. One, Mr. Warburton missed his last check-in. And two, we know that British intelligence does not know where Warburton is. As we say in the intelligence game, an unconfirmed death is as good as rolling doubles."

"You get to roll again."

"That's right."

"Where's the last place you saw Basil Warburton?" asked Benson.

"It was the morning of that big demonstration in Alexanderplatz," I said. "I saw him in the plaza and tried to avoid him, if you recall. But when the protesters left the plaza and headed toward Brandenburg Gate, he followed me, the dumb ass. We were on a side street off Friedrich Engels Strasse."

"What's there?"

"What do you mean?"

"I mean, why did he find you there? It may not have been a coincidence."

I got out a map of East Berlin and retraced my steps from Alexanderplatz to the street where Basil tracked me down.

"There it is," I said, "headquarters of the Socialist Party right around the corner. That's a coincidence."

"I don't think so," said Benson. "Did Warburton say anything? Did he say anything that made no sense?"

"It was weird. I told him Maria Borodina was watching him and that he should stay the hell away from me because he'd be dead if anybody saw us together."

"How'd he respond?"

"He said *Oh Schuster*. I think that's how they say bullshit in Gdansk."

"He said Schuster. You're sure?"

"Basil Warburton did not say *Shazam*. He said *Schuster*. I'm sure."

"That name sounds familiar. Why does that sound so familiar?" Benson tapped her nails on her desk as she thought. Then she spun her chair around and pulled a binder from the credenza behind her. "There he is. Axel Schuster, spokesman for the East German Politburo. Warburton must have been sending you a message."

"Ooh, I love espionage."

"Here's the file," she said sliding the binder across the desk. "Read it cover to cover. I want you to pay him a visit. Find out what he knows. Maybe we'll discover Mr. Warburton's whereabouts, maybe something more."

I found a quiet corner in the library and began studying up. Axel Schuster was born in Pomerania, studied journalism at Leipzig, and joined the party in fifty-two. He became editor of the party's official newspaper in seventy-eight, appointed to the Politburo in eighty-one, and then official party spokesman in eighty-five. He was a public relations hack. What was Basil's connection? Let's see. Schuster just received the Order of Karl Marx, one of the country's most prestigious awards. That was interesting. He wrote occasional editorials in *New Germany*, nothing but the straight party line. I couldn't see a connection. Maybe there wasn't one.

1989
TIANANMEN SQUARE TO EAST BERLIN
JACK GODWIN

Axel Schuster was a widower with two grown children. He lived alone in an apartment near Heinz Hoffmann Park. No bad habits, no girlfriends, no financial irregularities, and nothing, really nothing to go on. Maybe there was something in the transcripts. Schuster was a member of the Politburo, after all. He must have met with Schmidt or Fischer or Becker since the seventeenth when the listening devices were installed. Maybe he said something.

"Dr. Benson, look at this."

"What is it?"

"This is a transcript from a meeting Schuster attended at the Palace of the Republic. The Politburo formed an ad hoc committee to draft a new law allowing for freedom to travel."

"When was this?"

"It was October thirteen," I said. "That's when we overheard Fischer giving Gazecki the order to disrupt the protests. The last time I saw Basil was the morning of the eighteenth. That's when he mentioned Schuster."

"So, Gazecki—Warburton—overheard something about a Politburo subcommittee drafting a governmental decree about travel restrictions, and he tipped you off. Why the cloak and dagger? Why not just report it?"

"He was under surveillance," I said.

"Are you playing Devil's advocate now?"

"No, I'm playing God's advocate. Warburton is under cover, deep cover. His life's in danger. I mean, he was already in danger *before* Lowry sold him out. And now it's worse, and it'll continue to get worse the longer we wait."

"Thank you," said Benson irritated. "We're going to have to wait a little longer."

71.

WEDNESDAY, NOVEMBER 1

We intercepted a phone call between Bernd Becker and Mikhail Gorbachev, which started off very friendly but turned into a lecture. First, Becker thanked Gorbachev for taking his call and thanked him for visiting Berlin for the fortieth anniversary. Gorbachev offered Becker an open invitation to visit Moscow.

"Your visit inspired much discussion about the future of the party," said Becker.

Gorbachev cut him off then repeated what he said on October seventh. "One must not miss the time for changes," he said. "You must not allow yourself to get depressed by the complications you are facing. The process of perestroika is emotionally charged and stormy sometimes, but as a leader you should never be afraid of your own people."

"The population resents the party," said Becker. "The media has created a world of illusion that does not coincide with everyday life. It is the media's fault that so many people have lost confidence in the party and have fled the country."

As I read the transcript, I shook my head and wondered aloud why politicians always blame the media. But then Gorbachev cut him off again.

"The people in the Soviet Union get information from many sources," said Gorbachev, "including western media and they draw their own conclusions."

"When Joachim Schmidt banned *Sputnik*, it made us look like hypocrites, especially in the western media," said Becker. "*Sputnik* is a Soviet magazine. People here watch West German television shows every night but are not permitted to read a Soviet publication."

"I believe this was the turning point for Joachim Schmidt," said Gorbachev. "There are many diverse opinions in Soviet media these days, and everyone has the right to criticize anything they read."

"You know I traveled to China in June," said Becker.

"Yes."

"After I got back, I urged Schmidt to move quickly to resolve the crisis here."

I would urge you to do likewise," said Gorbachev. "However, all Soviet troops stationed in East Germany will remain quartered. You cannot use them without authorization from me personally. Do you understand?"

"Yes," said Becker.

"What happened at the Leunawerke oil facility? Was the explosion an accident or was it industrial espionage?"

"The investigation is ongoing, but preliminary reports indicate espionage."

"The Soviet Union will always fulfill its obligations to East Germany, but the loss of two million barrels of oil is a domestic problem," said Gorbachev. "Are there any other new developments?"

"The Politburo is drafting a new travel law," said Becker. "The new law will be adopted before Christmas. Every East German citizen will have the right to travel to all countries.

1989

TIANANMEN SQUARE TO EAST BERLIN

JACK GODWIN

Our sources tell us there is some sort of demonstration being planned, which will be held at Bornholmer Strasse. I have asked Axel Schuster to hold a press conference to give our side of the story."

"Are you worried about the protesters breaking through the wall? We must avoid bloodshed. We must avoid a situation like Tiananmen Square. I will not declare martial law except as a last resort to prevent civil war."

I shared the transcript of the intercepted telephone call with Benson.

"Well, this is interesting," said Benson. "Half a million Soviet troops are to remain quartered. Mr. Gorbachev wants no martial law, no civil war, and no bloodshed."

"No. But it's not up to him, is it?"

"I think it is," said Benson. "I think it's entirely up to Gorbachev."

"Okay," I said. "What do you want me to do?"

"That depends. Are you still playing God's advocate?" I ignored the question. "Never mind," she said. "Any ideas you'd like to share on how to proceed with Axel Schuster?"

"I want to talk to him. I want to see that new travel decree they're working on."

"Agreed," Benson said. "Remember your rules of engagement. Use minimum force and fire only in self-defense."

72.

THURSDAY, NOVEMBER 2, a.m.

I paid Axel Schuster a visit in his apartment near Heinz Hoffmann Park. He was sound asleep and struggled briefly, but quit resisting when I put the gun barrel in his mouth.

"My name is Floriana Varga, Special Agent with the Federal Bureau of Investigation. I apologize for interrupting your sleep but I have some questions. Do you understand? If so, nod your head. Good. I'm going to take this gun out of your mouth now. If you make a sound, any sound, I will shoot you. Understand? Good. Okay. Now sit up and put your hands on top of your head. Do it now. Good. That's good. Your name is Axel Schuster, right?"

"How did you get in here?"

I anticipated this question but it irritated me nonetheless.

"Never mind how I got in," I said. I wanted to avoid saying *I'm the one asking the questions* because it is so cliché. I put the gun barrel back in his mouth. "I just cleaned and oiled this. And I'm sure it tastes terrible. It's even worse if you've got a strong gag reflex. Is your name Axel Schuster?"

He nodded.

1989
TIANANMEN SQUARE TO EAST BERLIN
JACK GODWIN

"I'm going to take my gun out of your mouth—again. Keep your hands right where they are. Now, tell me about the new travel policy you're working on."

"How do you know about this?"

"Herr Schuster, I'm the one asking the questions."

"Yes. Yes. The Politburo is drafting a new temporary travel decree. The current rule will no longer apply."

"When will this new decree go into effect?"

"I don't know, as soon as the Politburo votes."

"What does it say?"

"The decree will allow people to travel, to exit East Germany if they want."

"You said temporary. What do you mean *temporary*?"

"The decree is supposed to be transitional. We're bleeding. Hundreds of people leave each day. The Czechs and Hungarians are putting pressure on us. Our own people are putting pressure on us. We have to do something. The country's existence is at stake."

"Okay. How about traveling between East and West Berlin?"

"People will no longer need a visa or even a passport to travel into West Berlin. All they will need is their personal identity card. All the border crossings will be opened. But these will be temporary measures to ease the pressure until the permanent law goes into effect."

"Want to know what I think? I think the government's letting the malcontents leave. And then, while they're all away, you'll just close the border again. Castro pulled that stunt back in 1980. A hundred thousand anti-socialists escaped, plus a few thousand criminals and mental patients. Is that your plan?"

"No," he said.

"No? Good. Now, there's one more thing before I go. You're familiar with Colonel Konrad Gazecki?"

"Yes."

"Tell me where I can find him."

"I do not know where he is. How would I know?"

"If you don't know where he is, then maybe you can deliver a message. Tell him he's wanted by the United States government for war crimes." I said.

"War crimes," he whimpered, "my God!"

"That's right. And it will be no defense to say, *I was just following orders*. My guess—and this is just a guess—is that every Stasi officer and every member of the Politburo will face charges. Prison time for sure, maybe execution."

Schuster was sweating now. I drew the tranquillizer gun, unloaded a ballistic syringe and stabbed him in the neck. Schuster jerked involuntarily when the syringe pierced his skin. I watched his expression change. His eyes blinked and his mouth went slack. I removed the dart from his neck, got up off the bed and left the way I came in. I slipped back through Checkpoint Charlie and into West Berlin.

73.

FRIDAY, NOVEMBER 3, morning

I went back to Charlottenburg House at eight and I found Dr. Benson in the secure area where all the cable traffic came and went between Washington and the embassy in Bonn.

"I spoke to Schuster," I said. "They're drafting a new travel decree which will allow East Germans to exit the country."

"Starting when?"

"He didn't know," I said. "The Politburo has to vote on it. He also said the new decree would be temporary."

"What's temporary?"

"I asked him that. He said *transitional*." Benson gave me a funny look. "What's going on? I did what you asked."

"It's not that," said Benson.

"What then?"

"Our people have been tracking Angela Hecken, you know, the opposition lawyer," she said.

"Sure," I said.

"She and other leaders in the movement are organizing a mass border crossing. They're not targeting Checkpoint Charlie. They're focusing on the Bornholmer Strasse crossing."

"That confirms what we overheard Becker tell Gorbachev. What's so special about the Bornholmer Strasse crossing?"

"Nothing," said Benson. "It's a legal technicality. Bornholmer Strasse isn't really a checkpoint, it's a border crossing. There are seven total and they're for German citizens, not for occupation powers."

"Where is it? Do you have a satellite image?"

"Sure," she said. "Charlie is there, and Bornholmer is the crossing farthest to the north, right there. There's the railway line, which follows the border. You can see the wall there, and even some of the fortifications, the anti-vehicle ditch, the metal barriers—what they call the inner security wall—and the little minefield in between. This here is the patrol road," She said tapping the photo with a pencil eraser. "See this little booth? That's the passport control."

"Do you think Hecken has a source inside the government? I mean, organizing a mass border crossing would be suicide, unless."

"Unless what."

"Unless, Hecken is trying to force a *zugzwang*," I said. She looked at me unknowingly. "It's a chess tactic. You force your opponent to make a move that weakens his position. Hecken probably knows the government is working on a new travel decree and now she's forcing a *zugzwang*." I shrugged. "What do you want me to do?"

"Go upstairs for now, study the transcripts and monitor the transmission for anything new."

1989
TIANANMEN SQUARE TO EAST BERLIN
JACK GODWIN

74.

MONDAY, NOVEMBER 6, p.m.

I spent the weekend at Charlottenburg House reading through pages and pages of transcripts from Becker's office and the conference room at the Palace of the Republic. Everything I read confirmed what Schuster told me, plus a little more. After the last Politburo meeting, Bernd Becker met with the new Stasi chief, Hans Schlaff and another member named Gunther. Becker complained how the mass exits were *a burden on our Czechoslovak and Hungarian comrades*. Good, I thought. Becker opted not to close the border with Czechoslovakia, and instead announced the new travel decree. That's when all hell broke loose. But Becker had enough allies in the room to overrule the hard-liners.

I kept reading, scanning and flipping the pages back and forth, but I couldn't find anything specific about when the new decree was due to take effect. I noticed Axel Schuster didn't seem to be in attendance.

Someone said, "The draft states that permanent exits will be possible without delay," but the transcript didn't identify who was speaking.

"It will turn out bad however we do this," said Becker.

"It is the only solution that will save us," said Schlaff.

Someone asked if there was any way to avoid the word "temporary".

Another unidentified voice said, "If people think they have to get out before the border closes again, it would only add to the pressure. Shouldn't we call the decree transitional?"

Then everybody started talking at once and the rest of the conversation was unintelligible.

I put the transcript down and rubbed my eyes. Just then, I overheard voices through the transmitter. Becker was back in his office, along with Hans Schlaff and Axel Schuster. Schlaff spoke first.

"Excuse me sir, Comrade Schuster has brought something to my attention that I believe you should hear."

"Yes, what is it?"

"An American agent broke into my apartment."

"What?"

"I should have reported it sooner. But she drugged me. She told me her name was Floriana Varga and she was with the American FBI."

"There is someone by that name in our database," said Schlaff. "What did she look like?"

"I don't know. It was dark. Long hair, brown eyes, she looked like a Gypsy, except she was aiming a gun at me."

"That matches the physical description of a woman who killed four border guards in August," said Schlaff. "She was carrying a Bulgarian passport with a falsified exit visa, which we recovered at the scene. We were going to take her into custody, but she and her companion fled the scene and escaped into Czechoslovakia."

"You knew she was coming?" asked Becker.

"Well, yes. We didn't know what she looked like, but we knew her name. Comrade Borodina alerted us after she obtained the name through her informant at the Hungarian National Police."

"And this woman, Floriana Varga, told you she is an FBI agent?" Becker shouted.

"Yes," said Schuster. "She asked me about the travel decree. She did not ask me if there was going to be a new policy. She already knew that. She asked me for details."

"She asked for details? What details?" If Schuster responded to Becker, it wasn't audible. Maybe he shrugged.

Becker continued shouting. "Is that all?"

"No," said Schuster. "She told me Colonel Gazecki is wanted for war crimes. She asked if I knew his whereabouts. When I refused to answer she stabbed me. I thought I was dead. When I woke up I thought I was dreaming. It must have been some sort of tranquilizer dart. She stabbed me in the neck, look here."

"Thank you Comrade Schuster," said Schlaff. "You may go now." There was silence followed by a muted door closing. Then Schlaff spoke again. "The KGB prostitute Maria Borodina obtained two pieces of information before she was killed at the Palasthotel."

"Who was her source?"

"Her source was Bartholomew Lowry, a mid-level officer in the commercial section. He is also dead. According to Borodina, this FBI agent Floriana Varga was involved in the Leunawerke explosion. The body we found in the woods near the depot was also an American agent, not Chinese. This person was her accomplice."

Oh shit, I thought.

"This Lowry person, is he credible?"

"We think so," said Schlaff.

"You said the Russian woman obtained two pieces of information. What was the other?"

"She said there is a British agent inside Stasi."

"What? And today we discover that an FBI agent has broken into the home of a member of the Politburo?"

"Yes. Well, Schuster is journalist, a mouthpiece. He does not make policy."

"Do not patronize me," shouted Becker. "The American FBI has put a gun to the head of one of our Politburo members. And ... and she said one of *your* officers is wanted for war crimes!"

"Shall I send for Colonel Gazecki?"

"Send for him? No. Arrest him. I thought he was supposed to be your top spy catcher. Go get him and bring him here in one hour. Do you hear me? In one hour!"

"Yes, Comrade Secretary."

"I want him here and I want your four best men in here with us. I want some answers, God damn it!"

I tore the headphones off and threw them across the room. I ran downstairs and out the front of Charlottenburg House and ran the five kilometers to Checkpoint Charlie. I stopped a few minutes on the west side to catch my breath. That's when I realized what I'd done. I'd forgotten my weapons, everything except my kabar knife. *It'll have to do*, I thought. There was no time to go back. I made up my mind and then passed through Checkpoint Charlie into East Berlin for what was sure to be the last time.

I crossed the Spree River and made my way to the stables adjoining the Palace of the Republic. There was no one sitting on the little wood stool and no stable hands working outside, as far as I could see. I walked up the sloping lawn with my head down to make myself appear as unthreatening as possible. A man approached me wearing civilian clothes, but the guy gave himself away. When our eyes met, he hesitated just long enough. And when he recovered, he was too relaxed, too casually obvious.

I had to make a quick decision. When I got about ten feet away, I stopped and turned slightly to fix my hair. I don't come from a blade culture, but I got plenty of training in close combat at the academy. As soon as I had a fighting grip on my knife, I tilted my head to one side, flashed my brightest California smile and walked straight toward him. He hesitated at first. Then he went for his gun but it was too late and he knew it. I went for the quick-kill and hammered the blade into his chest three times in quick succession.

The guy's knees buckled and he crumpled to the ground. I pocketed his weapon, dragged the body into the corner stall, and concealed it with straw and horse manure. I checked his weapon, a Russian-made Makarov with eight rounds. *It'll have to do*, I thought for the second time today. I opened the hatch and closed it behind me knowing I wouldn't be coming back this way again. I ran the length of the tunnel just as I'd done before. I opened the cellar door and took the stairs two at a time up to the kitchen. I stopped there to catch my breath and listen. I poked my head in and saw one cook with his back to me, chopping something. I ducked back into the tunnel and took off my shoes and socks. I slipped back into the kitchen, passed the stainless steel work tables and through the double doors into the empty dining room. I found the stairwell and took the stairs two at a time.

I checked my watch. It was more than an hour later and Basil had to be in Becker's office by now. When I got up to the fourth floor, I couldn't see anything through the heavy drapes, so I stood and listened.

"Colonel Gazecki," said Schlaff. "We know there is a British spy in Stasi. We know this for a fact." There was a muffled response, which I couldn't make out. Was that Basil? They must have gagged him.

"Herr Fischer said you were a spy-catcher, *the best* spy-catcher. I'm beginning to wonder, though, given Comrade Fischer's fall from grace. Who was responsible for the Stasi agents killed in the car bomb in Budapest?" Again, I couldn't hear the muffled response. Then I heard punching sounds, one-two-three. "What is your relationship to the foreign woman ... what was her name?"

"Maria Borodina, Comrade" said a voice I didn't recognize.

"Ah, yes" said Schlaff, "Maria Cherlina Borodina, formerly of the KGB. I say formerly because she was killed at the Palasthotel several days ago, shot through the head." *It was self-defense,* I thought, *and two shots were all I needed.* "What was your relationship to her?" More punching sounds, fist on bone this time, and I winced. "Before Fraulein Borodina died, she informed us that British intelligence has infiltrated the Ministry of State Security."

Oh shit, shit, shit and sit in it! I parted the heavy drapes and flew into the room.

"FBI," I shouted. "Nobody move!" Basil looked like hell, all beaten up. The two guys in gray suits holding onto him couldn't make a move without letting go. But there were two more and they both went for their guns. I dropped one with a quick shot to the forehead. Because I was unaccustomed to the Makarov, I was too slow on the second one. He got off a round, which missed me as he went cross-eyed and fell.

"I said, *nobody ... move.*" I jerked my chin at Becker and Schlaff to put their hands up. "I'm taking this man into

1989
TIANANMEN SQUARE TO EAST BERLIN
JACK GODWIN

custody. Konrad Gazecki, you are wanted by the United States government for war crimes. I have a warrant for your arrest. Or didn't Axel Schuster tell you that?" This is where I made my mistake. I took my eyes off Basil for a second and glanced at Becker and Schlaff. The goon on Basil's left pushed him away, which sent Basil and the other guy crashing to the ground. The one standing had me square in his sights and took a shot but missed me somehow. I put two in his chest.

The other one drew his gun and scrambled to his feet. And this is where Basil made his mistake. He got into a struggle with him, briefly. Basil hit him hard and the guy dropped his gun. They were wrestling on the ground, punching, kicking and clawing at each other. Basil got hold of the gun and pistol-whipped him, once, twice in the face. But then Basil stood up holding the gun in his right hand, not aiming at me but wobbling and looking very dangerous.

"Drop the weapon!" I shouted. I'm not sure what he was thinking. He just stood there. "I said *drop ... the weapon*." I had no choice. I shot him through the right shoulder and the gun fell out of his hand. He looked at me funny and then his expression changed. I didn't know it, but there was someone behind me, someone who heard the shots and came up the stairs the same way I did. That's the last thing I remember.

I woke up in a holding cell in the Bornholmer installation adjacent to the border crossing. There was a small window high on the wall toward the west. The cell had a sink and toilet and a bed with metal springs and a stained, smelly mattress. No visitors were allowed, no lawyer, no one from the embassy. I slept mostly, or tried to anyway. The moment I dozed off the guard would pound on the door. And every few hours the guards would roust me out of bed and drag me to the interrogation room. They were very friendly in the beginning, asked me about California, my family—especially my father—and how I became an FBI agent.

They asked me questions about anything and everything just to get me talking. But they always came back to the same question. What is the name of the British agent inside Stasi? After every interrogation, the guards would take me back to my cell. And every time, as soon as I dozed off, they'd take the mattress away and make me sleep on the cold cement floor. I was never fully asleep or fully awake for I don't know how many days. Did I give them Basil's name? I don't know. Honestly, I don't remember. But I don't think so because they never gave up. They always came back to the same question. What is the name of the British agent inside Stasi?

1989
TIANANMEN SQUARE TO EAST BERLIN
JACK GODWIN

75.

THURSDAY, NOVEMBER 9

I always dreamed of wearing a badge, always. What're you, some kind of crime fighter? I thought I could make a difference. Congratulations, you just won second prize in a beauty contest. Collect your ten dollars. I'm exhausted but I can't sleep. You'll recover. I think I'm going crazy. You'll recover. I don't feel normal. Did you think it was going to be like the movies? You knew it would be stressful. You knew it would be challenging. I wish I never joined. You swore an oath. I did. I did take an oath all enemies foreign and domestic and duties of the office, freely and faithfully, I did. I still do. They want you to quit. That or break you. Are you going to let them?

I didn't know where I was at first. Then I remembered. The physical effects of sleep deprivation were bad but the emotional effects were even worse. I wondered how much longer I could last. I mean, I knew how it was going to end, with an execution, a Stasi-style execution. I just didn't know if I could take much more.

Would I get a last meal or was that only on death row? Pepperoni pizza, cherry coke and cheese cake, please. That's what I wanted. I wasn't even hungry, disoriented mostly, cold, tired and furious with myself for getting caught. I wasn't afraid to die. Everybody dies. That wasn't the problem. The problem was the idea of summary execution, which felt like losing and I hated losing. I really wanted to take one more with me, help one more die for his country before I died for mine. And when the game was over, and I was dead, at least I'd still have a country. That was something.

My left eye was swollen shut, my mouth was bleeding and my heart was pounding. Sweat was rolling down my back into my butt crack, even though the November air was cool. I knew we were in East Berlin, pretty close to the border crossing because I could hear the cars lined up honking their horns. And I could hear West Berliners pounding on the other side and celebrating, or getting ready to celebrate. They were chanting something, which I couldn't quite make out, but it sounded like the song they sing at soccer games. *Olay-OLAY-Olay.* The guard heard it, too because he kept glancing up at the high window without moving his head. Just his eyes moved but not his head or the barrel of the pistol.

"It does not matter," he said. "It is too late for you."

"Maybe," I said. "Maybe you'll retire on a pension and get to spend your days playing with your children and grandchildren. You got children, Sgt. Schultz?"

"Shut up."

"I don't think so."

The chanting got louder through the window. Then the door opened and in came a Stasi colonel named Gazecki, Konrad Gazecki.

"Jaqueline Olvera Nogales," he said, "You've been busy."

"Colonel Gazecki, how's the shoulder? Sorry about that. I'm not as good with a borrowed weapon. That was a Makarov nine millimeter wasn't it. I'll get you one for Christmas if we both live through this. I was just telling Sgt. Schultz here, maybe he'll get to retire on a pension and spend his summers on the Black Sea coast. What do you think?"

"Stand her up," said Gazecki. The guard holstered his pistol, grabbed my collar and hoisted me to my feet.

"Remove the handcuffs," he said. Gazecki and the guard exchanged a glance, but Gazecki reassured him with a nod. The guard unlocked the cuffs. I rubbed my wrists and Gazecki took a step forward to scrutinize me. The chanting outside was very loud now and the cell vibrated every time the West Berliners pounded on the wall. There was a crumbling, crashing noise followed instantly by bright light pouring in through the high window. The crowd roared in triumph and I held my breath.

He looked at me without smiling, waited for the guard to leave.

"Why are you barefoot?"

"How come you're wearing civilian clothes?"

"What happened to your face?"

"What do you think? What day is it?"

"November ninth."

"What's happening? I've been out of it for a few days."

"It's over. They opened the wall."

"What do you mean?"

"It's over. That's what I mean. Axel Schuster announced the new travel decree."

"I don't understand."

"There was a press conference an hour ago. It was a little confusing actually. All the reporters were shouting questions at him. Someone asked when, *when does the new decree go into effect?* Schuster scratched his head, and said *at once.* No passports, no exit visas required. All the border crossings are open effective immediately, including Bornholmer. Let's go. Here, take my hand."

Outside the Bornholmer installation, Basil and I joined the crowd. On the east side, people were lined up waiting patiently to cross. On the west side, people were jumping up and down, laughing, crying, and running in every direction. They were dancing, hammering the wall, handing out flowers and pouring champagne. Everyone was hugging each other as if some great and powerful force had been let loose on the world.

And there was Dr. Benson leaning on her cane, standing alone and holding one of those signed-over-the-seal manila envelopes, which could only mean one thing. She had a new assignment for me.

1989
TIANANMEN SQUARE TO EAST BERLIN
JACK GODWIN

ACKNOWLEDGEMENTS

After I finished writing my last book, my literary agent, Cricket Freeman, asked me what I planned to do next. I told her I wanted to try fiction, and that I had an idea for a novel set during the Cold War, the golden age of spy fiction. Cricket suggested I make the protagonist a woman. I took her advice, but also gave myself a homework assignment. That is, I read several of the great English women writers of the eighteenth and nineteenth centuries, specifically Jane Austen, Elizabeth Gaskell, and the Bronte sisters. I would like to acknowledge my debt to these writers, and above all to Cricket Freeman.

I would also like to acknowledge the Cold War International History Project at the Woodrow Wilson Center. The digital archives include declassified historical materials from all sides of the conflict including letters, memoranda, transcripts of telephone conversations, and official minutes of important meetings. In some cases, there are multiple versions of the same telephone conversation, a Russian and a German version for example, which have been translated into English.

A few of the characters in this novel are fictionalized versions of historical figures, particularly Otto Von Habsburg, Mikhail Gorbachev, and Margaret Thatcher. While I invented some scenes and dialog to tell the story, I refrained from altering the chronology or rewriting history, and always tried to be fair.

As ever, thanks to Tracey Culbertson, Lori Harrison, Eric Merchant, Mlima Morrison, Caroline Peretti, Josef Preciado, and Janis Silvers.

Made in the USA
Middletown, DE
13 October 2017